RAIDEN

RAIDEN

SHELLEY CASS

To those who make me smile – you are the best magic.

And for Bronwen, a true warrior.

Eirian Isle
Margate Isle
Miridoon Cave
Jenra
Midroone Pass
Cursed Valley
Northern Province
Western Sector
Eastern Region
Southern Domain
Wastelands
Krall
Prison
Lixrax
Takal
Border Lands
Trune Territory
Willow
Bwintam
Scorched Land
Wrilapek
Wanru
Giltrup
Gangroah
The Jewel
Awyalkna
Sylthanryn City
The Great Forest

Locations and pronunciation guide:

Sylthanryn: (Sil-than-rin). The Great Forest. Where the Lady, or the Mother of Nature, and the Elves and Nymphs live.

Awyalkna: (A for apple-why-elk-nah). A mortal Kingdom under the reign of King Glaidin (G-laid-in) and Queen Aglaia (Ag-lay-ah).

The Awyalknian Palace is also known as the 'Awyalknian Jewel', and is protected by the internal Gwentorock (G-when-toe-rock) and external Gwynrock (G-win-rock) walls. The lands beyond the city are green and flourishing, with many self-contained villages.

Bwintam (B-win-tam) village was a key provider of Awyalkna's fresh produce, before it was razed by Krall. Gan-groah (Gang-row-ah) and Giltrup (Guilt-rup) are examples of smaller villages, while Wanru (W-an-roo, an isolated, hilly place) and Wrilapek (W-rill-ah-peck, a horse rearing place) are larger and more greatly populated.

Krall: (Crawl). A mortal Kingdom ruled by the immortal Sorcerer Darziates (D-are-zee-eights), who is the heir of the first Sorcerer to have lived; Deimos (Day-moss). Darziates is assisted by the psychotic Warlord Angra Mainyu (An-gra Main-you) and the Witch Agrona (Ag-groan-ah), and is responsible for the genocide of all of the *Larnaeradee* Fairies (La-nair-ah-dee), the Unicorns and Sprites.

Nature dies around Darziates' unnatural power, so he pumps his magic into Krall's earth to force a type of growth and food production. However this has corrupted Krall's seasons, which involve intense heat or extreme wet and cold. Sorcery has reduced the land to barren plains of wastelands or desert.

Jenra: (Jen-rah). A Kingdom circled by, and built into the mountains by the sea. The mountain Kingdom is isolated from the rest of the world, and was once known as *Karanoyar* (Karen-oi-ah), the original home of the Unicorns. It has lush valleys, but the peaks of the mountains are now infested with Griffin eyries, and King Durna's (Der-nah) brother – Warlord Aeron (Air-on) must work tirelessly to contain the infestation.

Lixrax: (Lix-rrr-axe). A desert nation, with people who have been tempered by the harsh environment. They are skilled survivors, and are a united family because of their surrounds. Their Emperor, Razek (Rah-zeck) regards all of the tribes and Takal residents of Lixrax as his children.

The Other Realm: a separate plain of malicious spirit beings. When King Deimos wanted to unite the world under one kingship, he used a piece of his soul to bargain with the demons of the Other Realm, who gave him powers to help him in his quest.

He became so powerful that the *Larnaeradee* Sylranaeryn (Sil-ran-air-in) and her Unicorn Kinrilowyn (Kin-ril-owen) had to fatally deplete their combined magic to defeat him as he faced the Army for the World.

Though he was overthrown by the first Army for the World, he made the first of the experimental Evexus beasts. The Evexus (E-vex-us) are creatures possessed by the spirits of the Other Realm.

Margate Isle: home of the Giants.

Eirian Isle: home of the Dargons (D-are-gone-s) and the Dwarves and Gnomes. A cliffy place of soaring heights and deep, tunnelling caves, perfect for creatures of flight as well as rock loving peoples.

1

One

The Witch

'Stop watching me like that Aggy. I can't stand it.' Agrona's mother had slammed an ornate comb down onto her dresser. Her eyes had been cold as they'd flitted to the reflection of her daughter – who was lurking at the door, and then back to her own reflection in the lavish mirror.

While her beauty had saved the woman from ruin, the illegitimate child had still become her principal regret in life. Agrona's real father had been a stranger who had left the cursed place. But that had become a boon, for while he'd been charismatic at first, he'd had strange abilities to control the things around him, and the people around him, too. Agrona had been an unwanted result of the brief relationship before a more normal, advantageous union had saved Agrona's mother from destitution.

'Your eyes are so dull. You make my skin creep.'

Steel vines had been wrought to frame the mirror. So detailed, the thorns truly had been dangerous to touch. The barbs had framed Agrona's devastatingly beautiful and cruel mother in a sharpness that matched her nature.

Agrona had herself been an uncannily striking child. Long, midnight plaits down her back and flawless skin. Deep, dark eyes, almost black. And an unpleasant personality.

'Get out!'

Agrona had sullenly stepped back through the bedroom door; stung. And for a few moments she had lingered, scrunching her hands into fists and glaring daggers at her mother's reflection. She had focused all of her icy, seething hate ... until suddenly the looking glass had groaned and broken with a jagged crack.

Her mother had whirled in fury.

'I despise you!' she'd hissed, her white cheeks reddening with fury. 'Disgusting Witch.'

Agrona had run through the cold, grey manor, her tears running hot with resentment.

There had always been something different about her. Something that others had unconsciously shied away from, even though she was the daughter of a wealthy lady who had married a lord.

She would never laugh, only smiling faintly at unpleasant things. Things that inexplicably seemed to happen to the people around her.

Even then, as Agrona had sat herself down with silent tears on the manor's stone steps, a group of urchins playing in the street had squealed and taken flight at the sight of her.

Agrona had watched them scatter and had stonily scrunched her fist again, frowning at the last child hurrying down a laneway to escape her presence.

She'd let a little spiteful energy go then – and the raggedy child had gone flying, making a satisfying thud as he'd hit a stone wall.

'Why are you crying?' a calm voice had suddenly poured over her like smooth silk.

And Agrona had stared at the man who had seemingly appeared on the steps beside her out of thin air.

She had never seen him before.

He had been young, and yet more self-assured than most gentlemen twice his age. His hair had been so light as to be almost colourless. His own skin was as pale as hers, like flawless porcelain.

In the distance, the raggedy boy had started to sit up and was sobbing feebly.

'I am not loved,' Agrona had answered, at once coveting this beautiful man. 'I am feared, because I am different.'

'I see,' the young man had answered. 'Have you considered that their fear gives you power?'

She had tossed her plaits back over her shoulders. 'I hate them. They don't understand what I can do.'

'Then why do they upset you?'

'I live here. There is nobody else like me, and I won't be accepted anywhere else.' Agrona's face had darkened. 'I am trapped.'

She'd glowered threateningly at the little boy; staggering to his feet and clutching his head as he cried.

'Agrona,' the man's voice had been like liquid gold as it had rolled over her. 'I am like you.'

He'd known her name without being told, and when she'd fixed her dark eyes on his face, he had not shied away from her.

'How are you like me?'

He'd turned from her and she'd followed his gaze. The little boy in the distance had shrieked – buckling and folding in on himself in a grotesque contortion. The crack of bones had echoed back to them before the child's body had dropped, unmoving, to the mud.

'What makes us different from other people?' Agrona had asked the man – curious and enthralled.

'Better than other people,' he had corrected. 'We are their betters because we can feel the Other Realm. We can manipulate its energy, to use it in this realm. One day you will be so strong that your mind will help you control things like your hands can. You won't need gestures. And the rest of the world will bow to us.'

Her dark eyes had become livelier than they had ever been.

'My mother will respect me then.'

'You do not need this place, or these people,' he'd answered. 'You can come with me, and I will teach you.'

'They would not let me go ...' Agrona had frowned, for the first time uncertain.

'They would not be able to stop you. And,' he had shrugged almost imperceptibly. 'Why would they keep you? They hate you.'

At those words, the hurt had played across her normally controlled face. 'My mother would not let her only child go.'

He had placed his hand upon her bony shoulder and she'd gazed at him with awe, feeling as if she had been touched by a God.

'Your mother would have a new child one day. One that behaves like the rest. A legitimate child to be her true heir. To her, you are wrong. As strange and fearsome as the man who fathered you.'

His words had tipped Agrona over the edge. She had long suspected it all herself.

'Will you help me leave here and be strong like you?' she'd asked him hopefully.

His eyes had been like grey steel and his grip had continued to hold her, but she had been held fast by something more. Agrona had been entranced by his power.

'You can join me. But to be strong, you must give up all mortal ties. Give in to your true impulses. And punish those who have made you miserable.'

His face had been hard. 'You can't run away from them in cowardice. They would only hunt us out of pride.'

'What should I do?' Agrona had questioned hesitantly.

'Use your power. Feel the Other Realm, and show these people how angry you are. Show me how powerful you can be. Impress me.'

'Will you come with me?'

She'd stood resolutely, gazing up at him.

'Of course,' he had taken her hand.

Agrona had led the way inside to find her mother, now sitting at the long dining table with her stepfather.

Her mother's glittering, harsh eyes had appraised Agrona first, before sweeping up to register the young man.

Her mother had launched to her feet, her chair falling backwards to the floor.

'*You!*'

Shock had coloured Agrona's mother's face and her stepfather had hurried to his wife's side.

'Why are you h –'

'Hush,' Agrona's new and only ally had cut her snarling mother off, and the stunned lord and lady had been pushed back to the stone wall. Their shoes had scraped audibly across the floor, but they had held their throats silently, their speech cut off.

Agrona had been confused for a moment. Her mother had known this man?

'Agrona, it is time.' His touch at her elbow had cleared her mind.

Raising her fist, Agrona had pictured her mother and her stepfather drinking something poisonous. She had imagined how the liquid would flow through their bloodstream. It would fill them. Burn their insides. Kill them.

As she'd thought about it, her negligent family had started to choke and splutter. The poison Agrona had imagined had begun forming inside them. She had created it. She was controlling it.

'Good, Agrona.' His voice had been the only approving one she had ever heard. 'Show us all what you can do. Concentrate harder.'

Agrona had watched as her mother's beautiful, cruel face had turned blue and her stepfather had begun foaming at the mouth.

Agrona had felt that, inside her two gurgling victims, something red and roiling was burning away their organs. Something magic. Her magic.

'Finish it, Agrona. This is necessary.'

His voice had taken her over and she had realised she would forever follow its commands as, at last, her mother's and her stepfather's eyes had rolled back.

His power had released them, and their bodies had slumped downward.

'Well done, Agrona.' He'd taken her hand again.

She'd smiled up at him.

The Witch of Krall had been only twelve when she'd met Darziates. But she'd given him her heart completely, to use as he wished.

And he *had* used it as he'd wished, forcefully shaping her ever after.

2

Two

K*iana*

A flood of sunlight.

I moved to shakily catch the rays on my fingertips, but frowned at my bony knuckles. They stood out, the skin stretching over them. The nub of bone in my wrist was too prominent, and my elbow was unusually knobbly.

My other hand was better to focus on. Covered beneath the comforting weight of Dalin's long, tan hand.

Dalin.

He was asleep; his head tilted back against the cushioned chair so that I could see the scar that ran across his ear and along his jawline. The sun poured over him so that he looked like some kind of Awyalknian prince, chosen by the Gods.

Though I was in a strange room, I had always been aware that it was Dalin by my side. Aware of how he had cared for me with every particle of his soul – holding strong the fragile thread of my own life. I stirred as I noticed the shape of a bulky bandage through the pants material over his thigh.

'It's alright,' he told me softly, sleepily. 'Still here.'

'I can see that,' I replied croakily. 'You were there every time.'

His green eyes widened and he sat forward more alertly now. 'You're really awake,' he whispered as if he hardly dared to believe it.

'Kiana?'

Noal climbed the last few stairs into the room. Shock and joy covered his face as he quickly crossed to sit with me on the bed.

'Gods, it's good to see you alive,' he breathed, and touched my free hand as if it were made of porcelain. 'There's so much to tell you. We've been so worried,' he went on earnestly.

'I shall be fine,' I reassured him, already feeling tired again. 'When one has had magical beings at their bedside – and has a guardian such as Dalin, there can't be too much to fear.'

'You remember the Elves and Nymphs,' Dalin affirmed with relief.

'Is there more to remember?' I asked.

'We'll tell you everything,' Dalin promised. 'But not just yet. It's not urgent.'

'Yes, the most important thing is food,' Noal reflected as I blinked heavy eyelids. 'You've turned to skin and bone.'

'You're right,' I nodded drowsily, conscious that my great loss of weight and strength would take time to regain. 'I'll need to get my strength back soon so we can move off again.'

'Move off?' Noal asked.

I frowned. 'To resume the quest.'

'We want you to recover,' Dalin said carefully. 'No need to rush.'

'It wouldn't be today,' I acknowledged, sinking further into the pillows.

'You look in need of rest again,' Dalin patted my hand, green eyes crinkled with concern.

'I could still best you in a contest,' I answered, but my eyes had closed before he could reply.

3

Three

N^{oal}

'I'm out,' Dalin grimaced, watching as Kiana listlessly took another one of his coins over a game of runes.

We sprawled with her where she was propped up in bed, and though she'd had a few days of rest since waking, her vigour had not returned.

'Evening, my dashing man candies,' Asha zipped playfully up through the stairway's opening in the floor. 'And my dear One.'

The little Nymph whizzed across to me and planted her rosebud lips on my cheek. Then she soared over to stand on Vidar's head as he ascended into the room.

Kiana sat up with a little more energy as the insatiable vitality of Asha, combined with the raw power that emanated from Vidar seeped into the chamber.

Vidar patiently took hold of Asha's tiny ankle and let her slide her way down his arm. Then she bounced joyously to the floor and walked, for once, to the bed.

She was tiny at ground level, and when she raised her arms, I picked her up to sit her amongst our lost coins and rune pieces on the cover.

'How do you fare today, One?' Vidar asked Kiana as Asha climbed instead into my lap, her gleaming red eyes on the gold that littered the white sheets.

'I am quite improved,' Kiana told the massive Elf, even though the only thing that had improved was that she was awake and eating. 'I'm sure Chloris and Frey will ease their frequent examinations of me sometime soon.'

'We did ask the Lady if we could get you out of here for a short spell,' Asha informed Kiana while stretching lethargically against my chest. 'But she decreed that you needed to gain more of your strength back first.'

Red Nymph hair tickled my nostrils, but when I tried to wave it aside, it drifted back up into my face.

'However, we would like to ask the Raiden and Noal to step out to see the city tomorrow,' Vidar went on diplomatically. 'So that we may give them their own tree tower of honour.'

'After all, the city is abuzz with desperation to see these two mortals, but all Noal and the Raiden do is camp out and rot in here,' Asha added.

'I see,' Kiana nodded, but I detected nothing good in her expression.

'Agrudek was fun to play with at the start, but really, we haven't been waiting for generations just to see him.'

'Generations?' Kiana asked.

'Do we get any say in this at all?' Dalin enquired, changing the topic. 'It sounds like you're asking Kiana's permission to take us out.'

'You get no say.' Asha floated out of the chair she'd made of me and pinched Dalin's cheeks. 'See you on the morn!'

She somersaulted her way to the window, waving with little fingers before spiralling out into the night.

'Be well,' Vidar added, following Asha's lead in bidding us goodnight as Kiana glared at us darkly.

'What's the matter?' Dalin asked.

'What's the *matter*?' she repeated very testily. 'You get to explore an enchanted city. A city not seen by any mortal for centuries. While I can't rise from bed without collapsing.'

Her eyes held some of their old power.

'Ah, self-pity.' Dalin shook his head with mock disappointment.

One of her eyebrows shot up in a dangerous arc, and in a flash, she had reached out and shoved Dalin off the bed.

'OOF.' He landed with a surprised laugh and thump on the floor.

'And you,' she said threateningly to me as she held her bad shoulder. 'Are lucky you're out of reach.'

'Amazingly lucky,' I agreed, feeling a fluttering of hope as she seemed restored somewhat to the Kiana I was used to.

'You know we will gladly stay locked up in here with you, if you wish it,' Dalin told her, gazing up genuinely from his position on the floor.

'I do not wish it. Off with the both of you,' she said with a flutter of her hand, and Dalin picked himself up. 'But perhaps after your adventurous day you can return to me, and then we can get back to thinking about the quest.'

'Perhaps,' Dalin yawned luxuriously.

'See you soon.' I skirted around the bed in case she tried to kill me, which made her smile a little.

'G'night,' she answered dryly, beginning to count her winnings as we left.

4

Four

D^{alin}

'Wakey, wakey ...' a high voice purred beside my ear, and I felt little fingers peeling one of my eyelids up. 'Arise, Sir Raiden ...'

I groaned as I blearily registered Asha's face, just inches from mine, and swatted lazily at the annoying Nymph. Her flaming hair tickled my skin before she soared in circles across Kiana's sitting room to where Noal was flopped across a couch.

'What'satime?' Noal moaned as she stood on his chest.

'It is morning time, and moving time,' she declared. Vidar came into view, having waited more respectfully. 'Good morning friends. Today you shall see some of the wonders of our vast forest city!' he told us warmly.

'So, get up, get up, get up, get up!' Asha sang, again taking flight and doing a loop the loop.

'Gods,' I grumbled, pulling on my shirt.

'You can leave the shirt off if you want,' Asha stopped to consider thoughtfully. 'It's warm out.'

'I'm all set,' I told her sarcastically. 'With a shirt on.'

'You're all set?' Asha asked, not resuming her usually endless movements. 'You're not going to neaten up?'

I rolled my eyes and crossed to a dish of water by the window to splash my face and scrub roughly at my hair, finally shaking the drops off while Noal did the same.

'Better?'

Asha observed us critically, floating upside down to scrutinize our scrubbed faces.

'I could do your hair for you,' she suggested at last. 'You'd look dashing with Nymph hair.'

'How do you get your hair like that?' Noal asked, interested.

'Ohh, with all of our momentum, our hair simply can't stay flat,' she explained as she squinted at us, walking upside down a few paces in the air.

'I don't think I'd have the energy to sustain it,' Noal reflected.

Then Asha clicked her tongue and snapped her fingers, flipping the right way up.

'New Elfling clothes!' she sing-songed, flitting out the window with empty hands one moment, and then zipping up through the stairway hole holding regal garments the next.

'What's wrong with these?' Noal asked, pulling at the garments he was wearing.

'These are more refined for a grand introduction, my silly dear,' she told him, tossing the silky materials in his face before dumping mine over my head. 'The forest dwellers will want you to live up to their dreams.' She watched us expectantly.

'We'll wait outside,' Vidar told her pointedly, and he led Asha out by her dangling ankle as she pouted sulkily and tugged at a tuft of his white hair.

'Spoil-sport.'

'These remind me of home,' Noal remarked, examining the simple, yet splendid make of the clothes.

I stepped into the trousers, and pulled my arms into the long sleeved, shirt-like vest, marvelling at the silky cloth as I laced the front. The material was light blue in colour, but became a shimmery silver as it moved in the light.

When I turned to Noal, I was startled – transported home for a moment. 'I forgot you could look so princely.'

'Why, thank you,' he answered dryly, following me down the winding stairs to the foot of the tree. 'It has been a while since you've appeared anywhere near that standard yourself.'

We found Vidar and the impatient Asha waiting in the bottommost room, and Asha let out a trilling whistle of appreciation while Vidar herded us through the mighty tree's doorway and out into a fairy tale city I felt I'd so far only seen in a dream.

I was at once struck dumb as we became more and more immersed in an atmosphere so rich with magic that the air almost crackled around us.

'Gods,' Noal breathed, as if he were tasting a wine better than life itself.

Everywhere were tree towers, vine bridges, rock pools, veils of leaves, flowers drizzling like curtains along the cliff walls ... and magical beings in a hive of activity.

To our side there was a particularly raucous burst of laughter as a multi-coloured swarm of Nymphs blurred past. But then they stopped. Back-tracked. And came to size us up.

"Ohhh, helllllllllllllo!"

Alarmingly, more Nymphs paused all around, then zipped in close to gather quickly.

'You know,' I mentioned to Noal uneasily. 'I'm not sure if I can handle a whole group of Ashas all at once.'

Vidar laughed and nearly knocked me over with a friendly pat on my shoulder. 'You get used to it.'

Asha smiled a wide smile and I noticed that her tiny, pearly white teeth were sharply pointed.

'Don't worry my sweet,' she purred. 'We're all quite nice when you get to know us.'

Then she gestured to the waiting magical beings and we were instantaneously swamped by crowds of Nymphs who chattered and hovered and hung off us like rainbow ornaments, and I couldn't help but share in their good cheer.

'Do you have a wench promised to you?' a violet haired Nymph asked in a baby voice, floating next to Noal and stroking his cheek.

Asha shot the Nymph a withering glare and said: 'not that one.'

The violet haired Nymph scowled and fell back, and all of the other hungry looking lady Nymphs who had been eyeing Noal off stopped their flirtatious cooing begrudgingly, while the male Nymphs appeared decidedly relieved.

'Do *you* have a girl?' asked a bold, blue haired Nymph beside me.

'That is the Raiden you are talking to,' Vidar chuckled.

'Mmmm. Perhaps I'm attracted to titles,' the Nymph stated, pressing fluttering lips to my temple so that I felt as though I'd been kissed by a levitating infant.

We nodded to politely smiling Elves and ploughed through the admiration of each Nymph group that hailed us in greeting, and eventually the little creatures settled into more playful behaviour – shouting to draw our attention to different things and competing to make us laugh.

As the sun set and the floating globes of light all over the city began to glow, Noal and I were surprised by how quickly the day had passed.

We were shown to our own tree tower to share, and reassured the Elves and Nymphs who were still hanging about that we wouldn't forget to call at all of their dwellings.

Then we at last tiredly found our own beds.

5

Five

D^{alin}

When I woke with the dawn, I ventured upstairs to find Noal, sprawled over his bed in an immovable condition.

'We said we would visit Kiana,' I told him.

'Oh … you go,' he yawned sleepily before rolling over. 'I'll catch up.'

'You'll be able to find your way to Kiana's tower in this state?' I asked doubtfully.

'Mph. Right behind you.' He waved his arm to shoo me away.

He wouldn't get lost, I decided. There were always gaggles of Nymphs available at all hours, and pleasant Elves out at more reasonable hours to help if he was desperate.

Even at this time, the fresh forest city was already waking up – though I did have to step around the odd Nymph hidden here and there in the glistening grass; sleeping without a care for the dew in their hair.

I successfully guessed my own way back to Kiana's tree tower door, which opened in welcome as I touched it and stepped inside.

'Kiana!' I called as I wound my way upward, but received no reply. 'It's Dalin!'

I poked my head up through the entrance to the topmost room, frowning at the lack of response, but the room was empty.

'Kiana?' I asked uncertainly.

'There's no need to warn me of your presence,' her voice carried in from outside. Kiana was standing on a balcony made of tree foliage and intricately woven, live branches. 'Apparently the doors of these towers only open for the actual dweller,' she went on, not turning from the view. 'Or when the dweller would approve of someone coming in.'

'Oh. Well, why not?' I started toward her with a pang of excitement as I realised that she was up. 'If a willow can talk, why not have a giant treehouse decide whether or not a person should be admitted?'

She was leaning out on the branch formed ledge, her back still to me.

She wore a fresh shirt and trousers, and her long hair was tied up as if for business.

'I'm so glad to see you out here,' I beamed. But my enthusiasm waned when she remained silent.

She sighed finally, and as if she felt incredibly fragile, she began to slowly turn my way.

She tightly clasped the branch ledge as she moved, and I was painfully aware of how thin her frame had become and how drawn her face was.

Alarmed, I took a step closer and then stopped when she looked away from me dejectedly.

'What happened?' I asked as my heart sank.

Her face hardened. 'I grew tired of being an invalid and decided to at least search my tower, if I couldn't see the city.' She spoke to the floor. 'I made it down through three rooms before I was depleted and lost consciousness trying to climb back up. Frey and Chloris found me and they had to bring me back up to bed. I couldn't do it for myself.'

At once fearful memories of the Lady's warnings that Kiana may never regain her strength raced through my mind. I pushed the thoughts aside just as quickly as they'd come.

I saw the hopelessness of Kiana's expression, as well as her un-spilled, angry tears, and I instinctively moved forward again, reaching to her with my arms outstretched.

For a moment she stiffened, returning to her fierce and independent self. But then the harsh tension in her broke, the hot tears escaped to run down her cheeks, and it was Kiana who closed the small distance between us. She buried her face against me and my arms enfolded her.

'I don't know what is wrong with me,' she uttered against my chest. 'I can't control this and it terrifies me.'

She stopped there, forcing down a sob so that I physically felt it shudder within her.

'Say it all. Just let it all out,' I answered softly, holding her shaking frame as she seemed to hold the rest in. 'It's alright.'

She was quiet a moment. Thinking.

'Well ... maybe it's worse that I *do* know what's wrong and still can't control it,' she admitted in frustrated sadness. 'Agrona is literally under my skin. Forcing me to stop being the fighter, and turning me into the weak thing she originally cursed me to be.'

I rested my chin on her head, feeling the sad line of my own lips pulling down.

At last, when her body grew still and her breathing became regular, I heard her muffled voice from against my chest again.

'Most people say 'don't cry,' then tell you why you're wrong about the thing that's upset you,' Kiana sighed. 'And for some reason that's not very comforting.'

I peered down at her. 'My mother is a wise woman,' I explained. 'She never used to tell me to stop making a fuss, no matter what troubled me.'

Kiana sagged against me slightly. 'It's just so frarshking hard to be unable to do anything by myself.'

I lifted her chin with a finger. 'So, if you are not a fighter and not independent, what are you doing out here right now?' I asked.

She shrugged and then leaned back to look me in the eye, roughly rubbing the tears from her cheeks.

'I couldn't stand it,' she answered almost defiantly. 'I forced myself out of bed, and to make it to the balcony. When you came up, I was recovering.'

'Not to tell you that you are wrong about the thing that has upset you ... but perhaps it's not really that you can't do anything by yourself,' I reasoned. 'It's that you haven't been pacing your efforts.'

She rolled her eyes as I moved, but she let me steer her towards the bed.

'You can't expect to regain your strength so quickly,' I soothed. 'You almost lost your life to Agrona's poison, and wouldn't have survived but for Frey and the Lady.'

'Yes,' she answered slowly. 'But I've come to the edge of life in the past. I've suffered the effects of cuts from poisoned talons and have had raging fevers, yet I've never been left so completely helpless. It's different this time.' The fear was only just being restrained from her voice as she bit it back.

'It is different this time,' I agreed. 'This time the poison was dark magic, not venom or some worldly toxin.'

She ducked her head. 'I'm afraid I won't get better this time.'

'You will,' I responded, because I had resolved that nothing could ever hold Kiana back. 'And you won't do it all on your own. I'll be here every step of the way to help. We need you.'

She gave one of her dry half smiles. 'If I've got you to help me, I will be unstoppable. And we can resume the quest as soon as possible.'

I gaped in exasperation. 'You've missed the point.'

'I understand that I won't recover immediately,' she placated me. 'But, yes. I must make myself strong again. Day by day I'll push myself further.'

'Slow sounds reasonable,' I agreed carefully.

'Of course,' she stated. 'Just not so slow that we miss the war and end up under Darziates' control. The quest must go on whether I am strong enough or not.'

I sat beside her on the bed in resignation. 'What's your plan, then?'

Kiana tucked a loose strand of hair behind her ear; thinking. 'Today I got down into three rooms. Tomorrow you'll help me get through the entire tower and then help me to make it back up.'

'Right,' I agreed. 'And from there?'

'We'll add exercises when I can start getting back up the stairs myself. And after that you'll be taking me out to see the city,' she said in a way that invited no disagreement.

'Oh joy,' I slumped mournfully. Then I gave her a sharp look. 'This will be a frustrating process. You'd best leave your knives up here in the closet.'

She grinned. 'I'll be awake the whole time, and as weak as a lamb. You have nothing to fear.'

I straightened her bed covering as I rose. 'Lambs don't get violent when they are angry and tired. They go to sleep and eat grass.'

6

Six

N^{oal}

There were roars of appreciative laughter around the rock pool while Asha told dirty Nymph jokes in her high, soaring voice.

She wobbled where she stood on my stomach as I chuckled – laid out comfortably on the grassy bank.

'No wonder we used to love the mortal race. This one's a good sport,' a dripping Nymph called Flash chortled, slapping the water surface with a small hand.

'We're a lovable bunch,' I grinned. 'Very likeable.'

'Have you got any good mortal gags?' Rebel, an orange haired male asked after resurfacing and floating above the water. 'I can store them up to tell Chloris for a laugh.'

I shrugged unhelpfully. 'I've got none as sickening as your Nymph ones, I'm afraid.'

'And it won't be Chloris laughing at jokes like that,' Flash kicked around in the water.

'It'll be me laughing at her face!' Rebel smirked. 'I got to do what it takes to keep her head away from the seriousness.'

'Is she having trouble with that?' rumbled a surprisingly deep voiced little Nymph called Ace, one of the council members and the Nymph army commander.

I'd thought he was cute at first, but his stout little body, pointed teeth and reverberating voice overruled his enormous green eyes, baby feet and dimpled cheeks.

'With all the excitement of having these humans and the One to take care of, she and Silvanus have been kept lively,' Rebel admitted. Then he snickered. 'But I can keep the jokes for a rainy day.'

'Frey has been quiet lately, with so much on his mind,' Shiva, with aqua coloured hair and eyes, commented from where he hung. He was upside-down in the air, drying off.

'You'd best do something about that,' Flash gurgled from behind a waterfall now, poking his head out through the falling water to speak. 'You know how hard he goes under when the seriousness starts.'

'Sati can fix him,' Rebel stated confidently. 'Frey has a soft spot for Sati.'

'So do I,' Shiva sighed dreamily.

'Is the seriousness still that bad?' I asked in surprise. 'I thought the coming of the Nymphs, and the Elves taking on a warrior lifestyle ended that problem.'

'Well, we've got to do something, so we spend a lot of time making sure all our past hard work on the Elves isn't wasted,' Asha explained good-naturedly. 'It's our duty to brighten up their sedate lives. But sometimes the seriousness can still creep over them again.'

'Once Frey was missing for two days before we found him in the forest,' Rebel chimed in. 'He just went out alone, sat down for a break and started thinking too much. Then he didn't get back up.'

'So, he'd fallen asleep?' I asked.

'No.' Flash appeared to be standing on the water surface as he flapped above it. 'He was just mulling. His eyes were open and he was breathing, but that was it.'

'Gods,' I uttered, amazed that someone could actually die of being too serious.

'We keep an eye on them just in case something like that happens,' Asha explained. 'It was worse when the Nymphs first came to the forest. We often heard of Elves perishing before old age, or being found half starved. Now it's less common because our dutiful antics help them stay wakeful.'

'For instance, yesterday Flash and I went to see Chloris and Silvanus,' Rebel told me. 'We put on an explosive fight for them, right on their kitchen floor.'

'And while Chloris did just sweep around us and Silvanus kept cooking – they were terribly entertained,' Flash added knowingly.

'Irritated, entertained – it doesn't matter,' Rebel grinned. 'Better than a case of the seriousness.'

'Well, this morning I helped enliven Vidar's drills,' Asha told the other Nymphs. 'I swiped his spear and we went on a nice dash around the city.'

'Of all the Elves, Ailill especially loves it when I visit to help him out,' Flash reflected. 'He acts like he really wants to be reading those books of his. And he acts like I'm this big nuisance. But he secretly enjoys me flapping around his healer head, pointing out what's going to happen in the next paragraph.'

'Speaking of healers and health, how are the One and the Raiden?' Ace growled in his gravelly tones.

'Kiana and Dalin,' I corrected, 'are better. Ailill took Dalin's stitches out and Dalin's helping Kiana to work toward getting slightly stronger every day. That's why I've been spending my time out here with you lot.'

'Aren't you invited to their training sessions?' Rebel teased. 'They need their alone time?'

I rolled onto my side to face the orange haired Nymph and Asha slid off my stomach with a squeal.

'Obviously with my sunny nature and fabulous humour I would be an asset,' I told the Nymph. 'It's more that I am wise enough to stay away.'

'Ah, yes, I made myself scarce after their first try, when Kiana made it all the way down to the last room in her tower, but couldn't make it back up,' Asha cringed as she lounged against me again. 'I couldn't endure the daggers of her sullen, blood-curdling stare over the Raiden's shoulder while he carried her up as

I followed behind.'

'Dalin has always been brave hearted,' I agreed. 'He endures her sharp barbs when she's frustrated, and they've progressed to doing some light exercises after they walk up and down the tower now.'

'She's definitely got spirit enough to regain her full strength,' Asha quipped as she rose, doing a flip in the air and diving with a dainty little splash into the water.

Flash swam over to where Asha had dived in. 'Every time I fly past, I hear the One cussing something awful at the Raiden,' he remarked, and he put his arms around Asha as she bobbed back up to the surface. 'So, she's got the spirit *and* the swear words to get her through.'

Shiva, the quietest of the males, floated over the water serenely. 'My little Sati is quite spirited too.'

Flash rolled his eyes and swam away with Asha in tow, kicking water at Shiva as he propelled. 'Why don't you just lay with her already? It's been a few hundred years.'

Shiva looked mortified.

'He wants Sati to be his life partner, not just to mate with her. They want to have their bond and try for Nymphlings,' Asha explained patiently, patting Flash's silver hair and giving him a kiss on the lips. He grinned, satisfied, and swam languidly away while she dipped back under like a playful fish.

'It's good to hear of the One regaining her strength,' Ace rumbled back to the previous topic.

He was every inch a miniature military general, with his straight posture and tough stance while he meandered up and down the pool bank. 'The Lady and council will surely soon wish to talk to the Raiden, the One and yourself.'

I sat up uncomfortably. 'About?'

'Your quest and the prophecy.'

My brow furrowed. 'We've explained that we're not the three you think,' I told Ace. 'And we truly are sorry for disappointing the two races who rescued us.'

Asha zipped from the water quickly to press her small, wet hand to my cheek.

'You, my dear,' she purred, 'could never be a disappointment.'

'But what if you *were* the Three?' Flash pushed. 'Hypothetically.'

'The One – Kiana – does have a talent for speaking *Aolen* ... the lost *Larnaeradee* language,' Rebel contributed helpfully. 'What if you were all destined to meet and save the world? If every good or bad thing that ever happened in your lives was fate, pushing you on a path to get to here and now?'

It was too much to consider, and I felt nerves bubble up in my stomach.

'If that was the case, what would that mean for us?' I inquired. 'Was this prophecy very descriptive, to help us know how we are supposed to save everyone?'

'Well, if it's your destiny, you'll probably just do the right things without realising,' Shiva speculated, tapping a teeny finger against his chin as he mused.

I crossed my arms.

'And seeing as we are most likely not anything beyond three unlucky, hopeful travellers on a quest of our own, what will we talk about at the Lady's council?' I asked dryly.

'The weather,' Rebel supplied, and I felt myself relax again.

'Good,' I remarked airily. 'I do love a good chat about the climate.'

'Sure you do, and out of everyone, the Lady would give you the most informed answers,' Asha piped up easily, toddling back into the water and splashing droplets at me with a little hand. 'But before you use the chance of a lifetime to speak with the oldest Lady in the world about that, why don't you join me for a paddle?' she smiled coyly, her little pointed teeth giving her a sinister appearance.

'Madam,' I scoffed haughtily, 'I am the master of paddling.'

Flash snorted as I stood regally, yanking my shirt over my head to toss it onto the grass – much to Asha's delight.

Rebel pretended to make room respectfully while I sauntered to the bank, holding my head high as I did professional looking stretches – before delivering a massive flop into the water.

Asha squealed with delight as her pint-sized body was swept easily away in the waves, and Rebel roared with laughter as Flash and Shiva were also enveloped by mini tsunamis.

I swam over to collect Asha from the swirling bubbles, and her little arms hugged around my neck as her hair sprang upright once more and I gave her a ride back to the others.

In this way the day passed quickly, and we carried on together until late afternoon, when I carried Asha out of the water, lounging in my arms as if I were a hammock.

'Should we go to see the little man before dinner?' Asha questioned from where she nestled. 'He's so cute.'

'Yes, we should visit Agrudek in his tree tower,' I agreed, heading in that direction at her suggestion.

'I feel sorry for the little man,' she remarked with a yawn, one leg dangling down to swing out of my arms while we walked. 'He's so timid.'

'He misses his family,' I told her, knowing that nobody could ever really recover from such a loss.

'Yet another victim of the Sorcerer and Witch of Krall,' Asha snarled, her pointed teeth suddenly gleaming. Then the creases left her face. 'Poor little man,' she crooned mournfully, throwing an arm over her eyes.

I sighed. 'Yes, I feel sorry for him too. He doesn't come out of his tower often, and when he does, he's jumpy and nervous. So, we'll go to him to make it easier.'

'Mmmm,' Asha's eyes were closing, and I marvelled at how Nymphs, after all of their trickery and energy, would simply fall asleep for short bursts to recharge. But it was always even more surprising when they woke abruptly, springing up from wherever they had drifted down to rest.

By the time I'd carried her to Agrudek's tower, where the door opened to us automatically, Asha was dozing like a cherub and Agrudek's tree felt overly hushed and sombre without her chatter.

'Good afternoon Agrudek!' I called cheerily as my head poked up through the stairway hole in the kitchen floor and I spotted the little fellow in the midst of making tea.

He quickly shuffled around to face me, trying a shaky smile as he reached for a second teacup with his one hand. 'H-hello friend,' he managed as the cup rattled on its saucer while he set it down next to his own cup, already waiting on the table.

I didn't have the heart to refuse as he hurried to pour the detestable tea.

'P-please, please take a seat.' He fumbled his way into a chair and I followed suit; holding the snoring Asha like a baby and trying to appear suitably pleased as he pushed the steaming cup towards me.

'I haven't seen you,' I commented conversationally to Agrudek. 'I thought I better check you hadn't been kidnapped by lady Nymphs.'

He hiccupped a nervous laugh. 'No, no. The w-wife wouldn't like that!'

His eyes grew distant.

'So, how have you been spending your time?' I asked hurriedly.

'... Just ... thinking,' he answered sadly.

'You shouldn't do so much of that,' I cajoled. 'Learn from the Elves.'

Agrudek tried to smile again. 'You-you're a good man ... and Dalin and Kiana ... tr-truly good people,' he said. 'You all d-did so much, I ... don't deserve ...'

'Don't say it,' I stopped him. 'You obviously are no friend of Darziates, so in my opinion you're the most deserving.'

His eyes lowered and he fidgeted uneasily with his cup. 'I - I just worry about my family. I don't know if they're alive or ... or ...' he quickly took a sip of tea to steady himself. 'I would do *anything* to free them.'

To be polite I took a gulp and set my cup back as the heated liquid was forced down in a torrent.

Was it apple flavoured herbal tea, of all things?

'You have to believe that Darziates will be brought to justice either way,' I said gently. 'That's what you can try to focus on.'

For a moment Agrudek stared miserably down into his cup, pulling at his carrot-coloured hair. Then he peered up at me questioningly.

'H-has Kiana examined the Krall general's scryer globe?' he asked.

'No,' I answered gladly, relieved at the change of topic. 'I think it's still out of harm's way with her other belongings. She hasn't lifted even a dagger since she woke.'

'And, the Elves and ... the Nymphs, they still think y-you are a prophesied Three?' he asked. 'They ... they believe Kiana has some kind of ... power?'

'They haven't really addressed the issue with Kiana while she's recovering,' I told him. 'But,' I sighed uneasily. 'Their claims are making me slightly nervous.'

'W-why?' he asked curiously.

'Because, our little quest has received much more attention than it should have. As soon as Dalin and I set out we were attacked by Darziates' beasts.'

Agrudek spluttered his mouthful of tea back into his cup.

I, on the other hand, tried to get another throat-coating gulp down.

'That's how we met Kiana. When she saved us. And at first, we thought it might have been coincidence that two of the Sorcerer's beasts somehow found us. But Agrona and those same beasts began to follow our trail, even before that entire Krall troop was sent out.'

Asha wriggled in my arms and rolled over to drool against my chest.

'I can't really believe that our quest isn't somehow important with all of that going on. And when the Nymphs and Elves mention what Kiana could be, I start to fear that we really are the prophesied group that the forest dwellers want.'

Agrudek's eyes had grown wide, and I supposed he was just as shocked as I was.

'I know,' I agreed.

He sucked in a breath. 'You r-really are the three? The two Awyalknian b-boys and their saviour ...' he gasped.

'It sure sounds like it,' I grimaced. 'But I find it hard to believe that I was specifically born to go on a quest that the world could depend on. I can't accept it.'

'Wh-what did the beasts look like?' Agrudek asked, and I realised that the ragged little man had finally become lively.

'They were gigantic, pointy, and insect-like. Grey. And colder than ice to touch,' I said. 'But worse, they were near impossible to wound.'

Agrudek sat back in his chair, as if rocked to his core. 'You are the three that Darziates wanted ...' he whispered.

I shrugged in bewilderment while Agrudek fell silent.

'It's not good for you to stay cooped up here so much,' I said after a time, noticing through the window that the outside light globes were glowing to life as dusk became night.

'You should come out with the Nymphs and I every now and then.'

Asha chose then to spring back to life, bursting from my arms and nearly causing Agrudek to fall off his chair in fright. She had hardly opened her eyes before shooting around the room.

'Hello, hello Agrudek!' she chirped.

'H ... hello ...' he managed finally, clutching his chest.

'I am STARVED,' she moaned, coming to tug on my hand like an impatient child. 'Noal and I are visiting my friends for dinner. You should come Agrudek, you look in need of a good meal. A whole heap of us will be there, and Vidar's coming too, the darling. It's in the vine rooms on the cliff face.'

'Perhaps n-not ... tonight ... But I'll m-make more of an effort,' Agrudek told her. 'Perhaps I will visit K-Kiana in her tower sometime soon.'

I stood and gratefully turned away from the detestable teacup. 'That's a great idea,' I told him amiably, nearly toppling with Asha's surprising strength. 'Thanks for having us, friend,' I blurted as fast as I could, tripping toward the steps.

And I barely managed to wave before we had whizzed right out of his tower and into the night.

7

Seven

*K*iana

I sat dourly on my bed, waiting for Dalin while Chloris packed away her tonics.

'Do not be too dispirited, One,' the willowy Elf told me kindly. 'There is an abundance of time for healing while you are with us.'

'The war will be over before we start on our quest again,' I grimaced.

'There is no fear of that,' Chloris replied calmly. 'The moment a being steps into the forest heart, where Sylthanryn City is hidden, time flows differently for them.'

Sheets of silken white hair glimmered in the sunlight as she came to sit beside me on the bed.

'What do you mean, exactly?' I asked.

A wisp of a smile touched her midnight lips. 'The power of the Lady makes time pass slower here than outside, almost as if the forest heart is separate to the rest of the world.'

Her words, and the beautiful aura that emanated from her were enough to mollify me as Chloris' elegant hand reached out to rest upon mine. I exalted in the thrill of her touch, and when her soothing voice continued, I had to remember to refocus on the words instead of the magic.

'The life force stemming from the Lady nourishes this forest and its dwellers. It seeps into our own souls, into the very air and earth here. Life is not extinguished so quickly with such an influence. Living is not a rushed experience. It follows its own pace. It is as if the amount of magic makes both the magical races and the flow of time last longer. And before Darziates came to be, when the magical races were spread throughout all of the lands, this phenomenon of vitality and better health was experienced by mortals, too.'

'I still feel like I have to hurry,' I admitted, despite being thoroughly intrigued.

'Consider, though,' she appealed to me. 'What would be the purpose of hurrying to battle when, while you are here, the battle is as good as years away from starting?'

I shrugged helplessly, struggling to fathom it.

'Take your time, for as long as time is not a concern,' she cautioned as she rose, both of us becoming aware of my tower door opening. She gave me one more smile before she descended the stairs, and I felt the ripples of her energy receding.

'Kiana! I'm here!' Dalin called up from the bottom floor, and I felt a new type of liveliness within my own self. I resolved to maintain my efforts regardless of Chloris' warnings, for the sake of my own sanity.

I smiled in spite of myself, and despite how slow my steps were as I carefully began my descent to the bottom floor to meet Dalin.

'Good morning,' he greeted me patiently when I finally reached the last step.

I grunted at him and determinedly turned around to start upward again. I was getting better at making it all the way up on my own.

'What – no break?' he asked.

'No break,' I grumbled.

He gambolled along behind me, making no comment as I gradually slowed. Eventually we made it to the room under the bedroom, where Dalin had cleared us an exercise space by pushing all of the sofas to the round walls.

'Today we'll be doing something different,' I told him, my face and voice controlled to allow no invitation for disagreement. 'We'll push the limits a little more.'

I saw his face fall. "Different' and 'push' how, exactly?'

'You remember when I showed you some weaponry exercises back in ...' I paused. 'Back in Bwintam?' I managed to get the name out.

'Oh Gods. Do you really think you're ready to get back into wielding weapons yet?'

I began to stretch, very gently. 'No. I acknowledge that wouldn't be able to handle the weight of the blades yet. So we'll be doing a weapons dance without the weapons.'

'Right,' he agreed warily.

'Come on,' I urged. 'I'll be taking it slow and easy so all you'll have to do is copy.'

He groaned as I took my first position, but he did as he was shown.

'Breathe deep,' I said. 'And hold your hands as though there are blades in your fists.'

He held himself appropriately so that I was satisfied. 'Now move fluidly.'

I moved my arms exaggeratedly slowly around my body, stepping carefully into an unhurried lunge as though attacking an invisible enemy – my 'blades' slicing across an unseen belly.

I let my breathing and my heart set the beat, straightening and stepping back on one foot, and raising my imagined weapons as if to defend an attack aimed at my head. I moved smoothly, but never left the dramatically slow pace.

I was aware of Dalin getting the hang of it beside me, but heard his left foot lightly brush the plush carpet as he moved.

'Quietly now, step lightly. Concentrate on every part of your body. Control every muscle,' I whispered.

I sensed he was imitating me as I bent backward and pushed my ribs to oblige while I sliced at the air over my chest.

My blood was beginning to pump now, so I picked it up just a little and spun slightly more rapidly to parry with the air. I crouched and ducked cautiously, trying to forget the dull ache that never left my shoulder.

Dalin was near silent now – a natural fighter.

With time, my heartbeat grew faster and my limbs began to move more quickly. Eventually my side burned and my shoulder seared, but I smiled. Glad to be doing something active again.

'Adjust your footing,' I panted at Dalin when I heard him wobble beside me. 'Right foot needs planting.'

'How do you know?' he gasped. 'You're not even looking!'

'You'll be steadier if you point your toes out straight.'

But it was only a small criticism. He was beginning to be able to judge my next move so that instead of copying my positions he was mirroring them.

A light sweat covered my body and my breath came quickly. Spurred by enthusiasm, I moved even faster to the rhythm of my heart beat. I could almost picture my imaginary daggers arcing through the air, slicing and tearing in a controlled battle.

I was burning with life, dancing like a flame, and I was myself again.

I thrust my right arm straight out in front of my body, stabbing an enemy, but drove my imaginary blade into the air with more gusto than I had intended.

And suddenly I couldn't see.

My breath sucked itself in, my face contorted, and I only knew agony as my shoulder, my chest, my back, everywhere, was on fire. Molten lava bubbled beneath my skin, clogging up my veins.

My legs buckled and I only distantly heard Dalin exclaim and rush to my side.

Everything I'd ever known had vanished from my mind in an instant. As if all I had ever been made up of was pain.

Alone.

Witless.

Darkness closing in.

Alone?

In the dark.

No. His firm grip was on my arms. Dalin's grip. And then I was back.

Dalin held me. The wound in my shoulder felt as if it had been newly opened. But this time by a white-hot stake instead of an arrow. I dragged my eyes up to focus on his anxious green ones.

'Kiana?' he asked, panicked. 'What just happened?'

'It's nothing,' I said, struggling to focus on just those green eyes. 'The pain I used to get in my shoulder is just a bit worse than it used to be.'

'*Nothing*?' he exclaimed incredulously. 'A bit?'

But he stopped when he noticed how hard it was getting to keep my head up. 'Kiana?' he asked uncertainly.

All of my energy was gone again.

'This isn't normal. I don't feel well,' I told him truthfully, and sank backward. Only his hands kept me upright. 'Can you help me get back to bed?'

8

Eight

K^{iana}

Distrustful of training with me again straight away, Dalin had instead suggested I venture into the city for our next activity, and he was now warily waiting for me to be ready to set out.

I stubbornly bent over to slip on my boots, but felt a twinge in my shoulder and unconsciously drew a sharp, nervous breath.

Dalin's hands came into my line of vision, resting on my hunting boots. I immediately shot him a heated glare, until I caught the expression of total care in those green eyes. He saw me soften, and slid my boots into place for me, wordlessly lacing them up before helping me down the stairs.

I forgot every worry, feeling the creases smoothing from my brooding brow and a terrible weight lifting from my posture as we stepped out together into the secret city of Sylthanryn.

The sizzling power in the atmosphere enveloped me, I saw joy on the faces of the Nymphs and Elves, and I moved out into the sunshine with a sense of elation that made my self-pity disappear.

I smiled gently back at Dalin, finding that he was watching my face with undisguised happiness. And I held out my hand to him, grateful for his support in many ways.

'Let's go,' I smiled.

9

Nine

D*alin*

I was whistling cheerfully as I strolled back to our tree tower. However, an odd prickling sensation at the back of my neck gave me pause, and when I heard a shuffling sound in the shadows behind me I whipped around; my hand instinctively braced over the hilt of my sword for the first time since entering the city.

I peered into the shadows and felt my heart quicken I made out something lurking a short distance away, just watching.

It was a small robed figure, too small for an Elf, too big for a Nymph, and not Kiana or Noal. That only left ...

'Oh, Agrudek!' I exclaimed in relief. 'You startled me! Why didn't you hail me down?'

I heard the sharp intake of his breath and I worried that I'd more than startled him in return.

'D-didn't want to d-disturb you,' his uneasy voice replied, and he shuffled into the light.

'Nonsense!' I told him. 'How have you been?'

'F-fine,' he mumbled, hanging his head so that I at once felt a pang of pity for him.

'Well, it's good to see you outside your tower,' I told him encouragingly. 'Where are you off to?'

He twitched apprehensively. 'I-I was j-just going for a stroll ...'

'You were headed toward Kiana's, weren't you? You're a good friend, Agrudek.'

He pulled at his scraggly orange hair fretfully and coughed. 'I was going t-t-to check in.'

'I've just left there and she's retired for the night. But you should come and have a drink with Noal and I.' I threw an arm over his shoulders and steered him around. 'I won't take no for an answer. Asha, Rebel and Vidar are coming.'

'... Really shouldn't ...' he protested feebly, glancing over his shoulder at Kiana's tower.

'It'll be fun!' I reassured him, and herded him all the way to our tower instead.

'Fun ...' he repeated weakly when we arrived to find that Asha and Vidar were already there with Rebel and a thronging cluster of other Nymphs who had tagged along.

Their laughter and the clinking of Nymph liquor bottles hit us as soon as we stepped inside.

10

Ten

D^{alin}

'Heeeeeelloooooooo??' a voice fluttering next to my ear called and I peeled one eyelid open with a massive effort.

A purple haired Nymph was grinning down at me. Her eyes, also purple, were so close I could see my rumpled features in them.

'Nova?' I grumbled blearily, throwing an arm over my face. She was a particularly cheeky Nymph. I couldn't handle such energy so early in the morning.

'Are we feeling delicate?' she asked evilly, and I heard the tinkling sound of her poking at the empty bottles of Nymph liquor littering the floor.

'Gods yes.'

'Well snap out of it,' she declared unsympathetically. 'The Lady has called the council to meet. I've been sent to fetch you.' I felt her little fingers plucking at my arm before she pulled it from my face and tossed it back down to the bed.

I moaned as the early morning light flooded my blurred vision.

'Come *on*! It's time to rise!' she yanked the covers back evilly. Then she changed her tone. 'Oooh wow,' she sighed.

'Mph,' I groaned as she started touching my bare chest and abdomen suggestively. 'Gerroff!'

'Dalin!' Noal moaned mournfully, stomping down the stairs and rubbing his eyes.

Naira –Nova's pink-haired twin – was catching a piggy-back ride as he came down, floating behind his neck like a scarf.

'Joy! Two of them shirtless!' Naira cackled, releasing Noal's neck.

'Hey!' Noal jumped when a Nymph hand pinched him on the buttocks.

'It's heartbreaking, but you've got to dress,' Nova informed us, already pushing me to the washroom with strength that did not match her stature.

'Chop chop!' Naira demanded, whipping us with a towel until we were scrubbed, dressed and wide awake.

'Is this council going to be filled with prophecy discussion?' Noal asked when Naira was mercilessly dragging him into the heart of the city.

'You're meant to be the one to put everything together for the Three, so *you* work it out,' Naira giggled unhelpfully.

'And if you could just use a bit of that Raiden-like speed, that'd be great.' Nova yanked on my hand, nearly pulling me off the ground.

'How far is it to the council room, then?' Noal puffed in annoyance, drawing a glittering, antagonising smile from Naira.

'You'll know it when you see it.'

He grimaced as we bustled further into the depths of the city than we'd ever gone before, until finally we truly did see what she meant – and the Nymphs snickered instead of complained when we jerked to a stop; our jaws dropping.

'Told youuu!' Naira tittered gleefully.

'*That*,' Noal gaped, 'is the most incredibly gigantic, most tremendous, most colossal tree I've ever seen.'

It was taller than all of the tree towers in the massive basin of the city, taller than the cliffs surrounding the basin, taller than the trees growing at normal forest ground level above the basin, and was so high that it in fact seemed to grow above the entire forest itself.

Its leaves and billions of branches rose so high above the canopy of the rest of the treetops that I could only make out a green ceiling-like blur which sparkled with filtered sun.

'Gods,' I breathed in awe. I could see hundreds of Elves and Nymphs moving about through different diamond shaped windows in the expansive trunk, or resting on ornate balconies. 'I can't believe I missed that.'

'I can almost bet where the meeting room is,' Noal commented apprehensively.

'Yup! It's the topmost room,' Nova supplied.

'But don't worry!' Naira laughed when he winced. 'This is where the Lady lives.'

'Her power runs through this whole tree. Nymphs and Elves join our own magic with hers to help us travel through its rooms,' Nova explained. 'We zoom straight up as if we were made of air,' she snapped her baby fingers. 'Just like that.'

'Right,' Noal frowned. 'But I'm not feeling very magical today.'

'Obviously that's why we have been sent to take you non-magical oafs.' Nova gleefully tugged on my hand to speed me up again. 'We'll channel our power through to you.'

We joined the Elves and Nymphs streaming into the massive tree's entrance hall, and I felt the overwhelming flow of the Lady's energy filling the tower, as though I could feel the pulse of the great tree itself.

'What is everyone else doing?' I asked. 'What's here apart from the Lady's home and council?'

'Everything,' Nova said, now pulling us out of the way of the streaming crowd. 'Libraries, histories, shops, a school room for the Nymphlings and Elflings.'

Noal spotted a sign with strange runes hanging on the wall behind him. 'And what does that say?' he questioned curiously. 'It's not in Awyalknian.'

Nova hung upside down next to the sign. 'It's a directory written in Nylvish.'

'It tells you all the levels so you can find which one you want,' Naira elaborated. 'But the topmost room is pretty obvious, isn't it? I don't think we need to look it up.'

'You have a separate tongue?' I asked in surprise. 'Why are you speaking Awyalknian?'

'Silly, pretty, young thing,' Naira teased cutely – pinching my cheeks. 'The Nymphs remember it from when we lived outside, but many Elves don't know it.'

'That explains why the Elves are not very talkative,' I realised in surprise.

'They're not super chatty anyway,' Nova interjected, flipping the right way up and brushing her floating hair in my eyes. 'Anyway. Hold tight!' she grinned, taking my hand as Naira took Noal's.

With a lurch, I felt my boots shoot away from the floor. We were abruptly sucked upward, whizzing at top speed through floor after floor.

I caught blurred visions of massive rooms, lounges and gatherings as I seemed to melt through the roof of each landing. My stomach was screaming as it was squashed down with the pressure of reality rushing past. Only Nova's grip on my hand assured me that I was still solid and real. Then the dizzying sensation was cut off and we stopped sharply, having appeared in a grand entrance way.

'That was ... disconcerting,' Noal gulped and staggered for a moment, before smoothing his mussed-up hair with a queasy expression.

'You're squeezing my hand,' Nova scolded me, peeling her squashed fingers free.

'Go on in,' Naira instructed. 'We'll be out here when it's over to escort you back.'

At the end of the spectacular entrance there were two polished doors that opened onto an opulent chamber. Near the chamber's high ceiling, with no strings or mechanics to work it, there floated an immense model of rotating art.

Coloured globes of varying sizes were levitating in circles around a central golden sphere. Some of them had rings encircling them that also spun, and smaller pale globes orbited all of them as they, too, circled the great golden sphere.

Below this masterpiece there was a circle of chairs in the middle of a gleaming, polished floor that reflected the decorative circling. There were ten chairs made of shining silver and an eleventh chair with a higher back made of beautifully stained wood.

Behind the chairs was a huge diamond shaped window from which streamed golden sunlight.

'Your mouth is hanging, darling,' Nova told me, giving me a little push to get moving.

'What is that?' Noal asked in amazement, his eyes on the rotating globes above the chamber we were to enter.

'It's a model of our solar system, silly. We're the blue, green and yellow ringed globe,' Naira giggled, and then stopped when she saw our blank expressions. 'Gosh. Mortals.'

'Forget it for now. We don't want to boggle them before they even speak to the council,' Nova told her, and then turned to us. 'It's just a pretty model.'

This time Naira and Nova shoved us so that we lurched across the entrance hall, entering the council room to find the Lady of the forest waiting.

Asha, Ace, Frey and a small number of other Nymphs and Elves were already there with her.

Thankfully Wilmont had spent years indoctrinating us with formal greetings – at last holding us in good stead with his methods.

Noal and I stepped forward together, and simultaneously swept ourselves into low, Awyalknian courtier-styled bows.

11

Eleven

D^{alin}

'Welcome friends.' The Lady's eyes were as green as radiant emeralds and her lined skin was as rich and dark as the earth. She was at once ordinary, yet extraordinary, and she captivated me almost completely.

Until I straightened to see that Kiana had also already arrived. She was dressed in something similar to her hunter's garb, and seemed almost back to her unshakable, usual self, even in the unusual setting.

'Please, be seated, and I will begin.' the Lady gestured, and I found that since we had last looked, the circle of chairs had been added to so that we could join the council members.

'You are the first humans to see our city and to be included in a council. And we are so glad to have you,' the

Lady informed the three of us simply, her voice musical and deep.

Her presence seemed to fill every inch of the large chamber with complex swirls and profound, incomprehensible power. I had to pull my attention to her words instead of fixating on her enchanting nature.

'Though we are less glad about the cause of this gathering,' she went on soberly. 'For we have called you here to discuss the threat facing our world, so that you may be better prepared for all that confronts you.'

Kiana leaned back in her chair. 'We are honoured and thankful that you would wish to help us even further than you already have.'

The Lady inclined her head. 'One thing we wish you to know is that the current threat to the world's harmony was something that was foreseen,' she confessed. 'The word was spread to all of the first peoples in the hopes of avoiding the danger. But as countless mortal lifetimes passed, the warnings were discounted or forgotten by many, just as people gradually stopped accepting that the magical races had ever truly lived among them.'

Kiana clasped her hands together pensively. 'Every Awyalknian child has heard what we all thought to be fictional tales of the Army for the World. However, Lixrax seems to still believe in yourself, at the very least,' she told the Lady.

'Lixrax remembers and believes some things, and perhaps some of our secretive Jenran neighbours do, too,' the Lady agreed. 'Though only Deimos and his descendant Darziates have ever truly acted on the warnings, with Deimos going so far as to begin the first War for the World.'.

'Darziates and Deimos are... ' I coughed. 'You're saying their actions are justified?' I had no idea what to do with that.

'They would certainly believe so. I will show you of what I speak,' the Lady said. 'Because I have the memory that spurred Deimos into action. The same memory that each of his heirs was passed.'

'The same memory?' Kiana questioned.

'My mind caught it by chance from a dying Sorcerer who had lived in hiding, readying to send it to his son,' the Lady explained. 'Perhaps it passed by me because I feature in it so heavily. More likely it was the will of the Gods.'

She gestured to the space in the middle of our circle of chairs, and I was amazed to see a patch of light breaking into spinning colours that joined to form the wavering shape of a woman.

I blinked at the real Lady sitting peacefully in her chair, and also the image of her standing in the middle of the circle.

Physically they were nothing alike. In the image her hair was auburn, she was tall and powerful, and her youthful stance was strong. Yet the spirit of both women was unmistakably the same.

She was *The* Lady.

The Lady of the forest.

I stared at the enchanting vision of the woman that I'd seen inked carefully across history books and embroidered gloriously on tapestries as the image began to speak.

'At the beginning of time I was created and given the knowledge and the will of the Gods. When I first awoke, I held in my hands two prophecies that would reveal themselves to me upon my arrival in the new world. The first prophecy was revealed only moments after my arrival, the voices of the Gods warning that the world's races would separate through the ages. The prophecy also told of a deadly threat that would be born into the world at the end of the ninth age. The voices of the Gods said that the world and her many races must be united to survive. If the world did not unite before the beginning of the tenth age, and the threat was realised, the world would be destroyed in a storm of ice and fire. I am now travelling far and wide to spread the warnings of the Gods, so that in thousands of years the world may be ready, and can be saved ...'

Before we could fully process this, the image of the Lady morphed.

We sat back rigidly in our chairs, shocked as the swirls of light reformed into the shape of a man's glaring face. His features were sharp and his granite gaze cold.

'Son. I have chosen this as my time to die. You will wake with the knowledge of all I have learned in my two hundred years, and with the knowledge of all of our ancestors. You will know that the first of our kind, Sorcerer Deimos, was a martyr who heeded the Lady's words. He devoted our bloodline to his cause of uniting the world. He sought the world's salvation, though his quest has remained unfulfilled.

'You will also wake with the knowledge of your true purpose and identity. You are the one that the line of Deimos has awaited, and already your darkness stirs. Grow strong in body, mind and magic. Be rid of the *Larnaeradee* and Unicorns who could facilitate the joining of any others against you. Reclaim our lost Kingdom in Krall. Rise to unite and lead the world. Be the one to save it all.'

The face distorted as the image broke apart, and I slumped in my chair as if I'd been released from a spell.

Noal let out a stunned breath and drew some more calming ones beside me.

The Lady sighed as if collecting herself too. 'That memory of myself was already centuries old back then, passed on along Deimos' line. The additional message from the dying Sorcerer was the spark that turned Darziates into what he is, giving him the same memories, feelings and goals as his ancestors.'

'This is much more than a war between Awyalkna and Krall,' General Ace asserted broodily then, with green eyebrows low. 'And Darziates has truly proven himself to be the most powerful one of his line.'

'Tell us,' Kiana invited when there was a moment's pause. 'We are ready to hear it.'

Frey's often serene expression was clouded when he spoke up to explain. 'Darziates has ruled in Krall for five hundred years. There have been no successors – it has been the same ageless Sorcerer. And in that time he has wiped out many magical races who might have opposed him. The *Larnaeradee*, Unicorns, Centaurs, Dryads, Sprites and water deities.'

Kiana's shoulders dropped slightly.

'So now the Sorcerer moves against Awyalkna. He will move on Jenra. And he'll cross the seas to take the other magical races,' Ace growled.

'What about Lixrax?' Noal asked with apprehension.

Ace scowled darkly. 'He already has Lixrax. Razek was forced into allegiance.'

'No!' I gaped in dismay. 'How could he coerce a whole nation to join him so quickly?'

'They have no choice but to follow,' Frey explained quietly. 'For the same reason that the people of Krall must follow his tyranny without rebelling.'

'Fear?' Noal questioned pensively.

'Sure. Many are controlled by fear,' Ace admitted, still glowering under a green, bushy frown. 'The peasants, the powerless and the weak. But an army of such magnitude could stand in revolution. They don't because...'

'They're as rotten as the Sorcerer,' I supplied, feeling certain of my response.

'Not everyone can be single-mindedly evil,' Asha disagreed with a tsk. 'The people of Krall were a fair race before Deimos and then again before Darziates. They weren't warlike and their land flourished.'

'The fact is that any who could stand against him were corrupted and conditioned into loyalty,' Ace stated flatly. 'Sorcerers have the power to corrupt even the purest of people to feel hatred and anger. Darziates has ingrained it into his soldiers to be loyal puppets and hateful enemies.'

'And Razek was forced to ally with Darziates to avoid a similar fate of mindlessness for his people,' Asha explained.

'Gods,' I muttered in horror. Noal had become pale beside me.

Awyalkna could not stand against the Sorcerer, his Witch, his army of beasts, his thousands of men and now also the elite Desert Storm of Lixrax. Even with the help of the Jenrans, if our quest *was* successful and they agreed on an alliance, there would be no hope of having enough forces to save Awyalkna.

Noal shook his head in disgust. 'Even if the Sorcerer thinks he's doing us all a favour, how can he be so deluded as to think that the entire world will just bow down gratefully and accept his reign?'

Asha crossed her legs where she sat in the air. 'The way that he sees it, he's the only one trying to do something to stop the 'threat', and is the only one able. He has worked hard, but he has made a very big mistake.'

'And ... what mistake is that?' Kiana asked heavily.

The Lady's eyes swept over the three of us.

'He never heard the second prophecy,' she answered gravely. 'It was revealed after I withdrew into the forest.'

'What did you learn?' Kiana asked warily. 'What is the second prophecy?'

'You,' the Lady answered with certainty. 'The Three.'

Kiana said nothing, Noal and I following her lead.

We'd all heard that title even before the forest. We'd been called 'the Three' by the Dryad spirit of the willow when she'd saved us from Agrona.

'Darziates thinks that he must be the one to unite the world against the threat warned of in the first prophecy. He seeks to end the boundaries between all peoples by imposing himself as the one ultimate King,' the Lady told us. 'He does not realise that by spreading his evil and suffering it is he who has become the threat.'

I rubbed my face, scrunching my brow.

Of course.

Kiana nodded slowly in understanding. 'He has become the monstrous event that he seeks to avoid.'

'Yet the second prophecy has revealed that there are to be Three able to stand against this threat and to unite the races against the Sorcerer,' the Lady stated earnestly.

'There is to be one to bring the Three together in their quest, and to keep the partnership of mortals strong. There is to be one to unite the lands of men. To bolster hope, respect and to lead all mortals of the world against the Sorcerer's storm. A king of kings – the Raiden. And there is to be the One, to summon and lead the magical races. They must join with the mortals led by the Raiden. The One will end the darkness. Thus, all races of the world will be united against the threat of Darziates,' the Lady finished.

Asha grinned a pointy-toothed grin. 'Can't be coincidence. The three of you ... out and about on your quest.'

Kiana shrugged doubtfully. 'That prophecy could be describing any three people on the planet.'

'No,' the Lady shook her head firmly. 'It describes each of you quite precisely. Noal ensured that, after the Raiden was healed, you did not part ways. Now he will continue to bring friendship amongst mortals. And the Raiden – to be able to rally and lead all men; a 'king of kings', must have royal blood. That is evidently Dalin.'

Kiana folded her arms in scepticism and a knife of guilt twisted in my stomach. I felt the blood draining from my face as Noal's stare met mine.

'And the One to lead the magical races must be magical herself. She must be a *Larnaeradee* at that, if she is to be a Summoner and able to speak the uniting tongue of *Aolen*. That is you, Kiana.'

Kiana drew in a deep breath. 'I don't believe that Dalin could be descended from royalty, or that I could be a Fairy without us having realised it.'

I felt sick.

The Elves sat forward in their chairs with the first signs of frustration I'd seen on their faces and the Nymphs buzzed in the air agitatedly.

'I see ... There is much for you to take in,' the Lady at last answered gently. 'Much has been revealed that must be processed.'

'Yes,' Kiana agreed diplomatically.

'Perhaps our council shall end for today so that you may reflect and rest,' the Lady acquiesced.

'Wait,' I cut in a little desperately. 'Can you first share any news of Awyalkna? Can you tell me how the King fares on the borders and how the Queen fares in the city?'

The Lady's eyes fell upon me, filled with empathy, and she nodded at the stout general, Ace.

The brawny little Nymph straightened from his mid-air, seated position to stand above his chair. 'The Nymph squads have reported that King Glaidin's troops have taken their first steps into Krall. The Queen has fortified the palace and the city is full of those who seek refuge. Some weeks ago, Darziates attacked the palace with two Dragons, but the city fought back and survived.'

The Nymph general cleared his throat. 'Beyond that, every day the surviving Krall soldiers continue their search within our own forest for the One. They have been getting closer to the city, but they cannot find us.'

At that, I hardly heard the Lady formally close the council. Or the murmured farewells that I received from the council members.

I vaguely knew that Noal had led me back to where Nova and Naira waited, and then back to our tower. He sat beside me when I slumped against my bed on the floor, lowering my head into my hands.

12

Twelve

Kiana

How could the Lady, all knowing and all-seeing immortal of the forest, possibly be wrong? With that disconcerting seed of doubt, I headed for Dalin and Noal's tree tower.

Their moss-covered door was already sweeping open as I approached, and I walked right in and across to the winding stairs. Pacing myself, I made my unaided way upwards to find them looking even more disturbed than I was by the council's revelations.

Noal was on the floor beside a slumped Dalin, and that nagging doubt suddenly sharpening with an edge of fear.

Noal peered up, though Dalin didn't lift his head, and I took an anxious step towards them. What had I missed?

Noal gave Dalin's shoulder a squeeze and stood, offering me a weak, reassuring smile before he quietly climbed the steps to his own bedroom.

Dalin at last lowered his hands to his lap.

His honey toned face was drained of all colour; so pale that the scar along his jawline seemed as vivid as if just freshly healed.

Nerves fluttered in my stomach as I crossed to take Noal's place beside him. He squeezed his eyes closed for a moment, steeling himself to face me.

'Kiana,' he at last said, his voice husky.

'It's alright,' I whispered encouragingly. 'Let it all out.'

With an anguished sound he took my hands in his.

'Dalin ...' I began gently. 'The odds were never in our favour. We never let it stop us before, even before our quest's grand fortune telling,' I tried to reassure him.

'There's such little chance for the survival of our country. And now, with these prophecies ...' he trailed off unhappily.

'Just because I'm no Fairy and you're no King, it doesn't mean we're useless,' I shushed him. 'We'll still do everything we can, as we always have.'

He shuddered. 'No ... that is the worst of it,' he managed. 'I have deceived you. I believe the prophecies are true.'

'What are you saying?' I asked.

His face was pleading for understanding and he gripped my hands desperately.

'I am the son of King Glaidin of Awyalkna. Prince Dalin. Heir to the throne.'

My heart seemed to fall away from my chest. My face had frozen into a mask of shock and a moment of silence passed between us as he searched my expression.

'The wealthy clothes,' I rocked backward. 'The never-ending supply of coin. The well-bred mares. The Awyalknian search parties. Darziates himself wanting you both so badly ...'

I suddenly realised that Dalin's hopeless grief right now was for his *family* as well as for his Kingdom.

Gods, I had been an out of touch fool.

What Awyalknian didn't know the names of the princes? Of course, the names had become fashionable since being associated with royalty, but as a young girl I'd known the original Noal's family had been murdered by Trune raiders. He'd been adopted as Prince Dalin's brother. I could not believe how spectacularly oblivious I had been.

I pushed myself away from Dalin's grip.

I stood and stepped back, reeling with sudden anger and hurt.

'I let you into my heart. Told you and Noal everything about myself. Things I've told no one else,' I said slowly. 'Yet neither of you trusted me in return.'

And if the prophecy was true for them ...

'Kiana?' Dalin moaned brokenly, scrambling to his feet and reaching out to me.

I turned away from him.

Just as I had for the two years before I had met him, I hardened my face, and brought the cold back into my eyes.

'Please Kiana, please forgive me,' he placed a frantic hand on my good shoulder.

I stiffened beneath his touch. I turned my gaze to burn across his face so that his hand slipped away, and he took a shocked step backward.

'No,' he gasped. 'Please don't shut me out again.'

I turned my eyes from him, staring straight ahead as I walked away.

'Kiana!' he cried after me.

I didn't look back as I exited their tower and stormed back to mine, where I retreated to the window seat in my bedroom to brood while the sky above the treetops filled with a net of stars.

I was still sitting with an iron grip around my knees, glaring outward when I heard the Lady and felt her presence fill my tower.

She came to me like mist coming into the fields at daybreak. Her power at once settled on every surface.

It seemed as if the world had become still and that the stars themselves were breathlessly watching as we both regarded each other.

I was not quite prepared though, for when she calmly uttered the phrase: 'Unana ren Tru *Larnaeradee.*'

'Unana ren, Ronden un Sylthanryn,' I responded – before my eyes widened.

What ...?

No, I knew what I'd said.

I *knew* what I'd said.

'Well met, Lady of Sylthanryn.'

How had I known to say it? How had I understood it?

With a stab of denial, I collapsed back onto the window seat's cushions. 'How ...?'

The Lady drifted to the armchair that had been Dalin's during my sickness.

'You spoke *Aolen*. The ancient tongue.'

'No,' I swallowed nervously, my mind stuttering forth from a jarring halt into a whir of uncertainty. 'How could I?'

'You are *Larnaeradee*. But more than that, you are the One *Larnaeradee* remaining to do what must be done,' she said calmly. She was willing me to feel it.

'No,' I repeated bluntly, shaking my head.

'No mortal could speak that tongue or understand it without a *Larnaeradee's* power to help them.'

'It was you who said all of the *Larnaeradee* and Unicorns are dead,' I replied defiantly, but the Lady's gaze remained steady, her eyes penetrating deep beyond my outer shell and into my soul.

I frowned under her scrutiny, feeling myself wavering under the sheer magnitude of her magic. The raw, savage, beautiful power of all of nature was harnessed inside her so peacefully. How could she ever be wrong? She was all know-ing. Ancient. Wise. A vessel of the Gods themselves.

'Kiana,' she said, her voice sending chills of energy down my spine. 'I will tell you the truth of who you are. When I am finished, if you still do not believe, then that is something I shall have to accept.'

I regarded her stonily. 'I will listen.'

She settled into the chair; her expression sincere. 'Then I thank you. And I will begin with what you must already know – that the *Larnaeradee* and Unicorns were the 'Summoners' and creators of *Aolen*, and were integral in uniting all of the races against Deimos in the first War for the World.

'But after Darziates' attacks began, and none could withstand them, the last of the Unicorns and their *Larnaeradee* parted for safety. The Unicorns returned to hiding in their lost, mountainous Karanoyar, and the *Larnaeradee* became wanderers. They disguised themselves as mortals and allowed their powers to become dormant – untraceable.

'It was only very recently that a couple descended from the *Larnaeradee* settled in Bwintam. They lived there with their powers dimmed – using them only to cloak their presence. They were the last surviving *Larnaeradee* family. Bwintam was their final refuge, for it was watched by the willow, and was close to the Great Forest.

'When your father Kires first visited the forest, there was such incredible joy and celebration. But no amount of pleading could bring him to stay. He and his wife Gwendis were the last of their clans, and they could not bear to step out of the world that they loved.

'The forest was solemn and quiet as Kires left, but he promised that he would send messages and, as promised, over the years we heard of yourself and your brother. Kires even returned to the forest when your sixteenth birthday neared so that, together, we could find your present. Though, again, Kires was gone too soon and I was not to see or hear from him again.

'When a Nymph squad found the ruins of Bwintam, it seemed that despite all efforts to remain hidden, the last of the *Larnaeradee* had been slaughtered by accident. But the squad told of the possibility of a survivor. They had felt the faint presence of a magical being other than the Witch, and our minds turned to the second prophecy. We hoped it meant that one of you had lived.

'I think, unknowingly, the Witch sensed your pure magic, too – and that is what made her want to lash out and to punish you so unwittingly. To make you suffer.

'I cast my mind out to feel for traces of you, but even in that state your power kept your exact location hidden. I could only send out my voice to try to spur you to find help.

'You healed outwardly and began to hunt again. And every now and then I caught glimpses of you on your journeys across the vast lands, until I deciphered that you were withdrawing to a smaller place – heading toward Gangroah.

'I watched over you while you were there, until one day a beast came to your cottage by mistake when it was looking for two princelings. And I was convinced that the prophecies were true as you came together, the Three questors the Gods had promised.

'Dalin, of royal blood. Noal – the one to keep you all together. And you, the One, final *Larnaeradee*.'

It felt as if my lungs had broken because my breath was coming in strange, winded bursts.

'I need to think,' I whispered hoarsely.

'Qui?' she asked steadily. 'Why'.

I flinched at how easily I had understood that word, again in *Aolen*.

Her tale brought terror to my heart. Because I could see it.

I had felt the truth of every single word that had passed her lips.

And once again, I felt terribly alone. The last of my kind. Alone within the darkness.

I stood; my face devoid of the emotion raging inside of me. I willed my mask to hold for just a few more moments.

'Please leave,' I said in a low voice. 'Give me time.'

The Lady rose and looked ready to speak, her lined hand reaching out.

'Please just get away from me,' I almost hissed this time.

Her gaze was filled with care, and she silently, respectfully turned. Leaving as quietly as she had come.

Her presence gradually faded from my tower, and at last I allowed my face to crumple.

My sight blurred with horrible tears as, in a sudden rage, I crossed to a vase filled with flowers from Dalin and thrust it furiously from the table.

But with that simple, aggressive motion, a familiar nagging ache began once more in my shoulder.

'Frarshk!' I spat, suddenly repulsed and afraid to be trapped in my own skin and in the city itself.

I had to get out. I had to think. I had to burn away this pain like I always had.

With the blade of my sword.

13

Thirteen

D^{alin}

'I can't be the glorified Raiden. I hardly measure up as a prince,' I told Noal hopelessly. 'And I don't know if Kiana will ever trust me again.'

Night had brought darkness to our tree tower.

'I had a hand in not telling her who we really are,' Noal reminded me.

'But you were following my lead.'

It was for safety at the start. But then we had never corrected the omission. I grew too comfortable with just being Dalin in her eyes.

Noal sighed. 'I hate to be predictable. But I might as well say exactly what I was supposedly prophesied to say. We'll have to find a way to come back together and overcome this. The three of us need each other and the quest needs each of us. The truth would have come out eventually, anyway.'

'Raiden!' Asha yelled then, crashing at top speed through the diamond shaped window on the opposite side of the room. Her hair was standing straight out from her head.

'Asha, what's wrong?' Noal asked in alarm.

'Have either of you seen Kiana?' she gasped as she tried to catch her breath, zipping around the room as if to find Kiana hiding in some nook or cranny.

'No.' My voice was strained. 'Not since this afternoon.'

'Oh Gods!' she blustered. 'GodsohGodsohGods!' she yanked on her hair in anxiety.

'Asha,' Noal addressed her in perplexity, fear now edging his own voice. 'What's happened?'

'I don't know, I don't know!' she wailed. 'I saw the Lady go into Kiana's tower, and I knew the Lady would want Kiana to confront the truth ... But just now when I went to see if Kiana was alright, her tower was empty. Her cupboard was open, and her sword was missing.'

'Frarshk ...' I groaned, feeling my stomach flip. 'How long do you think she's been gone?'

'Her power still swirled strongly about the tower, but I searched everywhere before I came here and I couldn't find a trace of her. She's not in the city.'

'She hasn't left for good or been taken. She's gone on a hunt to calm herself,' I stated, not feeling better at all.

It was Noal's turn to groan. 'Alone, still healing, and still weak from Agrona's poison.'

'Right,' Asha stated, her mood changing quickly. All fret-fulness dropped from her stance and she became the Nymph squad commander and council leader. 'Well, the weakened magic should make it easier for us to find her, calmed down or not. I'm going to get help. Ready yourselves.'

14

Fourteen

Kiana

'I heard a yelp,' a gruff voice whispered. 'A cry of pain. This way.'

As I pressed against a towering trunk to hide, I knew I had behaved idiotically.

A burst of pain like the one that had given me away only moments before exploded in my shoulder, and I tried desperately not to gasp. It ebbed for an instant and then shot savagely right throughout my body so that I had to bite my lip and grasp at the rough bark behind me for support.

I heard a twig snapping to my left and lowered myself quietly to disappear into waist high ferns, right as a line of figures in spiked armour stepped out from the trees to unconsciously surround me.

'I swear to the Gods I heard something from this direction,' a burly soldier grunted, pulling off his helmet and wiping his forehead with the back of his fist.

'Aye,' agreed a second stocky warrior, peering about himself.

'It could be her,' another brawny man squinted around the shadowy bushes and flowers. 'Or it could be those *things* ...'

'I tell you, they are Elves. They were exactly like the pictures in storybooks.'

'And those littleuns with wings? The ones that shot light and fire from their babe-sized fists? How do you explain them?' a different soldier queried.

'Much the same as you do anything else these days,' another said wearily, scratching his beard. 'It's magic. Good or bad.'

The sixteen surviving Krall soldiers had haphazardly encircled me by accident, and I had no way to escape. Yet, strangely, as I beheld them now I realised that they didn't quite resemble the brutal enemies I remembered.

They were formidable, but I could feel nothing foul about them. They were just men, as if they had been transformed or I was seeing them more clearly.

They were still, however, men who were specifically hunting for me.

'Well, if we don't find anything we can rest here for the night,' the bearded soldier announced authoritatively.

'And if we do find her?' asked the youngest looking one.

Some of them shifted, as if they were uncertain, or uncomfortable.

'You know any prisoners were meant to come with us to Krall ...' the bearded soldier replied, though with a lack of conviction.

'We take her back to King Darziates? So that he can befoul the only pure thing any of us have ever come across?' the youngest glowered.

Now they were all shifting in nervous unease.

'Enough ... we've discussed this,' the leader sighed. 'The only way we can get back to our homes without Darziates blaming this disaster on all of us is to have her with us.'

'Well I hardly have a home worth going back to,' the youngest scowled. 'And I know none of us feel any love lost when it comes to the Sorcerer. Maybe we should re-think our plans.'

'Shh!' hissed the one with his helmet off, glancing around as if Darziates might be listening. 'Just because you don't have family alive for him to threaten doesn't mean we don't.'

The younger one stalked angrily away from them, closer to where I was positioned.

'Thorin, enough,' the leader said again, more firmly. 'We find her first. Save her from those forest creatures. Then we decide what to do with her.'

I inwardly cursed. I would be found as soon as they inspected the area even a little more closely. There would be no chance for slinking away sneakily.

There was nothing for it.

Despite nauseating waves of pain, I wrenched myself up from a crouch; my sword raised to readiness while the majority of my would-be captors yelped or growled in startled incredulity.

'Well, you've found me,' I announced resignedly. 'But last time you had trouble keeping hold of me. Care to try your luck again?'

I was confronted by stunned silence, and when nobody – not even the open mouthed, staring leader moved, I went for the closest warrior. The youngest they'd called Thorin.

Impressively, he was quick to jump to attention and unsheathe his blade when I drove at him in attack. He hastily deflected each of my strokes as I forced him to give ground.

'Don't hurt, just disarm her!' the bearded leader yelled at Thorin over the clanging of our blades. 'Form a barrier!' he called to the others, placing me in a tighter, more purposeful ring.

Thorin was concentrating hard, but I drilled him with such intensity that he was growing breathless and panicked while he sought only to defend.

I feinted a jab at his ribs and had him empty handed in a moment. Not waiting for him to stop blinking in surprise, I delivered a high kick into his chest that sent him sprawling.

I was more exhilarated by my situation than I should have been.

I could still do this. I could still be me!

'If you insist on challenging one by one, it's your turn,' I told a curly haired soldier, and he had no choice but to raise his blade and engage with me as I stabbed and parried.

I had him disarmed and rolling away from me even quicker than I'd managed with Thorin, and I was grinning wolfishly as I chose my next victim.

I felt good.

Until, when I had engaged my fourth warrior, I felt a horrifying burning pang of fire inside, and I stumbled.

The agony crashed over me – clawing through my chest, my shoulder, my arms. As if Agrona herself was raking sharp fingernails under my skin at that exact moment.

The tip of my sword dropped as my grip weakened with the stunning shock, and my opponent's sabre nicked my arm.

'Oh! I'm sorry!' he gasped, and quickly flicked his blade away from me in confusion.

The rest of the soldiers had frozen in bewilderment, baffled by how fast the flurry of my attack had stopped.

'I told you not to hurt her, Phobos!' the leader reprimanded my adversary accusingly.

'I didn't mean it, she didn't block me,' Phobos protested earnestly.

A familiar trickle of weakness began to seep throughout my body, like a cold draught running through my veins. My mind whirled and I felt my knees buckle.

My sword slipped from my fingers and sixteen concerned enemies from Krall came rushing forward as I collapsed into darkness.

When I opened my eyes, I found Thorin propping me up in his arms. His fingers were pulling at my shirt and flitting over my chest, checking the wound.

Then, distantly but undeniably, I heard Dalin let loose a roar of outrage.

15

Fifteen

N*oal*

Dalin hardly slowed, even when he broke contact with Vidar to launch himself through the wall of Krall warriors looming over Kiana.

I kept by his side and the warriors seemed to give way before our blades like parting waters.

Dalin didn't risk using his sword against the soldier who held Kiana, instead thumping his fist so solidly into the warrior's forehead that the impact was grossly audible, and the warrior slumped backward to lay unmoving on the forest floor.

Dalin sheathed his sword – letting the Elves and Nymphs pursue the other soldiers. He pulled Kiana close, hugging her warmly as all around us the Krall warriors were driven off.

'I'm so sorry Kiana,' Dalin told her as he pulled back to meet her eyes.

'Me too! But you shouldn't go off like that without a word,' I told her worriedly. 'No matter how you feel toward us.'

Kiana shuddered.

'I *was* angry at you,' she admitted sickly. 'But, mostly ... I was just overwhelmed.' She swallowed thickly. 'I ... think the Lady was right,' she managed to add. 'I feel it.'

'What do you mean?' I questioned.

'I think I am a ... *Larnaeradee*.' She looked away from us as Dalin helped her to move into a sitting position. 'In fact, I'm terrified. Because I know I am,' Kiana admitted. 'It was all too much.'

'Oh, Kiana!' Dalin sighed, supporting her gently. 'Do you think it really makes a difference if you are?'

She frowned up at him, surprised.

'You're not exactly normal anyway,' I pointed out, and she glared at me, but with a glimmer of a smile.

'Kiana, it doesn't matter if you are magical,' Dalin told her seriously.

'It doesn't matter?'

'No,' he shook his head. 'You are still our Kiana. To us you've always been incredible.'

She shook her head with a scoffing gulp of wonder. 'It is my turn to apologise,' she said softly then. 'I should have accepted you, too. Nothing is different between us simply because of your titles. Though I'm embarrassed not to have thought more deeply on it.'

Dalin regarded her with relief. 'I will never again hide such a thing from you.'

'I should hope there is nothing else so surprising to know about you,' she replied, wincing as Dalin helped her to her feet, wrapping his arm about her waist in support.

'Told you you're the Three,' Asha purred smugly, whirring contentedly back to hover beside Vidar's smiling face.

The always fiercely intense Frey stepped forward then.

'One, can you walk?' he asked.

'Yes,' she answered firmly. 'And with my returning strength has come my returning senses. I apologise to you all for leaving without thought and dragging you all after me.'

For once Frey's serious face seemed taken aback. 'You have nothing to apologise for, Tru *Larnaeradee*. You are not a prisoner in our city, but a friend. You are free in this forest. And we only pursued you to defend and protect one that we love.'

Kiana's posture softened at the reverent, genuine expressions of all of the forest dwellers who had joined us.

'I am blessed beyond measure to have such friendship, and I thank each of you,' she told them; mollified as she took Frey's proffered hand.

'Alvar,' Ace rumbled at one of the quiet Elves, who was standing over the remaining, fallen Krall warrior as we readied to leave. 'Will you carry our new guest back to the city?'

Alvar knelt to bundle the warrior up, hoisting the man over his shoulders with ease, armour and all.

And after another Elf; Quidel took my hand, in what seemed like a blink we were all flashing through the forest and coming to a stop near Kiana's tower.

The city continued to buzz with night time activity as if nothing had happened.

'Please don't go out hunting so late again, Kiana,' Asha yawned suddenly, sagging down in the air. 'I'm tired all over.'

Flash laughed and whirred through the air to wait underneath her with his arms outstretched. Her eyes closed and she sank down into them, already dreaming.

'She'll wake in a few moments wanting to do something or other,' he told Rebel.

'We could pester Silvanus and Chloris,' Rebel suggested, and they drifted off towards the poor Elves' tree tower.

'Is all well with you now, Kiana?' Vidar asked, standing aside with Frey, Dalin and I as the Krall warrior was carried off and the rest of the group dispersed. 'I'm guessing when we found you that you hadn't been overcome in combat.'

Kiana's face grew troubled. 'You're right. I was revelling in the battle, and it was only Agrona's poison that stopped me.'

My heart sank.

'That is one reason that I hope to see the Lady now,' Kiana sighed grimly. 'Another is that I must hear everything else that she has to say about 'the One' of the prophecies.' She turned to Dalin and I. 'And I would like the both of you to be with me.'

'Of course,' Dalin replied at once.

'It is a good idea,' Frey conceded. 'The Lady never truly sleeps, and is probably waiting to see you. But you would do well to rest first yourself.'

Kiana shook her head. 'It's time I heard the full truth and accepted it. I need to do this.'

16

Sixteen

D^{alin}

The council room was glimmering with soft golden light and the model of rotating spheres turned continuously above.

The Lady was waiting, and for a moment she stole my breath away. The dazzling silvery green of her gossamer robes shimmered while she beckoned for us to come forward in welcome, and unlike the stooped, grandmotherly woman we had encountered so far, she now appeared in the form portrayed by artists.

Her rich, brown skin glowed as if it held the life of the earth itself, and auburn hair spilled down her smooth shoulders to brush her waist – all trace of greying age gone. I felt almost giddy from the aura that surrounded her.

'Lady,' Kiana inclined her head respectfully. 'I've come to hear you out with more accepting ears.'

'I am glad, and also impressed. It is no small feat to come to acceptance of such news in a day and a night,' the Lady told her compassionately. She stepped gracefully aside and I saw that there were now four cushioned chairs surrounding a merrily burning fire where the council had been seated earlier.

Noal, like myself, had become wordless and almost bashful as we came to take the chairs that the timeless messenger of the Gods offered.

'You have missed Noal, haven't you?' the Lady softened our awe with a more casual smile toward Noal's chair leg. 'Leaving you be during the council was very hard for her,' she confided to Noal warmly.

Noal guffawed as a hand sized spider pranced quickly up to sit on his knee.

'When you all left Gangroah together I found it almost impossible to mentally trace your steps,' the Lady informed us. 'I came home here, where I feel much healthier, and it was Granx who worked tirelessly to follow your progress in a literal sense. It wasn't until the willow sent two messengers that I was even sure the Three were coming to Sylthanryn.'

Kiana straightened where she sat then, her face clearing with dawning realisation. 'It is good to see you again, Gloria,' she huffed.

I frowned in confusion. 'You're the eccentric lady who lived in the second Gangroah cottage?'

I remembered the old green-eyed woman, and realised the Lady's previous, elderly form had been similar – if less human in appearance than the woman I had seen in Gangroah.

The Lady lifted her shoulders with an almost coy smile of an elegant admission in return.

'But everyone knew about peculiar old Gloria who lived in the Gangroah cottage!' Noal said in consternation, and then added: 'no offense.'

'I recall that we overheard a story about Gloria, and the 'empty' cottage, through a green-eyed, auburn-haired palace maid,' I turned to Noal, suddenly feeling a rush of realisation. 'The maid's chatter was what gave us the idea of heading to Gangroah in the first place.'

'So,' Noal eyed the Lady incredulously. 'Your youthful self was the one who informed us about your elderly self?'

The Lady regarded him patiently. 'Time and place do not restrain me,' she explained simply, as if that were not an extraordinary fact. 'I can be everywhere, though it is harder outside the forest now. So, while I manifested to present yourself and the Raiden with the idea to quest towards Gangroah, I also manifested as Gloria to keep watch over the last *Larnaeradee* and to make sure she would be ready and waiting for you.'

'You felt Kiana to be a *Larnaeradee*,' I remarked then. 'But the Fairies in the stories graduated into *Larnaeradee* on their sixteenth birthdays, and Kiana hasn't yet.'

'Yes,' the Lady acknowledged. 'While I could feel the truth about her, her earthstone is the key to accessing her wings and full magic. And though Kires and I found the earthstone he would present Kiana with for her birthday, I believe he never had the chance to unlock and explain the gift to her.'

The colour had left Kiana's cheeks as she listened. 'He put it in the Unicorn figurine?' she asked, aghast.

The Lady nodded. 'As Gloria I saw the figurine in your cottage, and felt certain that was where it was hidden.'

'Yes,' Kiana was nodding firmly now. 'There is a line, like an incision around the figurine's body, as if it were just a case that could be opened. But it is actually impossibly immovable.' Her brow creased with a puzzled frown. 'Why has it never opened for me?'

'Your situation is different to that of the Fairies who once lived,' the Lady explained. 'You knew nothing of your ancestry, of your powers, of being a Fairy when you were given that figurine. It did not open because Kires closed it protectively for until you were ready. It still may not open for you even now, until you have fully accepted who and what you are.'

Kiana sank back in her chair.

'Yet your situation is also different, and quite incredible, as you have already clearly begun to develop your powers, even without your stone,' the Lady reassured her. 'Confirming that you really are the One. The most powerful of them all.'

Kiana didn't respond, her face was pensive and grave.

'You can develop your powers further,' the Lady continued. 'But this will only be when you have your stone, and are ready for it. Then you will be endowed with the wings and powers of a true *Larnaeradee*. And only then will your body have the ability to fully heal itself of Agrona's magic.'

'Gods,' Noal breathed – absentmindedly stroking the deadly spider that had once terrified him.

'I do believe you,' Kiana replied with a glum sigh. 'I can no longer hide from it. I can feel that you speak the truth. But ...' her eyes trailed from the fire to the green gaze of the Lady. 'I do not understand why, if my family was so powerful, they did not use their magic to defend themselves in the end.'

I saw sorrow etch itself across the Lady's striking features. 'You were the One chosen by the Gods. Upon their deaths, your parents' powers and the powers of all of your ancestors were left to you so that you could gain the strength needed to face Darziates, as the Gods have selected you to do.'

The Lady seemed to reach toward Kiana without ever moving.

'While your parents did all they could to protect your family, hiding their identities and magic so they were not found by Darziates, this left them vulnerable to mortal deaths. And they could not undo what we now know was destined to be done, just as they could not predict or withstand such a surprise attack with dormant powers.'

'It had to happen?' Kiana whispered.

'It seems so,' the Lady affirmed painfully. 'So that all of their power could combine and become yours. Leaving you to be the One that the world so badly needs as the tenth age draws near,' she said sorrowfully. 'It is you, Kiana, with the magic of your ancestors alive within you, pure and strong, who can face the evil of Darziates. Not even I could do this as you can, as my magic, and everything about me, is the very nature that Darziates corrupts. You instead channel and wield nature's power, and I am part of that power that you draw upon to add to your own.'

Kiana was very still as she gazed at the Lady. 'And so, there are no Unicorns left alive either?' she asked stoically.

The Lady drew a deep breath before releasing it. 'No. You are the One, the only one, who can confront Darziates.'

Kiana's eyes lowered back to the flames before her. 'Then, in many ways I am as alone as Agrona cursed me to be.'

'But not in all ways,' Noal admonished her then. 'You have the two of us.'

'And you have the love of eccentric old Gloria, too,' the Lady added quietly, her melodious voice tender.

'Thank you,' Kiana replied heavily.

Noal sighed loudly. 'Though no love seems to equal what I am being shown right now,' he exclaimed, watching the Granx as it hugged its legs around his thigh, blinking its many eyes at him adoringly.

'She was disheartened every time she found you all, only to be sent on her way,' the Lady smiled at Noal again. 'Granx is enamoured by you especially, and is glad to reunite.'

'Well, why not?' he shrugged helplessly. 'It's understand-able.'

'Our days seem to be getting progressively stranger,' I mused tiredly.

But Kiana straightened with returning vigour. 'I would love to reunite with the two messengers you said the willow sent into the forest.'

'Who are they?' I asked, while the Lady stood with a smile.

'When they were transported here by the willow's magic, they told me their names were Ila and Amala.'

'Gods,' I uttered. 'The strangeness continues.'

17

Seventeen

Kiana

I had spent the last hours of the night nestled in the warm space between Ila and Amala's velvety bodies – finding solace and a growing sense of peace with my silent companions.

I felt almost accepting of the night's discoveries as the sun began to cascade down into the city and Amala stirred into wakefulness; peering at me with one big eye and whinnying cheerfully when she saw that I was really there. Ila chuffed groggily and nudged me so that I would rub her snout.

They only rose when I did, and then they trotted at my side like playful ponies while I made my way toward the clamber of the Nymph training grounds. The two mares only lost interest and meandered away, completely at ease in the city, when I stopped to observe General Ace's morning drills.

He paused his airborne pacing of the ranks when he caught sight of me waiting at the fence-line, and a number of bright heads bobbed up with many Nymphs breaking from their fiercely disciplined stances to shout joyous greetings.

'Asha,' Ace rumbled, and she toppled out of line to take up his patrol. Immediately the coy, cute smiles of the Nymphs disappeared; pointed teeth baring as the training resumed.

'Well met, One,' Ace greeted me in his gravelly tones.

'Well met,' I replied. 'I apologise for the disruption. I just wished to ask after the captured Krall soldier.'

Ace crossed his legs and sat mid-air. 'He was taken to an improvised holding bay,' he explained gruffly, leaning an elbow on his knee. 'We don't normally need to take prisoners, with the city being well hidden by the Lady. But we delved out a room beneath a part of the cliff walls.'

'And?' I prompted him to continue.

'And ...' he grunted. 'We left him to recover from the headache the Raiden had given him. He has been given food and water, but has refused to talk.'

'He has been questioned?' I asked.

'We mean him no harm,' Ace shrugged. 'He's a victim of the Sorcerer. But we also mean him no freedom until we have established whether Darziates still clouds his nature.'

'I understand,' I nodded. 'So, if we can establish that he is no longer a true enemy to us, he will be safe here?'

The general rubbed at his nose roughly. 'If we thought any of those confused soldiers out there were still a hopeless cause, we already would have torn the lot of them to pieces when they attacked you. In fact, it was quite a feat for the Nymphs to restrain themselves once they got the taste of the fight last night.'

'That's good, then,' I conceded gingerly.

'Very,' he agreed. 'We will only war with Darziates' mortals when it comes to that because they will be serving him against us and we cannot break his hold over them, not because we harbour any true hate for them.'

'Fair,' I asserted. 'But in regard to the warrior we hold now, I would like to talk to him.'

Ace stretched his legs out to stand in the air again. 'Perhaps,' he said slowly, stroking his wiry green beard. 'He may talk to you.'

'I can try. I may be able to help him to see more clearly.'

The general regarded the whirling combat practice that Asha was enthusiastically coordinating for a moment.

'Follow me,' he rumbled at last, leading me away from the training grounds, through a market place and toward the looming cliffs.

We stopped when the rocky wall was in front of us, and I could see three square chunks of the wall missing low down at ground level.

'Those are the cell windows,' he told me, and swept down to tug at the grass a yard from the wall. 'Stand here. The entrance will open for you. Hopefully he'll be responsive.'

'I appreciate it,' I told the stout general, and he nodded before heading back towards the training.

I stepped up to the patch of grass with some uncertainty, but a reverberating sound came from beneath my feet and I felt the ground begin to vibrate as magic danced in the grass underneath me.

I cautiously watched the turf and marvelled as the square of earth in front of my boots dropped away, revealing a ladder into a small underground chamber.

A door of sorts barred the end of the chamber from a slightly larger cavern on the other side, and though the door was made entirely of vertical vines and roots, they looked entirely too stiff to move.

I stepped closer to peer through the vines, and found that the forest dwellers had simply removed a vast cube of underground cliff rock to make a room.

Lush green grass had somehow been made to spring up from the rocky floor to carpet it, and the carved-out windows I'd seen at the base of the cliff were high in the wall – letting golden light flood over a small, plush bed. A mahogany desk with some books had been set against one rocky wall, with a large wooden basin of water set upon it, along with a platter of freshly picked fruits.

But most interesting of all was the prisoner himself. Despite his rather lavish surroundings he was sitting miserably on the grassy floor with his back against the wall. He still wore his armour but for his helmet and weapons, and was sullenly staring away from where I stood in the doorway, making a pointed effort to ignore any communication.

Even as the wish to enter occurred to me, I heard a whispering rustle, and all by themselves the roots and vines over the door loosened their hold on each other and began to part like curtains so that I could step inside, feeling the vines sweep gently closed behind me.

I leaned a hip against the mahogany desk, cocking an eyebrow.

'Have you really been in that armour all night?' I asked curiously, and the soldier's head whipped up.

'It's you!' he gasped with the rough sounding accent of the Krall brogue.

'You're right,' I told him calmly. 'It's definitely me.'

I saw the flowering purple bruise across his forehead and inwardly winced. That would cause quite the headache indeed.

'I am Kiana.'

'Kiana?' he echoed me with wonder, as if he'd dreamed of hearing my name.

I smothered a smile. 'And I recall that your name is Thorin?'

He flushed. 'Yes, Thorin,' he informed me hastily.

He appeared to be a little younger than myself. His hair was a shade lighter than Dalin's and his eyes were dark.

'Have they locked you up, too?' he asked, angered at a non-existent injustice. 'Where did they keep you before? Are you harmed in any way?'

I couldn't help but laugh in surprise. 'I'm no prisoner here,' I said as I eyed off his surroundings. 'Though it looks like it'd be a relaxing experience.'

He finally sat up properly.

'What do you mean?' he asked with an uncertain frown. 'Last night you escaped them and we found you. You were injured.'

I shook my head. 'Last night I was rescued by my friends from the Krall warriors who were trying to take me to their King.'

'The strange beings are your friends? How is that so? From the night they took you we have been searching...'

I frowned at how oddly he remembered things, wondering if Dalin's blow had seriously scrambled his mind. I crossed to sit on the end of the bed as Thorin's perplexed gaze followed me.

'So far, the only time I've been held captive was by the troop you were with,' I told him carefully. 'Your general's arrow wounded me as my comrades and I escaped your camp, and last night what remains of your troop nearly captured me again. The Elves and Nymphs aided us.'

Thorin flinched and slumped back. He appeared suddenly woozy and pale, as if all of these events were a blur that he had blocked out of his memory.

'But we were trying to find you. You were hurt.' He put his hand to his forehead, his skin growing paler, and I leaned forward in alarm.

'Why do you think you remember things differently to what I remember?' I asked, trying to bring his focus back.

His face grew confused, almost dazed. Then suddenly he took a sharp breath and squinted at me.

'I know all that you say is true,' Thorin whispered. 'We were the ones who hurt you. We were your enemies, meant to take you to Darziates, but then you … you showed us your power. And it was … pure.'

He shook his head, a vague cloudiness again coming into his gaze. Worry started to gnaw at my insides.

Something was wrong with him.

'All of us who survived and saw your power at once felt suddenly free, as if the darkness that Darziates has always forced upon us had eased, and we came after you because – we wanted to help you. Or … to give you to Darziates? Or to keep you for ourselves?' his voice trailed off and his body began to shake so much that his armour rattled.

'What's wrong?' I asked urgently, quickly crossing to crouch beside him. I saw his eyes roll back and all of the blood drained from his face.

'Thorin?' I asked, trying to snap him back into wakefulness.

I put my hand to his burning forehead. The instant that I touched his skin, his eyes flashed open and he lunged forward to grip both my arms. I cried out in surprise as his hands gripped my biceps like vices.

'Get off her!' growled a voice from behind me and then Noal and Dalin were charging through the vines at the door.

'Shush the pair of you,' I stilled them with a glance. 'He's not trying to hurt me, something's wrong with him.'

They both stopped at my words, but Dalin loomed angrily where he stood.

'Thorin?' I asked. 'What is happening to you?'

Thorin fought to keep conscious, and was gritting his teeth. 'It's as if admitting the truth is killing me!' he managed to gasp. 'But I need to tell you. Each of my comrades have felt the same, felt loyalty to you, but because of Darziates they have been too afraid to admit it. This is the first time I have completely admitted what has really happened and look what it's doing to me!'

I glanced desperately at Dalin and Noal to find that Dalin's anger was wearing off and Noal now wore an expression of horror.

Tears began to roll down Thorin's cheeks, though he didn't seem to notice them.

They were tinged with grey.

Watery grey trails leaking from his desperate eyes.

'I think I'm fighting Darziates' hold on me! I can feel his fingers around my mind, clawing at my brain, telling me you will only be safe if I take you to him.'

Thorin moaned and his hands started to lose strength and slip away from my arms. 'There's a war going on ... inside my head ...'

Abruptly he sank back, unconscious.

My heart was beating fast. 'Noal,' I spun around. 'Get help. Dalin, pull him up.'

With gritted teeth Dalin stooped to haul the armoured young warrior up and across to the bed while Noal dashed from the room.

I tried to check if Thorin was breathing clearly, though in the spiked armour he could hardly even be laid down comfortably.

'This is ridiculous!' I hissed. 'Help me get the armour off.'

But Dalin grunted. 'You do remember who this is, don't you?'

'It isn't his fault, he's under Darziates' power,' I retorted as he began to begrudgingly help me to unbuckle the chest plate. 'You heard for yourself that Thorin no longer wants to be an enemy.'

'And I pity that he is a victim of Darziates.' Dalin pulled spiked shoulder pieces and the breast plate away to begin tugging at Thorin's chain mail shirt. 'I mourn that nearly everyone in Krall is stuck under the Sorcerer's power, but as horrible as it is – it's the reality,' Dalin panted with the effort of helping me. 'The people of Krall are under the Sorcerer's power. And this particular Krall citizen has proven to be a violent warrior. Do you really think one of Darziates' own soldiers is converted? That he can suddenly be cured of Darziates, as much as he wants it?'

'Didn't you hear any of what Thorin said?' I joined Dalin in pulling the chain mail over the warrior's head.

'I heard his confession, but how can we ever trust someone who could be under Darziates' power? This could all be Darziates' trickery.'

I heard footsteps hurrying down the ladder outside.

'I've never seen you like this,' I said to Dalin then, disconcerted. 'I have never known you to be so hard toward another.'

'That was before I had to fight this same soldier to stop him from taking you from me twice,' Dalin answered heatedly.

I was speechless, and glad when Chloris and Silvanus rushed into the room with Noal.

18

Eighteen

N^{oal}

Flash and Rebel darted out from the trees, rushing toward us even while a fuming Dalin and brooding Kiana followed me out of the cave cell.

'Is all well?' Kiana asked, uncrossing her arms and softening her stance as they breathlessly jolted to a stop.

'One,' Flash gasped.

'Raiden,' Rebel wheezed.

'Noal,' they puffed, acknowledging plain old me together.

'We've lost an Elf!' Flash's silvery hair stood on end.

Dalin's countenance softened quickly then, too.

'Bard left the city to hunt,' Rebel garbled. 'Because he needed the challenge to stop feeling so serious!'

'How long ago?' I asked uneasily.

'Two days, and he would normally be back by now,' Rebel answered wretchedly.

'Frarshk,' Dalin rubbed his jaw.

'Bard should have stayed close in case the seriousness got the better of him,' Flash cringed, wringing his tiny hands. 'But groups of Nymphs have searched all of the nearest or most likely places, and there's no sign.'

'It's all this talk of war and Darziates stifling nature,' Rebel zipped this way and that. 'An Elf can't help but get serious with all of that looming!'

'It's worse for Bard, though,' Flash interjected. 'He's one of the oldest Elves in the forest. He didn't stop at two hundred. So, his mind already wanders and he has to stay regularly active.'

'If he's got trapped in the seriousness ...'

Rebel was breathing so hard that I wanted to take him down from where he agitatedly flapped so that I could rock him like a frightened child. I knew exactly how this type of anxiety constricted one's lungs and tightened their throat.

'Falling to the seriousness ...' the Nymph managed to croak. 'It's not like normal dying for an Elf, you know – they get trapped in their minds forever and their spirits don't return to nature.'

'We'll join the Nymphs in their search,' I promised. 'Is it best not to bring other Elves out into the forest at the moment, then?'

'It's why we took such a small group of Elves to find Kiana. And ...actually ...' Flash grimaced. 'The Nymphs have probably done as much as they can already without your specific help.'

'One of the only areas of the forest left to search is a place tainted by Sorcery,' Rebel cut in. 'Which hurts those who share their life force with nature.'

I blew out a big breath at how strangely fast paced the morning had become, with one urgent rush after another.

'Well, we best get a move on, it seems,' I stated blandly.

'Not Kiana, though,' Dalin surmised firmly. 'Not after last night's episode and ...'

Her dagger filled glare had his confident assumptions trailing off.

'I will of course be of service,' Kiana said in a steely tone. 'Last night was invigorating, and I owe the forest dwellers a debt.'

I cleared my throat awkwardly. 'We will trust you to decide for yourself.'

Dalin's lips pressed tightly together for a moment. But then he got back to the facts. 'Right. Would there be a handful of Nymphs willing to risk going to this place?' he questioned tersely.

'And even just a few Elves,' Kiana told Flash and Rebel. 'So that we can move with their speed.'

'We would also appreciate it if you could get someone fast to fetch our weapons from our towers,' I added quickly.

'As you say!' the two Nymphs saluted and at once rushed away.

'Those Krall warriors are still out there,' Dalin frowned. 'Bad or not.' The frown deepened to a scowl. 'They may not treat an incapacitated Elf kindly.'

'I know,' Kiana admitted and headed toward the ascent out of the city. 'We need to find Bard before anyone else does. And before he suffers a malady beyond revival.'

The three of us had not long wound our way up out of the sunken city and into the trees when five blurring forms materialised before us – Vidar and the Elves Alvar, Astor, Quidel and Rond.

'Thanks,' I told Vidar weakly, my eyes only just catching up to realise that he was holding my sword hilt out to me.

'Well met,' Vidar greeted us sombrely.

'We appreciate your aid in this search.' Astor's gravelly, deep voice was nearly a growl, and was heavily accented with Nylvish. 'To lose such a wise member of our kin in such a manner would be devastating.'

At that moment, a multi-coloured cloud broke out of the trees. Violet, magenta, lemon, amethyst, amber, turquoise, emerald, tangerine – the bright flashes quickly halted and became identifiable as a group of Nymphs. Asha, Flash and Rebel were at their head, determination on their cherubic faces.

'What do we need to know for this expedition?' Kiana accepted her own sword, quiver and bow from Alvar.

Vidar, usually so poised and unshakable, seemed to hunch in on himself a little. 'The place is on the mountain side of the forest. Toward Jenra,' he answered. 'We call it the Cursed Valley.'

The forest dwellers shifted and visibly blanched, even while Vidar was simply stating its name.

'Ah.' I swallowed. 'Goody.'

'The Cursed Valley is where our standoff with Darziates occurred.' Asha bared sharp teeth. 'The clashing magic disrupted the atmosphere, and never faded away. The lingering wild magic is neither pure nor dark anymore.'

'But now the trees and animals there are confused and warped,' Flash went on with a sick grimace. 'It is the one marred spot within the serenity of this forest.'

'I've never heard tell of it, or come across it on my travels,' Kiana admitted.

'The distorted atmosphere doesn't just act upon the animals and trees,' Vidar clarified. 'Mortals would unconsciously shy away from the place. Forest dwellers, on the other hand, must actively avoid it. Because of our introspective sense of nature, Elves can't help but be dragged to the beauty and corruption there. The wildness of it can ensnare our minds and lure us to it like a physical pull.'

'Bard may not have had his senses about him to stay far enough away,' Rond uttered in dismay. 'He likely lost track and the warring magic would have called to his engrossed mind most seductively.'

Vidar straightened his back with a hard expression on his face, clearly believing that this was exactly what had befallen the Elf.

'Even with your speed, it will surely take days for us to cross that much of the forest?' Kiana questioned bluntly. 'Perhaps Bard himself has only just made it all the way into the valley as you fear.'

'Whether he just got there or not, he doesn't have time to wait for us to dawdle our way after him,' Asha growled unhappily. The rainbow of Nymphs behind her uttered sounds of agreement and anguish.

'That is so. But the Lady knows all of this. And because of her, we may make time less of a problem.' Vidar now appeared both hopeful and terrified at once.

Rond rubbed at his brow pensively. 'I do not think we can ask this of her. Better to try without opening ourselves to her aid.'

'The Lady devotes her life force toward keeping this forest as our shielded haven,' Vidar countered solemnly. 'She loves us all as her own children, and would sacrifice much to save even one.'

'The Lady's magic would get us to Bard faster?' I asked. 'If we're open to it?'

'She could transfer us through the natural world so that we would lose barely any time,' Vidar confirmed.

'What's holding you back?' Dalin questioned.

Rond was shaking his head in worry. 'The world is failing under the spread of Sorcery. People are living shorter lives with shorter memories. Trees can no longer flourish to the great heights of these of the forest. The seasons are changing. And Darziates gains strength in these changes. But the Lady is as one with nature, and she too is fading. The war decides the fate of all races and the very essence of the world itself. It will mean the life or death of Nature herself, our Lady.'

Vidar winced. 'She is still the most powerful being in the forest. Yet,' he admitted sadly. 'It is becoming harder for her to stay separate from the nature that makes up her spirit. It is becoming hard for her to return to her physical body after calling on the magic.'

'After playing Gloria outside the forest, the Lady was in her own form of seriousness for a time,' one of the Nymphs told us. 'Her skin became translucent. As though she wasn't really here.'

'Healing Kiana was also a great feat for her, though once she could call upon the health and vitality of the world to heal any hurt,' Vidar finished.

Kiana looked stricken and my heart pounded at the implications of the Lady's condition.

This truly was a War for the World as we knew it. What was a world without nature? Life could not be sustained without it.

'Then, if we do ask this of her?' Dalin's voice was coarse with apprehension.

'It is her offer, rather than us asking,' Vidar corrected. 'She waits to know our will.'

'And if we accept, she may sever yet another link to her physical form, and be one step closer to leaving our realm,' Rond answered plainly.

'She would be devastated if we didn't include her in this and it cost us Bard,' Asha declared with certainty. 'Could you face her if we took that choice out of her hands?'

'She would be using our own power as well,' Vidar said. 'She would be enhancing it.'

'What do you mean?' Kiana asked.

'We must let her enter our hearts and minds,' Rond explained resignedly. 'So that we could share power and understanding. Only when there is a willing link within, can anyone truly control the physical body without damaging it.'

Kiana nodded thoughtfully. As if sharing bodies with a being of far greater power and foreign intellect hardly bothered her.

I cringed at the notion. I was happy in my simple little mind and restricted awareness.

'Would we even survive having such an enormous entity's mind linking up with our own?' Dalin sounded as hesitant as I felt.

'The enormity of the contact may mean that your minds retreat to hibernate throughout, or reject the memory of it afterwards,' Vidar told him honestly. 'Though that would be the only side effect.'

'And our bodies?' I asked nervously. 'Our very frail, mortal bodies?'

'Would be rejuvenated and enriched,' Asha answered. 'Though spending time in the city and being so connected with the One has likely already altered your lifespan and abilities in subtle ways. When we get back I can do a close examination of you to be sure.'

My mouth opened and shut at that.

'Do not fear,' the heavy voice of Astor rumbled then. 'We would continue to share our power with you while the Lady would share your mind and spirit,' he assured us nobly. 'Nothing would harm you.'

'I say we must trust the Lady to decide for herself,' Kiana finally declared, echoing my support for her wishes to join this search party earlier.

'Then let us reach out and try this with our Lady,' Vidar nodded.

Rond took mine and Dalin's hand, and I felt my body start to welcome in the erupting energy flowing from the Elf at once.

My limbs suddenly held more energy, and each of my senses became so sharp that the world almost seemed completely new.

There were more sounds, more life forms, more colours than I had ever realised.

Kiana took Vidar's hand, and the other Elves and Nymphs came together to form a circle.

'Don't freeze up,' I told myself silently. 'Come on brain. Got to be open.'

I focused on the leaves and dirt beneath my boots. I focused on the forest bird songs.

I took a deep breath.

Another.

And another.

Then accepted Astor's proffered hand on my other side.

19

Nineteen

N^{oal}

We were all linked now, tension and energy rippled in the air between us.

'Breathe the forest in,' Vidar instructed when we were quiet and in place. 'Feel its wholesome, unbounded life force inside you.'

I tried to do as he said, and was surprised when I found it to be quite easy. The radiating, pulsing energy of the Elves and Nymphs had completely absorbed into my bones.

The forest's own spirit was swirling about us in the air, in the water, the rustling leaves, pouring into me.

'Reach out to the Lady with your thoughts!' Vidar whispered intently.

My eyes had closed, but somewhere beyond us I knew a glimmering droplet of water was rolling slowly down the cool green skin of a nodding leaf. A lithe fox with twitching nose and clever eyes was stepping through the ferns. The wind was whispering through the blue feathered wings of a darting bird. The rich soil beneath me was drinking deeply from the moisture gathered by the plants above.

The forest was rippling with life.

I could taste it. Smell it. Understand it.

My thoughts reached out, seeking the Queen– for the pure heartbeat at the core of the forest, and the moment she heard us, I knew.

A collective shiver ran through the circle and rustled through the towering trees. I could feel her – not as the woman that she appeared to be, but as the entity that would live so long as the sun should rise and fall, as the entity that swept across the seas, that danced upon the earth at rain-fall, that kissed the petals of every flower open each morn-ing, and that loved all things thriving with life.

I wanted to share my love with her, and so it was very easy to succumb when her magic settled upon me. It was easy to want to share my own anchor to the world with her. My body almost didn't matter at all anymore, once my mind was touched by hers. I seemed to melt away beneath the weight of our embracing thoughts, until I was vaguely aware that my physical body was now being carried by an Elf while the rest of me was encased in ecstasy, floating in and out of mindfulness.

When I came into periods of clarity I glimpsed the nor-mally brown eyes of the Elf carrying me – now a spectacular green, glowing with the presence of the Lady's spirit.

It seemed we were passing through a blurring tunnel of green, made fuzzier by a veil of white mist that clouded everything. It was as if we were not moving through a world that was entirely our own.

And, thankfully, I wasn't entirely conscious of when it ended.

The Lady's vivid magic gradually faded from us like receding whispers, until the feel of it was just a hazy flash that flickered on the edge of memory, like a dream upon waking.

We were all lying upon the grass. Weeping with the joy of what we had felt, and with the sorrow that she had had to withdraw, becoming separate from us. Yet leaving us marked forever.

20

Twenty

D^{alin}

When I came back to awareness, I just sat with my head in my hands for a time while most members of our group stirred sluggishly or sat as I did after such a jarring loss.

Kiana came to lean against my shoulder and I inclined my own head against hers, feeling absurdly flat but otherwise returned to my normal self. Or perhaps more than my normal self.

The Nymphs and Elves had proven to be even less immune to the devastation of losing the wondrous lustre of the Lady's magic, as their minds had been aware and lucid while mingling with the vast consciousness of the Lady. We were the ones to rouse them to prepare to leave once more, and not even the Nymphs managed more than sombre expressions.

The border of the Cursed Valley was obviously marked by trees that grew in increasingly twisted and grotesque forms as we began our hike.

'The plants here are so ...' Kiana searched for the word, reaching toward the gnarled, blackened wood of a trunk but hesitating to touch it. 'Unhealthy.'

'They are all like that. Everywhere the magic of the battle reached,' Asha replied, glaring around herself with repulsion.

'We must be careful, and yet swift,' Vidar cautioned. 'We cannot be exposed to the magic for too long, or risk being drawn into it ourselves.'

A strange, broken yowl echoed out of the trees. It was answered by a similar shriek further away. My heart raced at the sound and my hand automatically sought the comfort of the hilt of my sword.

'The beasts here are deformed and brutish. However, they are generally content to stay within these bounds, where they feel strongest,' Rond told us. 'They are rarely large or crazed enough to challenge the forest dwellers, but we also rarely provoke them.'

'Perhaps they do not like us being here. Or perhaps our presence has awakened them and they have found Bard.' Quidel's hands were tight on his weapon.

'This place repels and ... enthrals me,' Alvar grimaced with distaste. 'This is a dangerous venture for us.'

'That's why you brought an unaffected hunting party with you,' Kiana answered supportively.

It was the first time I had seen the Nymphs looking anything but vibrant, and the Elves in any way uncertain.

The deeper we ventured into the looming murk the more that I noticed a strange, sweet tang pervading the humid atmosphere. But there was also an undercurrent of something rotten. The trees grew closer together, twisting so that their branches were strangling each other. It even seemed that those branches caught hold and scratched at the Nymphs with purpose, while sharp brambles stabbed and clawed at the base of every tree to hide roots that apparently sought to trip the rest of us up.

A nasty scratch on my forearm had begun to swell and throb and soon we were all covered in scratches from the stinging nettles.

At one point a bird squawked from somewhere above, sounding much too bulky as it shifted its weight on its perch. The tree tops swayed and creaked as the strange bird jostled the boughs out of sight, making a cascade of grey leaves rain down to slither coldly over us.

Vidar at last paused with an expression of sufferance. 'I must let my guard down so that I am drawn to anything that may have attracted Bard,' he told us.

'I will watch over you,' Asha promised.

'Everyone else should maintain as much control as they can,' Vidar instructed. 'Trust in the Three, for they can see more objectively than us in this place.'

As time passed, we slowed intolerably to avoid the treacherous roots and listened to the bodiless scufflings, creaks and tormented yowls of hidden creatures. Tears streamed down Vidar's midnight cheeks as he allowed himself to feel and hear what we could not. We followed his steps as he listened for the magic that sought to drag him into its trap like an enchanting song. Occasionally he would hiss and throw his hands up to his ears, and the effort of lowering them to listen again appeared agonising.

Many times, we heard the snuffling and heavy footsteps of something large stalking us, though we could see nothing. The air itself felt impossibly dense, and we cringed whenever we brushed against the sick trunks, feeling almost sickened by them ourselves.

Finally, Asha and Flash gave a warning cry that sent my pulse racing.

Noal and I were on either side of Vidar, and only just had time to catch him as he sank to his knees. We staggered under his weight, and the Elves closest to us quickly helped.

With a shuddering sigh, he made his shaking legs straighten again. 'Whatever it is, it's just ahead,' he announced in a thick voice, appearing barely fit to stand.

Something howled loudly from the direction he'd signalled. A series of answering, excited yammers echoed in response.

'If Bard is ahead, where you sense this power, then he hasn't got long,' Kiana said grimly, drawing her sword. 'That sounds like a hunting pack.'

We followed the tottering Vidar for no more than a few yards before the treetops suddenly erupted with a deafening surge of the yattering cries, and the boughs overhead shook with movement while we all ducked under further cascades of ashen, icy leaves.

'We need to fan out,' I ordered. 'Each Elf is to have three Nymphs to keep him safe and focused. We'll advance together, staying level. Remain hidden until we know what we're up against. For now these things haven't been interested in us, but that will likely change.'

'Steady,' I heard Kiana say soothingly to Vidar, who was shuddering with the effort to control himself.

We all carefully peered around the final trees before a clearing, trying not to touch their diseased bark.

I heard Kiana draw in a hissing breath when she saw the source of alluring power in the clearing, Noal stiffening beside me.

'A Dryad?' I whispered in wonder. It appeared as though it had once been as grand as the willow.

'That Dryad died before Darziates ever stood here,' Asha scowled with disgust. 'I know not what possesses its essence and body now.'

Its bulging trunk was massive, grey and diseased – bleeding milky coloured sap. Yet its leaves were green, and moss and lovely, bright flowers wound their way along the swollen grey bark. Other trees gave its snake-like roots a wide berth, but they still ringed in together tightly on the edges of the clearing. It was both repugnant and beauteous – a majestic nightmare perfectly symbolising the clashing powers that had battled here and that still lingered.

Even I could feel its intriguing allure. Its promise of wild power. But I easily tore my eyes from it when I heard Asha cry out, just in time for Vidar to shove me strongly out of the way. He was transfixed by the mighty tree.

'Wait!' Noal hissed uselessly, his grip not strong enough to pull Vidar back.

'Oh Gods,' I heard Kiana breathe, and I whirled around.

All of the Elves were stepping out of hiding to stride obliviously into the dim clearing. They gazed with blank faces at the mighty Dryad while their Nymphs whirred frantically around them.

And at the roots of the Dryad that had driven our friends senseless, was Bard.

Straight backed, legs crossed, palms up and resting on his knees meditatively. He showed no awareness of the fact that a group of odd, man-sized creatures were sniffing at him with hungry interest.

'Frarshk,' I uttered, eyes wide.

More bestial creatures began dropping from the trees around the clearing like oversized raindrops.

Soon the Elves would be surrounded.

21

Twenty One

D^{alin}

The ape-like creatures appeared in swarms, free-falling or climbing down the trees with iron grips.

Their feet were more like hands, and long tails twitched behind broad bodies covered with coarse blue fur. Blue lips curled back from protruding, wolfish jaws.

The Nymphs snarled and bared their own pointed teeth in challenge, bringing burning magic to their fists while the Elves remained in a state of useless wonder – oblivious to the creatures dropping from the canopy like wiry acrobats.

Kiana, Noal and I drew our swords to join the forest dwellers while a wall of gnashing fangs and muscled, blue bodies formed around us. There were shrill yips and deep hoots of primal hunger, but the swarm didn't advance.

Not until an incredibly bulky, king-sized ape creature dropped like a boulder from the Dryad itself. The crazed braying of the crowd eased slightly and the few that had already been sniffing at Bard scarpered away quickly with resentful or fearful huffs.

The king stood over Bard, claiming him, before loosing an echoing, terrifying roar.

Then suddenly the lines of dark blue broke. The first beast launched to snap at Vidar, then they were all pelting forward in a ravenous wave to try to score bites out of the stricken Elves.

Nymph magic blazed and there was the smell of singed hair and burnt meat. Kiana and Noal threw their blades into the slew of scrambling bodies. But I was instead distracted by a glimpse of Bard through the onslaught – a momentary window of horror. In that glimpse the largest of all of the monkey-like creatures took a brutishly strong grip of Bard's arm and snapped his wrist like a twig. Pleased by the prone Elf's lack of reaction, the king ape bellowed in delight before sinking its teeth into the Elf's wrist for a gory feast.

I didn't think. In a dogged battle through buffeting bodies and over rocks and roots, I closed the distance to Bard and swung my sword at the king ape before it could tear more deeply.

I got in a deep jab at its back before the brute leapt out of the way with a furious, booming cry. Elf blood and skin clung to the fur around its chin as it rounded back around with alarming speed for its bulk; launching to wrap me in a very human feeling stranglehold.

My blade jabbed into its shoulder at an odd angle and I was dragged to the ground under double my own weight – half smothered by coarse chest fur.

I wriggled savagely, drawing my legs up to lever the brute enough that I could free an arm and pound its ribs with one hand, while wrenching at my sword with the other.

The warped ape howled at my stabbing and sprang away once more, propelling all the way up into some boughs to disappear.

I pushed up and tried to gain better footing amongst the roots, hurrying to Bard's side and ducking as a smaller monkey thing went flying over us.

I glimpsed Asha lifting another creature and throwing it in a ball of fire into the trees. Rebel was ripping one animal's head off with a few efficient bites into its neck, and then with a wrench from his infantile arms. Flash had been crash tackled to the ground by a leaping blue figure, but in moments the thing was howling as a tiny fist burnt through its body to emerge at the other side of its back.

It seemed that Rond was rousing at the sounds of Flash's nearby struggle, while all of the other Nymphs continued shredding at their foes with both bloodied teeth and magic. The blue animals were being flung around like dolls, but still the treetops rang with chattering voices and more of the creatures leapt down to bound over the smouldering bodies of their kin.

I crouched closer to Bard, who had leaves on his shoulders and legs, and dew wetting his white hair.

'Gods,' I grimaced, examining the mess of where the Elf's broken wrist had been mauled.

Silver blood glugged from around the broken bone and shredded skin, so I quickly ripped the sleeve of my shirt to bind it as best I could – just tying a tight knot in the makeshift bandage when there came a dull thump from a creature landing on a bough right above my head.

In an instant a pair of strong, hairy arms had grabbed me round the chest and hoisted me upward. Branches flew past and my legs dragged along bark and moss as I hurtled high up along the Dryad's trunk, the ground below getting alarmingly further away.

The kingly primate crowed as our jolting ascent suddenly ended with me being roughly hauled onto a bough. The thing was on me immediately, its beady eyes fixed on my throat.

Fangs flashed and I resorted to bar-fight tactics, throwing a fist into its snout and then into its furry stomach and bleeding shoulder. I managed to slither around it and ram a fist into the original stab wound above its kidneys, eliciting a winded, keening grunt. Before it could flip us, I grabbed its head and slammed its face into the tree ... both of us pausing in surprise when I bashed a huge fang loose to rattle down at our feet.

There were some high pitched chitters of what could have been interest from smaller apes scattered about on different boughs like spectators. One of them darted forward to scoop up the dropped tooth.

The king pushed away from me to catch itself instinctively in a nearby branch, where it swung and held on with its tail, snarling bloodily and furiously at the other apes while I wobbled for balance.

The closest creature raised the tooth with a high pitched yip of defiance. It straightened to its full height, punching its thick chest with a fist, and then turned on me.

The king roared again in a rage that seemed to even still the sounds of fighting below for a moment. It dove for the tooth holding fiend before the smaller challenger could snatch for me. And in a moment that creature was missing the arm that had held the king's tooth aloft.

I hadn't noticed another ape swinging on the bough I stood on, until it was yanking on my ankle with an excited screech.

'Woah!' I cried out at the sight of the ground suddenly above me.

I hung upside down for one dizzying moment before the king was ploughing into us with a point to prove. We all collided with the Dryad's trunk and I went skidding down like a sack of bones to smack into a lower branch. My scrabbling fingers couldn't get a grip, and I plummeted again through two more branches that slowed my fall only slightly before the ground rushed to meet my body.

I had the appalling, wet sensation that my nose had sunken into my head as I hit the dirt face first and an explosion of budding lights filled my vision. I pulled my head back up with an immediate spurt of blood while my addled mind made out the sounds of Kiana's frenzied calls to me.

'I think I only broke my nose, of all things,' I called across to her thickly.

As my sight cleared and thoughts squeezed their way in between the throbs in my skull, I laughed at the sight of my sword resting right within reach. I'd landed almost back at the spot I'd been snatched from.

Staggering upright and limping to the still blissfully unaware Bard, I crouched beside him once more.

'Bard!' I yelled into his passive face, shaking his shoulders. 'I could do with some help!'

A glance above showed the king sized beast, and now also two other fast, blue shapes making their way toward us. One was fearlessly bounding down the trunk. The other was leaping and flipping from one bough to another. The third creature was jabbering loudly and swinging across from the fight with the Nymphs, clearly ready to try its luck elsewhere – perhaps even against its king.

It had a burn hole in its forearm, and half its tail was missing, but it dropped from the branches of its tree like a fur covered dancer, landing on all fours from an impossible height and sniffing the air.

'Please, Bard,' I shook the Elf again urgently. 'Gods, what will wake you?'

A short, sharp cry of pain rose from Asha in the distance, and my heart leapt into my mouth. I couldn't help but crane to see that she had fallen beside Vidar, and a blue beast was about to bite into her throat.

Then, with the sound of her pain, Vidar shook himself. He sensed the battle at last, responding to the threat to Asha.

With a savage roar, he burst into action, grabbed the large, lithe animal in front of him, and rent its shrieking body in two.

At the sound of Vidar's voice and Rond's calls, too, the other Elves were startled awake. They responded to their attackers with surprise and energy.

That left the senseless Bard as the most appealing Elf morsel in the area again. And it also left me, the one tasty snack who had been stupid enough to insult a king.

'Oh, for frarshk's sake –'

The king ape sprung out of the tree on a vine, arcing through the air to slam into me so we went flying together to land in a wrestling heap before the other challengers could come in and snatch me away again.

We tussled as if this had turned into a highly personal grudge match, and though the two others had used the opportunity to close in on Bard nearby, the king-sized creature no longer appeared to care about losing such a large meal.

Saliva dribbled in strings from its distended maw – highlighting its one missing canine fang – and I yelped as blue hands clawed for my mouth to pry my lips open. Snaking, hairy fingers pushed in to grab for my teeth and I gurgled in outrage.

I chomped down on sour, sweaty digits with a ferocity the Nymphs would have been proud of. Then I clawed its wiry body, grabbing a handful of tail and yanking hard.

The creature shrilled as if I'd nearly ripped its spine out. We both quickly scrabbled away from each other and I desperately dove for my sword.

When the brute launched again, spinning in the air with twisting muscles in a show of flexibility no human could ever achieve, I swung in one simple, violent stroke.

The creature slid past instead of into me. And it didn't bounce back up. It scrabbled in the roots for a few moments, dragging up and then collapsing.

Blood pooled from the hole my sword had made, much graver than the loss of any fang could ever be.

Then it stilled.

A chorus of screams and what could be described as cheers arose from the trees, and some of the attackers crowding my friends turned to see what the fuss was about. What I'd done to their leader.

Groaning, I hobbled upright and the two smaller apes scampered away a short distance from where I'd taken down the king. I lifted my blade again, but this time turned it on the real enemy in this glade.

Just as Vidar had woken when his beloved Asha was threatened, I had to hurt what Bard was listening to and caring for.

So, I hacked and gouged at the grey trunk of the Dryad tree, boring chunks of wood out until, as I had hoped, I heard a new voice raised in wrath.

Bard didn't seem to register his injuries or the battle filled valley.

He lifted his double-edged Elvish weapon and blurred upright, his deep eyes volatile as he rushed me.

I held my hands up. 'Bard, I'm a friend!'

Bard's glowing green blade stabbing for my chest was my one answer. He was awake and moving, but his senses had not returned.

Our weapons clanged in a harmony of ringing steel and the two fine blades of his spear darted, alight with his magic like striking green snakes. My own sword dashed against each blow, sparking from the heat of the power.

'Bard!' I heard Astor yell across the distance. 'Bard! No!'

'Bard, I am Dalin! Arh, the Raiden!' I tried to pant when he pressed close at one stage. 'I came to help!'

Gods, people were forever confusing me with enemies when they were delirious.

We whirred around each other in a series of parries and strokes; the Lady's magic perhaps still guiding my movements as I kept up in a fight I had no right to keep up with. I lost myself in the flowing motions and it seemed our feet hardly touched the ground.

Until a blue shape plummeted enthusiastically from the tree above, and landed on Bard's shoulders, sinking brutish fangs into beautiful Elvish skin, and forcing Bard to his knees.

I launched at the opportunistic creature, stabbing at its clinging hands and feet.

Yowling, it lifted its face long enough for me to sink my sword through its eye and I heard its skull crack before it toppled off Bard.

Then Bard blinked at me, and truly saw me for the first time.

'Raiden?' he gasped in the lilting accent of his kind.

I sagged. 'Oh, thank the Go –'

At that moment the last of our three foes, the one with the scorched arm and maimed tail, yanked me up from behind.

Like a weightless toy I was hoisted across strong shoulders and the thing hurriedly left the carnage of its pack behind, scampering toward the nearest tree.

As I fought to get free, trying to stab at its running legs, I felt it tense and jump.

'Fraaaarshk!' I groaned, knowing that I was at their mercy when in the trees.

My teeth jarred together and my head lolled helplessly as we launched upward. But as soon as the creature had touched down on a bough to eat, I stabbed with all of my might into a hairy blue calf muscle so that the creature yowled in a blood curdling cry and dropped me.

I caught myself with one hand, clasping onto the edge of the mossy wood desperately while my legs dangled in the air, threatening to over balance me and break my hold.

Furious, limping, the creature tried to lash out, but I swatted with my sword and lopped a blue hand off so that the beast tipped forward with a startled mewl and could not catch itself.

Crying wildly, it fell to the ground below and landed awkwardly in a heap, and while I had survived the same fall once, I wasn't sure that the Gods would be so charitable as to save me twice in the same manner within such a short space of time.

I gasped helplessly, my arm burning and shuddering under my own weight.

Thankfully any other apes in the trees seemed distrustful enough of me now to hang back and simply watch.

'Raiden!' I heard Bard call up from below.

I groaned in reply. Every breath was an effort that took energy away from my grip on the bough.

'Raiden, I shall catch you!'

All that escaped my lips was a hiss of rushing air.

Sweat dripped into my eyes.

But Bard was certain of his abilities, and he was an Elf, so I decided grimly, that so was I.

With a grimace, I released my hold on my sword first, letting it drop the great distance.

Then I released my hold on the bough.

I toppled through emptiness and waited for obliteration as my body spun of its own accord in a downward spiral. But with a grunt of relief, I felt Bard catch me easily with his good arm.

And when I opened my tightly closed eyes, I was against his chest like a damsel instead of a mighty king-ape slayer.

'Raiden,' the Elf repeated. 'I thank you, and I apologise.'

'No harm, friend,' I shook my head tiredly as he lowered me to the ground.

'I thought I was lost to this realm,' Bard said quietly, as he turned to where the others were finishing their battles with only a scattering of remaining challengers. Leaderless and battered, the apes' gusto had faded and apparently so had the appeal of us as a meal.

'No fear,' I told him through the coppery taste of blood. 'We will be free of this place soon.'

22

Twenty Two

K^{iana}

The Elves were exhausted as we finally staggered free of
the Cursed Valley. They had faced a fierce mental battle to
leave the calling of the wild magic, and were too tired to use
their inhuman speed. We worried that reaching for any kind
of power at all would break their focus and force them to be
drawn back into the recesses of their minds, and back to the
Valley.

Even I was wavering in the face of their fatigue; unsure
if we should simply let them rest. It was Dalin who gently
asked them to continue on away from that deadly, alluring
place – encouraging them to simply walk, slow and steady,
as far as they could. And I was glad, for as they followed
him unquestioningly, the hardship written across their faces
eased ever so slightly with each step.

'I think we've come far enough,' Dalin said at last; his voice thick and nasally through a broken nose.

I nodded in agreement. 'We'll be able to make do with this as a camp spot for the night.'

The Elves sank down vacantly, and when everyone had eaten and I had cleansed Bard's injuries, the Nymphs purposefully snuggled into their Elves to keep watch over them, lest their seriousness deepen and cause them to wander.

'My apologies and thanks to you, again, Raiden,' Bard uttered before sinking into an apparently immediate, deep slumber.

'Your battle with Bard will be a talking point for years,' Asha yawned while she nestled into Vidar's arm. 'Not to mention your trapeze fight to kill the king of the giant possum-apes.'

'He left without being defeated by another challenger. So, technically, he's still their leader,' Rebel mused just as groggily.

'Maybe that's what the prophecy meant, Dalin,' Noal teased lightly. 'You were meant to lead monkeys.'

'I don't even want to think about it,' Dalin groaned. 'Being an ape's plaything was never in Conall's training.'

I observed him closely. 'How is your nose?'

The remembered horror of watching him fall from that height made me inwardly shudder. He had been lucky. So very lucky. But I was the one feeling especially fortunate to have him sitting in front of me in one piece.

'The swelling makes it hard to breathe,' he answered ruefully. 'But at least it's not bleeding.' Dark circles had formed under his eyes.

'If it were still bleeding, or looked overly crooked and made a grinding sound, I would worry,' I reassured him in an even tone. 'But nothing seems to need to be moved back into place. The blocked nasal passages will clear up eventually.'

'I simply cannot believe how lightly you got out of that fall,' Noal told Dalin in wonder.

'Twice,' Dalin affirmed. 'I cannot believe it either. I should have broken my neck.'

'Be careful next battle. Your luck stores need time to replenish after that,' Noal advised sagely.

Dalin grimaced. 'I'll keep it in mind. For now I just hope the Elves will return to their normal selves soon.'

Flash squidged the dozing Astor's arm muscles as if fluffing a pillow. 'What you witnessed today was nothing compared with what we had to snap them out of years ago. They will be much better when they wake a distance away from the Valley tomorrow.'

Asha thoughtfully sat up from where she had been lounging on the sleeping Vidar's chest. 'Especially because I have an idea that might help them,' she rubbed her hands together with a smile.

'Oh dear,' Dalin sighed. 'Any idea from your devious mind is guaranteed to involve some kind of risk.'

'Yes!' the Nymph exclaimed animatedly.

'What do you mean?' I asked as her red eyes flashed with eagerness.

'As your strength is clearly greatly improving, the Three can get into some training,' Asha told me gleefully. 'You have already been touched by the Lady's grace, and training with Elves could be another great advantage to you all. Then at the same time, it would be a way to also help our serious friends to stay focused!'

'How so?' Noal asked, clearly intrigued by the idea of training with the Elves.

'Well, if you're all as apt as the Raiden proved to be against Bard in a sleepwalking fight, you may actually be able to keep up with the training,' Asha explained.

'No,' Noal laughed without insult, 'I meant how would this benefit the Elves as well?'

'This group of Elves alone will need something physical to focus on after this. Concentrating on both fighting and educating you will do that. But there are others around the city who need a cause to help awaken them, too!'

Noal and Dalin gradually became just as enthused as Asha – though she told us with regret that the Nymphs would have to stick to spectating to keep from getting carried away.

I listened to their discussion with interest, for it was an opportunity I would die for. But I couldn't help wishing that I didn't have to fear how my body would react.

When fighting the Krall warriors, I had been weakened by pain. In the battle with those creatures, I had felt nothing except out of practice. The unpredictability of it had me on edge.

And I felt that all I could do was wait for the next internal attack.

23

Twenty Three

K*iana*

'Fraaaaaaaaaaaaaarshk!' Dalin went flying in a graceful arc, soaring away from his fight with the now healed and sentient Bard.

Astor easily caught and placed Dalin on the ground for the fifth time in a row, and Dalin sprinted straight back to resume the duel.

Not far away Noal was in a similar situation with an elegant female Elf. She couldn't speak Awyalknian, but she made duelling look like an art form, and I watched Noal thud harmlessly into Quidel's chest. Quidel was Noal's catching buddy, and the Elf was almost having trouble blurring to each spot in time – Noal having experienced flight in every direction three times over.

Nevertheless, to everyone watching, it was clear that both princes had already been well trained by human standards. And in the days since we had returned from the Cursed Valley, it was also clear that they were beginning to gain new strength and speed. It was not so easy for the Elves to simply sweep them aside anymore, despite how often they did so.

'I cannot discern who has most benefited from this week's training,' a melodious voice commented from beside where I leaned to watch.

Perhaps she spoke in warning, announcing her gradual arrival when I would hardly ever have been able to miss it.

'The Nymphs, I would say. They've tracked down every 'drowsy looking Elf' in the city,' I replied with a faint smile. 'Now it's sheerly for their own entertainment. They're placing bets on whatever random notion takes their fancy.'

The Lady's presence was very slowly joining me, starting like a flickering sun ray or a star's sparkle rather than an actual shape.

'Oh?' the glittering voice asked, rolling over me like a cleansing spring.

From the corner of my eye I now caught the wavering impression of a white dress, tumbling auburn hair, eyes greener than emerald jewels, long brown limbs, and a wise and wistful smile upon beautiful lips.

'The Nymphs cast bets on how many curses might be pummelled out of the Raiden yesterday,' I explained. 'This morning they took bets on whether I could simulate flying, and how long I could go without touching the ground.'

'Though you are in need of a moment's break now?' the Lady asked with a touch of concern. I felt the very slight weight of her hand reaching for my arm, as if she would pour her healing magic into me before she had even been able to gather the full energy to tie herself here to the physical spot beside me.

The chaotic cheers and airborne manoeuvres went on, somehow nobody else being aware that the most incredible presence to have ever lived had come to enjoy being among them.

'I am well. I simply did not want to push my shoulder too far,' I answered firmly. 'It's a fear I'll need to work on. More pressingly, I hope *you* are well.'

I put my hand on hers, holding her here as a firm anchor. A sigh – a shivering breeze – and her touch gained more warmth and solidity. My mind in turn sharpened as if I had spent my entire life before now peering through clouds.

A lute that had been playing distantly now seemed to be amplified and to be emitting rainbows of visible notes that drifted through the trees.

I noticed Chloris and Silvanus walking serenely by, one cradling the Nymph Sati and the other cradling Shiva.

The Elves were stepping closely side by side, because the two Nymphs had fallen asleep with their fingers entwined. And I realised without knowing exactly how, that Sati and Shiva were finally truly bonded, and were expecting a Nymphling. The joy I felt at that was only half my own.

Somehow seeming just as important as that – I could almost hear a humming lullaby as a bumblebee kissed the pollen of a flower near my boot.

There was just so much to notice and appreciate, and I began to feel overwhelmed.

'Sometimes when there is much to notice, to appreciate or to say, it is hard to find enough words,' the Lady said softly then, picking up my stream of thought and soothing it. 'I will show you a way that you can speak without talking. You may do this, if you need to make your message clearer when you become the Summoner.'

I nodded my permission and held onto her a little more tightly.

With gentle mental steering and a flash of colour, a memory from the Lady flitted across my mind. A loud swarm of Nymphlings were giggling and wreaking havoc around the city. They were so naughty, and so devastatingly adorable, and even though they were few, they were hard to miss.

An image of a tiny newborn Nymphling cuddled against its mother brought tears to our eyes. That would be Sati's joy soon.

'The Nymphs rarely have babes because they know parenting is not for beings who can be selfish or wild,' the Lady's words played about my internal senses instead of my ears. Her voice felt stronger this way. 'Nymphs are unable to fathom such a commitment unless utterly bonded, heart and soul, with their life partner or partners.'

Like a river, I felt the Lady's thoughts flow on, and suddenly I saw a moonlit vision of two Elves I had never met sitting across from each other in a clearing. Their silvery white hair was glowing brighter than the stars above them, and the illumination swirled at their heart centres, too.

'Elves must make their children with just as much consideration, though in a very different way,' the Lady's voice described. 'An Elf is only capable of performing the act once in a lifetime, whether helped by a partnership or independently.'

In the moonlit vision playing through my mind, the two Elves leaned forward and took each other's hands.

'It has such risk involved that not all Elves who have chosen to bond decide to do it.'

The Elves both lowered their entwined hands to the ground, and I watched in wonder as the lights over their hearts – sparkling like silver flame – also appeared at their fingertips.

'Physically, they are infertile. But their connection to the world that made them is not. They must put some of their own souls, joined together, into the earth and use their minds to channel nature into forming a physical entity.'

I gasped in amazement at the cost of making an Elfling. To risk one's inner self was the mightiest feat of selflessness and the most monumental gift of life.

'If an Elf is utterly sure of who they are in order to pass some part of themselves on, a child may be brought to life with the energy of the earth and breath of the skies, and a grave connection with nature is formed.'

I realised that it was that exact connection that could sometimes cause an Elf to forget their physical self as they delved closer to nature.

'An Elfling's hair becomes white – the colour of the spirit given to bring their babe to life.' The image of the two Elves pouring themselves into the earth faded as the Lady spoke.

My vision cleared to show me that barely anything had changed and hardly any time had passed for anyone beyond the two of us. My eyes were drawn to the auburn haired being beside me. 'Could you share even more of what there is to know, and what you could never have enough words to say ... about yourself?'

'My own life has been as expansive as time,' the Lady agreed. 'Using mental images, and perhaps going even a little more deeply than that, would tell you much.'

'I wish to know of your life, as you have known and guided mine,' I answered truthfully.

Alright, she agreed inside my mind; a sweet caress of a word.

In a moment I felt as though I was no longer myself at all. My hair was auburn, my limbs were strong with magic, and I breathed every aspect of the world into my being. The Lady and I were completely one.

We watched time blur past. We were surrounded by flowers that grew, died and reappeared around us. Countless faces aged before our eyes – so many smiles and tears and friendships cultivated and lost. Eons of time skipped by in trickles and blinks.

But with a quick internal leap together, we were back at the start, standing up from where we had awoken. We had just opened our eyes to find ourselves in an empty, raw world, not yet overflowing with colour or life. No structures. No people. No animals.

We were the first. The first to come to the world. We spread the gifts of the Gods and saw peoples and civilisations being born, springing from nowhere while their buildings grew like living things. Wondrous, curious developments unfolded with the creation of language, economy, sickness, health, marriage, good and evil.

When Deimos gathered his storm of war we became sick. We became weak. Our body changed and aged as we felt tragedy make us and the world itself feel old. We were dying. Draining away. And it took a great deal of time, after the angry flame of the life of Deimos had been extinguished, for us to feel glad and strong again.

Then, like a staggering lash across the face, we had felt true horror when we had lit upon the mind of Darziates receiving his father's memory and power, and we had not recovered fully again.

We had lost the Centaurs, the *Larnaeradee*, the Sprites, the Unicorns ... And we were barely strong enough to expel the Sorcerer when the Nymphs had arrived needing aid.

But there appeared hope as a second prophecy spoke true. The arrival of the Three had renewed us, and now it was nearly time to face our next stage of life, and to release the burden of holding onto this physical stage.

The world has hope, and so do we.

There were tears on my cheeks as I realised, I was just Kiana again. The Lady's hand was still on mine.

'I understand you,' I said with a small smile.

'I thank you,' she replied gently, out loud.

I knew she was still keeping track of my mind, or the enormity of seeing the beginning of life itself and of being included in such vast thoughts would surely have overcome me.

'Kiana,' she said softly. 'You have done as much for me, as I have for you. I am at peace for the first time in many ages.' Her eyes held mine. 'But even before the hope I have felt more recently, I was able to go on in my long, sometimes lonely life simply because I knew myself and my place in this world. You will feel the same, when you embrace your place in the world. I feel you are getting close to that.'

I let out a long breath. 'I pray to the Gods I am. It would have been so easy when we left the Cursed Valley to ask the Elves to leave us, so near to Jenra, so that we could continue on. But I would have been incomplete and unable to offer everything I can to the quest.'

The Lady smiled warmly. 'You knew your time and learning here was not done. Your journey, your healing, and your friendships here are still unfolding.'

I nodded in agreement.

'You know, when your father came here,' the Lady went on tenderly. 'Kires explained that both his and Gwendis' power had dwindled without use, and without having ever known their Unicorns. They could feel nature and see more deeply than humans, but they had to reach for the magic with great effort. Kires still told me that he accepted this with gladness, because he understood that such transformations had been necessary. He was happy, and had embraced his place in the world. When you truly understand and accept who you are, and your connection with the world, you will be whole, too.'

I inclined my head respectfully, but saw the Lady pause, her eyebrows slowly drawing together in a light frown.

I realised the fighting exercises had halted abruptly and the clearing had stilled. I saw that a new presence had been the cause.

The Krall soldier, Thorin, had emerged, and was standing with Frey and Ace on the edge of the clearing. He had apparently been watching the fights until Dalin had caught sight of him and had ceased in shock.

Thorin appeared uncomfortable at the scrutiny of the Elves and Nymphs, though the only hostility seemed to emanate from Dalin.

'The training has been spectacular,' the Lady spoke sincerely from my side. 'And so has our guest's recovery. Welcome to the city, Krall warrior.'

The Lady at once drew all eyes, and the mood instantly settled at the appearance of the leader of the forest.

Thorin's mouth dropped open and he bowed in amazement.

'Please resume your tour of the city so that you may feel most at home,' the Lady said with a graceful gesture, and a flurry of movement in the clearing quickly resumed.

Only Dalin was slow to take up his position once more.

I felt a light touch of goodbye against my hand, and when I glanced back, the Lady had gone.

Twenty Four

Dalin

'Am I the only one who doesn't trust that man?' I commented gruffly to Noal, feeling an annoyed flush in my cheeks.

'I don't mind him,' Noal admitted as we passed the sight of the awkward soldier being surrounded once again by a cluster of Nymphs. As had become their habit, they collapsed playfully all around him while the Elves nodded and smiled.

'I am certain that he was one of the original soldiers who first ambushed and abducted you and I in the forest,' I told Noal, feeling my brow become heavy with a surly frown.

'What are the chances of that, when there were so many soldiers?' Noal asked lightly. 'And anyway, even if he was, the guy is happily converted now.' He was completely unconcerned, idly stroking the Granx's back. She was catching a ride on his arm as we walked.

'I've had to fight him off Kiana twice,' I glowered then. 'The worship he looks at her with is sickening. He could try to take her at any moment.'

'Well, the forest dwellers have accepted him,' Noal said reasonably. 'He's been allowed to live freely with Agrudek in his tower.'

'Has nobody else considered that Darziates could still hold some power over him? That he could still be the enemy?'

We entered our tree tower to put our weapons away for the day.

'Thorin seems to respect rather than detest the Lady. And he seems to respect *you*, too,' Noal told me as we climbed the stairs. 'It's not quite Kiana-worship level when he watches our training sessions, but he is impressed. And he also always listens in awe when the Nymphs recount your heroic battle in the Cursed Valley.'

'He's probably sizing me up for when we next face off with each other,' I scowled.

'You're being unfair,' Noal reprimanded me. 'The more people against Darziates, the more people with us. If we have a representative from Krall, that might also count as having an alliance with another of the races of mortals.'

I snorted. For once Noal seemed only too happy to be focusing on his role of bringing people together in the prophecy.

'Look,' I said heatedly as I leant my sword against the kitchen wall. 'I truly do feel pity for Thorin, for being a victim of Darziates. But the rest of the population of Krall are all victims too, and we will still have to fight them to defend Awyalkna.'

Noal sighed. 'It's awful. I don't even like to think of the soldiers I killed when we were escaping the camp.'

'Our captors,' I interjected darkly. 'Where we were imprisoned.' I stopped scowling as Asha drifted in through the window and kissed my cheek.

'That Granx adores you even more than I do,' she told Noal next, laying herself out comfortably in his arms, right beside the luxuriating Granx.

'Another male I adore,' Asha went on, 'our dear Vidar, is waiting outside. You've both been invited to come with us for another evening at Rebel and Flash's home, where there will once again be a great deal of Nymph liquor.'

'Of course,' Noal grinned cheerfully, following her back down the stairs and outside.

I grimaced and made my way after them.

The merry-makers already had the fire crackling in readiness for the food to be cooked, and for the comfort of the Elves and humans who couldn't fit into Nymph homes.

My mood lifted as I saw the usual Nymphs cackling and play fighting all over the place, and crowds of Elves taking in the scene and enjoying themselves in their quiet way.

Even before we'd managed to approach, there was a blast of coloured magic that whirled towards Noal. Asha caught it lazily before it pelted her in the head.

'Poor aim Flashy-boy!' she told the other Nymph reproachfully, then suddenly shot out of Noal's arms to careen after the now howling Flash.

A horde of other Nymphs all scrambled up to join in, and coloured lights and sparks began to sizzle all about us as the little beings did their best to knock their fellows out – not holding back or buffering their magic at all.

I followed Noal to the fire, spotting Kiana with the Elves. And talking to Thorin.

My mood dropped again but Noal chose to ignore the return of the stormy expression on my face, pushing me to sit on the opposite side of the fire.

Kiana nodded and Thorin acknowledged us with a smile before returning to his conversation about places she may have seen while travelling through his country. His speech rumbled with the Krall accent, which made his voice sound heavy and drawling compared to the flowing speech of Awyalknians.

I tried to focus on the antics of the Nymphs, but I couldn't help listening to Thorin as he greedily absorbed Kiana's attention. Some drunken Nymphs and the Elves about the fire had settled to attentively listen to Thorin speak as well.

'We can all see what it's like in Krall,' he was saying to his captivated audience. 'And deep down I know most of us hate it. It's as if his darkness has seeped into everything.' Thorin's face was entirely earnest. 'There are stories of Krall once having been a golden Kingdom and of how upon Darziates' rise the beauty vanished and the kind spirits of the people also faded. Now the harsh land seems as if it has been infected by a sickness. The weather is always so bleak – freezing with ice, rain and mud for one half of the year and blistering with heat for the other half – and the people have been twisted to distrust others, to war monger, or otherwise to obey out of fear. Friendships are either fiercely loyal and exclusive as a means of survival, or more like alliances out of necessity to get by. Often family can hardly even be counted on.' He sighed. 'But as miserable as it is, it's our normal day to day. It's what we know. And there are those who have been drawn to Krall *because* of these things. People like the Trune raiders,' he said, nodding to Noal. 'And warriors like Angra Mainyu.'

I stared at Noal, shocked that Thorin had felt comfortable alluding to the Trune raiders and how they had murdered Noal's family. Noal only confided in his closest friends about that time, and anyone else should know better than to mention it in his presence.

Either Thorin knew exactly who Noal was. Or Noal had confided about his loss to this man, when even thinking about it had crippled my brother for years.

Noal saw my stunned expression and shrugged as he stroked the Granx's back. I felt another spurt of anger towards the soldier.

'... I am fortunate. I have been so close to your pure magic and I have been freed of Darziates. But the whole of Krall is infected. I don't think they can be healed so easily in such masses. Even if deep down they know they are being controlled, their fear keeps them quiet and his power keeps them restrained. I think only with Darziates' death will those who can be healed become free,' Thorin shrugged. 'Many may not be healed even then. It is hard to allow light into your life after only knowing hate and darkness.'

There were murmurs and nods of agreement and I stood up unobtrusively, leaving them to their conversation.

I treaded angrily through the grass, kicking at tufts with each step. In the distance I heard another party of Nymphs talking about my fight in the Cursed Valley. At a glance I saw that they were flopped all over Bard, who had been dragged out of seclusion regularly recently, but I only waved when he called to me and plunged further onward in search of a more hushed corner of the city.

I finally stopped when I found a place free of anybody else.

I sucked in a big breath and slowly let it flood out of me, remembering Thorin's face from when I'd had to fight him. I'd fought him the hardest when I'd no longer been able to carry Kiana and we'd been surrounded. Thorin had charged over and over to get to her, but when he'd gone down, I'd relented. And in response he had quickly sat up to slice my leg open, targeting a weakness already there. Only with a quick block with my own blade had I stopped him from hacking the entire limb off, and only with a fast punch had I managed to stop him from getting around me.

How could he really have changed? He was free amongst those I held dearest, free to turn on them should Darziates again transform him into the crazed warrior I'd first seen.

I stopped tensely with that thought. And at that same moment, a twig broke to signal that someone was close.

I whirled savagely around to find *him* standing there, and didn't pause in throwing out my arm to shove him backward so that he slammed into a tree trunk.

I pressed my arm into his gullet to pin him there and I glared at his shocked face while he stared at me; trying to get his breath back but making no move to push my arm away.

I was taller and older than he was. He could probably have overpowered me with his bulk, but I was feeling so savage right then that I knew I would win if he chose to test me.

I pushed my face nearer to his.

'I don't trust you,' I said quietly. 'You may have been 'healed', but you have in no way made up for all you have done.'

I felt him swallow beneath my arm across his throat.

'If you hurt any of my friends again, you will have me to face,' I told him, releasing his throat and shoving him savagely so that he slammed back against the tree again. 'Understand?'

He nodded.

I turned to stalk away as he coughed and leant back against the tree, and I saw Kiana standing just beyond the scene.

She stared at me with startled eyes as I strode past her. But the stony glare I gave her left no room for challenges, and she let me pass her without a word.

25

⦿

Twenty Five

D^{alin}

I was sheathing my sword as I exited my tower early the next morning.

Noal had woken me and told me to meet him outside, but now I cursed inwardly when I saw Thorin conversing quietly with Kiana and a group of armed Elves near our door.

Noal approached and was studying my face almost worriedly when Kiana gestured for everyone to gather in close.

I drew in a deep breath, refraining from glaring at Thorin as he stood beside Kiana.

'We are going to catch the rest of Thorin's men,' Kiana announced bluntly, apparently only for my benefit. 'I am going to lead four Elves in a search and there will also be another party of four. Nova and Naira will act as messengers between the groups. This time the Elves will not have to go where harm may come to them, as the Krall warriors have simply been circling the city in confusion. And on this occasion, we will not take so many Nymphs in case they struggle to contain their joy for battle.'

I recognised some of the Elves who had come along to help us in our fixes so far. Alvar, Astor and Quidel were amongst them, along with Vidar.

I said nothing, but regarded each of them as I waited for Kiana to finish speaking.

'We are going to find the warriors in the hopes that they can be cured of Darziates' hold, rather than just leaving them to wander in search of the One for the rest of their lives,' Vidar explained.

'Most likely there will be fighting involved, but we want only to stop and bind them so that they are not hurt and can be brought safely back here,' Kiana continued. 'Bringing more Elves could mean a real battle. Bringing Nymphs could end in too much death. And Nova and Naira have sworn not to get involved.'

'It's hard to keep your magic blasts on 'stun' when there's a battle on,' Nova admitted sweetly, stroking Noal's cheek.

'We really do get a little bloodthirsty in a real fight,' Naira agreed, somersaulting happily above our heads. 'But we will try to refrain.'

'Thorin is not coming because his comrades wouldn't understand his change of sides,' Kiana added, and then she addressed me directly. 'Are you in?'

I blinked in surprise, and noticed all of those around me were waiting expectantly for my reply.

'Of course I am. We're in this together,' I told her adamantly, glancing from her to Noal with a frown.

Noal clapped me on the back and the Elves smiled in appreciation.

'Good,' Kiana answered. 'You'll lead the second party. Noal and Nova will be with you, as will Quidel, Alvar and Rond,' she told me. 'The rest will be with me.'

There were nods of affirmation before the small crowd dispersed to complete any final preparations, and Vidar handed each member enough rope to bind the wrists of a few captives each.

'Cheer up!' Noal said, slinging a comforting arm around Thorin's shoulders as the warrior watched the planning glumly. 'You can fight your friends when we bring them back if you like.'

Thorin laughed, and I tried not to stare after them, instead turning to Kiana, who was silently fastening a loose buckle on her belt.

'Are you sure you want to fight again so soon?' I asked her quietly when the others had begun to move out of earshot.

'I'm fine,' Kiana replied shortly. Then her face softened when she saw my expression become blank and angry once more. 'Really, I am,' she told me.

'We're all ready to go,' Vidar informed us, and Kiana turned away from me to signal for everyone to get moving.

Kiana and I led the party out of the city and at the top of the cliffs we split into two groups.

We would both head in the direction that the Krall men had fled towards after our last encounter, but would search in different areas to cover more of the forest.

I almost wished we were all sticking together. Just so that I could reassure myself that Kiana, Noal and I were still a cohesive 'Three'.

26

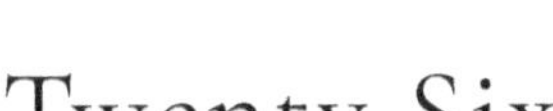

Twenty Six

Noal

My stomach was grumbling by noon.

'I'm sure someone brought an apple or something,' Dalin deadpanned flatly when I complained of my malnourishment.

I grimaced with distaste. 'I've done very well avoiding those things for a while now,' I informed him disdainfully. 'I choose to continue to starve.'

'Suit yourself,' he answered distractedly, and fell back to silent watchfulness. 'But stay forward with me. Our eyes need to be ahead.'

Dalin had placed Quidel and Alvar at the party's sides, and had instructed Rond to follow at the rear while Nova was to continually sweep all surrounding areas.

The Elves he led, who were doubly experienced, more than three times his age, and incredibly powerful, never hesitated in following his requests. In fact, they looked to him respectfully for direction, though he didn't seem to think twice about assuming the automatic command of 'the Raiden'.

I, on the other hand, was patting my stomach wistfully when Dalin held his hand up to stop us, catching sight of Nova zipping back in a flurry.

'All fifteen of them are up ahead,' she whispered. 'Armoured up, though not prepared for us.' She grinned with delight. 'They're resting for a moment, out of formation, with their focus on their water flasks and their weapons put aside. But I wouldn't wait. The opportunity will be gone the moment they stand and regroup.'

Dalin considered this and nodded. 'There are five of us to face the fifteen of them until the others get here. So the best way is to do this with the element of surprise,' he said softly. 'Noal and I will stun and then distract any big ones to time waste for as long as we can, and everyone else will need to use Elvish speed to restrain as many as possible.'

I took some deep readying breaths and rolled my shoulders. 'While I feel that nobody is ever outnumbered when they have Elves on their side,' I whispered. 'Let's all try not to get hurt while avoiding injury to our opponents.'

The Elves gave us returning grins and Dalin drew his sword from its sheath with a soft shing.

'You have until the count of sixty to spread out and encircle them. After that count, wait for a further count of ten to make sure we are all ready. On ten, we go.' He turned to Nova then. 'You should tell Kiana's party where we are.'

She saluted with an: 'Aye Raiden,' and whizzed off through the air.

When we had approached as stealthily as possible and could hear their voices ahead, Dalin eyed each of us and started quietly counting down. We all nodded when we got the count, and he became silent.

I took up my position a distance away to Dalin's side.

The fifteen warriors seated and spread out in the clearing didn't sense us watching as we counted down.

They went on talking, gulping from water flasks and wiping at tired brows.

Until we all swept out from the trees in synchronicity – and charged.

27

✺

Twenty Seven

D^{alin}

I easily stunned the nearest soldier before he could even swivel where he sat. I tapped him on his curl covered head with the hilt of my sword and he simply fell backward to lie on the grass.

I saw Noal move to do the same with his first soldier, but as the surprise wore off, our next opponents had drawn their sabres.

A massive soldier with a beard went for Noal before my brother had finished knocking out his first man, and I swung myself into the lunging warrior so that he tumbled at Noal's feet.

Noal pushed past me and sprang at a man who had rounded on me as well.

The bearded soldier I'd sent sprawling lumbered up at me without bothering to scrabble around in the grass for his dropped sabre. He moved quite nimbly for his bulk, immediately thrusting his big fist into my ribs and then clubbing me in the face.

I aimed a bone cracking punch into his temple in return and shoved him off – quickly glancing over to see Noal pinning his own opponent, face down, while he bound the struggling warrior's hands.

The majority of the Elves were also each handling a few warriors at a time, simply keeping the soldiers busy until Quidel could bind them, or until Kiana's group arrived.

A retrieved sabre instead of a fist was lobbed at my face then, but I skipped to the side and deflected, making my large, bearded soldier whirl. I instinctively caught the swinging sabre against my sword, but marvelled at the sheer power of his arm.

The man thundered after me and threw himself into a series of attacks that were each aimed at taking my head off as I strove to deflect.

'Too scared to attack, boy?' he growled. 'Or do you only know how to defend?'

I smiled politely, circling our blades and spinning his arm into the air when he jabbed at my belly in a flash blow. He had to scramble to keep a grip on his hilt.

'Perhaps I'm just playing with you,' I answered as he stared at my sudden show of ability. 'Seeing if I can hold you off for as long as I managed last time.'

When they'd all wanted to take Kiana from me.

I had definitely been able to hold my own, with gargantuan effort, on that night. But the Lady's touch and training with the Elves had given my old skills stunning finesse. It felt almost easy to face this clearly experienced warrior.

'Fight me!' he spat. 'You know how!'

He lunged viciously forward with his blade aimed straight for my chest, and I quickly spun aside to avoid having to meet the blow with a killing stroke of my own.

'Scared to get hurt?' he laughed jokingly. 'Or you don't want to hurt me? Is that it? Scared of blood?'

'Perhaps I like you,' I said in a tone that suggested otherwise.

I ducked another swing of his sabre, only to have him aim a kick at my head while I was low. His steel covered boot crunched into the already aching side of my face and I dropped and rolled to escape his sabre as he chopped up the ground after me.

'I doubt that!' he grunted, pulling his blade from the grass. A piece of my shirt fluttered away from where it had been pinned to the ground by the point.

'You're right. I do dislike you,' I remarked sourly as I bounced to my feet in readiness. 'That was a good shirt.'

He threw himself at me, aiming shattering blow after shattering blow while all I could do was defend; my arms weakening under the strain of stopping his incredible strength while not being able to do anything to diminish his own.

He worked to batter me into exhaustion so he could finish me off, and I swore darkly when he pulled a curved, lightning shaped dagger from a sheath at his hip so that I had to focus on two deadly weapons while keeping us both alive.

'No!' Thale bellowed.

But Nikon ignored him and turned back to face me – and my fist.

I clipped his eye with my knuckles and quickly caught his dagger hand to stop it mid-air.

Unconcerned and lightning fast, he dragged his other armoured wrist over my face, scraping the spike lined cuff of his armour down my already ruined cheek, then drove a quick succession of savage thumps into the wound in my pinned arm.

I felt the hole in my skin gape wider.

I desperately, angrily thrust Nikon's own dagger filled fist up into his face with a mighty punch that drew a yelp from the soldier.

I smashed another huge blow into his temple before he could recover, and shoved him sideways as he sagged. Finally, he lay prone upon the grass, stunned – but also unfortunately weighing down my still stuck arm.

I groaned blearily. My head felt like an inflated balloon that was swelling to bursting point.

'Frarshk, frarshk, frarshk, frarshk, frar – '

I cut my curses when I heard the familiar voice of someone else swearing nearby.

Craning my neck, I caught sight of Noal being driven to the ground by a warrior more than twice his size. The man was a monster. And he was ready for murder.

A furious cry exploded from my mouth. In a rush of adrenaline I dragged my injured arm out from under Nikon's weight, the spikes along his armour raking my skin.

I sprang to my feet, enraged, and sprinted back to snatch up my blade from beside Thale.

'You can't take on Vulcan,' he ground out from where he laid. 'You're about to keel over.'

I charged ferociously, skidding to a halt over Noal and ramming my blade under the soldier's sabre as he swung it down like an executioner's axe.

'Back off,' I spat, driving at the monster so hard that he had no choice but to retreat.

I continued to pound after him as he desperately sought to parry and block, until finally he stumbled and went down with a loud crash of armour and mountainous muscle. I immediately slammed my hilt into his head, making his eyes instead of his head roll – despite the death he had been about to deliver to my brother.

I staggered around to face Noal, who was leaning up on his elbows, pale with exertion, and sweating from his close call.

'Are you hurt?' I demanded, worriedly striding back to him.

'No,' he puffed cheerily. 'Thanks for that.'

I saw him grin at someone over my shoulder and I checked to see Kiana standing there, a picture of calm against the fuzzy backdrop of struggling or unconscious soldiers behind her.

Everything had been so drawn out by our need to make prisoners out of people intent on killing us. But now both our teams were finishing up their prolonged scuffles – the

Elves closing in on any soldiers who were still loose, ropes at the ready.

'Sounds like you did well,' Kiana told me.

I was feeling shaky and sluggish, but I managed a smile. 'You took your time getting here.'

'Yes. Well ... we'd gone further than Nova expected. And I regret that.' Kiana eyed my battered face, which was pulsing with heat. Then her eyes went to my crimson shirt sleeve. 'You look a mess.'

'I feel a mess,' I grimaced and extended my good arm to pull Noal to his feet.

Instead, he quickly reached up and put a steadying hand on my chest as I swayed. Kiana rushed forward and I felt her grab me from behind.

'Perhaps you're as bad as you appear,' she said, and Noal clambered to his feet beside us.

'It's a stab wound.' Thale watched us from where he was bound a distance away.

I glared at the bearded warrior as Kiana helped Noal to lower me to clear ground.

'I was fortunate it was nothing more than a dagger and some spike wounds,' I admitted begrudgingly. 'Even after all that Elf training. How embarrassing.'

'The knife was edged with a toxin,' Thale croaked. He was looking decidedly conflicted over whether he was betraying his comrades by speaking – or if it would betray his conscience not to. 'It is a Krall toxin that thins the blood and weakens a foe.'

'Let me see,' Kiana instructed, sitting down on my other side and unsheathing her own dagger to cut away the remaining ribbons of my sleeve.

I wearily closed my eyes while Noal kept me upright with a hand on my shoulder.

'Oh DISGUSTING!' I heard Nova declare and I opened my eyes with a start. The Nymph had taken a seat on Thale's chest.

'You're a bully, aren't you?' Naira said matter-of-factly, also sweeping down to sit on Thale. 'That one, too. He finished off the job,' she added, nodding her pink hair toward the unconscious Nikon.

Thale was turning green. Noal and Kiana just stared for a moment.

'This is why it's best to be on the team who fights to kill,' Nova shrugged.

I squinted at my arm and winced at the grizzly sight of the torn skin all around the original stab wound. It was like it had been scraped back with a peeler.

Muscle was exposed and the dagger hole had torn wider after my exertions. The blood was still leaking in fast streams, creating an odd tickling sensation that mingled with a hot throbbing feeling.

'Lucky the spike ones aren't that deep,' I commented. 'And lucky the dagger wasn't very wide.'

'But not so lucky, the dagger was long and curved,' Kiana said. 'It has gone right through, and has left an uneven trail.' She turned then to the guilty faced Thale. 'Is the toxin Krarx?' she demanded.

'Nothing so immediately deadly,' the warrior answered quickly. 'It's Kilto.'

'Don't be too hard on him,' I sighed. 'I think he's going through the awakening that Thorin went through.'

Vidar led the other Elves across to us then.

If they'd been in a fight to the death, I was certain that the Elves would have been untouchable and unscathed. But as it was, even Quidel, Rond and an Elf from Kiana's team had managed to get assorted bruises, scrapes, bloodied noses and gashes that bled luminescent silver.

The Krall men had been smart enough to flood their powerful Elvish opponents in groups while Noal and I had faced only independent foes before Kiana had arrived.

'Sorry I won't be much help getting home,' I grinned.

Vidar knelt down, examining my arm and tilting my face before he lifted my shirt to reveal my side, which was scraped raw and already black and blue.

Noal hissed sympathetically. 'Perhaps you shall have to be carried yourself,' he told me.

I noticed Kiana was pulling cloth for bandages out of a pack to bandage my arm and exclaimed in surprise. 'Is that your healing pack?'

She nodded with relief. 'I found it with the rest of their bags. They must've kept it for me while they searched.'

I winced as I felt the pressure of the bandages tightening around the wounds, and noticed that I was now leaning almost completely on Noal – my nose inches from his chin.

'Gods,' I heard Thale utter sickly. 'I just don't understand.'

Nova and Naira glanced down at him in curiosity.

'You're in shock,' Nova told the warrior helpfully.

'This will help.' Naira flicked her hand and a globe of light appeared over her palm. It floated gently down to sink into Thale's forehead, and his eyes closed at once.

I stared at Naira blearily while Kiana wiped at my burning face, but the Nymph just shrugged and yawned.

'We can't really afford him to blow his top right now. I just put him to sleep. Deep sleep.'

'In fact,' Nova elbowed Naira to get up. 'We should make sure they all stay in the land of nod.'

'Ready?' Kiana asked Noal over my shoulder.

'Great,' I said wearily, as Kiana got up and took my good arm in her hands so that I could sit forward and Noal could stand.

Then together they helped lever me to my feet.

I felt as if someone had packed my arm full of salt and stones, but I stayed quiet as Noal slung my good arm over his shoulder, and wrapped his own arm around me.

'We're organised,' Kiana told Vidar.

'Are you going to be able to lug this many heavy bodies back to the city?' Noal asked, glancing at the soldiers who were littering the forest floor.

'It will be no trouble – Nymph magic will keep them sedate, and we can make trips quickly,' Rond assured me, crossing to scoop up a couple of unconscious men and their discarded bags with ease.

'I am, as ever, glad to be on your side,' Noal told the Elf in wonder.

I simply concentrated on walking as the party readied to leave, slinging bodies and bags up as they went.

I managed for a moment, but I heard Noal call out to Kiana as I finally slumped against him.

'Just need a quick rest,' I mumbled.

Nova brought another ball of light to her fist.

'No, you don't!' I said, trying to swat her away, but she easily flitted around my arm and pressed the glowing ball to my forehead.

As my eyelids drooped, I heard Vidar step comfortingly close. 'Don't worry Raiden. I will support you.'

28

Twenty Eight

N*oal*

Thorin and a crowd of Elves and Nymphs were waiting when we finally descended the slope into the city.

Thorin stared at his floppy comrades as they were paraded past him, but Asha whirred gleefully up to meet me and showered my face with kisses before contentedly burrowing into my arms.

'They're fine,' Kiana reassured Thorin as the Krall warriors were marched toward his original cell – with Naira now perching disinterestedly on an unconscious warrior's bobbing, bald head, examining her reflection in it.

'They escaped with only minor bumps, even if others didn't,' I added, peering back with a frown to where Vidar had paused.

'What's wrong?' Kiana asked with concern, moving to Vidar's side as he laid Dalin on the grass.

'He's waking up,' the Elf replied in surprise, and Asha and her fellow Nymphs noticed Dalin for the first time.

Asha sat up hurriedly in my arms, her face switching from contentment to anger. 'Is it bad?' she asked, eyeing Dalin's blood-soaked shirt as Thorin and our welcoming party drew closer.

'He was stabbed with a poisoned dagger,' Vidar explained. 'But the Nymphs put him to sleep, and he's not meant to wake for hours,' the Elf added with raised white brows.

Flash and Rebel landed next to Vidar to examine Dalin.

'He added a fractured cheek bone to the broken nose,' Rebel observed with a crinkled-up expression.

'Nova and Naira put him to sleep?' Flash asked with amazement. 'That's incredible! Not many can wake up from that before they're meant to. The One must really be rubbing off.'

'More like the Lady,' Kiana sighed. 'But he needs the rest.'

Dalin's eyes weren't open but his bruised features creased with a frown. 'Oh frarshk,' he moaned, and struggled to sit up against Vidar.

'What is it Raiden?' Rebel asked with pity.

'It's not that incredible at all,' Dalin answered mournfully. 'Nobody could sleep through all this racket.'

His skin was so pale that the scar along the un-bruised side of his face stood out. His green eyes were feverish when he blinked at us.

'Well, grumpy or not, I'm putting you back to sleep,' Flash told him, and pressed a glowing palm to Dalin's forehead before he could protest.

'I'll get Chloris,' Rebel added as Vidar hoisted Dalin back up.

'Do you know the name of the poison on the blade?' Thorin asked after Vidar had carried Dalin back to his bedroom in our tower.

'Kilto,' Kiana replied while Dalin was set down.' I know it's not the worst toxin of Krall, but it will need our attention.' She began to unwind the stained bandages around Dalin's arm then.

'What are you doing?' I asked her, pushing Dalin's hair back from his pale, marked face.

'Chloris will want to inspect and clean it,' she told me, carefully pulling the cloth away from the still bleeding gouges.

Thorin winced when he saw the mess of holes and spike wounds. The skin gaped open like torn meat. 'Ouch,' he wheezed in sympathy. 'It's gone right through.'

'Ouch,' I agreed, feeling queasy at the sight of the mess again myself.

Kiana inspected Dalin's ribs and the gashes along his face more closely now. 'At least he won't need stitches for the face.' She lightly drew his eyelid up to inspect his swelling eye then. 'And the damage around his cheek shouldn't cost him his vision.'

Dalin tried to turn in his sleep, but I pressed him down gently to still him.

'Is there anything I can do?' Thorin asked earnestly, but Kiana shook her head.

'I could definitely help to heal this, but Chloris is much more experienced, so I'll leave him in her hands. It's fortunate it happened in the forest. In some less medically able villages, this kind of wound would have become infected enough for the victim to lose the arm.'

I shuddered as I was reminded of the struggle Agrudek suffered over the loss of his hand, but turned as we heard Chloris ascending the steps.

'The Three are keeping me quite occupied of late,' she smiled at us as she climbed into the room. Ailill was following her.

'I only just removed the stitches from his leg,' Ailill remarked dryly, and I noticed Thorin ducking his head awkwardly at that.

'More stitches?' I asked, mortified on Dalin's behalf.

Ailill examined the dagger wound. 'Only some,' he told me while Chloris nodded. 'To seal up both ends. Now shoo,' Ailill told us. 'Give us some peace.'

'Can't I stay with him?' I asked the Elf.

'We need a sanitary environment,' he remarked archly, with a Wilmont-esque sniff.

And when Thorin put a comforting hand on my shoulder to guide me from the room, I followed glumly.

29

Twenty Nine

K*iana*

'I would have preferred to give them more than a day to settle down,' I told Thorin as Noal, Asha and I led him to the patch of ground over what had once been his cell. 'They have hardly started their first night in the city yet.'

'I can't stand listening to them yell the forest down anymore,' Thorin answered tensely. 'They might start to feel threatened enough to actually take their Krarx.'

'You'll try to make them see the truth?' Asha asked Thorin with interest, swinging from her grip on Noal's hand while the Granx sat on her forehead like a bonnet. 'A mass awakening?'

'I'll try to reassure them and prepare them to hear it from Kiana,' Thorin grimaced. 'I don't think I'm inspiring enough on my own.'

'We need you with us in case we have to put any of them back to sleep in a hurry,' Noal told Asha. 'And because we love your company,' he added.

When the patch of grass disappeared to reveal the ladder, Asha, Noal and I waited quietly in the side room while Thorin cautiously approached the vine barred door.

Almost as soon as the vines had parted there were cries of disbelief.

'Thorin!' they yelled, and I heard scrambling feet as they ran to hug him and thump him on the back.

'We thought you were dead!' came one voice.

'Where've they been keeping you?'

'Are you harmed?'

He cleared his throat with an uncomfortable cough. 'I'm not a prisoner.'

And suddenly the glee and welcome faded to silence.

'You've joined them?'

'No. Well, yes. But it's not like that,' he fumbled to explain. 'They've accepted me as a friend.'

'You've betrayed *us* then?' one soldier accused.

'No, they wish to be friends to you, too,' Thorin clarified.

'How can they be friends?' protested another. 'We're being held captive!'

I heard Thorin trying to be patient, perhaps remembering his own reaction not so long previously.

'Look around. This room is more like a palace bedroom than a dungeon. They've given you food and water, they've even bandaged your wounds,' he pointed out.

'So, they aren't trying to kill us yet, they're even feeding us,' argued a voice.

'They're magical beings! Who can say what they're planning? Perhaps they're fattening us up like livestock!'

Asha clasped a hand over her mouth to keep from giggling while the Granx waved about on her forehead.

'They're not farming you all for food,' Thorin managed to sound placating.

Noal was trying to appear serious, but he was failing.

'They ambushed us!' argued another.

'Yes, but none of you are even really hurt,' Thorin countered. 'We know that's strange. Enemies kill.' I heard him take in a breath. 'And you would have eaten your fatal dose of Krarx if you truly thought you were in danger.'

'Clearly we didn't think to eat it because we planned on fighting our way free' someone replied stubbornly after a pause.

'You thought you could easily escape the magical beings who have so effortlessly thwarted our every move in the forest?' Thorin asked dryly.

'Well that just reminds me of another reason why they must be enemies,' came another's voice. 'They've captured the girl we've been trying to rescue for so long.'

I shrugged at Noal and Asha before I crossed to lean in their doorway, finding a much bigger room than before, with many more beds and people in it.

'Actually, I'm not a prisoner here either,' I informed them, and fifteen pairs of eyes flew to the door to stare at me.

'It's her!' someone whispered.

'Kiana,' I supplied.

'Kiana!' they echoed wistfully, and Thorin blushed, likely recalling that he'd reacted very similarly.

'You're not trapped here?' one soldier asked from where he was sitting on a bed.

I shook my head. 'You're not either,' I told them all. 'You'd be free if you wanted and accepted what it means.'

'What?'

'It's true,' Thorin affirmed grimly.

'And you weren't searching for me because you wanted to help me. It was because I'd escaped you and your king. It was in fact the Elves and Nymphs who saved me from *you* and from the arrow wound your general had given me.'

'Stop!' a bald man groaned, growing pale.

'I can't stand to hear all of this!' one cried fretfully. 'I remember all of this but there is something telling me not to believe it!'

Another one collapsed back upon his bed and moaned, his head in his hands.

'It's all true,' said a hollow voice from a bed by the wall, and I noticed the bearded leader who had stabbed Dalin.

'I feel the same,' cried another man dejectedly, and sank down against the wash stand.

'You're saying ... we are the threat to you?' one asked me, mortified and blinking around at the blanched faces of those around him.

'You aren't the villains,' I said compassionately. 'Your king is. Darziates has blinded you, and as his soldiers you had no choice but to obey.'

'I know,' said the bearded leader in a flat tone, eyes on the floor. 'I've felt that and not admitted it for as long as I can remember. But we had to submit to him ... our families ...And it was just the way things were. That was life.'

The room fell into silence as each man sank into his own thoughts.

'For tonight you can sleep here and get used to things,' I told them gently, choosing to withdraw to let them think. 'In the morning if you feel up to it you can meet all of the friends waiting to greet you in the city above.'

'Gods,' one of them muttered in disbelief, as if winded.

The vines over the door didn't close again when Noal, Asha and I left them.

After all, these men *weren't* really prisoners.

30

Thirty

D^{*alin*}

'You've slumbered for two days,' Chloris told me. 'You must take things slowly, Raiden.'

I squinted at her with one eye swollen mostly closed, and even the shine of her silvery white hair seemed too dazzling in the sun.

'More like I've been made to slumber for a couple of days,' I grimaced as I sat up stiffly.

'Yes. And if you are not careful of your fragile health, I might call on the Nymphs to send you to sleep once more,' Chloris warned.

'I will be entirely careful,' I promised, and waited until after she had left before kicking off the sheets and pulling myself up to face the looking glass.

'Gods,' I muttered, touching the puffy purple bruises and jagged slices along my cheekbone.

The skin stretched over my damaged eyelid in a particularly gruesome lump – and I could only see through a tiny slit in the swollen purple mountain it had become.

I found more bruises in a stunning array of colours when I lifted the clean linen shirt I'd been dressed in, and knew that I wouldn't be able to tolerate any of the fitted outer garments I'd been given to wear in the forest so far.

Instead, I foraged around until I found a loose tunic and my weather-stained trousers from our journeys. I managed to pull the pants up and to step into my boots with the aid of my good arm, but I cursed when I tried to thread my arms into the tunic sleeves and felt my bicep throb and burn.

'You know, I'm sure Chloris actually meant for you to be careful when she said that you should be careful,' Noal commented from the doorway.

'I'm not doing anything strenuous,' I told him.

'Ah,' he nodded thoughtfully. 'That's why that nasty tunic is getting the better of you.'

I sighed with exasperation. 'Are you going to help, or reprimand?'

He grinned. 'I don't know why I bother,' he declared as he came across to help me drag the tunic over my head, guiding my arms through.

'Did you let Ailill put stitches in me again?' I asked him with distaste as I felt my skin tighten against them with the movement.

Noal ducked his head guiltily. 'Your mother always told me not to argue with the healers.'

'That was in regards to *you*. She never told you not to protest on my behalf.' I shook my head at him and ran my fingers through my hair to try to bring it into some semblance.

'So, what are you planning?' he asked finally when I was dressed and headed for the steps. 'Seeing as you won't stay in bed.'

I buckled on my sword more out of habit than anything else, finding it difficult with one good arm.

'I don't know. I just feel like getting out and about.'

'I shall accompany you out as well as about then, my brother,' he professed cheerfully, following me as I descended.

Yet, despite my determination, I regretted stepping back out into the city immediately when I spied two Krall warriors nearby, surrounded by a mass of doting Nymphs.

'Seriously?' I paused in shock. 'It seems like every time I wake up a new Krall warrior is walking about the city.'

'They've all come to their senses much like Thorin did,' Noal explained calmly. 'For the past two days they've been settling in while you've been recovering.'

'Of course.'

'Really Dalin. The Elves and Nymphs have accepted these men and are trying to help them adjust. I don't mind them.'

'In two days, you've got to know the people who wanted to take us to Darziates?' I asked wearily. 'How about the big one who tried to chop your head off?'

'I've talked to most of them,' Noal answered patiently. 'And you should too. Then you would feel what I do, that they really are different now.'

'Where is Kiana then?' I tried to change the subject.

Noal sighed. 'Asha convinced Kiana to go with her to her favourite water pool.'

I nodded. 'Should we visit?'

'The Nymphs will cheer you up,' Noal answered in agreement, and we made our way into the quieter part of the city where the water pool was.

However I again regretted my choice when I found that not only was Kiana there, but also Thorin and four of his comrades.

Asha squealed with delight and whizzed out of the water towards me at top speed.

'You're awake!' she cried, wrapping her little arms about my throat as I caught her, one armed. 'Your beautiful body is all in one piece! Though it's a real shame about your face.' She wrinkled her nose at my mountainous eye.

Flash and Rebel shot across and pumped me on the back in a congratulatory way.

'Nova may never forgive you for pulling that early awakening stunt,' Flash praised my efforts. 'It was quite disconcerting!'

'The One might not forgive him now either,' Rebel chortled then, and I squinted over to notice that the group sitting on the opposite side of the water had stopped talking, and Kiana had a dark expression on her face.

'Good morning,' I greeted her across the water.

'You were meant to stay in bed,' she replied warningly.

'Perhaps I am sleepwalking,' I answered. 'Gods know I've been pumped with enough magic to make that happen.' I shot a dry one-eyed glare at Flash.

'Are you going to swim with us?' Asha crooned. 'I'll help you get your shirt off.' She immediately started unlacing the front of my tunic.

I could see by the startled warriors' faces that they hadn't yet got used to such actions from this gorgeous, tiny being.

'I wouldn't,' Rebel warned. 'Ailill would kill you if you wet his stitches.'

Asha paused, and then exhaled dramatically. 'Another day then.' She turned to Noal. 'But handsome here has no excuse.'

'Oh, all right then,' Noal gave in with hearty self-sacrifice, and quickly tore off his shirt and boots to chase the squealing Nymphs. He dived like a whale, sending each of the Nymphs tumbling about in the foamed water from the shock waves.

'Well?' Kiana lifted her eyebrow at me from across the rock pool.

'Oh frarshk,' I said under my breath, and began to walk around to the group.

Kiana patted the grass beside herself at the end of their line along the bank.

'This is Dalin,' she told the soldiers evenly. 'The forest dwellers refer to him as the Raiden.'

For once they were not encased in spiked armour and were managing to appear more human.

'I've got a bruise that says we've met, I think,' said one of the men with a wide smile, tapping his shock of curls.

I nodded coolly and sat down, feigning great interest in the playful banter going on in the water as Kiana resumed their conversation about Krall training routines.

Eventually I laid back upon the grass and closed my eyes, ignoring them completely while my arm throbbed horribly.

'You look spent,' I heard Kiana say, and realised I must've fallen asleep. 'You know, your face really is a mess.'

She was leaning over me, shielding my eyes from the sun with her hand, and I frowned at the light.

'It's afternoon already?'

She nodded. 'You might as well have stayed in bed after all.'

'Gods, I'm sick of sleeping, but I can't seem to stop,' I moaned, pushing myself up with my good arm.

'That's because you kept forcing the Nymphs to outdo each other,' Noal informed me. He was now dry and sitting next to Thorin. 'They gave you a few really impressive blasts to keep you unconscious. Nova was especially passionate.'

'That explains it,' I agreed, sitting forward and rubbing my forehead.

'I could hardly see straight when they put me to sleep just once,' one of the soldiers joined in politely then.

'Yes. Well, I might walk it off,' I said by way of excusing myself, and I pulled myself to my feet.

'I'll come with you!' Asha chirped, kissing Noal on the nose and then flying across to hover next to me.

Kiana stood too. 'A walk would be good,' she announced.

'Are we going to visit the little man?' Asha asked as we began to walk back around the water. 'Agrudek seems even more agitated lately.'

Already with some distance from the new invaders, and with Asha and Kiana by my side, my mood was lightening. In fact, it improved with every step.

31

Thirty One

N*oal*

'You should all stop by at my place tonight,' Flash innocently remarked to the five men of Krall sitting along the edge of the water.

'It'll be fun,' Rebel encouraged, just as adorable as his mischievous friend.

I snorted and flicked some water at them. 'Don't be fooled by their coaxing,' I warned the warriors. 'Whenever I join them, I wake up the next morning surrounded by empty Nymph liquor bottles and with a headache like an axe to the forehead.'

'You've always had fun getting into that state,' Flash protested good-naturedly, rolling over to lay more comfortably in the air.

'Have I?' I asked. 'I can't remember.'

'Sounds like I'd enjoy visiting you tonight,' one of the men grinned at the Nymphs. His name was Tane, and he couldn't seem to stop being jolly to save his life. Everything about him was energetic, even his hair, which was wildly curly.

It was hard to imagine him in Krall at all, and impressive that he'd kept the joyous attitude.

'That's my boy!' Flash crowed joyously.

'Actually, I am a father. Very adult,' Tane demurred at the 'boy' title.

'Aww Rebel, do you actually think he's old enough to drink with us?' Flash asked his orange haired friend.

'Dunno. It's pretty potent stuff for a child to handle,' Rebel speculated. 'But the baby over here survived,' he added on the bright side, nodding at me.

'Child?' objected one called Wolf, looking mildly offended. 'I've reached my thirtieth year. Thale has reached his fortieth. He's considered a veteran.'

Rebel held his stomach and lolled about in the air laughing. 'Flash, do you really think these novices can handle it?' he wiped at his eyes exaggeratedly.

'Novices?' Wolf was hurt. 'Now that's a bit harsh.'

One particularly massive man leaned back on an elbow. 'I'm wondering,' he drawled in a baritone. 'If we are so fresh in your eyes, how old does that make the both of you?'

He happened to be the one who had been trying to remove my head before Dalin had fought him off and, after recently apologising profusely, he'd introduced himself as Vulcan.

Flash picked at a pointed tooth. 'I was in my fifteenth year when Darziates chased the Nymphs into the forest.'

The furthest warrior from me, Purdor, spluttered loudly. Then coughed erratically when he tried to stifle his reaction. Rebel obligingly thumped him on the back.

'But,' Purdor gasped with watering eyes. 'That would make you ...'

Flash nodded and winked. 'Over five hundred years old. But don't tell Asha, she thinks I'm older. She likes older Nymphs.'

There was a stunned silence.

'You hold your age well,' Vulcan complimented him finally in a mellow voice.

'You hold your age well?' I echoed him with a chuckle.

'Well, what would you say to that?' Vulcan defended. 'They look like infants.'

'That's so that big folk underestimate us and wonder what went wrong while we tear your throats out.' Flash grinned nastily; his sharp teeth abruptly appearing a lot more sinister.

I remembered watching the Nymphs ripping through the ape beasts in the Cursed Valley, and the Krall soldiers now glanced at each other with sudden unease.

'We meant no offense, Flash,' Thorin told the Nymph in a placating tone.

Flash's expression rapidly transformed again as he burst into peals of laughter.

'See?' he chortled to Rebel, who was guffawing as he circled us. 'This bunch can't handle us. You should've seen your faces!' Flash roared at the soldiers, nearly falling out of the air.

'You should've seen yours,' I reprimanded him, swatting at his leg.

'They know I'd never hurt my friends. We never even hurt them when they were enemies,' Flash complained, floating lazily down to stand on my shoulder.

'Sure, we knew,' Tane agreed weakly.

'I'll make it up to you in liquor,' Flash waved us off. 'Mine's the best home brew you'll find.'

Rebel chuckled. 'I think not.'

Flash stiffened. 'Pardon?' he crossed his little arms.

'You heard,' Rebel answered in all seriousness.

Flash pelted into Rebel so fast that Purdor barely had time to flinch beside them.

There was an 'oof' from Rebel, and then a wrestling swirl of silver and orange was zooming about us in ferocious circles.

'Should we try to break that up?' Wolf asked in consternation.

The smell of burnt Nymph hair wafted over the water as one of them lit up a tiny fist.

'Wait for it,' I shook my head. 'They're just getting some energy out.'

Soon we heard a high pitched shriek of laughter as the quarrel evolved into play wrestling.

'Look what I got!' Flash crowed, holding up a tuft of Rebel's hair like an orange moustache.

'You dolt!' Rebel gleefully pulled Flash into a flip in the air by yanking on his silver mane now, and Flash repaid the favour.

'Wow,' Wolf deadpanned as we watched their whirling tussle slow from a blur of colour and pinwheeling limbs, to a slow hit here and there while the two Nymphs floated back over. They were chattering about the night's gathering as if they'd never broken from the conversation.

'Well, anyway,' Rebel said as he glided down to the ground next to Thorin. 'This infant is ready to drink all of you big manly men under the table.'

Vulcan snorted. 'You're on.'

Rebel smiled fearsomely. 'Bet I can outlast all sixteen of you.'

'I'll round up the lads later and we'll see,' Wolf agreed to the challenge, rubbing his hands together.

'Ugh, Flash?' Thorin asked, watching the other Nymph with a frown. 'You alright?'

Flash had abruptly halted, while mid-airborne somersault. His eyes had glazed.

I shrugged. 'This is what happens. Sometimes they just fall down on the spot to sleep for a burst.'

Flash slowly drifted downward, already asleep before he'd reached the ground.

'Gods!' Purdor started at the sight of Rebel, who had also stopped and was now snoring gently next to Thorin.

I nodded at their amazement. 'It's best to watch where you step around here,' I warned. 'If you look carefully there's often a bunch of them burrowed in the grass all about the place. And as soon as they're awake they've got double the energy they had before.'

Wolf scoffed, finding that hard to believe.

'Are you coming tonight?' Vulcan asked me then, sitting up.

'Course I am,' I grinned. 'Drinking with Nymphs is the most fun you'll ever have.'

Tane clapped me on the back. 'I think we're going to get along.'

Wolf nodded. 'I never thought I'd like an Awyalknian,' he admitted with feigned distaste.

'I never thought that Elves and Nymphs were real,' groaned Purdor. 'But here they are.'

'I never thought I'd be glad to see someone in any way magical,' Thorin mused. 'But it turns out not all magical beings are like Agrona and Darziates.'

There was silence for a moment as the tone became grave.

'Come on Thorin, I'm dashing and funny, but I'm not magical,' I said, batting my eyes at him in good humour.

They chuckled and the mood lightened.

'Awyalknians being friends ... drinks with magical beings ... I guess more bizarre things have happened,' Wolf shrugged.

'It's true,' I agreed. 'I've stopped bothering to be shocked these days, after so many outrageous things have happened.'

They looked to me questioningly, but I didn't explain further. Now wasn't the time to elaborate about our quest, the prophecies and why Darziates had sent them to catch us in the first place. Instead, I pushed myself up to my feet and stretched.

'You're leaving?' Tane asked.

'I'm off to tell Dalin and Kiana about Flash's invite. You should probably pass the message on to everyone else, seeing as you said you could all beat the Nymphs in a drinking game.'

'Would your friend Dalin really want to come?' Purdor asked. 'He doesn't seem to have taken a liking to us.'

'Which is understandable,' Wolf added to avoid offence.

I shook my head. 'Dalin will come round. He is one of the best friends you could have, once he sees that you *are* friends. He's looked out for me ever since I can remember, and even the Elves and Nymphs trust him as a leader, as young as he is.'

Thorin looked glum.

'Don't worry,' I told him. 'You'll see a different side of him when he relaxes. I'll drag him along.'

'See you soon, then,' Vulcan smiled, probably still feeling bad about getting so close to killing me.

3 2

Thirty Two

N^{oal}

'Kiana! You and Dalin here?' I called as I climbed the steps to Kiana's tower. 'Party at Flash's tonight!'

There was a scuffling sound and something heavy was dropped distantly overhead – Kiana's room? It apparently began to roll, and then thunked its way down the stairs.

'You ok?' I called again, jogging up the steps now. 'Wha –?'

I wasn't expecting to see a cloaked figure scuttling across the kitchen to pick up whatever had dropped, and pocketing it furtively.

I nearly fell back down the stairway with a start, until I saw who the hooded figure was.

'Agrudek!' I exclaimed, skipping up the final steps and across to him. 'Did you drop something?'

'D-d-didn't mean to alarm you,' he answered quickly. 'Kn-n-ocked over an ...um...'

'Never mind that,' I reassured the poor man. 'Are you well? I haven't seen you!'

'Y-y-yes – I know,' he said nervously. 'S-sorry. Should have come to visit ... I heard of all the ... er ... heroics!'

'Well you're making up for it by visiting Kiana now,' I surmised. 'You can keep me company while I wait for her, too.'

'I'll j-just go,' he countered fretfully. 'I c-can come another time. D-don't want to be a -b-bother.'

After my own experiences, I hated to think of the small man being in a state of constant anxiety on his own. But I tried to be welcoming instead of pitying.

'Nonsense! I won't hear of it.' I put my arm around his shoulders and steered him towards the table so he couldn't squirm away and return to his isolation. 'You stay right here and I'll get you something,' I added. 'Kiana won't mind. She's used to providing food for Dalin and I.'

Agrudek patted my arm awkwardly. 'Oh n-n-no, let ... let me do it.' He crossed the kitchen to put a pot full of water over a hot globe of Nymph light that was always alight in the corner.

'That's nice of you,' I took a seat while he grabbed a cup and a plate, both with one hand.

When he placed them on the counter, I noticed him pulling out a pouch from a pocket in his brown cloak, and then sprinkling small grey leaves from it into the cup before pouring the warmed water in.

'You brought tea leaves? Is that tea that you're making?' I asked with an effort to conceal my distaste.

'Ah ... yes,' he answered shakily. 'I b-brought them from my tower in c-case. But now they're just for you.'

I glared up at the heavens as he turned away to stir the hot fluid. The Gods always seemed to find humour in cornering me into having things I hated.

'We c-can have an apple each with it ...' he told me. 'You said – Kiana won't mind.'

I plastered a smile across my face when he carted the cup of tea over.

I stared at the murky brew when he next carried the apple laden plate over and set it on the table.

I was sure I was imagining it, but this tea seemed particularly nasty. The floating leaf remnants had turned the water a horrible greyish colour.

'Are you sure you want to sacrifice your personal tea leaves, just for me?' I asked hesitantly. 'You can have the cup instead.'

'Oh n-no – it is for you.' He sat down opposite me and fidgeted with whatever heavy thing he'd stowed in his pocket, seeming even jumpier than usual. His eyes darted to my cup and back to my face.

'Kiana and Dalin are both on the mend. You should join us tonight,' I told him amiably, trying to postpone having to drink. 'I'm sure the two of them won't be long, and we can all go together. Then you'll be glad I didn't let you get away!'

He glanced back at me, reaching for an apple but then putting it back. 'Y-you haven't touched your tea,' he said then, and I inwardly cringed.

I lifted the cup with dread, trying not to appear overly repulsed. 'It looks lovely.'

Agrudek watched as I brought it to my lips. And, seeing as there was no escaping it, I took a massive gulp.

It truly was worse than any tea I'd ever had the misfortune of tasting, and I set the cup back down with a shudder I couldn't quite mask. But he was satisfied enough that I'd only had one gulp.

'Thanks,' I managed. 'That's great.'

Agrudek sat back as if relieved, and watched me so intently that I started to feel slightly uncomfortable.

'How ... how do you feel?' he questioned, scrutinising my face – a twitch at his eye.

'Ah, I'm fi –' I began, and suddenly stopped to draw in a sharp breath.

A stabbing pain shot through my stomach, as if my insides were coiling themselves into knots. I gasped and doubled over, clutching my middle.

'Gods!' I cried.

Another blast of agony radiated through my core. I felt my frame spasm uncontrollably, my intestines twisting with a wrench, and I slipped sideways off the chair – curling up on the floor.

I heard Agrudek stand.

'Yes ...' he said quietly and sorrowfully. 'Pain for n-now, but it will be over quickly. I'm s-sorry. I have ... so little time.'

I couldn't seem to control my body anymore, shaking all over as I was wracked with searing jolts.

'I hadn't p-planned … I just needed to get …' Agrudek withdrew a smooth, dark globe from his pocket.

The Krall general's scryer globe, which had been stowed away in Kiana's bedroom cupboard.

'But, perhaps d-doing this will help me in his eyes …' Agrudek gazed down at me sadly. 'I w-would do anything t-to get them back, you s-see. I am s-so sorry.'

And then he turned and hurried down the steps to flee Kiana's tower.

33

Thirty Three

D^{alin}

Asha dozed in Kiana's arms while we headed back, walking companionably as the sun began to set.

'I feel better,' I told Kiana with a sigh. 'I'm glad we walked together.'

'You're a frightfully battered patchwork,' she replied. 'But you seem much calmer.'

I smiled tentatively with sore lips. 'Any tension inside me slipped away as we walked.'

'The forest does that for me, too,' she agreed.

'*You* do that for me,' I informed her as we neared her tower door, and I was glad to see her blue eyes crinkle with warmth.

'Hi guys!' Thorin's voice called and I glanced up to see him loping across to us. 'I've come to see what's held you up.'

At once my annoyance twinged again as he threw a grin at me.

I nodded back.

'Are you both nearly ready?' he asked.

'Ready for what?' Kiana questioned, swaying Asha gently to and fro.

Thorin tilted his head, confused. 'To go to Flash's place. Rebel bet all sixteen of us that he could out drink us all.'

Kiana gave her half smile. 'He probably can.'

'Noal was going to let you know,' Thorin said. 'Everyone's already headed over to get started.'

I grimaced. 'Poor Noal has probably been waiting for us to get back.'

'Poor Noal has probably been eating through my cupboard,' Kiana countered dryly. Then she started off. 'Come on then, we'll go collect him.'

Thorin bounded after her like a lovesick puppy. I hung back for some space, pausing to unbuckle and lean my sword against the wall of the sitting room.

'He's probably fallen asleep,' I remarked as Kiana continued up. 'It's so quiet in here.'

There was a pause.

'Noal?' Kiana gasped as she peered into the kitchen and I glanced up hurriedly. She sprang up the rest of the steps and into the room above. 'Noal!'

'What? What's wrong?' I asked, my heart skipping a beat as I pounded up after her, half shoving past Thorin to find Noal lying on the floor.

His skin was sapped of all colour, his eyes were closed and he was as still as death.

'Noal?' I sank to my knees and gripped his hand. 'He's cold! How is this possible? He was fine earlier!'

'What is it?' Asha asked sleepily, rubbing her eyes and climbing out of Kiana's arms.

In the span of moments her little face underwent a series of changes from confusion, to fear, and then to rage.

She hissed savagely; her enormous eyes suddenly gleaming with red fury. 'Who did this?!' Asha demanded, rising into the air like a wasp.

'We don't know yet, Asha,' I told her, barely hearing my weak voice. I held onto Noal's hand as if I could warm it with my own.

'I'll raise the Nymph armies! Let everyone in the forest be on the hunt for the one who hurt him!' Asha screeched in a voice that echoed with sudden power, and Thorin teetered for balance while Kiana and I were nearly blown backward by the physical force of the Nymph's explosive animosity.

Cups and plates in cupboards rattled and the table and chairs screeched along the floor, as Asha hurtled to the window in a gale, screaming furiously for the forest dwellers to rise to arms.

'Noal?' I asked again, stupidly, and clasped his hand in both of mine as Kiana knelt to try to listen for a heartbeat. 'Please my brother ...' I cried. 'Wake up!'

Kiana now searched for any kind of wound or mark to signal what could have hurt him and I closed my eyes and began to pray to the Gods, begging them not take his spirit.

'He is breathing,' Kiana said briskly. 'And there is no wound. Nothing.'

'No wound?' I heard Thorin question, and I opened my eyes as he knelt beside her with a worried frown. His face showed more dread now that he had heard there was no injury.

'What is it?' Kiana asked. 'What are you thinking?'

Thorin leant forward and smelled the air. Then the colour drained from the soldier's face.

'If there is no wound that has caused this,' he said haltingly, his voice shaking. 'Then it is poison.'

The air deflated from my lungs and I rocked back.

Kiana's eyes grew wide and she stared at him with understanding. 'Krarx?'

Thorin hurriedly stood and swept the room with his eyes. His gaze settled upon an overturned cup on the table and he moved to examine it, sniffing its spilled contents before grimacing.

He lowered the cup back to the table slowly.

'It is Krarx,' he said weakly. 'The fatal leaves that Krall soldiers carry in case we are caught and tortured. But I don't understand. Krarx should have killed him at once.'

'Gods!' Kiana breathed, slumping backwards to the floor.

My eyes went from Noal to Kiana to Thorin. 'Stop!' I cried in a frenzy. 'He is alive. Surely there is an antidote!'

Thorin gazed at me sickly and I had the urge to shake him, to force him to admit there was a cure.

'There is no antidote,' Kiana answered hollowly.

'The Lady, then,' I grasped for answers. 'She helped when you were poisoned. And the Elves helped to remove the Krall toxin from my wound. We must simply be quick.'

Kiana swallowed her emotions. 'I was poisoned with dark magic. The Lady could try to match it with her own. And the toxin you were given can be cured with natural remedies. It is not so with Krarx. Though perhaps the Lady's lingering touch upon his soul has saved him so far.'

Suddenly Thorin straightened, his expression hard. 'We don't know for sure that there is no remedy,' he said adamantly. 'We have never properly tried because the poison is only ever used on purpose, chewed as leaves, as a means of consciously choosing death. But I have heard speculation that there may be a cure. Thale will know!'

Barely finishing his sentence, he sprinted from the room. But within moments he was breathlessly skidding back into the kitchen, flummoxed.

'No need to look for Thale, they've all come to us,' he gasped. 'And –'

A tremendous whirring sound filled the air outside, a storm of voices approaching.

'What's happening now?' Kiana asked, rushing to the window.

I stared beyond her and gaped as I saw the sky about Kiana's tower filling with teeming, furious Nymphs all screaming and growling savagely over each other.

It seemed like all of the Nymphs in the city were there, Asha at their forefront.

The Krall men who had been celebrating at Flash's grove had followed the abrupt stampede of Nymphs in confusion, but they hurried towards Kiana's tower as she leaned out and waved urgently at them.

General Ace flew directly towards Asha, and with a commanding sweep of his hand the storm of noise and sizzling, angry power dimmed.

Asha's face creased with a snarl of fury.

'We want the blood of the one who has hurt Noal,' she screeched, and the crowd behind her bayed and hissed.

'You cannot have it,' Ace told her, and she lashed out at him like a tiger. Flash zoomed out of the crowd and caught her furiously struggling arms.

'The Lady has forbidden rashness,' Ace said in a low voice. 'We have no facts, and we can't tear through possible culprits without reason.'

'I will know the facts when I find the traitor!' Asha screeched. 'I will punish him!'

'When we know for sure who has betrayed Noal we will decide,' Ace rumbled so that the crowd all heard. 'Now is a time for us all to bend our minds and magic toward Noal so that he may recover,' Ace said. 'The Lady's will is already fixed towards him.'

Then, as bewildering and awful as her rage had been, Asha's cries of grief were even more horrific. Asha sagged and turned, letting Flash wrap his arms around her while she wept brokenheartedly.

I turned from the crazy scene as thunderous footsteps began climbing their way up through Kiana's tower, before fifteen stunned and overwhelmed warriors piled into the kitchen, with Ailill, Frey and Vidar in their midst.

'We swear to you, we have not harmed Noal,' the bearded soldier named Thale at once burst out.

'These soldiers were at the gathering,' Vidar confirmed. 'Please, help us all to understand what has befallen Noal.'

The three Elves and the soldiers listened, aghast as Thorin and Kiana explained.

'But we have no clue about what could actually cure Krarx poisoning!' I heard Thale exclaim as Thorin got to that part of his story. 'It's all rumour and guesswork. We might sicken him further by feeding him experimental concoctions!'

'Surely it's worth trying,' Thorin argued. 'It is that or we allow him to die without any attempt to save him.'

'I can feel that the Lady and the forest dwellers are sending healing magic even now,' Frey said. 'Yet without an antidote it's likely that this will slow the damage rather than restore Noal completely. Perhaps the Lady could have helped before, but she has not been well herself,' Frey admitted.

'Try it Thale,' one warrior encouraged.

'The lad does not deserve this death,' another said. 'Especially if we do not at least attempt to cure him.'

I know, I know.' Thale rubbed his brow. 'We can try. I did once hear whispers from some of the higher-ups ...'

Their talking washed over me as they bustled about, going through Kiana's healer pack, some of them leaving the tower and coming back with plants from the forest.

I was staring numbly when at last Kiana knelt beside me and gently helped them take Noal from my arms, resting him carefully on a blanket on the floor.

Vidar sympathetically led me to the end of the kitchen where I could watch from a distance. And I thudded into the wall, sliding down it miserably while sixteen strange men, three Elves and Kiana gathered around Noal to discuss ideas that could, just possibly, bring him around.

34

Thirty Four

D[alin]

The kitchen had cleared until only the Eves, Thale, Thorin and Kiana remained.

The other soldiers had left to wait in the room below after having poured different concoctions into Noal for most of the night.

The faces before me were now without hope, and I had almost given up completely when I heard a weak voice.

'Dalin?' Noal groaned faintly, and my head shot up.

'Noal?' I cried in disbelief, pitching forward and skidding across the kitchen floor to his side.

Noal's eyes were open and the others had sprung to their feet, rousing from their own misery as I clasped his hand tightly.

'Brother of mine you gave me a scare,' I admonished him shakily.

The colour was still gone from his skin and he was fighting to stay awake. He tried to say something, then coughed dryly and tried again.

'Agrudek,' he rasped.

I tried not to seem taken aback. 'He's not here, Noal,' I said. 'But Kiana and everyone else is. Asha nearly started a war on your behalf.'

Noal shook his head.

'No?' I uttered, puzzled. I didn't think he was referring to the Nymph war being averted.

He forced each word out as if every single one pained him. 'It ...was ...Agrudek.'

For a moment I sat in stunned silence, feeling my nostrils flare and the tendons in my neck tighten as my jaw clenched. The entire kitchen was still as everyone else absorbed what they'd heard.

The words echoed horribly in my head, etching their way into my comprehension.

It. Was. Agrudek.

Anger began to throb in my chest.

'Can you tell us about it?' I asked softly, my voice low.

He drew a deep breath. 'Came here ... found him. Said ... was waiting for Kiana.' He stopped and licked his lips, his skin looking stretched across his face.

'Made me tea ...' Noal grimaced. 'Felt sorry for him ... But it was ... toxic.' He sighed. 'Agrudek just wanted ... to get away with Darziates' globe.'

He seemed to sink into himself when he'd finished. He'd said all he had to and had exhausted himself.

'It's alright brother,' I told him. 'Rest easy now. You've done well to tell us.'

Noal nodded gratefully, his eyes closing as I stared into his face for a moment, but he was already asleep.

Then my gaze flashed up to Kiana's.

Her face was drawn with shock.

'Agrudek took the communication globe I stole from your general,' she said to Thorin and Thale. 'And he nearly killed Noal for it.'

'He's gone to talk to the Sorcerer ...' Thale breathed.

'We did so much for that man,' I ground out through gritted teeth. I carefully laid Noal's hand down next to him and slowly stood.

'Vidar, will you please help take Noal to my bed and make him comfortable?' Kiana asked the Elf, who immediately moved to oblige.

I was smouldering inside. Hatred in its purest form was spreading through every particle of my being. Outwardly, I felt a cold mask cover my features as I moved to the steps and quietly started to descend.

'Dalin,' Kiana said in a warning voice from behind me.

All eyes in the room below swept to me.

I noted that the room was dark, though none of them slept. They were all fully clothed and seated on furniture or sprawled on the floor, and they'd heard everything. They were as stunned as those in the room above.

'Dalin!' Kiana repeated, this time more forcefully.

My sword was still leaning where I'd left it what seemed like an age ago. I was halfway across the full, silent room when I heard footsteps down the stairs, following me.

'Where do you think you are going?' Kiana asked icily.

My eyes were fixed on my sword. Just half a room away. Once it was in my hands it would remove Agrudek's traitorous head.

'After we saved his life, he nearly robbed Noal of his,' I said in quiet fury. 'He will try to tell Darziates that his men are here. That there are hundreds of Nymphs and Elves helping us. That the Lady is vulnerable.' My fists bunched tightly. 'He will try.'

'You are in no condition to do anything about it,' Kiana said. 'You are still recovering yourself.'

'The Elves shouldn't risk themselves again so soon and I don't need a Nymph getting carried away and ripping that man's head off for me.' My jaw was clenching as I thought about what Agrudek had done. I could feel my stitched muscles and skin throbbing, but it simply didn't matter. No amount of pain would hold me back. 'He left Noal to die. I am going to return the favour.'

The room was tense and I felt every eye upon me as I began towards my sword again.

'Phobos,' I heard Kiana say.

I could hardly believe it when one of the massive warriors nearest me stood up, blocking my way.

I glowered at him darkly. 'Step aside.'

Phobos swallowed, and glanced nervously over my shoulder at Kiana.

'Raiden,' a new, calm voice came from behind me, and I growled.

You would weaken with infection and perhaps even die before you ever found him.' It was Ailill's voice.

Phobos stood a little more resolutely, and I glared.

'And it is not a good idea to pick up that sword just days after I have put those stitches in,' Ailill continued. 'Because if you were even to break just one of those stitches, I would send you to sleep before you left this tower myself.'

I turned slowly, to Phobos' relief, and faced Kiana, Thorin, Thale and Ailill.

'The man that tried to murder Noal,' I began in a low, controlled voice. 'Can betray us further. Information costs lives as much as poison does.'

Nobody spokes for a moment.

Then a deep voice spoke from my left. 'We will find him,' an impossibly large man said resolutely.

I regarded the soldier in surprise. It was the monster called Vulcan who had also nearly killed Noal – though in a fair fight we'd invited upon ourselves.

'It is plain that Agrudek took the poison from one of us. We shall be the ones to bring him back for you.'

I frowned, staggered by the offer.

'Noal needs you by his side now. He is fortunate to have survived,' Thale said from the steps. 'Agrudek will not have got far. A party of us will leave before the hour is out.'

I felt a light hand on my good arm and looked to see Kiana there. 'Please,' she said.

I regarded the men about me, struggling to process their kindness – and to trust their words.

'Leave it to us,' the wall of a man called Phobos reassured me, and there were nods of affirmation around the room.

I drew in a very long breath. Hoping we were not about to release an entire band of Darziates' men to do as they liked ... But at the same time, knowing they were no longer his.

'For doing this, I thank you, my friends.'

35

Thirty Five

A^{grudek}

'Engrark.'

He didn't have to wait very long – the Sorcerer had probably been focusing on this scryer, hoping for it to become active again.

Grey, stormy light illuminated from the globe in answer; the foul, cruel chill of his master's magic seeping out into the surrounding beauty of the forest and at once making the inventor feel filthy.

Agrudek. You've kept me waiting.

Agrudek's mind immediately seemed to crumple in on itself – all lucid thoughts breaking apart as if against jagged rocks.

I wasn't sure how long I'd have to gift you glimpses of your family, before you would be brave enough to reach out.

'Th-th-they l-l-l-l-l-live?' Agrudek whimpered.

For now. While you still hold use.

'W-w-what can-n-n I d-do? How can I g-get them back?' Agrudek whispered.

Be my spy.

Agrudek closed his eyes sadly. 'Th-they will not t-t-trust me n-now. Th-they will t-t-take the scryer away. How will I c-c-contact you?'

Agrudek knew that Darziates' magic was weak in the forest. The Lady weakened it. But the grey light around him swelled for a moment, and something small, cold and heavy pressed into existence against his chest.

A necklace now hung about his neck. It had a miniature scryer globe attached like a spherical pendant.

Do not fail. Information on the one called Kiana will pay for your family to be fed.

The grey light and the awful, suffocating stain of Sorcery began to fade. Eventually the original scryer was just a dull globe again, and Agrudek let it slide from his fingers.

He flinched as yet another flash of his daughters' little faces, all bloodied and sunken, was sent his way. His wife's screams echoed in his ears.

Button noses broken.

Pigtails shorn off.

Baby teeth knocked out.

Roly-poly roundness now just skin clinging to barely animated bones.

Agrudek shivered uncontrollably while he waited. He coughed roughly, and red stained his hand.

When they found him Agrudek regarded the stony faces of the soldiers.

These men of Krall had also found joy and love, but were free to keep it. For Darziates did not know, or have interest in which men out of the ambush party had lived to be converted, and so their families were safely anonymous.

One of these blessed fools now came forward to grimly take the scryer from where it laid at Agrudek's feet.

Then without a word, but with hard eyes and hands, Agrudek was dragged back towards the city.

Where he would have to play his new part.

36

Thirty Six

D^{alin}

My head ached over all of the things it was coming to terms with, and my swollen, dry eyes desperately needed sleep. But it seemed it would not come.

Noal, on the other hand, had slept a peaceful, healing sleep for a night and a day. Kiana also dreamed serenely; squashed in beside me in the same armchair I'd frequented during her illness. Her arm was linked comfortingly around my good one; her fingers entwined with mine as she slept, and I was loath to move.

But I needed to get out of the claustrophobic room and away from my chaotic thoughts, so I wordlessly shifted up out of the chair without waking Kiana.

I didn't bother straining my arm to get a tunic over my shirt, going straight down to the kitchen. I stopped in surprise at the sound of murmuring voices still in the room below, and realised that the soldiers must have stayed in Kiana's tower for all of that time out of care for Noal.

Listening, I heard a few lazy conversations and a couple of others occasionally calling 'strike' in a gambling game. Thale must have been talking to Thorin closer to the stairs.

'The Elf healer, Frey, just told me that if the Lady had not slowed time for Noal while we worked to save him, Noal's organs would have shut down.' Thale had a grimace in his tone. 'We have been ridiculously lucky.'

'At least some good came out of all of this,' I heard Thorin reply. 'We know there *is* a cure for Krarx poisoning.'

I could imagine Thale shaking his head. 'I tried so many things that I don't know which was the actual cure that worked. And I felt magic around the lad. As Ace and Frey said, the Lady and every forest dweller in the city was bending their will towards helping Noal to recover.'

I continued down the steps to descend into the room where the soldiers were lounging casually. They were spread across the floor, sprawled in chairs, leaning on furniture, sharpening knives, tossing coins into piles of gambling wins, eating fruit, and one was even smoking comfortably in an armchair. But they stilled when I entered – their faces unsure as they regarded me, and I realised they thought I had come with news from the sick room.

'All is well,' I told them – reassuring men who had once been my enemies. 'I'm just going to get some air.'

I saw one of the warriors share a look with his friend and then they both glanced at where my sword still leaned.

I tried not to scowl. 'I'm not going to take revenge upon Agrudek right now. I'm just getting out.'

'Do you need company?' Tane asked, eyeing me as if I were about to fall over.

'I'll be fine,' I answered the curly haired soldier stiffly. 'Thank you.' I tried to ignore the oddity of thanking a man of Krall.

I wearily turned and continued down the steps, moving out and through the still strangely subdued city until I found a rock pool that was quiet and deserted.

I gingerly pulled my shirt over my head and kicked off my boots to step into the water. Making my way slowly deeper, I was careful not to wet my bandaged arm when I poured the water over my head and let it run down my face, back and chest so that the cool droplets soothed the aches along my cheekbone and body. And watching the sun begin to lower and set over the glimmering water also began to soothe my soul.

At last, feeling less turbulent, I made my way back to the bank and sat upon the lush green grass to let my trousers dry and watch the sky turn a fiery orange.

I had to do better, I resolved pensively.

I had to be smarter.

The smallest man of Krall, who I had pitied, helped, and underestimated, had nearly robbed me of my brother. I had never even considered Agrudek a threat. Meanwhile, the ferocious warriors of Krall, who I had condemned and judged, had stayed happily in the city, alongside their magical captors, and aided in saving Noal's life. They had thrown off the mental influence of Sorcery, and had chosen to save their enemy, despite my disdainful behaviour.

I, myself, had been unfairly judged and fought even now to be more than my own father expected. All while I was letting my prejudice against anyone in Krall's armour blind me to the true men hidden beneath. A brown robe had concealed something much more sinister.

Gods, how Glaidin must be condemning me for taking Noal out of the palace for a quest that frequently put him in such danger. Yet we now knew that my mother was besieged within that very palace while my father marched to nearly guaranteed death, and nowhere was safe.

'You look to be turning over some hefty thoughts,' a voice speculated, shattering the silence. I didn't need to turn to know it was Thale.

I inclined my head in agreement, gazing out at the spectacular colours reflecting on the pool's surface.

Thale seemed to take that as an invitation, lowering himself down to the grass beside me with a grunt.

Another man sat down by my other side, and four others – one who I remembered to be Nikon, came around from behind me to sit on the grass as well.

I recognised them, and even remembered their names after having overheard them talking. Cadell, Phobos, Ferron and Phrixus.

'Bad day?' Ferron asked.

I regarded him. 'Rough year,' I replied, letting a dry smile touch my sore lips.

They were quiet for a moment, unsure of how to approach.

'I thank you all for what you did for Noal,' I said softly, staring back out to the water. 'I actually cannot thank you enough.'

I felt the tension and uncertainty in the men ease a little.

'We thought we owed it to you after the ambush and capture business,' Cadell answered.

'Also, for trying to kill you so we could snatch Kiana that time,' Phrixus added.

'And for *that*,' Nikon indicated my arm, but his eyes observed the older, long scars from the beasts on my back, and the bruises down my side. 'Though it looks like you already had some good injury stories. Perhaps they explain why our King was after you in the first place?' he hinted with interest.

'A few good stories,' I agreed, and they waited expectantly. 'Tales to tell some other time.'

'Perhaps the next time the Nymphs concoct another party,' Ferron suggested. 'I was having fun until everything else started.'

'The Nymphs are almost back to normal,' Cadell winced. 'As if they hadn't been about to spill into an uprising just yesterday.'

'You look exhausted,' Thale told me then, reminding me of how I ached all over from our fight days ago, and how my head throbbed from the broken nose I'd received just before that.

I shook my head with the first real smile I'd been able to give to these men.

'I never would have thought that I would have men of Krall, meant to be killing me, mothering me instead,' I said wryly.

'We never thought we'd appreciate an Awyalknian enough to care,' Ferron shrugged.

I let out a big breath, wincing, but feeling more at ease now. 'I am fortunate then.'

A moment later we heard calls in the distance, and I turned carefully to see more soldiers –Tane, Wolf, Vulcan, Purdor and Thorin coming to find us.

'Good news!' Tane announced as they drew closer.

'Noal is awake,' Purdor said.

And immediately the last ounce of tension in my body relaxed.

'He's definitely recovered,' agreed Wolf. 'He was eating a feast with Kiana watching in disbelief when we left.'

I laughed softly.

'They both sent us out here with a message, though,' Vulcan said then, and I glanced at him with the smile still on my lips.

'And what was that message?' I asked.

Vulcan crossed his arms. 'Go to bed.'

I raised a disbelieving eyebrow at him.

'Noal awoke miraculously, and his first words after rising from near death, were for me to go to bed?'

Vulcan shrugged. 'Actually, he demanded to be fed anything but apples first. And Kiana said 'tell Dalin to go to bed'.'

'Was there anything else?'

Purdor nodded. 'Kiana said to hurry if you want to eat before sleeping. Noal's devouring all the good stuff.'

I grunted. 'I best leave you all then. Or I'll have Kiana to contend with.'

I pulled on my boots and scooped up my shirt from where it lay beside me. Then I put out an arm to push myself up and winced as hot pain shot through it.

I'd used the wrong arm.

'Are you alright?' Thorin asked with concern.

'Fine.'

'Here,' Vulcan said respectfully, giving me his hand and pulling me up with my good arm.

I nodded my thanks and pulled my shirt on delicately, not bothering to lace it back up.

'I'm glad we talked,' I told them sincerely. 'As you say, perhaps next time the Nymphs are having fun we can share stories.'

'Be glad to,' Phobos replied eagerly, and the others agreed.

37

Thirty Seven

K*iana*

'I feel magnificent,' Noal declared, patting his stomach comfortably. 'I want to go and thank the Krall warriors for their help.'

It was dark outside, and Dalin had finally passed out by the bed while I'd watched the incredibly restored Noal ravenously consuming everything in sight.

I couldn't help but frown in consternation. 'I can't believe how completely rejuvenated you are,' I remarked helplessly. 'I can't find any excuse for you not to go.'

'I feel better than perfectly fine,' Noal shrugged in disbelief himself. 'I know that the Lady hasn't been here physically, but I swear by the Gods her magic is even now restoring me.'

'You're also upbeat because Dalin admitted he is getting used to the soldiers now,' I commented, feeling relieved myself.

'That is definitely cause for celebration,' Noal agreed, peeling himself free of the bed while I turned so he could dress fully again.

'I'll go with you to find them,' I told him as he finished dressing and happily bounced down the steps as if nothing had ever been wrong. 'In case you start to feel as someone normally should in your position.'

I glanced back to Dalin's exhausted, battered figure, resolving not to disturb him now that he had at last settled to rest. Instead, I quietly pulled a spare blanket down from my cupboard and lightly laid it over his sleeping form.

I stroked his forehead gently, pushing his hair away from the cuts there, and bent over him to softly kiss his cheek where the corner of his mouth was turned down.

Then I lightly kissed his lips.

He sighed in his sleep but otherwise didn't stir, and I slowly drew away from the warmth of his face in surprise at myself.

'Kiana? You coming?' Noal whispered up the steps, and I quickly turned and followed him down.

'The men are likely still where Dalin said they found him.' I made sure my voice was level as I followed Noal out, quelling the desire to stay in the tower with Dalin.

'They do seem content to gather wherever there is space,' Noal commented agreeably while we moved in the direction Dalin had mentioned.

'Noal!' Tane yelled joyfully when he spotted us, and there were shouts of welcome and cheer as we were drawn warmly into their circle. It seemed that their group had swelled – all of the Krall soldiers now sitting together by the rock pool where they had made a bonfire.

'Thought you'd still be eating – you were that famished when you woke,' Wolf joked.

'I only came out here because I'd eaten everything in there,' Noal confided.

'Where's the Raiden, as he's called around here?' Thale asked. 'Did you badger him into sleeping?'

I sat amongst them comfortably. 'Now that there's no one left to worry about he could finally shut his eyes.'

Phrixus nodded. 'We found him out here, mulling away. But less surly towards us, at least!'

'He wore the weight of the world on him,' Nikon sniffed brusquely, whittling away at a piece of wood with his knife.

It sounded like Nikon was speaking from experience, and as much as these men were wholeheartedly embracing the joy of the city, I could guess that all of them had lived most of their lives feeling much the same weight.

'If anything is not well with Dalin's friends, Gods watch out until he makes it right,' Noal answered whole heartedly.

'He burst out of nowhere before I could take your head off that time,' Vulcan remarked to Noal light heartedly. 'That's true friendship.'

Phobos stretched out on the grass, his bald head resting on his arms. 'I didn't enjoy getting between him, his sword and vengeance upon Agrudek last night. But Kiana scared me into staying put.'

I shrugged. 'It is a talent of mine.'

Noal grinned. 'Dalin's always looked out for me. And he's saved my neck a million times on this quest alone.'

'He actually bested me by saving my neck, too,' Thale admitted uncomfortably.

'What do you mean?' Noal asked, and I listened in interest.

'Well,' Thale coughed. 'When you came for us in the forest, I saw the Raiden strike Tane down with a thump to the head, and you had clobbered Aiolos,' he told Noal. 'Elves were everywhere, my men were being taken prisoner, and I wanted blood. But I was infuriated as the Raiden easily fended off nearly all of my blows without returning any. And any blows he took were because he wouldn't attack in return,' Thale explained.

'You knew us as the enemy. You were justified in fighting back,' I reassured the bearded warrior sincerely. 'Dalin understood that.'

'Yes, but he just refused to properly engage, and it confused and incensed me. It seemed arrogant rather than kind. I became so enraged that I made a stupid move, and he had to twist and catch my dagger in the arm, or spit me through the throat with his sword. I couldn't understand why he chose to take the dagger instead of the kill, and why I'd suddenly begun to change my mind about him.'

'That's why you kept hollering not to kill him,' Nikon recalled with a snort. 'I thought you were insane.'

Thale shook his head. 'The wonder of it is that he risked himself for a sworn enemy. All of you did,' he added, looking at Noal and I. 'You could have just left us to rot in the forest. Or you could have killed us all.'

'No,' I said grimly. 'We knew, after seeing Thorin, that you were not really our foes.'

Noal rolled onto his stomach on the grass, gazing enthusiastically at the men around him.

'So, we know how many Dalin got. How many of you did I get?' he asked, breaking the sober mood.

Two raised their hands and Noal became crestfallen.

'Well, I don't really count, because Dalin finished the job,' Vulcan explained pityingly.

'You're the size of a house. I tired you out so he had an easy job,' Noal protested. 'And it took me ages to do that, so I didn't get to deal with anyone else.'

I huffed. 'Vulcan can count for two, so you and Dalin can both add him to your tally.'

'We're fortunate you all took a chance on us anyway,' Cadell announced, and Ferron, who was beside him, nodded.

'You would not have found such charity from us if this had all taken place in Krall under our King's orders,' one of the quieter men, Roth, reflected.

'We would have obediently been doing any slight thing that our Lord ordered,' another called Gideon said a little bitterly, peering up from where he was leafing through a book of art that Frey had given him. 'Many of us would have been happy to.'

'Not all of you seem like the typical soldier types, though,' I remarked, eyeing two other reserved soldiers called Aiolos and Rendor, who were completely absorbed in books of their own.

'Yet that is what we've been made to be,' Phrixus stretched lethargically. 'So honestly,' he went on. 'These few days in the city, with a clear mind, and with beings who trust us – or who forgive and accept us – have been the best of my life.'

'Even the Raiden, who clearly had misgivings, went out of his way to help us. I am grateful to have earned some respect from him now,' Cadell remarked.

'The Raiden still really doesn't like you though,' Purdor laughed at Thorin. 'You must have done something to really get on his nerves before we got here.'

Thorin seemed to physically deflate. 'I know. All of you may have gained his trust, but I don't think I ever will.'

'What'd you do?' Phobos asked.

Thorin sighed, 'I was part of the ambush that first caught you both,' he answered, turning to Noal.

'Can't remember,' Noal shrugged. 'Was getting knocked out at the time.'

'I threw your food on the ground in your prison tent.'

'Well, that's a jerk move,' Noal agreed. 'Dirtying up our stale bread.'

'And when the Raiden was trying to carry Kiana away from us that night, I was the first to charge and continued to charge while trying every foul trick I knew to get around his sword,' Thorin admitted, eyes on me now. 'I wanted to kill to punish this spoilt Awyalknian for the ones he'd killed back in the camp. And I wanted to kill to get to you, to keep the purest thing I'd ever discovered all for myself. So, at one point, when he drove me down again, I pretended to be badly hurt, and he relented. When he was back to facing everyone else, I sat up and aimed at a gash that was on his leg, seeking to widen that gash and saw his leg right off to be rid of him.' Thorin appeared deeply upset as he concluded. 'He has seen me at my darkest, and is justified in his distrust of me. I would never trust a former enemy either, especially one who has proven himself to be such a threat.'

'No, I know Dalin,' Noal cut in then. 'He doesn't hate you specifically. He just hates what you seem emblematic of: the ferocious threat Krall poses against Awyalkna and the world. He'll come to see you clearly, and you'll gain his respect.'

Thorin shook his head. 'I wish I could believe it. But I have come to suspect why Dalin has earned such a title and such regard amongst the forest dwellers. And I have come to suspect why he has the best reason of all to condemn someone that he sees as an emblem of Darziates' control.'

'What do you mean?' I asked him, sharing a glance with Noal.

'While we held the three of you in our camp all that time ago,' Thorin said slowly, 'a great friend and mentor of mine, a much older soldier, began to speculate on why two lads of Awyalkna would be wanted by our King. And he remembered the names of Awyalkna's princes.'

The group had become completely silent, and even the quieter soldiers had broken from their reading.

I slowly took in a deep breath and let it out.

'Yes. Accepting people usually comes easier to Dalin,' I said. 'But it is hard for him to accept people from Krall ... when he is Prince Dalin of Awyalkna, the first place Krall threatens to destroy.'

'He's royalty?' Vulcan choked.

Thale deflated. 'I stabbed royalty.'

'The green eyes and tan skin should've given it away,' Tane chortled in disbelief.

'He doesn't seem cold enough to be royal,' Purdor commented.

'So, what does that make the both of you?' Tane asked curiously.

'I am his cousin. His family officially adopted me when my parents were killed by Trunes,' Noal answered.

'And I have been a hunter and healer by trade, and saved these two when Darziates sent his beasts after them.'

'Is that why the King was after you?' Phrixus asked in awe – despite only knowing the half of it. 'Did the Sorcerer mean to capture the future heir of Awyalkna?'

Noal and I resigned ourselves to patiently outlining our histories and quest to get to Jenra.

I found it surprisingly easier to briefly recount my own past, and what was expected of me according to the prophecies. I also found the Krall warriors to be surprisingly accepting of every unbelievable detail, though in Krall they were of course more readily exposed to magic and strange happenings.

'And when Kiana was stronger once more, we found you lot,' Noal concluded at last.

Thale's eyes were wide as he stared at us. 'You are showing us incredible trust right now,' he commented. 'You have shared critical plans and personal information of great threat and value to Darziates.'

'Somehow Darziates seems to have already been quite aware of many of our plans,' I grimaced.

'We're still honoured,' Wolf said seriously.

'I can't believe we have been made part of prophecies that originated from the dawn of time!' Tane clapped his hands together excitedly. 'I mean, we've been saved by two different ancient races, we've met the Lady of the forest, and now we are going to fight for the Three. A Fairy, a King of Kings ... and a Noal.'

Noal laughed.

'Fight for?' I raised an eyebrow.

'We have seen the wrath of the Sorcerer and what he can do to the world,' Phrixus told me. 'We have never had any cause to believe that there was any way to stop him, and just assumed that eventually he would have everything, and everything would die. But now we will fight for you, to save the biggest source of hope for our world that we have ever known.'

There were cheers of approval and agreement, and I realised that once again I was far from being the proficient lone hunter anymore. Now I was a member of a rapidly swelling band of friends.

And I was glad.

Because it felt like this had been meant to happen all along.

As if everything was at last coming together.

38

Thirty Eight

D*alin*

Feeling stiff and unforgiving, I stood beside Kiana, Noal and Thale as the Lady took a seat across from Agrudek.

We had all been led to his tower to be present when she questioned him.

His skin was ashen and his frame was visibly shaking as he stared miserably at the floor.

He was a piteous creature, reduced with shame as he huddled beneath her gaze.

'Agrudek, you have told us that Darziates drew you into what you did,' the Lady began.

'Yes,' Agrudek whispered, but continued to hang his head and look wretchedly at the floor. 'He w-was driving me ... insane.'

Noal watched the inventor's face intently, seeming determined to believe that Agrudek hadn't wanted to hurt him.

In contrast, the Granx sat protectively on Noal's shoulder, and appeared decidedly hostile as they faced the small man.

Agrudek tugged at his scraggly orange hair in agitation. 'I felt I h-had no choice but t-to obey Darziates ... just as it had been during my days as h-his scientist.'

Kiana crossed her arms, her face blank.

'Tell us more,' the Lady said.

Agrudek shifted nervously in his chair. 'I ... I had to do experiments for him ... make things, back in K-Krall ...'

'We know,' Thale growled, and then restrained his own suspicion, remembering that he, too, had been ruled by Darziates. Doing all the Sorcerer bade.

Agrudek flinched and darted a desperate glance at Noal. 'You know ... those beasts ... the ones that ch-chased you?'

'Yes,' Kiana interjected rigidly.

'I ... he made me m-make them ... their bodies ...'

'What are they, and how did you make them?' Kiana questioned.

Agrudek shuffled his feet sadly. 'I made a-all of his experiments – their casings – and he would bring them to l-life ... Then they would become something more. Take on their o-own appearance and behaviour. But those beasts he sent after you ... were different ... more sinister ... s-smarter. He would fill them with real spirits ... icy shadow be-beings from the Other Realm ...' Agrudek whispered the last words and a chill rippled through the room. 'And they would c-come to life, the shells that I had made suddenly becoming like skin, the s-s-sockets of their eyes filling with the frost of their presence.'

Every face, even the Lady's, showed dread.

'He is trying to remake the Evexus of old, then,' the Lady stated, closing her eyes and sitting back. 'Deimos made these things too. Though making them came at a terrible price. The power it took to bring spirits from the Other Realm into ours and into the bodies he had made for them drained him terribly. He aged and weakened every time he did it. But their power was great – for he gave them parts of his soul to anchor them to this world.'

Kiana had grown pale. 'There were five of them chasing us. But I don't think they were finished.'

The Lady looked to Agrudek to explain.

'It is one reason why my h-hand was cut off and why my family was taken,' he said quietly. 'I-I couldn't perfect them. It seemed that the process of ... taking the s-spirit from its realm into this one left it reduced. Though I a-a-am sure ... the Sorcerer has been working to fix that. To find them that ... 'anchor'.'

The Lady was aghast, and for all of her glorious brilliance, she appeared weary.

The little man seemed to be withdrawing further into himself, getting even smaller under our scrutiny.

'They are the p-purest of evil and c-completely unnatural,' Agrudek whispered at last. He coughed wetly. 'I believe that the darkness and ice that w-w-would make up a perfected Evexus ... could only be destroyed by the warmth of the p-p-urest of nature's magic.'

The Lady stirred after a moment. 'It is helpful for us to know these things.'

When she rose to lead us from his tower, Agrudek searched Noal's face anxiously, but the Granx reared back threateningly and I stepped in front of Noal to cut him off from view. We left without looking back.

'I feel that he speaks truthfully of the Evexus,' the Lady remarked sombrely as Agrudek's tower door closed heavily and unmovably behind her. 'But it is impossible to know if he really was under the power of Darziates. I will not enter his mind to find out, as I fear that would break it.'

As we parted from the Lady, Thale turned to us in confusion. 'I thought she could do anything,' he commented. 'She even made the forest safe from Darziates' power.'

Kiana's voice was quiet and sober as she answered. 'When the Lady was explaining why there had to be Three, and why she couldn't face Darziates herself, she described that her magic is a part of nature itself, and Darziates' magic is everything unnatural, and kills nature. And it took all of her might, and the united might of all of the Elves and Nymphs, to banish the Sorcerer from the forest. So perhaps she can't see through his deceit should it be upon Agrudek.'

'I guess now that I've finally had a chance to be surrounded by nature, and have seen its vibrancy in the Lady and Sylthanryn, I just assumed there wasn't much that could beat it if the Lady chose to fight,' Thale admitted a little despairingly. 'Krall is starved of life, though it goes on living.'

'Let's find the others,' Noal told him comfortingly. 'They were going to spend their afternoon at Flash's.'

'They're finally taking up that drinking challenge with the Nymphs,' Thale allowed himself to be cheered as we crossed the city.

'Darlings!' Asha's voice cried out as we drew closer to the vine homes that covered the cliff walls at the edge of the city. She sped out of a tussle she'd been having with Rebel and crashed into Noal adoringly.

'Come and join the fun,' Rebel invited us, now lazily lobbing a ball of light to scorch Shiva as he floated past with Sati.

As we moved to sit about a fire with the men of Krall, I realised that I really didn't resent the majority of them anymore. I even felt comfortable sharing words with them as they joked boisterously around us.

It was only Thorin who drew wariness from me now as I listened to him talking to Kiana and Noal with reverence. He likely wished he was the other member of the Three, instead of me, so that he could have them all for himself.

'Will you tell us more about your life back in Krall?' Kiana was asking him. 'Was there anything there that brought you joy?'

Thorin shrugged, but regarded her sincerely. 'Life in Krall was survival and obedience, not happiness. Not for anyone. My own story is that, when I was eight, my father was killed for speaking against the King and for gathering a following of others. My mother was stoned to death to set a further example, and I was scorned because nobody wished to appear traitorous. I lived as a beggar until a warrior called Marn got me off the streets by joining me up with the army. I was ten when I joined, and Marn bribed his general to let me be in his regiment. I in turn helped him as things got harder for him with age. He had to hide a growing sickness in order to be sent with me for the forest mission.'

'Gods,' Noal breathed. 'You have been a hardened soldier for seven years.'

'What happened to Marn?' Kiana asked.

'He died a warrior's death,' Thorin answered proudly. 'It was the Raiden's blade that did it, when you were escaping the camp. I hated the Raiden for it then, but am grateful that it wasn't the sickness that took him, as would have happened soon.'

The breath seemed to leave me, and a weight settled in my stomach even as the other warriors all raised their mugs full of Nymph liquor in respect for my having given Marn a good death.

I tuned their voices out then, reflecting on the many 'honourable' deaths of Sorcerer cursed men I had given out that day, and how many more times I might have to do the same.

When Tane began speaking about how his infant son would likely be bound into a life of soldiering too, I quietly withdrew from the group and left to walk by myself.

My wanderings carried me to a private corner of the city, at the foot of the waterfall that tumbled majestically down the cliff.

I pulled myself with difficulty up onto a rocky ledge that jutted out from the wall, sitting by its edge and gazing out at the city. I was lost in my thoughts for some time, listening to the musical tune of the rushing falls and staring at the silvery water as it gushed past me.

The sky was darkening when I at last refocused at the sound of someone approaching – only audible over the water as the figure carefully climbed closer – and I saw with surprise that it was Thorin.

I regarded him wordlessly while he pulled himself up onto the ledge beside me.

He caught his breath, but it remained quiet between us for many moments before Thorin broke the silence, saying: 'it is alright, you know.'

I processed the words numbly.

'I would have done everything the same in your place. Marn knew, and every Krall soldier you fight knows that death will inevitably come. And dying in battle is the most honourable death, for we are warriors. And war and dying is all we know.'

I could faintly make out his earnest expression in the light cast by the stars.

'In fact, it is I who should feel guilt over the deaths of Krall soldiers,' he said then. 'Because I will be by your side next time. Against Darziates' people, killing my brethren. There is no way to avoid it. They are under Darziates' power.'

I frowned at him, not understanding.

Thorin sighed. 'I know you don't like me. And I wouldn't either if our places were swapped. But Kiana and Noal told us everything last night, and we want to fight for you. We ... I ... will follow you.'

I sat back in wonder, considering his unexpected overture for a few moments.

Then stretching, Thorin at last got to his feet. 'I shall rejoin the others and leave you in peace,' he said. 'Though I mean what I've said.'

He turned to begin his descent. But my heart skipped a beat as he lost his footing on the lip of the ledge.

I saw the rock crumble under his feet, and his body start to drop as he lost his balance and swayed forward with a cry over the open air.

I lunged to my feet and caught hold of a handful of his shirt, abruptly hauling him back so that we fell together to land across the ledge.

He was panting with shock against me, but I winced and drew my throbbing arm out from under him, sitting up as my own breath came quickly.

'Be careful,' I croaked, speaking to him finally. I flexed my bad arm experimentally, but somehow it felt as if none of the stitches had popped, so Ailill would have no reason for an apoplectic fit.

Thorin stared at me with wide eyes. Then, slowly, a grin spread across his face.

'Thank you.'

I nodded in exasperation.

He held out his hand with a smile and I evaluated it for a moment before I took it in my own and shook it.

'If you can't manage to find your own way down, I'd better escort you,' I said gruffly.

So together we climbed our way back down from the ledge, going carefully in the dark.

39

Thirty Nine

Kiana

I easily blocked Phobos' sword and followed it with a thrust that he in turn blocked, finding our drills simple and invigorating.

My eyes flitted across to where Dalin was leaning against the fence surrounding the grounds, talking casually to Purdor and Ferron. Thorin was listening attentively at his side.

My heart flipped at a sudden memory of my lips on Dalin's.

Phobos grunted and I slowed it down.

Now Dalin was testing his arm, trying the weight of his sword. He swung his blade about himself cautiously.

I blinked distractedly when my opponent spoke, and only then realised that I was now exchanging blows with Phrixus.

'Sorry, what did you say?' I asked Phrixus.

I forced my attention forward, and was relieved to be able to get absorbed into the drills.

Aiolos, one of the quieter men, proved to be a particularly beautiful swordsman. I broke from routine to make things more interesting, and he cried out as I suddenly used his lunge as a foothold. I stepped on his thigh, swung myself around his neck and slid down his back.

'Gods!' he gasped as I sprang away.

'Your bladework is stunning,' I complimented him. 'It's too good to hide behind mindless blocks and blows.'

His friend, Gideon, tried to startle me then, but I heard his little chuckle as he crept up. I easily slid out of his hold, through his legs and used his ankles to propel myself away.

I smiled gaily as the soldiers around the yard all began to consider the challenge of my new game, and I felt so lively that I wondered if perhaps Agrona's poison had worn off.

I threw Wolf over my hip and shoulder, then did a tumble and somersault away from Phobos to avoid being dragged down by his bulk when he dived in to crash tackle me.

I ran up the length of Thale's back, and ducked around Vulcan as his big arms made to catch me.

I was laughing with the fun of it as, with angles and leverage, I bested every bulky warrior who tested me, and I was feeling invigorated when I faced Nikon next. But, with just one more thrust of my blade, a searing stream of fire suddenly shot from the scar that Agrona and the general's arrow had left me with.

I gasped and staggered forward and Nikon gave a startled cry, redirecting his blade as I doubled over, clutching the old wound.

'Are you well?' I heard the warrior splutter, and felt his hands steadying me.

I couldn't reply or even think over the harrowing waves of pain, feeling as if someone was driving knives into my chest – twisting them in.

I groaned and slid down from his grasp, landing on my knees upon the grass.

I felt another pair of hands catch me from behind, cradling me as I tried to stay conscious over the lashes of agony.

'All she can do is wait for it to end,' I heard Dalin say, and I felt him draw me close to try to comfort and shelter me for a semblance of privacy.

I vaguely made out Noal crouching beside me and dully heard the voices of the other men bubbling around us, but everything other than the pain seemed suddenly unreal.

For a flickering moment I saw a flash of a bony white hand slapping my face, heard the shrill cry of a raven, and felt the sickening, rotten stream of Agrona's power surging through my shoulder. I slumped heavily against Dalin as he held me until, finally, it all ebbed away to leave me drained and shivering – the searing bolts of agony dulling to throbbing spasms.

'What was that?' I heard Thale whisper over us.

'That was Agrona's poison,' Noal answered blankly, and I felt him put his hand on my knee reassuringly as I tried to regain my breath, my face still hidden against Dalin's chest.

'But Kiana was fine a moment before,' Thorin fretted. 'More than fine.'

Slowly, I sat a little straighter and lifted my face. 'I am nearly fine again,' I told them, but just the effort to talk made nausea roil in my stomach.

Noal sighed. 'It feels like all the lot of us do lately is get hurt, poisoned, or into trouble,' he complained. 'I'm fast tiring of it.'

'Does Agrona's poison affect you that badly every time?' Ferron asked, pale faced on my behalf.

'Much the same,' I said shakily. 'I never know when it's going to happen.'

'Is there anything that can be done?' Cadell questioned, just as appalled.

I shrugged my good shoulder. But I knew that there *was* something that would help me to overcome Agrona's dark magic. Something I had to try, if we were ever to be the Three of the prophecies.

'Gods that was awful!' Tane told me reproachfully, and I laughed despite myself.

'You're exhausted.' Dalin gave me a quick squeeze. 'I'll help you back to your tower.'

I nodded gratefully, and Dalin supported me to stand and walk back.

'It will be less of an ordeal if there isn't a crowd of mothers following her,' I heard Noal say good-naturedly, and I appreciated when our new friends returned to their exercises.

40

Forty

Kiana

'Where are you going?'

I bumped into Noal and Thorin almost the moment I left my tower.

'Hmmm?' Noal prompted suspiciously.

Thorin put on a serious face and crossed his arms when Noal elbowed him.

'For a walk,' I replied.

'For a walk?' Noal repeated incredulously, as if this were the most preposterous reply he'd ever heard.

'That's what she said,' Thorin told him helpfully. 'A walk.'

Noal took a deep breath, smoothing his golden hair in irritation. 'Have you forgotten the severe pain you were in earlier?'

I shrugged. 'I need to think in peace. I'm getting out of the city.'

'And what is it that you need to think about that you can't mull over in the city? This nicely lit and perfectly safe city, now that it's nighttime?' Noal enquired.

I lifted my hand and opened my fingers to show them the Unicorn figurine, and Noal stared at it with his mouth open, understanding dawning upon his face.

'Is that ...?' Thorin regarded it curiously, remembering what we'd explained about it to the Krall men.

Noal's face softened. 'You want to see if it will open? Because of today?'

I gave a single nod. 'I've got to work out how to do it sometime anyway. And you know I am at my best when I am roaming amongst nature.'

I didn't mention how I'd been trying different ideas all afternoon, grappling with growing despair as the Unicorn figurine remained as whole as ever. I also didn't mention that it felt like something in the forest was calling to me, wanting to help me to solve this problem.

Noal pinched the bridge of his nose worriedly. 'You can't go out there alone,' he said finally, but I smiled a half smile.

'I've been through the forest many times alone.'

'Plus ... *we* were what made it dangerous for her last time. That's not going to happen now,' Thorin admitted.

Noal glared at Thorin. But then he groaned. 'Dalin won't forgive me if anything goes wrong.'

'And I won't forgive you if you try to stop me,' I told him with a wider smile.

'I am not comforted,' he said to my back as I left them. 'If you haven't returned in the morning, we're sending a search party!' he called warningly after me, and I waved over my shoulder.

'Noted.'

Soon I had climbed to the top of the cliffs – calmly following my feet in a steady amble through moonlit trees that had grown to boggling sizes in the forest heart.

Almost as persistently as the Willow had compelled me to come to her, I felt as if I was being pulled along a specific path. If I listened carefully, I was sure that I heard magic whispering on the wind, circling through the trees, beckoning me on.

The Unicorn began to grow warmer in my hand, buzzing in my palm. The buzzing increased when I quickened my pace; the prickling, ticklish sensation spreading up along my arm. When I stepped my speed up to a jog, the tingling enveloped my entire body. At the same time, the leaves on the forest floor started to lift and dance in front of me, swirling crazily as a light breeze grew into a gust of wind that thrust me forward almost eagerly. My hair played about my face and with a terrible longing I ran on.

Skirting trees and leaping over bushes, I moved faster as I felt the magic growing, until the forest – and my entire being – seemed to pulse with it.

Then suddenly the dense trees widened out into a circular clearing and I skidded to a stop. The wind eased, the whispering faded and the dancing leaves settled at once.

I panted, hands on my knees, as I took in the starlit glade. A round pool reflected the glimmering sky, and the lush grass grew right up to the rim of the clear water. Beyond that, overlooking the basin, was a small grassy hill and a marker stone.

That mound was where the magic that had been calling to me still danced, while everything else had fallen still.

Drawn, I stepped slowly around the brilliant pool to stand before the rise, gazing upon the white marker stone. And though the runes engraved across the stone were faded and foreign, I realised I could read them.

It was written in *Aolen*.

Unra olen de merdon rendaers,

Silrinae un dera Kinrunda.

Unredon maros, perdu amoeren.

'Here lie the cherished saviours, Sylranaeryn and her Kinrilowyn. Together always, forever loved,' I whispered.

This was where the *Larnaeradee* and Unicorn who sacrificed their lives to end the threat of Deimos had been brought to rest, blanketed with earth and grass together.

I held my Unicorn tightly, though I was somehow comforted instead of chilled by the idea that I had been called by my ancestors to come to this site when I most needed to be close to them. When I was to confront the truth and accept what I was.

I bowed my head before sitting gingerly at the foot of the slope, gazing at my shifting reflection in the water, and noticing how certain I finally appeared.

I slowly opened my tingling fingers to gaze at the Unicorn figurine my parents had given me on my sixteenth birthday.

'I'm ready,' I announced – surprised at how true that was.

And in response, a shot of energy pelted up along my fingers and a small ray of white light burst from the horn of my Unicorn, coming from within it.

I watched with wide eyes as the bright beam started to move – down from the Unicorn's horn, between the ears and eyes, tracing the long nose, the slender neck, the muscular shoulders, across the belly, along the tail and the back, circling the entire figurine.

I was transfixed when at last the light began to approach its starting point at the pinnacle of the horn again – the figurine vibrating frantically until the Unicorn split itself into two perfect halves that laid separately on my palm.

I gasped as the white light that had traced the outside of the Unicorn swelled to envelop something round and no bigger than my thumb, which had fit perfectly inside the stomach of the figurine for all of this time.

The light began to rise, carrying the small object upward with it until it had reached eye level. Then it simply floated, suspended in mid-air before me.

I lifted my chin and the light floated closer. Then, as the dazzling light started to fade, I felt a delicate chain drop about my neck, and a slight weight settle between my collarbones.

A weight that felt natural. As if it had always been meant to be there. As if I'd been missing it all my life.

I blinked back down to my reflection in the pool to stare at the stone resting comfortingly against my skin.

Rubellite tourmaline.

With steady fingers I lifted a hand to my earthstone, and felt a shiver of power dance from its surface to kiss my fingertips.

The figurine had fused itself back together as if it had never contained such an incredible secret. I pressed it to my heart with a bittersweet pang, but mostly I felt ... whole. I felt greater in all aspects than before. Happier. Free.

And I drew a deep breath.

I focused my mind, visualising the one thing that I now wanted above all else. Yearning to be unlimited even by gravity.

There was not a noise in the forest – as if the entire world was holding its breath in anticipation.

Then, as simple as breathing, I felt my wings flicker and rise behind me. So light I would barely have noticed them, so right they felt as if they'd been there all along.

The silence of the forest vanished with a great clamour that suddenly exploded from every treetop, every burrow, every nest.

Birds called ecstatically, small scavengers squeaked, the trees rustled and their leaves danced.

And with complete exultation, and not one doubt, I sent my newfound wings whirring into action as easily as I might move my hand.

I shot into the air, whirling ecstatically up through the treetops to soar across the stars.

41

Forty One

The Sorcerer

Eyes like granite flashed open.

The Sorcerer refocused, straight backed, breaking from his meditation.

A strange, painful pulse of power had just jolted across his senses.

This power had suddenly awakened, pulsing exultantly to life, and had swept outward across the lands.

Her.

Kiana.

It had to have been Kiana, embracing her gifts.

'Master,' he heard Agrona sobbing fearfully – pawing at his door. She had felt the tremors of pure magic as he had.

The Sorcerer sent the Witch backwards with an impatient, magical push so that she fell away from his door, through walls and floors, to be dumped back into her own room.

There was no denying now that Agrona would not be enough to help him unite and rule an entire world and Other Realm.

Kiana, though, would be more than enough.

He had always known that he would eventually need to hold the hearts and souls of all peoples. It was why he had spent so long perfecting his influence in Krall, where it had seeped into the mortals' thoughts to shape their feelings, too. But Kiana's awakening had been like an awakening of his own. An epiphany.

Darziates now saw that, most importantly of all, his control would need to go beyond physical boundaries, and flow through nature itself. He would need to break even the boundaries of nature to defeat the threat of the tenth age. He would need the last *Larnaeradee* to join his cause.

To successfully establish a new way of life – one massive community, connected by their obedience to a single crown and banner – people would need to breathe Darziates' power in from the air, drink it in the water, see it storming in the clouds, and feel it in their land.

'Kiana,' he uttered the word reverently out loud.

She was the key he had unwittingly been waiting for.

With her magic, they could thrust their control into every fibre of every being, and every inch of land, sea and sky.

The Sorcerer closed his eyes once more; returning to his meditation. Though this time a faint smile played about his cruel mouth.

For the future beckoned.

And it was going to be better than he had ever expected.

42

Forty Two

Noal

I woke to Dalin shaking me urgently. 'Get up!'

It was still dark and there was a roaring sound in my ears.

I frowned groggily as Dalin pulled me into a sitting position by my shirtfront. He saw I was awake and moved across to do the same to Thorin.

We'd tried to wait up for Kiana, but had fallen asleep in the sitting room of our tower. I blinked blearily and noticed that the loud noise hadn't just been a rushing in my ears – swells of voices were pouring into the room from outside.

'Frarshk,' Thorin groaned. 'I'm off duty.'

'Get up!' Dalin repeated, now trying to pull his own shirt on over his bandaged arm and getting tangled in a rush.

I yawned and rubbed my face as Thorin stumbled up to help Dalin pull it over his head.

'What's going on out there?' I asked. 'It sounds like the mightiest party in the history of the world.'

'I don't know!' Dalin cried in exasperation. 'I've been trying to rouse you two so we can find out!'

'It sounds like every Elf, Nymph, bird, horse and rabbit in the forest is making as much noise as they can,' Thorin darted me a wide-eyed look.

'Oh ...' I breathed. 'Dalin, last night Kiana –'

'Yes, yes, I've already pieced all of this together, let's just go and see!' Dalin said, herding Thorin ahead of him.

'Gods. Do you think ...?' Thorin asked as we squeezed our way out of the tower door.

But we stopped in our tracks incredulously.

It looked like it truly was a gathering of every single being in the forest.

The whole city was full to bursting. Birds rushed around in trilling swarms, and despite the hour not a single Elf or Nymph seemed to be indoors.

The vine bridges hanging over the city were swinging, crowded with dancing Elves while Nymphs drank and laughed wildly on every branch.

Every lit-up doorstep had someone carousing crazily on it, or magical beings clinging happily together. Some were crying tears of joy. Some shouted jubilantly to the heavens.

'Quaray!' an Elf close to me beamed when he turned around and saw us standing there. 'Quaray un Tru!' he laughed, shaking my hand vigorously, almost making my teeth rattle until Thorin and Dalin pulled me away through the thronging crowd.

They'd spotted the Krall warriors, all bunched together and as confused and bleary eyed as we were.

'Hello there!' yelled Tane, being the brightest of the lot as usual. 'Come to join the impromptu party?' he had to shout to be heard over the noise.

'I've never been in a place where parties are so frequent!' Wolf announced whole-heartedly, while rubbing sleep from his eyes.

'Or so lively,' yawned Vulcan. 'Before it's even first thing in the morning.'

'Does anyone have a clue what we're celebrating?' Purdor asked, accepting a mug of Elf ale as big as his head with enthusiasm.

'Not the foggiest!' Thale cried, almost drowning himself in his own mug.

'We can only guess,' Thorin began. 'But we think it's Kiana.'

'She left with her Unicorn figurine last night,' I added with a raised voice.

Ferron almost choked on his drink.

'You mean you think she's become ...?' Cadell asked, thumping a spluttering Nikon on the back.

'Well, good for her! Darziates should watch out!' Phobos grinned, sloshing his drink down Lydon's shirt as he raised it.

'There's hope for the world!' Phrixus cried, tipsy already and sauntering off to hug a lady Elf twice his size.

They all cheered, thoroughly immersing themselves in the celebrations, and Dalin laughed, accepting three more mugs from a grinning Elf, handing two to Thorin and I.

'Raaaiiiideeeeeennnnn!' Nova and Naira zoomed across to Dalin.

'Congratulations to the Threeee!' they cried drunkenly, which suggested they'd had quite a lot.

Nova kissed an off guard Dalin rather passionately and Naira wrapped her arms around my neck.

'I wouldn't.' A testy voice stopped Naira in her tracks as she made to do the same to me.

I glanced up to see Asha, Flash and Rebel floating above us.

'You're as ... jealous as ... the Granx!' Nova pouted with a hiccup.

'Kindly remove yourself from my princes,' Asha replied daintily, her sharp teeth glinting.

'Ohhhhh, so now you own both of themmm,' Naira rolled her eyes.

She pecked me on the lips and spun away giggling, becoming a blur of pinks and purples as she launched into a jig with Nova.

Rebel went off in pursuit of the two Nymphs, not complaining as they turned their attention to him while Flash joined the Krall warriors in drinking from a mug over half his size.

'So, you've heard the news?' Asha chirruped blissfully, taking Naira's place in my arms and stroking my hair contentedly.

'We've guessed,' Thorin answered.

She gasped dramatically, but the evidence of delight to be the news bearer was clear on her impish face. 'Kiana has found her earthstone. She's a *Larnaeradee* at last!' the Nymph crowed gleefully. 'The entire forest was vibrating with life!' Asha went on. 'Every tree, every blade of grass, every insect woke up with joy and shivered with her power the moment that it happened! I nearly fell out of the air with the force of it! I can't believe you didn't you feel it!'

Dalin, Thorin and I blinked at each other.

'I was pretty tired ...' Dalin replied weakly.

'I may have felt something,' Thorin shrugged, scratching his cheek.

'I think I do remember waking up hungry at one point,' I reflected.

Asha sighed. 'Mortals.'

'So, what are we going to do now that it's happened?' Thorin asked. 'Keep partying until she comes back?'

'Oh, I think this party will be ongoing for a few days at least,' Asha mused, languishing comfortably in my arms. 'This is one of the greatest moments in history. It has to be celebrated accordingly.'

'Of course.' I grinned at the scenes of wild abandon all over the city. 'And we'll all do our bit to help.'

But as the remnants of the night waned and the sky started to lighten, the Elves and Nymphs began to gaze eagerly upward.

The first rays of the sun crept over us, and my eyes widened as the forest dwellers broke out with roaring cheers.

Because with those first rays of sunlight, we finally saw the last, One, Tru *Larnaeradee.*

There were cries of hope and overflowing joy as the entire city craned up at the sight of the figure soaring high in the golden sky.

'Gods ...' Dalin breathed in awe.

The Krall warriors were speechless, the Elves held each other and the Nymphs hung mid-air, holding their arms out lovingly.

For she was everything good in the world.

Her pure magic washed down from where she hovered to touch all of us.

43

Forty Three

*K*iana

'You look enchanting!' Asha purred with satisfaction.

She was floating above me, her chin propped dreamily on her hands as she gazed at the teal-coloured dress Chloris had just helped me into.

The material flowed down my chest in a 'v' to a belt of material before the light, rumpled cloth again flowed freely out to an uneven, wispy hem.

My hair spilled in waves down my shoulders, and Chloris pushed a ruby lined flower comb into the hair beside my ear to lightly pin it back.

My own eyes lingered where, on my bare shoulder, the blood red brand of Agrona had become a silvery colour that nearly matched my skin, like a testimony to my transformation. It was now the brand of my rebirth.

And even as I stood still, I was sublimely aware that magic now pulsed not just around me, but through my veins. Like sparks dancing in my blood, energising me.

The power of my lost kin was alive again within me.

'Lovely,' Chloris smiled as she moved back. 'You're ready.'

'Kiana!' I heard Dalin call up the stairs.

He, Noal and I had all been whisked away to be dressed 'properly' for the occasion, and now the party was building to an even greater extreme.

Thanking Asha and Chloris, I descended the stairs to where Dalin was waiting in the lowest room.

'You should see how outrageous it has become out there ...' His words petered out as he turned from the window. 'Gods Kiana,' he coughed. 'Wow.'

I smiled. 'You look princely.'

He truly exuded the image of royalty in the magnificent, deep green garb he'd been given, but the green of his eyes was fixed on nothing but me as he came to where I stood on the last steps and offered his hand.

I took his hand in mine and we paused for a moment, remembering how many times I had worked so hard to reach him on this same bottom step, before Asha zoomed down the stairs to sweep us back outside into a world of music, dancing and laughter.

'Come on!' she crowed, sending us hurtling forward toward where Thorin, Tane and Noal were waiting outside the tower door, and their eyes widened as they saw us.

'Gods, you all polished up nicely!' Tane whistled, taken aback.

Noal was as regal as Dalin, and Thorin regarded the three of us almost hesitantly.

'I've suddenly been reminded that you are the heir to a throne,' Thorin commented to Dalin.

But Dalin didn't seem to notice the effect he'd had upon our warriors, and he slung an arm good-naturedly around Thorin's shoulders.

'Lead the way,' Dalin said with a grin. 'We've got to show the forest dwellers that we're committed and just as supportive of Kiana as they are.'

The uncertainty at once dropped from their faces.

'Right-o!' Tane agreed merrily, and he and Thorin bounded off to where the other soldiers had gathered already, drawing Dalin and Noal with them.

I only wandered away from the noisy pack of males when they were happily sloshing their way through tankards of Nymph liquor and Elf ale – trying to outdo each other with toasts to my success, all while hardly noticing I was sidling off.

I sat myself aside with my back against the trunk of a tree, cushioned upon the grass and surrounded by the revelling of those around me.

The sound of the music was so loud that it soaked deeply into everything. The ground shook with the power of it as if the earth was resounding with a heartbeat.

It felt as if my own heartbeat was changing to pulse with the rhythm of the music and the air itself seemed to swirl with the power of all of those gathered in the city.

I felt the joy of the Lady. I felt the energy of every Elf and Nymph pumping through the atmosphere. And I was aware that my own power rose to join theirs, stirring the air around me so that waves of my hair kept lifting slightly to float in the lightness of the environment.

I ran my fingers over my tourmaline stone, and rested my head back against the trunk of the tree with a faint smile lifting the corners of my lips.

The future beckoned. And it no longer promised to be so dark.

44

Forty Four

D^{alin}

Phobos, Ferron, Thale, Nikon and Thorin were all lazily offering me advice when Ailill unwound the bandage from my bicep.

Kiana had recovered as quickly as the forest dwellers when the city had settled back to near normality for the first time in days, and she was as invigorated as ever while talking with the Lady a short distance away. But we tired-out mortals had been sitting in an exhausted, defeated looking circle when Ailill had approached with his healer bag.

'I find it's best to look away while the healer pokes and prods you,' Ferron remarked sagely as the bandage loosened. 'Act as if nothing's wrong.'

Ailill rolled his eyes.

'No, no, it's better to look at the wound while it's being seen to, so you know what's going on,' Phobos disagreed.

'It's true,' Nikon asserted. 'One of my friends thought he was recovering nicely because he believed the healers when they said he was going to be fine.'

'What happened to him?' Noal asked curiously, stroking the Granx's back after she'd scuttled away from the Lady and climbed up his leg.

'I attended his funeral pyre very soon after,' Nikon answered ominously.

'I don't think it's quite that serious in this case,' I informed them all.

'It depends on how I'm feeling towards you today, Raiden,' Ailill commented mildly in his willowy voice.

Noal lifted his eyebrows. 'Was that a joke from Ailill? I'll have to tell Flash and Rebel.'

The Elf just sighed, world-weary, and continued to unbind my arm.

'I hope it was in jest, for the Raiden's sake,' Thorin laughed.

'And for Awyalkna's, seeing as he's the heir,' Noal added.

'You could always fill in for me. Wilmont trained you too,' I told him as he scrunched his nose in distaste.

Finally, the bandage came away from my arm and I felt fresh air touch my skin.

'Gods,' Ferron commented, eyeing my healing flesh.

Phobos whistled appreciatively.

I glanced at it and huffed. 'Never mind.'

There were six jagged lines running down my arm where Nikon's armour had torn. The marks were purple and raw, and spanned diagonally down from just below my shoulder to near my elbow. They'd been stitched back together in the deepest spots.

'You told us you'd only put a few stitches in!' Noal accused indignantly. 'Chloris agreed!'

'Chloris lied,' Ailill replied with the ghost of a smile.

'She wouldn't!' Noal scoffed, wounded at the thought of the sweet, kindly Elf who always helped us.

'Told you,' Phobos said logically. 'You should always watch what the healer is doing.'

Ailill lifted my arm to inspect the other side of the stab wound, where the dagger had come out. The cut was about as thick in width as the length of my thumb after Nikon had widened it with his fist, but all of the raw flesh was sealing back together in healing scars.

Ailill wordlessly set to work, and despite his stern exterior, he was gentle.

'You are fortunate this happened in the forest,' Ailill told me as he worked. 'The time flow here has helped you to heal much more quickly than in normal mortal time. Otherwise, the muscles inside and the skin on the outside would still be fragile and knitting together.'

Ailill picked up a thin, silver instrument with a sharp tip.

Thale and Nikon were looking decidedly apologetic as they guiltily watched Ailill slice through each knot, and then tug each loosened thread free.

Finally, Ailill rinsed my arm before handing me some more bandages.

'You are to be bandaged again when you have given the wound a short rest. But beware,' the Elf glared at me. 'The skin is still not strong enough under pressure.' Then he glared at each of my companions.

'What did we do?' Thorin muttered defensively.

'You will most likely be the culprits should the muscles inside his arm tear back open,' Ailill said in a pre-emptively scolding tone. 'So, I'm glaring at you ahead of time.'

'You *are* all awfully rough on me,' I agreed.

Ferron hiccupped loudly on a laugh as the Elf brought his glare back to me.

'The skin will regain its strength slowly, so protect your arm from injury.'

I nodded reassuringly. 'I'm always careful, never fear.'

Ailill got to his feet. He shook his head and left us, muttering to himself as he went.

'I think he really likes us, deep down,' Thale laughed while I flexed my arm gratefully, glad not to feel as restricted anymore. It only felt a little tight and tender.

'I can finally train properly again,' I said with a relishing stretch.

'Not with us,' Thorin held his hands up innocently. 'We're the culprits who will reliably break you.'

I glanced up with a grin as Kiana approached, sitting herself between Ferron and Phobos.

'That's all healing nicely,' she commented.

'Nicely?' Thorin exclaimed, put out on my behalf. 'It's like he's been hacked to pieces and slapped back together. He's a battered piece of man meat!'

'Well, it all looks nice considering that, doesn't it?' she answered him with her half smile.

'What were you talking about?' I asked her, nodding to where the Lady was now conversing with Ace and Frey.

'The Lady was offering me advice,' Kiana replied with relief. 'Helping me get to know what I can do now that I have my earthstone.'

She stroked the dazzling red stone at her throat and our eyes were all drawn to it as it glittered.

It was a polished oval shape, half the size of my thumb.

'Of course, as we already know, the greatest thing that the stone has given me is my wings,' Kiana went on. 'But the Lady was explaining how I've always had magic inside, which the stone now helps me to channel. The wings will naturally appear in whatever shape needed, yet they're not really a part of me. They aren't hidden anywhere at the moment, it's more like the magic reacts to my desire, and makes them manifest in reality when I wish it.'

'So, they don't sprout out of your back? And they don't get stuck in your clothes?' Nikon questioned.

'It seems they just appear at my back, whether there are clothes there or not,' Kiana mused. 'But once they are there it's as if they are a part of me, meant to be there. I control them just like you control an arm or leg.'

'You'd have to be careful then,' Thorin remarked. 'That means they can probably be hurt.'

She shrugged. 'Probably. But they feel as strong as a shield. I think I could decapitate someone with them if I wanted, they're that tough.'

Thale's face paled. 'Let's not test that.'

'There you all are!' a cheerful voice called out.

Tane, Cadell and Purdor were wandering out of the trees behind us.

'We've been searching for you lot everywhere,' Purdor exclaimed, and then his eyes flickered to my arm. 'Gods doesn't that look ...' Cadell elbowed him in the ribs. '... effective.' He finished with a grimace.

'You certainly have the image of a hardened warrior with marks like that,' Tane told me.

'And all I had to do was have Thale fall on me, and Nikon sit on me,' I teased.

'Perhaps you shouldn't tell the story quite like that,' Phobos advised.

'So why were you searching for us everywhere?' Noal yawned at the three newcomers.

'The rest of us have all been busy testing our sabre skills against the Elves,' Cadell replied. 'Thought you should know.'

'What?!' Thorin whined. 'Without us? We've been waiting forever to train with the Elves!'

'Yes well, we've come to get you so you can be in on the action now, haven't we?' Tane said in a placating tone. 'We were startled at how quickly they got through the lot of us. We've each been defeated about eight times each. But it's fun.'

'Fun?' I repeated. I'd found body jarring defeats against the Elves to be enlightening, but not entirely fun.

'Gods, learning from the Elves would be priceless ...' Thorin breathed.

'Just a moment sparring with Bard changed me forever,' I agreed.

'Can we challenge the Nymphs too?' Thorin asked enthusiastically, but Tane glumly shook his head.

'They only train with other Nymphs. So that they don't accidentally get carried away and kill us all.'

Almost on cue, a colourful swarm of Nymphlings zoomed by in a blur, making loud explosions and erupting into cackles of laughter before disappearing amongst the trees.

'Even challenging one of the Nymphlings would be epic. Despite the risk of a horrible death,' Ferron watched after them wistfully.

'The Nymphlings endure few rules and wreak havoc wherever they pass,' Kiana told him. 'It wouldn't be a risk of horrible death. It would be certain horrible death.'

'But we're definitely invited to challenge the Elves?' Thale questioned, boyishly eager.

Cadell nodded with a grin of excitement.

And within the blink of an eye, they had all scrambled up, barely able to contain themselves. Even Noal, who had had plenty of battles with the Elves, was getting carried away by their gusto.

'Are you coming?' Ferron asked Kiana and I as we remained seated.

I shook my head and let my breath out in a big regretful gust. 'I would hate for any of you to break me and upset Ailill.'

Kiana folded her arms. 'And I shall supervise the Raiden.'

'See you later then!' Ferron replied gaily, and rushed off as the group almost kicked up a cloud of dust while galloping towards the training grounds.

But when Kiana slid herself across the grass to lean her back against the tree beside me, I felt far from left out.

She gently ran her fingertips along the long angry wounds on my arm, and then rested her head against my shoulder contentedly.

'Everything's different now, but the same too,' she reflected, and I tilted my head to rest mine on hers.

'What do you mean?'

'Well ...' she answered slowly. 'I feel like my strength has doubled. Like I could lift the world, run for days, battle a giant. And I feel so much more aware. Everything is more vivid. But I still feel like my normal old self at the same time. I'm still me, even with magic and wings.'

'I knew you would be,' I told her honestly. 'Really all that's changed is that you can now channel your power.'

Kiana nodded. Then a note of pleasure touched her voice. 'And I love it.'

'What's it like?' I asked. 'To be so weightless that you can fly?'

'It's freedom,' she breathed, as if she relished the words. 'It's like nothing I've ever felt before. I hate that my parents had to sacrifice it.'

I sighed wistfully. 'You make me wish I was the One. We could swap. I'll fly and you can be the future King of Kings.'

She laughed. 'Or perhaps I could take you with me,' she suggested lightly. 'When I've perfected my abilities.'

Suddenly Kiana sat forward, turning to face me. She focused for a moment and then I blinked in amazement as, in a silvery flash, her wings had appeared.

I shook my head in appreciation. 'It's incredible,' I whispered, gazing at the iridescent silver wings in awe, and seeing through them.

They were almost as long as the length of her body this time, though last time I had seen them they had been smaller, shaped to be sharp and fast.

She took my hand and guided me to reach over her shoulder and gently touch the smooth, shining wing there. Instantly a tickle of warmth pranced along my fingertips.

'You're a wonder,' I told her.

'That's not the half of it,' she beamed as she stood, her feet lifting from the ground. With a grin she darted away from me, spinning at top speed high into the air and out of the clearing.

I was stupefied as she soared across the sky, darting and slicing faster than my eye could follow, spiralling elegantly around some clouds in the next moment.

The Lady had finished talking to Ace and now she and Frey watched Kiana's antics as well.

'Already the One has stunning control,' I heard the Lady comment gladly. 'Her skill is natural.'

'It is good that she has advanced more quickly than would have been expected of the other *Larnaeradee*,' Frey said. 'It shows how capable she truly is as the One.'

'Yes,' the Lady agreed softly. 'And she needs such skill now, to be able to Summon the other races later.'

'You both know I have great hearing too,' Kiana spiralled down to where they stood. 'I can hear you discussing me,' she said reproachfully. 'But your words are comforting, and I'm ready to train to use this great power you keep talking about.'

'To train, you must simply become comfortable in who you are. You already channel nature's power of growth, life, rejuvenation and purity,' the Lady said. 'It is a wonderful gift. The opposite of every power Darziates has ever known.'

Kiana's face grew solemn. 'Good.'

'Now you must simply learn to allow things to come to you naturally as you need,' the Lady continued. 'From any part of nature that you set your mind to, you can draw energy to help you manifest a thought.'

'Though surely spending time with the guidance of your wisdom will be an advantage to me?' Kiana frowned.

'Your time in the forest is coming to an end,' the Lady's voice was sad, and I felt my own heart jump a little at the thought of leaving the sanctuary we'd found in the city 'There are not enough moments in the world for me to share all I wish to. But you are more than ready to go on from here and learn as you are tested.'

Kiana sighed. 'I've felt that things were coming together. Coming to an end.'

'Do not fear, One, your time here will never be over. You will always be welcome in Sylthanryn,' Frey answered warmly, but I was feeling morose as I listened myself, feeling as if a stay in the heavens was coming to a close.

When they parted, agreeing that a final council should be organised as soon as tomorrow morning, Kiana crossed back to me.

'I know,' she told me wistfully at the sight of my expression. 'I'll miss all of this too. But we have to get back to the quest. Awyalkna needs us.'

I lifted my good arm and put it around her shoulders as she nestled back against my side.

'And so does the rest of the world I guess,' I agreed tiredly.

'Hmmm,' Kiana exhaled gently, resting her head against my chest. 'But not right now.'

'No, not today,' I said, now feeling complete contentment.

45

Forty Five

K^{iana}

The sun was setting when I finally forced myself to sit up, peering back over my shoulder at Dalin. 'Should we see how the others are faring against the Elves?' I asked.

'It's best we check they aren't tearing each other apart,' he agreed, leaning forward.

'Wait,' I told him, tracing along the line of one painful scar and then holding my hand out.

Dalin grimaced and handed over the new bandage he'd been given so that I could carefully bind the fragile skin and pull his sleeve down for him.

'I was so comfortable that even walking to the training grounds seems harsh,' he told me, standing and reaching out to pull me up.

'At least I'm deigning to walk along with you,' I cajoled. 'I could just fly over.'

He tightened his hold on my hand instead of letting go when I was on my feet. 'You could try,' he bantered. 'But we've just had multiple feast days that even the God of Gluttony would applaud us for. I think I could successfully keep you grounded.'

I was a little rueful when he did at last let go as we found the others – now just the sixteen Krall warriors and Noal having the time of their lives. They were play wrestling like children while the Nymphs Nova and Naira catcalled from the sidelines.

'Raiden!' Tane yelled joyously while Dalin put his good hand on the fence and propelled himself over to join them.

'Did you miss me?' Dalin asked, before Wolf grabbed him in a headlock.

'We did miss you, but now that you're here ....' Wolf began, then wheezed as Dalin spun free and shouldered Wolf to send him sprawling backward.

'Now that I'm here?' Dalin inquired as Wolf chuckled from the ground.

Vulcan wrapped his massive arms around Dalin's waist then and tackled him to the ground in turn.

'Now that you're here, you can join in the fun!' the other colossal warrior finished.

Dalin rolled out from the big man's grasp and promptly sat on Vulcan's stomach.

Vulcan spluttered.

'Yes. I am having fun,' Dalin decided.

'Dalin, we were warned not to break you,' Noal commented, and pulled Dalin up from Vulcan's gut.

'At least not on the very same day that Ailill warned us against it,' Thorin resolved.

'Ailill's not watching,' Dalin protested.

'We won't test it today,' Phrixus informed him. 'There'll be plenty of chances for us to challenge you in the future.'

Dalin gaped in exasperation at the unyielding men surrounding him. 'You've all turned soft,' he criticised, throwing his hands up.

'And don't you love us for it?' Tane joked, pinching Dalin's cheeks and steering him toward where I leaned on the fence beside Nova and Naira. The others began packing up to follow.

'Pooh, is training over?' Nova's purple eyes were mischievous as usual.

Naira twirled her floating pink hair flirtatiously. 'We just loved your physical displays,' Nova pouted.

Lydon blushed furiously and Roth's eyes were boggling as Naira puckered her lips suggestively at those two shy warriors specifically. Their even quieter comrade, Rendor, appeared ready to suck his head right down into his shirt to hide like a turtle when the Nymph winked at him next.

'It's over, and they won't be in the forest much longer for you to perve on,' I informed the Nymphs dryly, rescuing poor Rendor. 'Will you be escorting Dalin and Noal to the council in the morning?'

Naira tore her eyes from the soldier with a sly snicker, and shifted her attention to Noal. 'Absolutely.'

'So, our stay in Sylthanryn is coming to end,' Noal reflected disconsolately, hardly even flinching when Nova swatted his butt cheek with an audible 'thwack.'

'We'll be back to having the time of our lives, getting chased and hunted on the quest in no time,' Dalin promised, just as downcast.

Yet while I was dismayed as I rose early for the council the next morning, I was aware of how far the three of us had come since entering the city. My own progress was clear as I returned to the Lady's colossal tree tower, where I was able to use my own magic to travel up to the council room.

I was also now able to plausibly outline my flight reliant plans when it was time to share our next steps.

'We will hold to our original course,' I explained. 'We'll pass through the forest to reach Jenra and ask for their allegiance, as was our initial quest. And I will be continuing on from there alone,' I finished carefully, managing not to grimace.

'Beg your pardon?' Noal sputtered, and the Granx waved her legs indignantly from her perch on his hand.

Dalin's composure slipped just a little as his shoulders lowered. He'd known this was coming, and deep down, so had Noal and all of the forest dwellers.

I took a deep breath. 'This has of course been part of the prophecy, though I only considered it seriously when I was granted my earthstone and first formed my wings. Now it is clear that I can, and that I must be the Summoner. I must go to the other lands beyond the seas to at least try to gain the support of the remaining magical races.'

'But, Kiana,' Noal argued weakly. 'We're a team.'

'Yes,' I nodded. 'But I am the only one on the team who can fly across oceans to reach the other races in time.'

Noal slumped back in his chair, at a loss.

Dalin was unhappy ... but understanding.

'It is the course of action that has the best chance,' the Lady affirmed.

One of the Elves motioned as if to speak, but then stilled again – knowing we would not understand when, though he could comprehend our mortal tongue, he could not speak it.

I pondered him for a moment, and then I caught his eye. 'Try it in *Aolen*,' I suggested encouragingly.

'I don't know if I can,' he responded apologetically in perfect *Aolen*.

The Elf started in shock.

Dalin turned to me with amazement 'I just understood exactly what he said,' Dalin declared in flawless *Aolen*, a smile covering his face.

Noal's eyes were wide. 'So did I,' he grinned suddenly himself, forming words of the ancient tongue without trouble.

Asha laughed and clapped her hands.

'It is a wonder!' another Elf called elatedly.

'Tree tower! Nymph liquor! Squirrel! Cake!' Ace cheered in *Aolen*, soaring into the air.

Everyone in the circle began to speak at once, testing the words in an enthusiastic rush.

'It seems the One's powers are beginning to affect us all,' the Lady spoke in *Aolen*, too. 'Now we can spread the lost language of the *Larnaeradee* all around the city, and it will come back into the minds of all who have forgotten it.'

'What was it you were going to say?' I politely asked the Elf who had first spoken, and he composed himself as best he could.

'I meant to say that the Elves may help to speed you to your next part of this journey,' he replied, still beaming. 'We can escort you to the end of the forest.'

The others nodded.

'It is risky, though,' I replied. 'Any Elf who comes would need to run close to the Cursed Valley again.'

'All Elves must be stronger than ever now,' Frey stated adamantly, despite his especially serious nature being one that was most at risk. 'There are tremendous things calling us forward more clearly than the enchantments of the Cursed Valley and our own internal thoughts. The world is drawing us out, and we must look outward.'

I inclined my head, trusting them. 'We accept your offer then, with great thanks.'

'It would be a great asset to have the Elves speed us through the forest,' Dalin agreed gratefully. 'It would take weeks off the journey. And even if time flows differently within the forest, our own bodies would feel the impact of such an expedition without magical help.'

'I can also offer further aid,' the Lady assured him then, settling her hands in her lap placidly. 'I can extend my magic to adjust when in time you leave the forest to re-enter the world beyond.'

'That would be a mighty blessing!' Noal breathed appreciatively. 'We have spent a great span of time here, but if we left the forest and time had not passed on the outside ...'

'I can make it so that barely a week has passed beyond these trees,' the Lady affirmed. 'Yet you must also treat this blessing as a risk and be cautious, because though the storm will have passed, the beasts and Agrona may still have been hunting you a week after you came here.'

The three of us considered her point gravely as the reality of our situation, and the danger we had evaded while in Sylthanryn, started coming back into focus.

'Gods, I can't believe our time here has ended,' Noal sighed, stroking the Granx again while she held onto his wrist as if in a hug that could anchor him there with her forever.

The Lady regarded him kindly. 'The Elves and Nymphs shall not meet with you again for a short time,' she acknowledged. 'But when you have re-joined with your Awyalknian forces, our troops will be marching to join you. Perhaps by then the whole Army of the World will again be rising.'

'You will not be coming?' Dalin asked the Lady.

She shook her head gently. 'Playing Gloria was my last venture out. My hand in this has passed. I have done all that the Gods sent me to do, and now my power remains here. I am as much a part of the forest now as it is a part of my magic. Yet if the world is healed again, I will be able to touch every inch of nature, and be reborn.'

Asha crossed her legs at the ankles, inches above her seat. 'I personally would like to offer my support to the questers, and have had many Nymphs ask if they could go with the Three when they leave. While I know the forest dwellers ought not to give away their strength to Darziates until the right moment, is there something I could do as we wait?'

Dalin suddenly straightened with an ardent expression. 'There *is* something you could do for us Asha!' his voice now held a keen note. 'You could give King Glaidin a message. In fact, you could give the whole of Awyalkna a message,' he said eagerly. 'You could tell them that we are alive and mean to bring help. You don't have to do anything that would tell Darziates how strong the forest dwellers have become, but you could still give them hope when they think there is none. They'll believe you, when the words are coming from a being straight out of the stories of old,' he finished enthusiastically.

'I love it!' Asha cackled. 'If it's only me out in the open the Sorcerer will hardly notice. But the Awyalknians have to learn about us before we turn up to help them, so they're not too shocked to fight when we arrive anyway,' she grinned impishly.

'It's settled then,' the Lady agreed calmly.

And when the council ended, I was glad to see that another weight seemed to have been eased from Dalin's shoulders.

While the room began to clear of those still buzzing with chatter in *Aolen*, Dalin and Noal bowed before the Lady in deepest respect.

When they had also withdrawn I lingered for a moment more, warmed by the Lady's tender expression as she turned to me.

'Kiana,' she put her hand upon my shoulder so that I felt her magic dance through my body. 'I want to remind you that I have already begun to heal, simply because of your presence. You are everything this world needs. The *Tru Larnaeradee*. And I know that you have the pride and blessings of all who came before you.'

I took her hand in mine, as if reaching for my own mother.

'Thank you,' I whispered. 'For everything.'

46

Forty Six

D^{alin}

I was sitting across the bonfire from Kiana, watching as she concentrated with all of her might.

She was glaring down at a rock in her palm.

A pensive mood had settled over the three of us after the council, but we had joined a gathering of the men of Krall to inform them of what had gone on. Now they weren't making much of a racket either.

'How long do we have to prepare?' Thale asked, already used to the fact that he was miraculously using Kiana's gift of *Aolen*.

'A couple of days,' she answered gruffly, not taking her eyes from the rock.

'It's a bit sad,' Purdor commented thoughtfully. 'I've never had such fun, or even such stability in my life. Despite all of the uprisings, surprise battles, poisonings and the like.'

'That's because you've never been anywhere but Krall and the battlefield before you came here,' Ferron told him, breaking some branches for the fire.

'I was not always completely miserable in Krall,' Cadell noted. 'It's the King who makes the land so rotten.'

'I admit,' Kiana grunted, 'the first time I travelled to Krall, I was taken aback that it wasn't *all* bad.' Her gaze still did not waver from the rock. 'Granted, the borderlands were as barren and foul as predicted. And when I reached the city sectors themselves there were patrols and strained, unhealthy looking citizens. But aside from the fact that I was there in the week of the cycle change, there weren't lurking villains and dark spirits on every street corner as I'd expected.'

'What is the week of the cycle change?' Noal asked curiously.

'In Krall there are only two seasons,' Phobos explained. 'And the change between them occurs in just one brutal week.'

'In a week it changes from bitterly cold, muddy and wet, to sweltering heat, with vicious sand storms from the wastelands, and dry earth,' Wolf elaborated.

'Darziates' unnatural power has confused nature in Krall. The seasons are too corrupt to follow the natural pattern and simply move from one extreme to the other.'

'How does the population survive if the weather changes so drastically?' Noal asked in perplexity. 'Surely agriculture is impossible in such conditions.'

'The land is arid, but not dead,' Tane told him. 'And Darziates continuously pumps dark magic into the earth so that it keeps producing.'

'Ruining the natural cycle further,' Vulcan commented dryly.

'A-HA!' Kiana cried abruptly so that our entire party jumped.

'What do you mean, 'A-HA'?' Thorin gasped, clutching his chest.

Kiana was grinning as she held her hand out for us to see her rock. Or what had been her rock.

My eyes widened as I saw that it had become smoothed into a beautifully streamlined arrow head.

'Gods!' Phrixus breathed in awe. 'You just made that stone morph with ...'

'With my mind and magic,' she finished, now examining her creation critically. 'Though I still prefer using my own skills to make them, it will be helpful to stockpile some before we go.'

'If the Elves and Lady are going to aid us by adjusting time, there may not be a need to rush,' Thorin speculated.

'If they are helping us all to exit the forest at the time when you described, our troop would have been marching into the forest to intercept the three of you at that point ... So will we also be marching into the forest somewhere else at the same time as we're leaving it?' Gideon pondered.

Purdor shuddered.

'Best not to think about it,' Kiana surmised.

'We won't,' Thorin remarked, before glancing around at the other men. 'Are we all in agreement, then?'

Thale nodded his head slightly.

'On that note, let me be the first,' Thorin announced, standing up. 'To swear my allegiance to this quest and to pledge to do all in my power to help and protect the Three, or accept my death upon defeat.'

I was surprised by how formal he sounded, until Tane stood beside him, his usually grinning face now solemn.

'Let me be the second to swear my allegiance and pledge my strength,' he said, and then Wolf stood.

One after the other, each of the sixteen warriors repeated the same oath.

But when Thale had finished last of all, a noise from the dark bushes behind us made us all glance up. And a dark, small figure shuffled timidly out from the trees, his shadow dancing across the ground from the flames – wavering and broken.

'Agrudek ...' Thale growled with warning in his voice, for the inventor was meant to remain in his tower.

The little man's patchy orange beard twitched nervously.

'Please, I,' he sounded close to tears. 'I want to p-p-pledge myself ... I want to help.'

I glowered at him and his eyes darted away from me, to Noal.

'P-please let me redeem myself.'

Thorin stepped forward angrily. 'You cannot be redeemed in this way. Innocent or not, how can we trust you enough to come with us?'

'And what use would you be in your condition?' Vulcan questioned bluntly.

Agrudek flinched. 'I-I cannot live with myself. I have to make up for what I did.'

'We would not help you in times of danger,' Ferron told him. 'We'd be busy.'

'You'd be a liability,' Phobos scowled. 'You'd be more help staying out of this.'

'No ... I w-would take care of myself ... if anything should h-happen, I can simply leave the group. I w-would not stay if I was s-slowing you down,' he begged, his face haggard and remorseful.

'Is there nothing we can say or do to make you stay in the city?' Thale asked, knowing the forest dwellers wouldn't hold him.

Agrudek appeared unsure of himself, but shakily nodded. 'I w-would follow.'

We were all quiet for a moment, until Noal spoke.

'It is worthy of you to step up,' Noal said quietly. 'And we cannot stop you.'

The soldiers stayed quiet, following Noal's decision despite their darkened expressions and reservations.

I contained my own contempt for Agrudek with a great effort, forcing the anger in my voice down until I could clearly convey my own reply to the scientist.

I leaned forward and he couldn't help but draw his eyes to me as he felt my stare.

'I respect Noal's choice,' I enunciated every word distinctly. 'But should you ever hurt one dear to me again, you will not be human in my eyes. You will be exactly the beast that Darziates sought to have. And you will be treated as such.'

He squirmed where he stood, licking his lips. But he nodded, and after darting a glance at the hostile faces around him, he fled back into the trees.

47

Forty Seven

D^{alin}

The morning dew was still wet upon the grass and the city had a sombre feel as we climbed our way out along the slope for the last time.

The Krall men were not boisterous now, but had their armour in bundles tied onto their packs, and their sabres buckled back in place.

Agrudek kept out of the way of the hulking soldiers – his small legs stepping quickly as he bent under a satchel on his back. His own bags were as heavy as everyone else's, filled with supplies that would not spoil in the damp mountain air.

Ten Elves had come to escort the twenty of us, and they each offered their hands to two of us at the top of the slope. Frey took the lead, bursting into a sprint and burning away the distance so that the city disappeared quickly behind us.

I forced myself to look ahead and to focus on our next phase, rather than on what we were leaving behind. And the power of the Elf holding my hand helped me to be distracted from all sadness, as – through our blurring motion – I could make out every amazing thing worth appreciating.

I noticed even the finest hairs on each slender, green blade of grass that rushed past, and it felt as if I was barely touching the ground itself as I moved my legs.

When we stopped at night, we felt an odd mixture of serenity and bone deep weariness after an entire day of enhanced movement. We collapsed around a fire that Alvar made and ate what Vidar put in front of us.

I only dimly heard Frey conversing with Kiana as I stretched out to sleep, and he asked which path through the mountains she planned to take.

'The Midroone Pass?' he repeated her answer. 'It is known to be hazardous.'

'In colder months,' Kiana admitted. 'But the Lady will have ensured it is still warmer outside.'

'Even in summer the mountains are perilously cold and wet. But you are likely right to take that road,' Frey replied. 'It will not be snowed under for much of the way, and the scarcity of growth and shelter on that path deters the Griffins from haunting it.'

'It means that we will have to head in a more westerly direction tomorrow,' said Kiana.

'And that circles us further away from the Cursed Valley,' Vidar noted in appreciation.

'Running with Elves is amazing,' Thorin yawned then, sprawling out dreamily near me. 'But sleeping it off will be even better.'

'I certainly wouldn't mind feeling like that every day,' Tane agreed.

'I'd get a headache if I had that many thoughts and details to register every day,' Thale closed his eyes.

I was on the very edge of sleep when I heard Kiana speak again. She was as untouched by the day of running as the Elves were.

'I'm going to see if I can fly and keep up with you tomorrow,' she was saying. 'It'll show me how fast I can travel, and it'll be good training with quick twists and turns.'

And it seemed she had only just uttered those words before a deep voice, very different from Kiana's, was waking me.

'Raiden.'

I stirred and blinked up at Quidel's face hovering in the dark, his bone white hair standing out against the early morning sky.

He clapped me gently on the shoulder as I nodded and sat up, then he moved on to Noal as the men around us stirred into wakefulness too.

'You're flying today?' I yawned, checking I hadn't dreamed it as Kiana appeared at my shoulder to press an apple into my hands.

'Yes. I may tire of keeping up by myself eventually,' she reflected, biting into her fruit. 'Right now, flying seems comparable to running, where the wings take energy from the rest of my body just as my legs do. I need to learn to take energy from nature.'

'All set?' Phrixus asked, scratching his stubbled cheek. 'Frey said the Elves are ready when we are.'

'We're ready,' I groaned, stretching my spine and taking some quick bites of the apple.

I shouldered the weight of my pack once more, crossed to Frey, and was soon hurtling through the forest again – but this time with Kiana soaring with ease along beside us.

I could appreciate in infinite detail how gracefully she was able to glide through the air, spinning easily around every tree and over every hollow log as if she'd been flying for all of her life.

48

Forty Eight

N*oal*

'Oh Gods ...' I heard Lydon gasp as we slowed to a halt within the last trees of the Great Forest.

My own eyes were wide as I beheld the dark Jenran mountains, soaring upwards before us like mighty houses to the Gods themselves.

I'd never imagined that nature could create such massive landforms, and I found myself tilting backwards as my eyes travelled up the stark incline, which started just beyond the trees and ended at last with snow-capped peaks.

'No wonder they don't make contact with the outside world,' Dalin commented, squinting up at the rocky slopes in front of us. 'And no wonder we know next to nothing about them.'

'It's definitely not as welcoming as Sylthanryn,' Thale grunted, tearing his gaze from the intimidating sight.

'We have to cross those?' Ferron huffed incredulously, blurring to a stop with Vidar and Aiolos. 'That'll take years!'

'We'll manage,' Kiana remarked, letting her wings disappear.

'Do any of you want to help us speed over those big nasty things?' I asked the Elves with chagrin.

'Alas, we would not want to reveal our strength yet,' Vidar answered regretfully, and I could see the worry in his expression as he regarded the brutal, miserable climb ahead of us. 'The Griffins would happily report to the Sorcerer if they thought they might gain favour. And he would be highly interested to know that the Elves have not continued to dwindle in their seriousness.'

'For now, this is where we must part,' Frey agreed with a heavy tone. 'But we will see each other again.'

'And we can only thank you with our love and friendship in return.' Kiana told them. 'We will miss you on this journey.'

'Be well, and I hope we shall meet again,' Thale saluted his new-found friends.

'Be well, and I hope we shall meet again,' Frey nodded in answer.

I felt a wave of sadness as they hesitantly backed further into the trees, until finally they turned from us and disappeared into the dense forest.

Silence descended over our glum group as we lost sight of them. But Kiana stepped forward resolutely.

'We can't remain,' she told us. 'We have to be careful and move on swiftly.'

'Alright. It's time we set out,' Dalin agreed with growing resolve, and we all turned towards the two of them. 'It's best we head into the mountains while daylight is still on our side.'

'We don't want to be without shelter when night comes,' Kiana affirmed. 'I'll be leading us through the Midroone Pass, which is a lonely, treacherous passage even in the light.'

'Goody,' I shivered.

Despite the sun shining gloriously above, I felt the chill flowing down from the high, snow peaked caps.

'I just can't wait,' Tane informed Kiana cheerfully as he adjusted the weight of his pack. 'You make the climb sound so appealing.'

'It's even worse in real life,' she said over her shoulder as we followed. 'But I attempted a number of paths in the past, and discovered it's the shortest, least Griffin infested passage. And we do need to get to Jenra before the tenth age begins.'

'G-g-griffins?' I heard Agrudek almost squeak to himself in apprehension.

'Murderous, winged beasts that haunt Jenra,' Kiana explained.

'Not goody,' I groaned at my first step onto the slope of the mountains.

It wasn't at all long before my calves started to burn as I slipped over countless loose pebbles that shifted under my shoes. I heard some of the other men already panting and cursing too, as they skidded on the wet rocks and slid back down the distance they'd just toiled up.

'Step carefully,' Kiana cautioned as we followed her in a begrudging line. 'We can't afford to be slowed down by one sprained ankle.'

So, we all pushed to keep up, placing our feet warily without ever seeming to get closer to even the knees of the mountain.

It was not until the shadow of the second mountain began stretching grimly across the one we were so very gradually climbing, that we neared the place where the two looming formations joined.

'The pass is close if I remember correctly,' Kiana announced, stepping lightly around a series of boulders and peering at the rocky walls between the two joined mountains.

'We aren't going through there are we?' Cadell asked, eyeing the dark, narrow gap suspiciously.

Kiana pulled up onto a ledge, frowning through the shadows beyond where she perched.

'I can't see if that's the path there or not,' she answered. 'Wait here a moment.'

She expertly slid down the rocks and disappeared behind them, and we heard a light echoing thud as her feet landed on the crumbly, rocky ground on the other side.

Moments later she flew back up and beamed at us. 'We've found the beginning of the trail. You'll have to drag yourselves over. There's a bit of a slide down to the bottom.'

Dalin was first to grimly move forward to tackle the boulder Kiana had climbed. He manoeuvred his way up until

Kiana was within reach, helping him to haul himself over to sit on top of the rock with her.

'Come on,' he beckoned before wiping his brow. 'One at a time.'

Thorin went next and Kiana and Dalin helped him before sliding down to the other side, and we each followed the same process of helping the next man.

I waited until last, with only Agrudek left to go up before me, and he thanked me timidly as I helped to boost him upward to Vulcan's waiting hands, while I tried not to think about the early death that the inventor had nearly granted me.

Then it was my turn, and I was sliding down the other side of the boulder, into the dark, to land amongst the rest of the men.

Dalin and Thorin held out their hands and both caught one of my arms each as my feet came upon slippery stones. And abruptly I found myself cut off from outside warmth, surrounded by a dim, roofless cavern.

Impossibly high walls of hard grey rock hemmed us in and the trail ahead ran off into a series of twists and turns so I couldn't see very far along it.

'Well, this is nice,' Tane commented.

'Who votes on going back into the forest?' Purdor asked dryly.

But Kiana was already moving forward again and we obediently trailed behind her, walking in single file between the high, looming walls.

'It won't always be this narrow,' Kiana called softly back to us. 'Or this easy to follow the path. Sometimes the trail is wide from storms, snow or floods. Sometimes the whole path has broken away beneath falling boulders.'

'Welcome to Midroone Pass,' Phobos muttered bleakly ahead of me.

'Where boulders can obliterate both you and the solid rock path you stand on,' Ferron added behind me.

'I'd planned on us singing some cheerful marching songs,' I heard Tane remark in disappointment. 'But the echo might loosen things up top. What a shame.'

'A tragedy,' Wolf's voice carried back in a wry tone.

'It'll get harder than missing out on choirs and symphonies,' Kiana warned. 'But,' she said, peering the long distance up to where a slit of the sky still showed above us, 'we'll be stopping soon. Before the light is even near failing.'

'It's long before sunset,' Vulcan protested from down the line. 'We normally use every moment of light to cover distance.'

'We will need time to ensure we find shelter every night,' Kiana explained. 'As we climb into higher altitudes the temperature will drop, and when dark comes it will be near freezing out in the open. We can't risk being unable to find refuge. I did that once in one of the other passes, and it wasn't pretty.'

The echoing, crunching sound of our feet was all the response that she was given as an increasingly morose mood fell over our group.

'It won't be so bad for the next couple of days,' she said in an effort to be reassuring. 'We'll cope with just setting up camp against the walls. After that we'll need to burrow down.'

Then, just as she'd said, we stopped barely an hour later and began to roll out our cloaks. And even though the sun was only just setting, the light faded fast as it was blocked by the rocky walls. Then, as the light fled, so did any remains of the day's warmth.

We shuffled closer together as we chewed unenthusiastically on our dinner, each of us staring about ourselves as night crept through the tunnel-like road.

Eventually the darkness was so deep that it seemed as if we sat on a precipice surrounded by nothing.

Adding to the eeriness of the pass, the wind picked up to whistle and moan through the rocks, echoing mournfully up and down as if someone was crying out. Warning us that we should have stayed in Sylthanryn.

49

Forty Nine

D^{alin}

In a matter of days, it felt as if we'd been surrounded in unchanging rock, falling streams of pebbles, and whining wind for all of our lives.

The hours felt endless, and our calf muscles strained at the hard and dreary work of following the jagged turns of the winding upward slope. Every time we rounded another bend, we found a new length of path identical to what we'd just left.

We had been fortunate each night as, just as we all felt too depleted to continue, and just as we began to worry that we would freeze in the unbearable dark, Kiana would lead us into a shallow nook in the rock wall that she'd sheltered in on her own journeys.

We would rise just as exhausted as we'd been the night before, and each night grew colder than the last as we climbed higher, where the air made our clothes feel constantly damp.

We shivered in the gloom at night, with no comfort against the bitter chill.

But then, despite the freezing cold, we grew so hot from climbing during the day that steam seemed to swirl about our bodies.

I was also beginning to feel starved of colour. There were no patches of green and no flowers to break up the sight of grey rock, until finally the narrow path widened and one of the walls declined in a dip so that we could see the sky and the world again.

The sight invigorated us, and the path had opened far enough for us to walk as a group instead of in a line.

But as the days passed, the relief of seeing the sky was almost forgotten as we climbed to such heights that all we could see was mist that swirled through the gaps in the rocks, as if souls from the Other Realm were reaching out with beckoning fingers to claim us.

Worse, we discovered that the twisting and winding road had in many places been blocked by fallen boulders, and time had to be spent climbing over them.

Then sometimes deep, bottomless ravines would suddenly open on one side of us as the path fell away altogether, forcing us to inch our way over the remaining ledges as they crumbled and groaned beneath our feet.

At one point a quieter soldier, Rendor, nearly slipped into the deadly drop, and only a lightning-fast grab from Ferron saved him from the fall. Then later, while I glumly filled my flask from a trickling trail down the rock face, I felt Thorin roughly push me aside. When I lurched sideways a fist sized rock missed my head to crunch upon his knuckles instead, immediately leaving a flourishing purple bruise.

'We're even,' Thorin winced, shaking his already swollen fingers and referring to when I'd saved him from falling from the forest ledge.

But as we trudged wearily onward it began to feel that memories of the forest could not truly be real. Surely the entire world was unchanging rock and life was just a series of shuffling feet, cold fingers and noses, white clouds of breath, and saturated faces.

We were hardly surprised or upset one night when Kiana grimly warned that the path ahead would become even more hazardous, and that shelter might become increasingly rare.

50

Fifty

D^{alin}

'Does she always have to be right?' Wolf groaned as he saw another pile of boulders beyond the pile he'd just climbed. 'Frarshk it all to the Other Realm,' he gasped; his hands on his knees, his dark hair scraggly and clinging to his face from condensation.

'How many more obstacles are ahead?' Thorin called, yet to join Wolf at the top of the current climb.

'I could count them for you. But we don't really have the time,' Wolf replied.

'That many?' Thorin winced.

Then when we'd conquered those countless piles, it felt like only moments of being back on our single-file trek along the narrow path before Kiana was stopping us again.

'What is it?' Thale called from the back of the line.

But I was close enough to see that before Kiana's feet there yawned a massive break in the stone floor where the entire path now dropped down into nothingness, and it was too far to even leap across to the other side.

I heard Vulcan and Phrixus' echoed curses as word of the problem spread, because we all knew that edging our way all the way back from where we'd come was not an option.

'I've got a good length of rope,' Aiolos called.

But Thorin frowned upwards at the rock face we huddled against. 'There's nowhere we could tie it,' he answered. 'There are jagged rocks jutting out, but they're all too sharp.'

Kiana had been silent in thought for a few moments.

'I think I can take care of that,' she remarked at last, dropping her packs to the side and out of the way. 'Pass the rope forward.'

Aiolos obliged and we passed it from man to man until it reached her and her wings suddenly appeared at her back to lift her high above us.

We craned our necks to watch as she soared upward and then stopped at one of the bigger rocks jutting out from the wall, which she inspected and ran her fingers along.

Then I heard gasps and laughs as, without warning, the rock she touched began to grow, widening and lengthening outward from the wall beneath her fingers while its jagged edges smoothed and started to curve upward.

Satisfied, Kiana withdrew and the rock stopped transforming at once. She looped the rope over the smooth, strong hook she'd just created so that it was securely bound and dangling down in front of us.

'Kiana, you're brilliant!' Thorin called up to her.

'If I was confident enough to create an entire bridge, I would,' she admitted. 'But what if the rock I would take to make a bridge came from the rock you're already standing on?'

'Let's stick with the swing.' Tane reached out boldly to catch the rope in his hands, tying a handhold in its length.

'Wait,' I called, evaluating what strategy would be best for all of us. The rope would certainly hold us, and so would the rock anchoring it. The only danger we would face was the possibility of missing the ledge when we let go.

'Vulcan,' I called down the line of men. 'Do you think you could make it up here?'

Vulcan considered for a moment, judging the narrow ledge and the deep ravine that would meet him should his foot slip from it. He was about halfway down the line.

'I can do it,' he answered confidently.

'I want you to get across first. You have the strength to catch us once we swing, so there is no chance of anybody not landing on that other side.' His bulk would also mean he had the greatest ability to launch himself and weight the rope all the way to the other side.

Vulcan nodded, assuring me he could do it. But I held my breath as he sidled away from the wall at his back and carefully began to edge around Phrixus, the first man in front of him. Phrixus, and everyone he passed, pressed themselves as flat as they could against the mountain wall, trying to leave him with as much ledge to balance on as possible.

Vulcan grunted with the effort of squeezing around Cadell's bulk next, and Cadell took a hold of Vulcan's belt as he passed, steadying him. Thorin took hold of Vulcan's belt next, and then the next man copied.

Kiana hovered so that she could help him regain his balance if needed, until Vulcan finally managed to edge his way to the front. He wiped the sweat from his brow and shook his shoulders to disband the nervous tension from his body before he accepted the rope from Tane.

'Careful,' Tane warned as Vulcan tested the rope and took a deep breath.

Then he leaned back and let his feet launch away from the ledge, grasping the rope grimly as he swung across the deadly abyss ... and was carried all the way across to where the ledge began again.

We all gritted our teeth as we watched him extend his legs to land on the other side, at last standing firmly once more.

Tane glanced back at me, a little pale faced, and I inclined my head. His turn.

'You better catch me,' he called across the gap to Vulcan. 'Or you'll hear me cursing you all the way down. And then I'll haunt you.'

Vulcan let the rope swing back across for Tane to catch. Then he raised his arms, ready to catch and steady Tane when he came across to land.

'I won't let anyone drop,' the big warrior told Tane soberly. 'Or I'll go down too.'

'I'm also great at catching,' Kiana asserted for further re-assurance, though I had no idea how she might catch the bulk of someone like Phobos or Thale.

Tane looked at the rope in his hands, and then stepped up to the edge. 'Frarshk,' he groaned mournfully, and let himself swing out across the nothingness.

Vulcan leaned as far forward as he dared and caught Tane firmly around the waist, dragging him onto the ledge.

'Nothing to it,' Tane croaked, and sent the rope back across to Ferron, who was next.

We swung across one by one, each of us braving the sickening swing over the void to be caught by Vulcan, until only Thale and the ever-withdrawn Agrudek remained.

'Should I try to swing him across with me?' Thale asked with doubt.

The scientist had been thrown and caught or carried for every rock pile climb we'd faced so far. But the drop beneath the rope was a new problem.

'I can carry Agrudek myself,' Kiana said then, and my eyes shot across to her.

'I will fly him over. He's light and it won't be for a great distance.'

'No,' Thale argued stoutly. 'If he is too heavy for your wings to support then you both could fall. I will carry him.'

Agrudek just stared miserably at the rocks at his feet, clutching a globe pendent around his neck for comfort.

'The same risk applies to you,' Kiana stated. 'But if you should fall, you have no wings to save you. And,' she firmly cut his next protest. 'We can't afford to waste more time arguing, or we won't find shelter before the sun goes down.'

Thale frowned at the watery globe of light hanging above us through the mist.

'Thale,' I called as he glanced desperately from the sun to the rope. He looked at me. 'Swing now,' I told him. 'Trust Kiana. She will take Agrudek.'

His shoulders slumped, but when Vulcan held out his arms for the last time, Thale grudgingly swung across the deadly drop below, and we all turned nervously to watch Kiana lightly land back on the other ledge in front of Agrudek.

'Hold still,' she warned the small man sternly. 'I'm going to shoot across fast.'

I heard him whimper faintly and saw him squeeze his eyes tightly closed as she stepped behind him and wrapped her arms under his. She braced herself, and then in the blink of an eye she had launched off the ledge to speed towards us.

Agrudek dangled in her grasp, before they appeared on our side of the path in a flash, where Vulcan caught hold of them to stop them from careening into the rock wall.

When Vulcan let them go, Kiana released the gaping scientist from her vicelike hold, and he staggered to the wall and clung to it.

Yet Kiana simply floated lightly back, picked up her packs, unhooked the rope, and flew to head our line again.

5¹

Fifty One

D^{alin}

'Frarshk. Again?' Wolf's voice carried downwards. 'You'll never guess what I've found now,' he growled, scrambling back up his side of a pile of boulders to shout down to us.

'I don't think I really want to,' Nikon grunted, hoisting his pack and armour into a less sore spot on his shoulders.

'Surprise, surprise,' Wolf cried sarcastically. 'We've been blessed with another gap in the path, right at the foot of this pile of boulders. A double catastrophe.'

'Great. So now we get to climb and swing,' Purdor gasped, leaning against the massive boulder he'd just scaled and staring up at the others he had to conquer next. 'At least now we don't have to do them separately.'

Our strength was flagging after being continuously met with one setback after another.

'FRARSHK!' Thorin's voice rang back to us when he climbed up next to Wolf to observe our next obstacle. 'FRAAARSHKFRAAARSHKFRAAARSHK!' we heard his echoes rebounding musically through the mountains.

'You seem disgruntled,' Noal commented blandly.

'The next gap in the road is MASSIVE,' Thorin called down darkly.

Thale sighed. 'We all hate the gaps, but we've got past them before, and we can again.'

'This one is three times the size of the others we've faced,' Thorin continued.

The smile dropped from Noal's face. 'Three times?'

'But this time I can see what's at the bottom,' Thorin added. 'And it's not very nice.'

We waited for a moment. Weighing up if we really wanted to know ahead of time.

'What's at the bottom?' Purdor gave in at last.

'Sharp rocks,' Thorin supplied. 'Very jagged. Very, very far down. Perfect for impaling warriors on.'

And we soon got to see the monstrous challenge for ourselves, after carefully lowering ourselves from the boulders to gather on the small space of intact road at the edge of the drop.

'The Gods seem set on placing every possible challenge in our way,' Phrixus moaned, but Kiana shook her head.

'I crossed this once, and it has not grown much. It can be done – and must be done.'

'But there isn't enough rope this time,' Phobos protested.

'We wouldn't reach the other side. It is too wide to swing across,' Nikon agreed.

'We brought more than one rope,' Kiana scolded our downhearted responses.

Her wings flickered and whirred into action to carry her up to the rock wall, and she pressed a hand to the rough surface. As she drew her hand away from the rock it again seemed to follow – bulging and stretching outward towards her fingers.

She swept back down to us, scooped another rope from Roth's belt, and with a thought, she confidently fused the ends of the original rope and the new rope firmly together as if they'd been one length all along.

Then with only a little hesitation, sweating nervously and praying to the Gods that we would live, each of us again managed to swing across the colossal break in the road before sinking down on the other side as if our bodies had turned to water.

Our nauseous reverie was only broken when Aiolos looked over at Kiana.

'Was that really there when you came this way?' he asked weakly, his voice wavering.

The soldier beside him, Rendor, had a green hue to his face.

Kiana, who had already recovered after carrying Agrudek safely across – glanced up from where she was sharpening her dagger.

'Yes,' she answered Aiolos simply.

Cadell wetted his lips and focused on her, keeping his eyes from the fall we'd all just escaped. 'How did you cross?' he asked. 'You didn't have your wings.'

She shrugged, putting the dagger away. 'I climbed.'

Thale choked on the water he'd been sipping. 'What do you mean you climbed?' he managed, the water dripping from his beard.

'It was all I could do at the time,' she deadpanned, as if that explained everything. 'And not crossing was not an option. I was on a Griffin hunt.'

'How could you possibly climb that?' Phrixus husked. 'There are no handholds that wouldn't have sliced your hands to ribbons, and surely it is too far to scale that wall all the way across to the other side?'

We were all waiting for some sign that she was in jest, but there was no trace of humour about her face.

'Surely even *you* wouldn't survive a climb like that? It would be torture. It would take too long!' Phobos exclaimed.

Now her eyebrow arched. 'It wasn't an easy night.'

She showed us the palms of her hands and her fingers, which were lined with the many scars that came with her trade. She calmly traced some of the longer ones that would have been quite deep, but that were now faint upon her skin.

'I had wrapped leather strips cut from one of my packs around my hands to protect them. But after a span of time spent clinging to razor sharp hand holds, the leather wasn't tough enough to protect me fully.'

We all stared at Kiana in silence before she stood once more.

'Let's move,' she said then. 'Our next challenge will be finding shelter.'

52

Fifty Two

A^{sha}

Asha stared intently from her perch amongst a cluster of sparse wasteland bushes, finally forgetting how nauseated she felt within Krall's borders.

Instead, she was enthralled by the sight of so many vast masses of big people in one location – lumbering about and gathering together in their camp.

They were slowly assembling to hear the Awyalknian King talk, and the Lady had helped Asha to time her arrival so that she could hijack his speech and address everyone at once.

When King Glaidin got started before the massive crowd – all shifting and listening loyally – a glittering grin of pointed pearly teeth covered her face.

She broke from the cover of the bushes and soared effortlessly towards the massive crowd.

Conall was standing at Glaidin's side as he addressed his men. And with all soldiers focused on the King, Conall was the first to notice the small shape hovering over the army.

Glaidin faltered when Conall spluttered, and then the King himself choked on his own inspiring words to gawk upwards.

When the masses cringed and peered skyward, expecting perhaps that the fabled Agrona had appeared ... they found that a tiny child with floating red hair was flying over their heads.

It was an image of such incredibility, and a being that exuded such wholesomeness compared to the foulness in Krall – that the crowd remained almost stock still instead of bursting into shocked pandemonium.

Asha just adored attention, especially on a mass scale, and lapped up every moment.

'So sorry to interrupt,' the Nymph beamed delightedly at the mortal King, who blinked back in bewilderment.

She swept down to his level and bowed before she held out her hand for him to take as the mortals did. He automatically raised his own and bent over her small one.

'Well met ...' he stammered with uncertainty.

'Asha,' she supplied. 'Well met King Glaidin. Good choice of location. Great audibility,' she congratulated him in the Awyalknian tongue, and then turned purposefully to face the gigantic crowd. 'I've come with an important message.'

She spoke in her battlefield voice, but there was no need, as every astounded Awyalknian listened raptly.

'You have no need to fear me,' she reassured them unnecessarily, holding out cherubic little palms. 'All I ask is that you listen and believe.'

The silence continued to grip the crowd of wide-eyed soldiers as they hung on her every word.

'I am a Nymph of the Great Forest, sent as a representative of the forest dwellers and the Lady of Sylthanryn herself.'

Wonder filled murmurs at last broke the spell of surprise.

'Your stories are all true. I am proof that pure magic is real, despite the Sorcerer's best efforts to drive good magic to extinction. But,' she paused for dramatic effect. 'While I represent the beings of the forest, I have in fact come to you on behalf of another,' she soared a little higher. 'Prince Dalin of Awyalkna wanted his people to know that hope is not dead.'

Murmurs grew into exclamations and cries of surprise, as many Awyalknians had come to believe that Darziates' Sorcery had done away with the heir of the royal line.

Asha saw the Awyalknian Warlord catch his swaying King. Glaidin's legs seemed to have lost their strength.

'Prince Dalin and the companions accompanying him have become very dear friends to the Nymphs and Elves. But they have moved on from us now to continue with their quest, which has been prophesied to be the quest that will even the balance between Awyalkna and Krall,' Asha continued.

She went on to revel in the undivided attention of the mortals as she outlined the Three's mission.

She floated in various positions of comfort before her captive audience, sometimes even elaborating with a show of lights and shapes to depict the scenes of her story.

'And so, brave soldiers, do not despair for your country. This is not a war you will face alone, because Awyalkna's victory means the safety of all lands. We will march together with united banners, and, if the Three are successful, Darziates will face a threat as great as his own.'

She leant back in the air to rest then, crossing her legs to await a reply.

And after only a momentary pause, the crowd erupted with feverish, fierce cries of relief and joy that made the entire camp rattle.

Asha turned to the two stunned Awyalknian leaders as the army rejoiced.

'King,' she said. 'Speeches make me thirsty for something strong. And I have more to tell in private.'

Glaidin straightened shakily. 'Of course, friend, please follow me to my quarters.'

Conall wasn't entirely sure that this dazzling, babe sized creature was old enough to be drinking a strong brew, but Asha was watching Conall pour her a goblet of wine with anticipation. He was less sure of the safety in denying the request of a magical creature sent by the Lady of Sylthanryn.

He tried not to stare as he handed her the cup, but he was greatly disconcerted by the sight of her floating above the chair that the King had pulled out.

'You're just as dashing as the Raiden, even with that stunned expression,' Asha told the King while Conall sat down while Glaidin made a great effort to draw himself together.

'Please, if you can pass on any news of my sons, I would be grateful.'

'Oh yes,' she told him knowingly. 'I have some incredible things to tell you about those two young men ...'

As Asha described the exploits of Noal and Dalin – or the Raiden – Glaidin felt as if his entire world was being rocked. Even knowing they had lived had struck him to his core, though beyond that, he was hearing tales of his boys that he could hardly process.

'So now the Raiden is leading the Krall warriors with him to Jenra,' she was saying matter-of-factly. 'He has earned their respect, and because of the One's magic, they have undergone a dramatic change.'

'What kind of change?' Glaidin asked in a husky voice, trying to concentrate on the facts at hand.

'They have turned from their King.'

Conall sat forward with wide eyes. 'Now that's a very interesting development.'

'It must be a trick!' Glaidin gaped. 'No man of Krall would unite with an Awyalknian! They are in danger if they think those men, are their friends! Dalin is young and too trusting ...'

'No man of Krall has had an opportunity to follow his own free will for centuries,' Asha countered Glaidin's disbelief. 'The One's magic has freed them, and the Raiden's cause has inspired them to follow him. It is no trick. And the Lady of the forest saw goodness in them herself,' Asha reassured him, and the truth of that statement was enormous. The Lady was surely the most ancient and powerful being of the natural world.

'This is not just a war between Awyalkna and Krall anymore,' she told the mortal king. 'This is another War for the World. And if we have people of Krall supporting us, then we may find a way to truly be completely united against the threat of Darziates.'

'Friend,' Glaidin at last said quietly. 'You have no idea how welcome you are as your kind again comes to share this world with us.'

Conall rubbed his hands together. 'Yes,' he grinned boyishly. 'You are very welcome, indeed.'

53

Fifty Three

K*iana*

'Frarshk,' I breathed.

It was already late in the day, but the hollow in the wall that I'd hoped would serve as our shelter was filled in with rocks.

I turned to face the trail of glum, exhausted men still catching up behind me, all of them cold and sodden from the damp air and chilled wind.

It wasn't going to be easy to tell them we would have to keep going. It was going to be even harder to tell them that we might not be able to find anywhere else tonight – which would lead to possibly fatal exposure.

'Why have we stopped, Kiana?' Roth panted as he caught up to me.

He didn't seem as robust as the others. Would I be mourning his death by the morning?

Definitely Agrudek. He would be first.

I swallowed my thoughts sickly.

'Is the shelter close by?' Ferron asked wearily as the group clambered together, bumping against each other blankly.

I took a deep breath. 'That was the shelter,' I answered regretfully, gesturing to the build-up of rubble from a rockfall.

I saw shoulders slump and the passage reverberated with their foul words as they grimaced miserably with battered, chapped lips.

I hated that I wasn't confident enough to try to use magic to hollow out a new cavern, in case I might cause a worse rockfall myself.

'We will just have to continue on for a while until we find something else that is suitable,' I told them, as if I didn't doubt that we would find safety from the freezing night in time, and as if I couldn't see the worry in their already ragged faces.

They trudged along behind me, the temperature dropping steadily as we found nothing but unending walls and icy wind.

The thin, watery light of the mountains was waning and I pressed them on at an even greater pace. They were already shivering more dramatically than before as the dark began to chase us down.

The men were starting to move sluggishly, their ragged breaths echoing around the pass and over the wind.

Purdor fell wearily forward, knocking into Thorin. Thorin had been drinking from his flask, and the water spilled down his chest, but he caught Purdor, who shook himself determinedly and started moving again.

Then the dull light was gone.

'Kiana!' Thale called at last as he helped Tane to his feet from where he'd tripped. 'We cannot see.'

'Right. Halt!' I called, and the sounds of the lagging footsteps behind me stopped.

'We don't have your keen eyes, Kiana,' I heard Noal rasp, and I could just make out his slender figure stooped over in the dark.

Gods, I could see them all swaying where they stood. They were slowly freezing on their feet. They couldn't go on, but we couldn't stop without shelter. They wouldn't live through the deepest part of the night. None of them.

Yet while every part of my body was bitterly icy; my exposed face and hands feeling burnt and stiff, there were constant sparks of magic in my blood that seemed to be keeping me from getting as dangerously cold as they were.

'I can continue on and search in the dark. I will find what I can and come back for you,' I told them, turning at once.

'It's not safe for you to go alone,' Dalin managed through chattering teeth. 'If something happened, we wouldn't be able to find you.' I saw his outline straighten with an effort. 'I'll come with you.'

'No,' I answered firmly. 'I can be faster alone. We need haste.'

I didn't wait, but turned and jogged away from them. 'Stay close together!' I called over my shoulder as I swept away into the dark. 'And keep moving your arms and legs!'

'Are you sure we should let her go alone?' I heard Thorin through his shuddering.

'She'll be … fine,' Noal told him between gasping breaths. 'It's Kiana.'

I sped on desperately, and reached out with all of my senses to scan every nook and every cranny, listening to the wind curving around every rock and throwing out my intuition in the hope that I would find something. I gauged the slopes in the path with my feet, hoping to feel a slant that would indicate a hollow.

I feared that if I stopped running for too long, I would lose any lasting heat in my body, and would end up shutting down myself.

I was becoming frantic when, finally, some instinct told me to stop.

Backtracking, I strained to see if there was an opening in the wall, but everything seemed black.

I reached out and forced myself to patiently run my nearly numb hands along it.

'Frarshk,' I cursed, finding absolutely nothing as I made my way back and forth.

Gritting my chattering teeth, I angrily kicked at the looming mountain, but nearly fell forward as my leg swung crazily out in front of me, not connecting with anything solid.

With a croak of delight, I fell to my knees and inspected the base of the wall, finding a low, arched opening that surely led into a cavern inside.

I laid flat on my back and pushed forward, sliding into the dark hole to find myself hurtling down along a short slope before I hit a rocky floor below.

'Thank the Gods!' I whispered to the heavens.

I could just make out that the dark space was a protected cave, big enough to fit our group. The galling wind did not reach this space, and I hastily felt my way around to ensure there were no other occupants or dangerous crevices.

I quickly left my packs, bow and quiver against a wall before scaling hurriedly back up the slope to be lashed by the cold outside again.

I ploughed urgently back along the pass to find my group, instinctively vaulting over obstacles, and heard the wheezing of their breathing as I drew close.

I rounded a bend and skidded to a halt, nearly sliding right over Nikon, who stirred dully.

I could make out each of their forms, huddled on the rocky path as if they were only half alive, and I immediately stepped amongst them, briskly pulling them to sit up.

'I've found a place,' I cried with false cheer. 'It's not far, and it's warm and dry.'

The air felt as if it had already dropped well below freezing point, and nobody acknowledged my words.

'Enough!' I snapped like a commander. 'To your feet! NOW!' I made out a couple of heads lifting in the dark. 'MOVE!' I bellowed, my voice whipping around us in the howling gale.

One figure started to stir, and used the wall to pull himself sluggishly to his feet. Dalin.

He leaned down and pulled the feebly stirring figure next to him up as well.

Noal.

I was sure that it was Thorin and Vulcan who helped each other up next, and Wolf pulled the shuddering Agrudek to his feet.

They were rising as if from a deep sleep. As if from death. And after what seemed like an age, they were all standing, sagging against each other where they stood, waiting to be told what came next.

'Follow,' I growled. 'Do NOT stop!'

I felt a shaky hand on my shoulder as they formed a line. I turned and began to lightly jog back the way I'd come, listening to their stumbling, lurching steps as they held onto each other.

'KEEP MOVING!'

Like marionettes they flopped and dragged themselves in a senseless shuffle after me.

Thorin collapsed and I had to pause to drag him to his feet and roughly push him on before doing the same for Gideon and Purdor.

'DON'T STOP!' I roared when they slowed without my direction, and they managed a burst of speed.

My heart was racing as I finally cut them off, holding out my hands and putting my palms on Thale and Tane's chests so that they slowed, their bodies heaving.

The cold felt like knives carving grooves into the lining of my own lungs as, like sheep, the rest of them milled around me.

I turned to Tane. 'Get on your back. Lay with your feet pointing to the wall.'

Unquestioningly he obeyed, dropping down and folding in on himself like he'd just been holding out for my permission to collapse.

'Trust me,' I told him sternly, and knelt to put my hands on his shoulders before thrusting him towards the wall.

I heard only a few interested stirrings from the others as Tane seemed to disappear into the wall, sliding down into the cavern, and I turned to Thale.

'You're next,' I instructed.

His chest was broader than Tane's and he almost didn't fit, but he scraped through with my help, and I pushed man after man down into the hole, hearing them collapse inside when their feet touched solid ground. I had to give Phobos and Vulcan more forceful shoves, and then it was just Dalin and Thorin.

'Come on Raiden, it's not the palace, but it'll do,' I teased, and he slid down into the cavern as well.

Thorin didn't move to follow him immediately though, standing against the wall with his head back and his eyes closed.

His breath was wheezing and laboured, his chest fighting to rise and fall in a more extreme way than I'd noticed with the others.

'We need to get you inside, right now,' I told him as he opened his eyes and I pulled him to lean against me. His stocky build dragged along with me as I walked him to the gap and helped him to lie before it and slide in.

I heard Vulcan catch him and whisper with an effort up to me that the slope was clear.

I slid at long last back into shelter, but in the darkness the sound of everyone's excruciating breathing seemed loud and ghastly.

'Please Gods,' I mouthed silently, 'let me be able to give them heat.'

I cast my eyes around the darkness uselessly, wondering how I could make fire without anything dry to burn. Unsure, but determined to at least try, I picked my way over and around the trembling bodies scattered across the floor, and found a clear spot in the middle to sit in, thinking furiously.

I closed my eyes and tried with all of my might to will a fire into existence.

Even just a small flame at least. Yet nothing appeared.

Perhaps I couldn't create fire without anything to build it off, I considered – thinking of how I could make rock change shape simply because the rock already existed.

I frantically felt the ground around myself to find two pebbles, which I hastily beat together so a little flicker of light sprang up in a flash between them. I beat them together again, but this time I pictured the spark growing, and the flicker of light seemed bigger. Eagerly, I beat them together one last time, now picturing that spark exploding into a flame, and I jumped when a burst of light and heat exploded from the clashing rocks in my hands.

This time it didn't fade, but stayed stretched between the rocks as I held them in a small, flickering ball of white flame.

Some of the men were rousing at the sight of the small fire, and I pulled the rocks away and set them on the floor while the flame globe stayed up in the air where they had been, levitating and creating a floating ambience in the middle of the cave.

I focused on the white brilliance and pictured in my mind what I wanted it to do, before it obediently swelled to more than double its size. Now all it needed was: 'heat,' I whispered to it, and suddenly I felt radiating warmth touch my cheeks.

Heat trickled tenderly through the cave, settling upon the hushed, shivering figures like a comforting blanket.

I put my hand out to touch the flames with my fingertips, feeling nothing but waves of lovely warmth before I took a handful of it out to sit on my palm. Then, with a sense of newfound confidence, I sent out a new thought. At once some of the swirling light broke away into pieces to cross the room and float at intervals along the walls of the cavern.

Able to see clearly at last, I dragged all of the packs and bundles of armour to a spare space and left them there. Then I uncorked a flask of alcohol and rustled up some frugal snacks, putting a touch of my newfound skill with heat into each portion.

Some of the men were stirring and a lot of them were sitting up by the time I was passing the flask and the snacks around – quietly, blankly chewing while they recovered their senses.

Vulcan was the first to speak, croaking to Thorin that he should be making an effort to get up too, as Thorin was the only one who hadn't sat up yet. But the young warrior didn't respond.

Vulcan frowned and nudged his friend, who was lying motionlessly next to him.

'Thorin?' Dalin asked. He took hold of Thorin's shoulder and gently rolled his friend over onto his back, gasping when he saw that Thorin was not conscious, though his purple lips were parted with the terrible effort it took for him to breathe.

'What's wrong with him?' Vulcan cried, and scrambled to pull Thorin into a sitting position against himself, away from the icy rock floor.

I lurched across to Thorin's side and noted the condition of his tunic in consternation.

A thick layer of icicles lined his collar and was growing down along the material across his rasping chest. It was much thicker than the dusting of frost that everyone else had already shaken off.

'There's ice all down his front that hasn't melted,' I said in confusion. 'How did that happen? No one else got that much ice on them, did they?'

'No,' Dalin said. 'None of us got wet enough for the cold to make the ice that thick.'

Suddenly Purdor gasped. 'Oh Gods! The water!' he cried in horror. 'I fell against him and he spilled his flask! His chest was wet the whole time we were out there!'

Thorin's clothing and chest had been slowly freezing for that whole time.

'Will he live?' Wolf asked apprehensively.

'Are his lungs still working?' Thale asked, his face drained of colour.

'He didn't complain. I didn't even notice,' Tane said guiltily, as if they hadn't all been witless and on the edge of life themselves.

I brushed the ice from Thorin's shirt.

'Dalin, get the shirt open and tell me the damage. Vulcan, keep him warm,' I rose and scooped up my healing pack, rustling around in it.

'It all seeped through to his skin,' Dalin gave a commentary as I dropped down and began hurriedly chopping ingredients. 'His throat and chest are blue all over.' His voice was hard, trying not to panic.

I nodded. 'How blue?'

Noal was crouching by them now. 'Not as blue as Dalin looked in your cottage after the Evexus attack,' he responded, guessing what I was going to try to do.

'Alright,' I replied. 'I don't think there's permanent damage. I can still hear him fighting. But we need to warm him up.'

Dalin rubbed Thorin's hands and chest, trying to bring heat back into his skin. 'You're going to give him that fire drink you gave me?' he asked as the soldiers watched tensely and I mixed ingredients furiously in one of the bowls from my pack.

'It worked for you; it'll work for him.'

I used my new talent to send heat through the bowl and warmed the liquid up so that it bubbled thickly.

'Get his mouth open,' I ordered, rising with the concoction and crossing back to them.

'It won't hurt him, will it?' Vulcan asked uneasily over Thorin's head, giving the smaller warrior a bear hug.

'I sure hope it does,' I told him seriously. 'It's got to be hot enough to heat up his blood and organs.'

Vulcan let Dalin take Thorin's jaw in his hand to open his mouth.

'Sorry Thorin,' he told his friend.

I slowly poured the drink down Thorin's throat, massaging it down until it was gradually all gone, but other than the automatic reflex to swallow, Thorin didn't twitch.

Dalin started to rub Thorin's arms and hands in his own again and I followed suit, now trying to put my hands over his chest and sending waves of magical heat from my own body into his with the friction.

'Come on ...' I muttered as everyone else held their breath, watching for any sign of movement.

Then he spluttered weakly, and stirred in Vulcan's arms.

The men let out a series of whoops and cheers, and Thorin blinked painfully.

Then he raised a shaking, unsteady hand to his throat.

'It feels like ... I've swallowed lava.'

Vulcan squeezed his comrade tightly in relief as Dalin and I sank back in euphoric, dizzy exhaustion.

'Just wait until Kiana gives you a second dose,' Dalin told him.

54

Fifty Four

A^{glaia}

Aglaia was working beside her young soldier, Elan. People called him Friendly.

They were in a dining hall brimming with other volunteers who were counting out rations for the city's midday meal.

'Majesty?' a page boy's soft voice said from near her elbow, and she peered down with a start from where she had been levelling off a cup of grain.

'Yes?' she asked kindly.

'A royal messenger from King Glaidin has arrived.'

Friendly paused in his carrot chopping as her cup tilted and the grains spilled.

The Queen lowered the cup to the bench.

'The messenger just rode in. He'll meet you in the private council chambers,' the page continued.

Aglaia nodded. 'Thank you.' She swept immediately away from her chores, with Friendly keeping pace.

The Queen didn't slow until she had crossed the throne room to a small council room attached to the great throne hall.

She was about to step inside with Friendly behind her, but the first thing she saw through the ajar door was Wilmont.

Wilmont, of all people, standing over the messenger, who was slumped in a chair at the table.

'I asked you a question,' Wilmont was hissing, leaning over the exhausted messenger. 'The rumours from abroad, are they true?'

'My message is for the Queen and her generals,' the messenger replied, then his eyes flickered to the doorway. He fumbled to put down a flagon of water and quickly tried to rise. 'Majesty!' he greeted her respectfully.

'Stay seated,' she instructed the tired man as she entered. 'You have travelled far and I can see you are fatigued.'

He sank back with relief while she turned a frowning gaze on Wilmont, who was suddenly back to oily composure.

'Wilmont, why are you interrogating my messenger before I have spoken with him?' she asked the frilled, powdered man, anger seeping into her voice.

Wilmont lowered his head in deference, as if ashamed. 'I beg forgiveness your Majesty,' he said silkily. 'I had hoped to hear and then soften any painful news before you had to hear it from someone less adept.'

'In what world has that ever been your right or your responsibility? I do not need a filter for my messengers, and do not need to be handled like a sensitive damsel. Do not make such assumptions again, Wilmont,' Aglaia warned. 'No matter the intentions, you have overstepped your authority.'

His ringlet framed face became drawn. 'Of course, my Queen,' he simpered, but his eyes were penetrating and she felt the already tense frame of Friendly behind her stiffening further.

'Leave now,' she told the brash official.

'Majesty ...' Wilmont began to protest, raising hands that were surrounded in lace cuffs.

'*Now,*' she said firmly. It was only when she felt the tightness of the gold band ring on her finger digging in that she realised her fists were bunched by her sides.

'Very well, my Queen,' Wilmont replied more tersely. And he gave a slight bow that was more like a jolt before sweeping past them to the doorway, where he had to squeeze around one of the generals who had also just arrived.

'Good riddance,' General Sumantra rumbled from where his barrel-like frame was almost completely filling the doorway. 'Thinks he's more important than he is. Bloody presumptuous.'

He moved into the room, followed by the other three generals left in the city. The archer Dren also entered, for Aglaia had been becoming aware of the brilliant people at her disposal, and had begun to be more inclined to choose loyalty, trust and talent over titles and rank when it came to advice.

'I've never really found that fellow endearing,' Dren commented to Friendly as they watched Wilmont skulk away and closed the doors to the room.

Aglaia turned once more to the messenger. 'We are glad to see you, despite Wilmont's less than welcoming reception.' She seated herself at the head of the table and gestured for the others to sit. 'Please proceed with your message.'

He took a deep breath. 'King Glaidin said that he knows this will all be very hard to believe, but that every word of it is true. And I can myself swear to it all ...'

Hard to believe was an understatement.

'So, the princes are alive,' one of the generals uttered when the messenger had been taken to find rest.

'And they are questing to form alliances amongst mortals and – immortals ...'

Aglaia had remained outwardly calm as she had heard of her boys, but she knew that Glaidin would not have sent such news unless he was certain of its validity.

Sumantra stabbed an eager finger into the surface of the table. 'If it is true that Jenra and these so-called magical races might be coaxed to join our numbers, Awyalkna just might have a chance. It is a slim chance, but better than what we all had up to an hour ago.'

'Lucky the princes came across the last *Larnaeradee* and became part of these prophecies,' Friendly contributed, and then blushed when his superiors shifted their attention to him.

'Thank the Gods they're all right. Thank the Gods they made friends with the right people,' Aglaia nodded.

'Or the right creatures,' Sumantra chuckled. 'I always did like telling Fairy stories to my little-uns.'

Dren rubbed his chin thoughtfully.

'What is it?' Sumantra asked him, a little more soberly this time.

The archer leaned forward and looked the general and then the Queen in the eye. 'I'm going to be leaving you.'

'What do you mean?' Aglaia asked in surprise. 'We need you here. You comfort the people. They see you as their hero against the Dragons.'

Dren shook his head. 'Both Sumantra and yourself have made this city one of the safest havens in the lands of men.'

'You want to join Glaidin on the frontlines?' Sumantra asked gruffly.

'I mean to fight for our country, but first I intend to search out Prince Dalin and offer my services on his quest. I am almost certain my four friends will want to join me,' Dren said, referring to the other Dragon fighters.

Aglaia felt torn as she regarded the archer.

'The only way I could bear to lose such a talent would be for my sons. There is really nothing more I could have hoped for you to say.'

55

Fifty Five

The Witch

Even as a girl with hateful, hurt eyes and long plaited hair, Agrona had known that she would kill any who threatened her master and all they were working for together.

'You should not need physical gestures for your power to work,' his hard voice had often said. 'Your mind is weak, I can read every thought.'

He pushed and pushed.

'Be better for me. Be better than everyone.'

Pushed and pushed.

'I will. For you. I love you.' Her heart had been completely his all the same. He had saved her.

'Yes.'

'I will be everything you need,' she had always promised.

'Of that I must be convinced.'

Oh yes, he had always pushed. Not afraid to demand more. Making her want to be stronger, crueller, and to convince him – to earn her place with him.

He had always been present in her life. He had given her purpose, he had appreciated the sadism she enjoyed for sport, and had freed her to be the creature she yearned to be.

In fact, unlike her scornful parents, he had forced her powers to grow. And the mild disappointment on his face when she had never achieved as much as he had hoped had only made her yearn to impress him more.

She was devoted beyond reason to Darziates and to his cause. He had a destiny beyond all others. She had bound herself to him totally, loving him with all of the passion and demented lust that her dark soul was capable of. She knew every nuance of his nearly expressionless mask, and knew what every shift in octave in his voice might mean.

And so, she knew almost immediately when he started to get sick.

She sensed the shift in his iron will, and the tiny fissure of weakness in his heart.

Agrona had been warned that there was one other woman in the world who might be a threat. And that woman had somehow sent an invisible dart of lethal, pure magic into the Sorcerer to disrupt his quest.

Agrona's beloved Sorcerer King had begun to turn from her, under the spell of another. He had heard from Agrudek, and he had ordered his Witch away to resume her search over the accursed forest and mountains, to look for the Awyalknians.

Because he wanted the girl who hid under a magical shield.

So now, while the mountain air tore in stinging blasts, ripping at her wings, shredding her feathers – Agrona's fury and terror swelled inside like a diseased growth. Bitten by icy wind, and driven by malicious, demented jealousy, all Agrona could do was gnash her beak and search.

She craved Kiana's death with her entire being. Just as much as she craved her King. Her master.

The Witch must save him. She must protect her Sorcerer.

In a fit of wrath, the raven let loose a horrendous screech that cut across the wind, and she felt Griffins shuddering all throughout the mountains as they recognised the unnatural sound. Even all the way down in their mountain eyries, they cowered low and stayed hidden while Agrona swooped over the jagged peaks.

Agrona sent out all of her anger and hate to fall upon every Griffin and every mortal in the mountains. She may not have been able to see through it at first glance, but Agrona's magic could still seep beneath Kiana's shield.

She could still do damage.

She would send enough malice into the mountain passes to make Kiana and all of her cronies cower under barrages of their own self-doubts and the very worst of their memories.

56

Fifty Six

N*oal*

Thorin was playing with a little ball of flame that Kiana had given him to keep heated as we walked. He threw it casually from hand to hand as if holding fire was a normal thing to do.

Nothing else seemed out of place, and none of us were expecting Kiana to abruptly halt in her tracks – causing Tane to almost trip over her. She narrowed her eyes, glancing around the tops of the rocky walls framing our Pass.

'What is it?' Dalin asked, skirting around Gideon and Lydon to come to her side.

'There is a nasty scent on the wind,' she answered quietly, though when I sniffed the air, I could smell nothing, and ahead of me Purdor shrugged apprehensively at Phobos.

She stepped forward, lowering her packs and taking bow and arrow in hand.

'Hands on weapons,' Thale ordered, and the soldiers all took on ready stances.

'Yes. We're going to have company,' Kiana warned over her shoulder, and her wings blurred into shape at her back.

The air above us suddenly burst with shrill, echoing screeches.

'Griffins?' Thorin rasped, clutching his ball of fire in shock.

We squinted upwards but the amplified sounds were disembodied and we could see nothing.

'Kiana!' I heard Dalin call as she lifted into the air, though all we could do was clasp our ears in a desperate attempt to block the growing, nightmarish noise out.

She spiralled upward and soon vanished beyond the top of the rocks and we all listened with dread as the keening screeches rose in pitch when she was spotted.

There may have been a twang from her bow before the screeching of one of the creatures was abruptly cut off. A choking, gurgling sound replaced it, ahead of a thunderous crunch as a body hurtled down to land somewhere on the rocks above.

The squawking of the other invisible beast amazingly managed to increase with fierce intensity and there was the sound of rushing air under massive, swooping wing beats.

I heard Kiana curse, but then there was a second howl of animalistic pain, and another horrific crunch of a plunging body impacting upon rock. Then the pass was almost quiet again, except for the wind.

'That was quick,' Wolf whispered.

Dalin and Tane stepped back as Kiana dropped expertly back into our midst, hauling two massive carcasses with her.

'Gods!' Cadell cried at the sight of the corpses as Kiana heaved the weighty Griffins up by their tails for us to see.

Dead or not, they were fearsome things to behold. Not animals or magical creatures, but a blend of the two. And in the tales of old, they had allied themselves with Deimos of Krall, delighting in war and in feasts of mortal flesh.

'There were only two of them?' Phobos exclaimed. 'It sounded like an army!'

'That croaking is what they do to panic their prey,' Kiana answered.

'It was working,' Phrixus remarked sourly, rubbing his ears.

'Frarshk, they reek,' Ferron complained, covering his nose.

'Are you in one piece?' Dalin asked Kiana grimly.

'Of course. These are some of the smaller ones, but they can do as much damage as the large ones,' Kiana replied. 'I am hoping that these two scouts did not sound off long enough to let any lurking hunting parties know of us.'

Tane coughed in shock. 'Those are the small kind?'

The two bloodied bodies were over an arm span long, and their eagle-like wings were double that in length. They each had vicious, sharply hooked beaks and talons, and the ears and matted body of a lion.

'The bigger kind are less common,' Kiana told him, hoisting them over to a break in the rocky wall and dropping the rancid bodies over the edge and into the abyss.

'The larger breed are huge creatures that could easily carry someone as big as Vulcan back to their lair for dinner. Very strong.'

Vulcan swallowed uneasily as she rinsed her hands of the pungent smell. 'Nice to know,' he managed.

Kiana brushed her hands together in distaste. 'I hope that their scent won't be traced and we can move off without drawing further attention.'

'I hope never to smell such things again,' Phrixus said with revulsion as Kiana picked up her packs again. 'Those things were festering long before you killed them.'

But we walked on for only a short while before Kiana held up her hand in an indication that we should halt once more.

She craned her neck and peered sharply up through the great distance to the opening above us again, scanning the sky.

'Stay calm,' she said simply. 'We are about to get more visitors than I can stop in time.'

And in barely a heartbeat, four expansive shapes swooped with thundering wings over the lip of the cliff and plummeted down towards us.

Horrific, airborne predators.

Two of them pounded along the rocky wall, loping easily on a vertical path, their sharp orange eyes fixed keenly on us. Three of them landed heavily on the road just beyond us, lashing their tails alertly as they blocked our path. The other one was clearly one of the larger kinds, and it sank in an almost graceful way down to perch on a shaft of stone that extended from the rocky wall a few yards above us.

It was so huge that if it had reared up it would have been twice as tall as Vulcan, and probably powerful enough to carry a small army home for dinner.

I was alarmed to see that it observed us intelligently, its bright, unfeeling eyes sweeping over our faces.

'Are you going to speak or just sit there like a dumb animal?' Kiana asked it, her voice sounding foreign as she broke from *Aolen*.

'Just seeing what all the fuss is about,' it replied conversationally, its gravelly yet human voice making the hairs on the back of my neck stand on end.

Agrudek let out a fearful squeak.

'Oh?' Kiana asked sceptically. 'What kind of fuss?'

A hungry gleam was in its eye as it looked her over. 'You only recently killed two of our kind. We fuss because we are upset.' Its beak clicked menacingly as it spoke.

Kiana laughed brazenly. 'Please. You're always killing each other off for food or territory. What's the fuss really about?'

Its tail lashed behind it.

'Griffins have been searching all through the mountains and have found not a trace of your large group until now,' it purred. 'Which is curious. Seeing as we can catch the scent of food from miles away.'

'So, your sense of smell is dying,' Kiana scoffed. 'Why are we being sought?'

It clicked its beak and made a croaking sound that could have been a laugh.

'A raven told us to look out for you.'

Instant dread nibbled at my insides. Dalin's face paled and I heard the men shifting uneasily behind me.

Kiana's voice became colder, her face hard. 'Is that so?'

'I was interested in the challenge of seeking such a well-hidden group. A group that has survived this altitude when even the elite Jenran guards must train to do so. And a group that has piqued Agrona's interest.' The Griffin eyed us beadily. 'And now I see I've found weary soldiers with a female who is more than she seems. I feel the magic around you, saving you. It's disgusting.'

Kiana gave her half smile and the massive Griffin ruffled its speckled feathers.

'And what do you intend to do now that you have so bravely inspected us for yourselves?' Kiana enquired. 'Flap back to the Witch? Or attack us for her?'

Its orange eyes flashed, the elongated pupils sharpening. 'We will not get ourselves killed for the Witch just yet. It is best we do not involve ourselves until we have learned what we can win and lose.'

'How very noble,' Kiana remarked dryly.

It shook its feathered head and crunched the rock under its feet, readying to take off once more. 'It is in our nature to be anything but noble. Even Agrona doubted we could be trusted to serve her when she ordered our kind to find you.'

Kiana gazed stonily back at the horrible creature, her hand on the hilt of her sword.

'We can see that you are not a very good food source, and it would be unwise to challenge whatever power you have before we are assured that we will win,' it finished.

'So, you will leave us unhindered along this pass?' she asked it in a low voice.

'For now,' it croaked, stretching wings that would have been longer in span than an Elf's body. 'But you will probably see us again. We do live for battles we can't lose, and there's a lovely war coming up that the Sorcerer has invited us to.'

Kiana scowled. 'Bloodthirsty self-serving wretch.'

It squatted on its hind legs and lifted itself off into the air, the fetid wind from its wings sweeping around us.

'Yes,' it uttered languidly, and then swooped back up the mountain wall and out of sight.

Its silent cronies followed suit, hissing and spitting at us until they disappeared, leaving our stunned silence behind them.

'So Agrona has found us?' Thale asked, rubbing his beard with worry.

Kiana shook her head. 'No. She sent those things to find us because they are the best scavengers in the mountains. All she knew was that we would be in the mountains and would have come from the direction of the forest.'

'But those things will tell her where we are. They work for her,' Nikon grunted in frustration.

'They work for none but themselves. They will only fight for Darziates because he looks the most powerful and because war means food. They are treacherous. We can believe the Griffin's statement that we are not yet in danger – not if it might mean harm to itself. It won't be hasty in taking a risk either for or against the Witch.'

'So, we're somewhat safe for now?' Dalin asked.

'From Griffin attacks, because they fear my magic as a threat that might be comparable to the Witch's. But now we know that Agrona is closing in again, and I don't even know how I'm magically shielding us. We likely don't have long.'

For the rest of the day, we trudged on grimly, with that very thought making us fear every shadow and making us jump at every birdcall from high above.

57

Fifty Seven

Noal

The carriage was bumping peacefully along the winding road, and the sun was strong and bright. It sparkled on my mother's honey blonde hair, and glinted in my father's sandy beard.

My sister was teaching me the runes to spell each of our names, marking the funny lines on parchment with charcoal.

I was eight, she said. Time I at least spelt my own name and hers right. Then she blinked up from the parchment spread between us in surprise.

I heard a cry and a thud from the driver outside, and the cart veered off the road while the horses panicked.

My father put his arm out to steady us, but then his eyes widened as he stared past my mother to the window.

'Thalia!' he cried in warning, and his hand went to his sword hilt. Up until then it had only ever seemed like a part of his clothes. But he didn't have time to draw it before my mother screamed and was dragged by her lovely honey hair through the window of the carriage. Then my father roared as he was torn away from my sister and I.

'Do what the Trunes say,' my sister whispered to me. 'Be still and quiet and you'll be safe.'

I felt her tears on my cheek and her arms around me. She was breathing fast in gulps and sobs. Then they took her from me too.

I cried as they kicked me down the steps of the carriage and I fell onto the dirt road.

A heavy boot crunched into my back and pinned me to the ground.

'Watch.' The owner of the boot told me with a bark of laughter.

And I watched as blows and blood made my mother's honey hair turn red. I watched as a quick slit silenced my sister's cries. I watched as my father was felled.

I was struck mute and the boot in my back moved and kicked my face down into the dirt.

My wrists and ankles were bound tightly while the murderers were hacking the heads from the bodies of my loved ones, before the Trunes kicked the heads across the dirt into a pile in front of me.

The face of the Trune who put the letter in my pocket was smiling. And when they all left, I still did not roll away from that place, away from the heads. I just lay there and gazed at the faces of the ones I had lost.

I stayed frozen and bound, crippled by the horror.

I'd be frozen there forever it seemed.

Frozen in a nightmare.

'Noal! Noal, wake up, you're fine!'

I woke with a violent jerk to Dalin and Thorin leaning anxiously over me.

Everyone else was awake already. The howling of the wind outside our shelter seemed even more foreboding than usual.

My head sank wearily back down to the ground and I held my brow with a shaking hand, my breathing ragged.

'Are you alright?' Thorin asked.

I nodded. 'Just a bad dream. Sorry if I woke everyone up.'

But I noticed that Nikon, who had been sharpening his blade during first watch as I'd fallen asleep, was now releasing his hold on Thale. Thale sat up, pale and shaken.

'If it was just a dream, then everyone had it. All of you started moaning and thrashing about at once, and I nearly sharpened myself instead of my blade,' Nikon grunted.

I took a long breath. 'Everyone had a night terror?'

I saw Dalin glance at Kiana, who was stony faced and dangerous looking. She shook her head and focused her eyes. 'These weren't ordinary dreams. What I just experienced was nothing like the nightmares I used to have. It was like reliving the attack on Bwintam, reliving the death and fear. Every sensation, everything was the same. As if I was truly back there again.'

'Aye,' Thale said in a low voice. 'I was reliving the day that Angra Mainyu forced my troop to trap and burn an entire field full of villagers he said were plotting against the Sorcerer.'

'And I was back to the day my parents were taken and I was cast out,' Thorin told us grimly.

I noticed that Agrudek huddled, haunted and withdrawn, behind Thorin.

'Mine was simply a parting argument with my father over my level of competency,' Dalin shrugged grimly. 'But it seems somehow our worst memories or insecurities have been used as weapons to hurt us.'

'I think,' Kiana said slowly. 'That this is our second warning that Agrona isn't wishing us well.'

58

Fifty Eight

D^{alin}

'I am so sick of these accursed mountains,' Thale muttered to Thorin and I after a particularly hard climb over a massive fallen rock. 'It feels as if I've been wet and tired and surrounded by howling wind for years.' He wiped at drops of misted rain that had begun to cling to his beard like ornaments.

'I swear I'll turn into a rock if I see nothing else for much longer,' Thorin groaned.

'You'd make a lovely boulder to sit on while we eat lunch,' Noal told him.

'Believe it or not,' Kiana announced, 'we have only a few days of this rock left before we see Jenra.'

Tane frowned as he slid down the boulder Thale had just struggled with. 'Shouldn't we be starting to descend soon then? It doesn't feel like we're going downward. The easing pain in my buttock muscles would surely tell me.'

'Midroone Pass keeps climbing until the very last stage before it opens to Jenra,' Kiana answered. 'When that happens, you'll definitely feel the downward slope.'

'Gods,' Phrixus moaned. 'There's no relief in this place. It goes from one treacherous extreme to another.'

'Yes,' Kiana agreed. 'A steep incline for the entire climb up, and then an extreme slope down at the end.'

'I don't even have the energy to be excited that this will end,' Purdor said gloomily.

'Because there's no sign that it's really going to,' Phobos answered as he caught Agrudek effortlessly. The scraggly scientist had just tumbled down the boulder. 'Every rock looks the same.'

There were sour mutterings of agreement all round, and our group's mood was morose as we toiled along the dreary path, until Kiana led us to settle into a melancholy camp in a cave for the night.

But despite the dreariness and exhaustion, after the previous night's dreams I lay listening to the others breathing deeply instead of settling for myself.

I sighed and rubbed at my eyes.

I didn't really want to face the judgment of my father again, even in slumber.

'Can't sleep?' a soft voice caught me by surprise in the dark.

I hadn't noticed Kiana crossing to kneel by my side, and as I made out her shape, I regarded her ruefully.

'Perhaps I am too tired to sleep.'

She held her hand out from where she crouched and I took it, allowing her to pull me up.

'Why aren't you resting?' I asked curiously.

'Perhaps I am too magical to rest,' she teased. 'Here,' she wrapped my cloak around my shoulders and clasped it at my throat. She had been so quiet that I hadn't even heard her draw it from where it was drying beside my pack.

'Where are we going?' I whispered, though I knew I didn't care.

'To be awake together,' she breathed back, and I followed unquestioningly.

Wolf was puffing away on his dwindling stash of pipe weed. He was wrapped up like a smoking, swaddled babe, keeping watch at the entrance, but he nodded quietly to us with a small smile as we stepped past.

I shivered the moment we were outside, feeling my face become pinched in the harsh chill straight away, and I rubbed my hands together roughly.

Then a warm hand rested on mine and I stopped.

Kiana entwined my fingers with hers and she watched my face expectantly.

At first, I was simply gratified by the gesture. But then I felt my mouth become an 'O' of amazement as a tickling sensation started in my fingertips.

It moved up to my elbow, spread across my shoulders, and bloomed through-out my core so that heat swelled through the lengths of my legs, and blushed warmly in my cheeks and ears. Even my damp cloak suddenly felt as if it had been touched by the sun's rays.

'Kiana,' I breathed in wonder. 'You are a treasure.'

'I've been wanting to try this,' she told me. 'But don't let go of my hand,' she warned. 'The wind is less mournful tonight. But if our connection breaks, you'll freeze.'

'I won't,' I assured her contentedly, and followed her as she led me along the path we would continue on tomorrow.

For once we were high enough in the cliffs to be close to their peak, and their walls did not tower high above.

'The stars have missed seeing us,' Kiana said quietly, gazing at the glittering, silver fires burning almost within reach.

'I've missed every part of the world beyond this Pass,' I answered.

'Well wait until you see what else is out there.' She pulled me along more quickly until we crested a steep slant in the path and found ourselves at an opening in the cliff face.

It was as if a portion of the cliff top had fallen away from there, and now there was just a yawning dip in the rock. A window in the cliffs.

'Woah ...' I was breathless at the sudden appearance of the world beyond the encasing of the rocky walls, and could not take my eyes from the great, incandescent moon that soared magnificently before us.

Beyond the gap in the cliff, and below the moon, there was a fatal drop. But the drop was obscured by the swirling mists of the clouds hugging the mountains below. The mists looked like a stretch of endless, rippling water – as if we could plunge in and swim across the white tendrils, weightless and free.

'Spectacular,' Kiana agreed softly.

I could imagine what our two figures would look like standing there. Dark, small shapes surrounded in the glory of the moon, hand in hand.

'It's like we're standing on the edge of the world. As if we could just step away into the mists and be amongst the Gods,' I smiled and turned to Kiana. 'But I wouldn't want to lose my life in the process.'

'Oh, there's worse ways to lose your life,' Kiana shrugged. 'There *is* a war coming up,' she reminded me.

'This world is worth fighting for,' I answered, pulling her down to sit, our legs dangling over the edge so that the mists swirled beneath our boots. But I felt completely calm and safe with Kiana by my side, and we held each other steady.

'Tomorrow as we get closer to the top, things will be harder.' Kiana leaned her head on my shoulder. 'There will be ice to make the paths even more hazardous. Perhaps even snow.'

I rested my cheek against the top of her head. 'I should be frozen right now. Somehow, you've kept me alive. You always look after us.'

Kiana was quiet for a moment. 'The cold won't be the hardest part. Once we've finished the climb and descent, we face the real task. In three days, we face our original challenge.'

I took a deep breath. 'Jenra.'

The idea of coming upon a new civilisation beyond the rolling mists seemed surreal.

'Imagine we have come all of this way, and are not able to convince the Jenrans to form an alliance,' I winced at the thought.

Kiana squeezed my hand. 'We already have the Elves and Nymphs. That's better for Awyalkna than when we first started.'

I frowned. 'But not quite the full unity of all races that the prophecy asks for.'

'I have every faith that the Jenrans will follow you,' Kiana answered simply. 'You are a prince after all.'

'I can impress them with all of my protocol and training,' I smiled.

'Perhaps a nice courtly dance?' she suggested.

'Well, my dancing is quite polished,' I agreed.

'Oh, of course.'

'Don't believe me?' I teased, pulling her up with me again, away from the edge.

With trained confidence, I launched her away from myself in a twirl and pulled her back so that she was tucked in my arms, and for a moment her face was surprised. Then she laughed lightly in delight.

Her hand was still in mine and my other hand rested on the small of her back.

'Amazingly graceful, Your Majesty,' Kiana smiled and moved in to rest her head against my shoulder again.

I held her gently and we moved slowly to a silent tune that only we could hear, relishing the simplicity and peace that came with there being just the two of us.

'What do you miss about home?' Kiana asked me quietly after a while, and I thought about it as I turned us gradually.

'I miss my land. The green planes of Awyalkna, and the energy of the people before all of this happened. But if you were to ask me what I miss about my life,' I grimaced. 'There wouldn't be much to say.'

'Your family?' Kiana regarded me now with concerned eyes, her face close to mine as I looked down.

'I love them. But my life was politics and expectations. I was an orphan to council halls and Wilmont's training. I was too immature or there was never time to discuss the important things, and I was surrounded by officials and servants.'

'Now you're the Raiden,' Kiana said.

'I have become the self I want to be,' I affirmed. 'Anywhere the quest has taken us has become home.'

She came in closer, sending thrilling pulses of magic throughout my core.

'I'm glad we have found home together then.'

I hugged her gratefully, but then noticed the shapes that had begun to dance in the air. 'Look,' I told Kiana in fascination.

Tiny white flecks were dancing about in the night. Floating slowly, as if the Gods had sprinkled little pieces of the clouds over us.

They landed on our eyelashes and in our hair, tingling on my skin in contrast to the warmth from Kiana.

Already they were starting to fall more quickly.

'Tomorrow promises to be harsh,' Kiana observed in a low voice, seeing through the beauty of the moment to the bleak challenges that snowfall would cause for our path.

'But we love the quest, it's our home,' I reminded her, trying to break her seriousness.

'Shall we return to our physical home for the night?' she asked.

Wistful that our escape was over, I bowed as our dance ended, and allowed her to lead us back.

It was almost heart breaking when our hands parted and the full force of the mountain's chill came rushing in as we moved towards where Phobos was now on watch.

59

Fifty Nine

N^{oal}

'Gods ... snow on the pass...' Ferron sat back in astonishment when Kiana and Dalin described how the snow would add a slippery, deep coating to our upward path.

'So, there is likely to be a deep layer of it by now?' Purdor mulled the news over slowly.

'Probably deep enough to sink in as we walk,' Kiana affirmed grimly.

'And it is going to be all cold and thick?' Wolf questioned.

'We'll be even colder, wetter and more miserable than before,' Kiana admitted. 'It'll be hard to see snags and rocks in the road.'

'So, this is going to mean a lot of breaks and rest stops?' Phrixus was rubbing his hands together.

'A lot of time will be wasted,' Kiana sighed apologetically.

'Right.' Thale looked serious as he thought.

'We'll follow your lead,' Tane encouraged his bearded leader, putting a hand on the grim warrior's shoulder.

'Whatever you decide,' Thorin added his support.

'Yes,' Thale frowned as if he was feeling the weight of a terrible decision.

'I know it will be hard, but I am positive I will be able to find our way through,' Kiana promised them in concern.

'We don't doubt you,' Cadell told her reassuringly, but then turned back to Thale expectantly.

'We will split into two teams. Nikon will lead one and I will lead the other,' Thale declared at last. 'The winning team gets out of the watch tonight.'

'What in the Gods' names are you working out?' I interrupted in perplexity.

Kiana appeared as confused as Dalin and I as she spoke again. 'We can stick together and all make it.'

Tane snorted. 'Oh, we would never let one of us die, this is all in good fun.'

Dalin gaped at him. 'I don't think I fully comprehend how you feel about the snow.'

Phobos was grinning. 'We've never seen real snow. When the Sorcerer's snow does fall it is filthy and becomes like mud immediately anyway.'

'So of course, we must test our strength against the challenges of the snow, the cold and each other alike,' Vulcan explained.

'We must battle in an epic snow fight,' Nikon finished for him.

They gazed at us excitedly, waiting for the enlightenment of the venture to dawn on us.

Kiana had her hands on her hips.

'Certainly, it will only occur during breaks and when it is safe,' Thale implored her.

'Please Kiana!' Tane begged. 'It'll break the monotony!'

'Fine,' she granted with a roll of her eyes. 'I'm sure I've developed my little fires enough that they can dry everyone off and prevent harm.'

'Hooray!' Wolf exclaimed gleefully, and our group preceded to break camp more quickly than ever before.

We lumbered out into the blistering ice and calf deep snow, which was deepening as white flakes fell to blanket the path – and the men bounded about joyously.

'It's so white!' cried Ferron.

'Dazzling!' Thorin laughed.

'Duck!'

Thale yelped as a white missile struck him in the forehead. 'I didn't say we could start yet!' he growled in protest. But Nikon was already scooping up a new snow ball.

'You're like a bunch of children,' Kiana scolded their antics. 'The altitude has made you all soft in the head.'

But by the second rest stop she was calling out tactical advice to both teams and criticising their foolhardier moves.

Later, when Tane had fallen down 'dead' from a snowball to the head, she sent a white globe of heat floating his way. 'You're going to have a wet behind,' she warned.

He spread his arms and legs out to leave an imprint of himself in the snow before the white globe thudded into his chest. He sat up to take hold of it gratefully.

'My boy would love this,' he said wistfully, his curls sticking to the back of his head as he tossed his little ball of magic from hand to hand. 'I wonder if he will ever see the beauty of nature like this. Rather than the unnatural wasteland that the Sorcerer has made out of Krall.'

'What is your son like?' I asked Tane.

'Locke's like me,' Tane laughed. 'If he ever falls over, he shall bounce back up with his curls.'

'You'd be worried if he didn't have curls,' Thorin teased, coming over to huddle next to us after his own snow fight demise. He was dusting the ice from his cloak.

'I'd never be worried,' Tane grinned. 'How could my Milara ever love another man after being married to the likes of me?'

'How does Mil not, after being married to the likes of you?' Thorin jested.

'If Locke's anything like you, that's great,' I told our most cheerful soldier. 'The world could do with more Tanes in it.'

Tane's face became solemn for once. 'I pray to the Gods he doesn't need to be exactly like me. Forced into soldiering.' Tane grew contemplative, stroking the handful of fire with a finger. 'Locke wasn't even a year old before I was called to go. Mil was so upset. He hadn't even called me father yet. I've never heard it.' He passed his magic globe to Thorin. 'When I go home, after we win this war, I'll hold them both, knowing that we stand in a safer world. I'll know then that this lost time has been worth it.'

'That child is the luckiest little one in the world,' Dalin replied. 'He misses you now, but he will live without fear in the future because of it.'

We became quiet for a moment, watching Vulcan and Nikon battle for the winning position of the latest snow war while the rest of the men cheered them on.

And finally, a white, wet ball engulfed Vulcan's left ear, and because it would have been a debilitating battle wound Nikon's team roared victoriously while Thale and his men scuffed at the snow glumly.

'I think it's time we get moving again,' Kiana announced. 'The day can't only be about fun and games after all.'

60

Sixty

D^{alin}

The men had exhausted themselves after two days of snow antics, and were now lying about in wet heaps, each with their own little globes of white magic.

Phobos looked the most comical, spreading his like a lit-up snow hat over his bald head.

Even Noal had tired himself out, having joined Nikon's team, and he had somehow emerged as the victor.

Agrudek had found a protected spot to huddle in, while Kiana and I had refrained from joining their most recent manic battle. I instead sat cleaning my sword, making sure no trace of rust could form on the blade in such a damp atmosphere.

'Join me?' I glanced up to find Kiana standing over me. 'It's early enough in the day that the others will find us.'

I took her offered hand and stood, sheathing my blade.

'We're going to scout ahead,' I told the prone figures sprawled about in the snow.

'Whatever you say, Raiden,' Wolf replied lazily, flapping a hand in our general direction.

'You all have to catch up when you've found your warrior strength again,' I warned.

To that, I only got a tired wave from Noal this time.

Kiana shrugged. 'That covers it.'

I followed her lead and we moved off down the trail at a more relaxed pace than normal.

'Are we looking for anything in particular?' I asked her as the others were lost to sight around a bend.

'The end of the path and the edge of a cliff,' she responded easily.

I grimaced. 'Are they the same thing?'

'The path ends with a cliff face,' Kiana affirmed. The path closed in again, becoming a winding trail as we followed it, and the cold rock walls pressed in.

I shivered, but then I felt Kiana's hand take my own again and a smile spread across my face despite the thought of the horrific descent ahead. Heat rushed from her hand and into mine, spreading along my arm and warming every inch of me.

'You're ever so kind,' I told her appreciatively.

'I know.'

Kiana squeezed my fingers, her hand sitting comfortably in mine as we walked side by side, our footsteps playing out an echoing rhythm. She began to hum softly, and I found myself becoming increasingly enamoured with the idea of the two of us just continuing to walk without finding any fatal drops leading to Jenra. Yet, much too quickly, we rounded a bend like any other, and suddenly found that there was no more path to follow.

'Oh Gods!' I gasped at the sudden lack of ground, and Kiana hurried to pull me backward as I regained my balance.

My breath came in ragged gasps and I heard cascades of stones and snow falling from where they had been loosed by my boots, sent to hurtle down the cliff face.

'I thought we still had a few more turns to go,' Kiana mused. 'It's fortunate we'd kept our wits about us.'

'Fortunate ...' I agreed weakly, my head swimming as we stood on the brink of the monstrous cliff.

'It's an even bigger drop than I remember,' she commented, leaning over the side and peering downward. 'It's good we weren't up to this bit when we were stumbling around nights ago.'

'Yes ...' I put a hand to my forehead, swallowing thickly.

Kiana turned to face me. 'Look beyond the drop,' she urged. 'Look at Jenra!'

Screwing up my face in an effort to make my head stop swirling, and clutching her hand tightly, I stepped back toward the edge and peered out.

'Fine,' I admitted, calming a little as I was drawn by what I saw. 'Apart from the lethal fall beyond our toes, the view that has so suddenly opened up is breathtaking.'

'It feels like I'm standing before one of the most detailed paintings ever created,' Kiana replied appreciatively, eyes on the sprawling valleys of glorious green, and towers that sprang majestically from the mountain peaks themselves. And beyond the city towers that had been carved into the mountains, there was the expansive blue ocean, rolling and lashing in the distance. It looked as though it would reach to the ends of the world, and I could only just make out the surging white foam of the waves.

I felt Kiana's hand pull at mine, this time more gently, and I tore my eyes from the land to focus on her smiling face instead. She beckoned for me to sit with her, and we both slid down with our backs against one of the rock walls.

'Can you see those people farming below?' Kiana asked after a moment, and I strained my eyes to pick up on any moving shapes.

'My eyesight isn't as good as yours,' I said in consternation. 'What can you see?'

'I can make out lots of specks working away down there,' she answered.

'Sharp,' I complimented in surprise.

I noticed an expression of curiosity cross her face, and that was the only warning I was given before a shot of tingling magic surged from her grip, bolting up my arm and seeming to shoot straight up to my head.

In a dizzying, lurch, my eyes felt as though they were burning, and my vision became sharper, brighter and closer at once, my eyes picking out movement below.

'Woah!'

In confusion, my head whipped back, connecting with the rocky wall, and I dropped Kiana's hand as if I had been stung.

At once my vision snapped back to normalcy.

'Kiana!' I groaned, clutching my head to still the sickening spinning.

'Dalin, I'm sorry!' she gasped, sounding truly aghast.

I felt her fingers rub the back of my head, but I was focusing on stifling sick waves of nausea that had begun to grip me.

'Dalin?' Kiana asked more quietly, and I forced myself to peer at her through my fingers.

'It's alright,' I mumbled dazedly. 'Just a surprise. I had your eyesight for a moment. You let me see them.'

'I promise I will not experiment on you again without your permission,' she told me earnestly.

She held out her hand, and I gingerly took it in mine once more.

'Definitely not without warning,' I chided.

'Definitely not,' she affirmed with a gentle half smile that played subtly on her lips and that warmed her brilliantly blue and gold flecked eyes.

I floundered for a response and again felt quite breathless. Our faces were incredibly close together, and I hardly registered myself impulsively leaning forward to press my lips against hers and away again.

We stared at each other. Our eyes were wide and my mouth tingled from the contact, prickling with her magic.

I tried to make myself breathe properly as she looked away from me with raised eyebrows, but she kept my hand firmly in hers, continuing to keep me warm.

'Kiana ...' I said softly. 'I am sorry ... I ... I promise I will not experiment on you again without your permission.'

She regarded me for a moment, and I waited in distress for her answer.

Then finally: 'definitely not without warning,' she chided.

'Definitely not,' I affirmed with a grin.

But then she leaned forward. And this time it was Kiana that brushed her lips against mine – before, in the distance, the sound of our approaching comrades carried along the path towards us.

Kiana pressed my hand and released it before standing as the Krall warriors, Agrudek and Noal rounded the bend in the path.

'Hello lads,' she greeted them, her voice steady, and I stood too, dusting the damp from the seat of my trousers.

'Did you find something?' I heard Thorin call from the back of the crowd.

'Not another gap to swing across?' Tane's voice carried forward as well, full of disdain.

But the men at the front had stopped short, taking in the epic descent and the city below with gaping awe.

'We've found the end of the pass,' Vulcan exclaimed to the men at the back. 'To get down, though, it looks like we have to freefall from the top of this cliff.'

'Oh.' Tane's voice was a little more subdued this time.

'Welcome to Jenra,' Kiana told everyone. 'The next stage in our battle with the Jenran mountains is about to begin.'

61

Sixty One

N^{oal}

The path had opened up to give us a spectacular view of green valleys at the basin of Jenra, and the open ocean beyond the mountains on the other side.

The city itself was also colossal – with spiralling towers of rock built into the mountainous cliffs opposite to us, their pointed tops making a jagged outline against the clear blue skyline.

'Gods,' Tane breathed through chattering teeth, breaking our stunned silence as we stared at our first view of anything other than mist and stone.

'Imposing,' Thorin commented with an enormous smile. 'I like it.'

'We've got to climb our way down there?' Thale swatted the snow from his beard in agitation as he glanced down from our great height. Cadell stood beside him, green faced.

The quieter group of the sodden soldiers – Rendor, Roth and Aiolos, grew even quieter still after having peered down. Gideon and Lydon had simply chosen not to look.

'I'm so ready for this,' Nikon commented sarcastically, his clothes saturated and his heavy pack making him hunch.

'I can't even pretend to feel ready,' I grimaced, trying to shake the snow from my trouser bottoms but instead feeling the wet material clinging back to my backside.

'Such a feat is normal for us now,' Phrixus hit me across my sopping back with a friendly, loud slap.

Purdor paused in biting his nails. 'Kiana, this is impossible,' he said fretfully. 'We don't have wings if we fall.'

Kiana was unphased. 'I managed to scale my way down before I had wings. But you will all have me hovering close in case you need catching.'

'We're not you,' Nikon told her seriously. 'I don't think we can do it. Not with our packs, with our little skill in scaling, and with so few safe handholds. We just won't be able to hold on for so long.'

'Plus,' Phrixus groaned as he flexed his fingers, 'I'm so frozen I won't be able to grasp the rocks.'

Kiana regarded us all earnestly. 'I've been thinking about this part, and I am confident I can ensure everyone will make it.' She lowered her packs to the ground and let her wings appear so that her feet lifted effortlessly from the path. 'We know I have some ability to manipulate rock, so I can make handholds and ledges in the rock face for you to use. But not only that,' she lifted higher into the air, her hair being plucked at by the wind as she closed her eyes in concentration.

Then suddenly the wind stopped tugging at her hair and clothes.

The gales seemed to avoid her and instead buffeted us as a satisfied smile played across her lips. 'I'll make this wind support you, holding you in place.'

There was an uncertain silence as we all apprehensively contemplated the drop.

'I swear I will catch anyone who should fall,' Kiana promised, her face unflinching.

'Alright,' Thorin told her begrudgingly. 'We trust you. You've got us this far.'

There were groans of both assent and dread as everyone resigned themselves to the seemingly unachievable task.

'Good,' Kiana smiled. 'Now you need to flex your fingers, kick the snow out of your boots and warm your arms and legs up,' she ordered before disappearing downward to examine the cliffside.

We all obediently began performing half-hearted stretches and uneasy flexes.

'I can carry you down,' Vulcan said gruffly when the large warrior noticed the unhappy scientist eyeing the edge.

'Th ... thank you,' Agrudek replied warily.

So, while Kiana was working her way down the cliff wall to create hand holds, Thorin and I used Aiolos' length of rope to tie Agrudek to Vulcan's back. The tiny man was barely as high as Vulcan's waist, and he could have been mistaken for a bag.

The rest of the men began bundling everyone's packs together with another rope so that Kiana could bring them down after us.

'Right,' Kiana shot back up, panting slightly. 'I've created handholds for about a quarter of the way down, and then made a massive, sturdy ledge at the end of that where you can rest while I start on the next quarter. Moving that amount of rock didn't appear to undermine anything important.'

Wolf's shaggy hair was wind swept as he peered over the edge apprehensively. 'How long do you think it will take before we make it to the first ledge to rest?' he asked.

Kiana's expression softened. 'You'll be too busy concentrating on your hands to notice. And you won't take as long as I did because you don't have to search for places to grip, and it isn't dark. We'll get this done.' She regarded us a moment.

'I'll be ready when you are.' Then she launched herself a distance away from the cliff lip and hovered in the air as we milled towards the edge in a nauseas bunch.

'I'll go first,' Dalin said with a sigh, and made his way forward.

62

Sixty Two

D^{alin}

The palms of my hands were prickling as I stood at the brink, and then, praying silently to the Gods to let us survive, I lowered myself over the edge of where the Midroone Pass ended.

'Be well everyone,' I said gruffly, and then gripped the first perfect handhold, lowering myself down along the mountain wall.

I huddled into the rocks and gritted my teeth against the first burst of wind that tore at me, but then the air seemed to settle around my form, supporting instead of fighting to tear me off the mountain.

I followed a rhythm to lower one foot down after another, and moved one sweaty hand after the other, refusing to think about how little there was between me and a plunge into oblivion. I kept my eyes on the rough cliff surface in front of my nose, only glancing up once to make sure Noal was above me. When I saw his ankles, I quickly refocused on the descent.

'Frarshk, oh Frarshk, oh Frarshk,' I heard Thorin above Noal as he began his descent too, and already my own arms and fingers felt tortured.

After a span of time I paused to momentarily wipe the sweat from my eyes, but felt my innards leap with fright when I accidentally caught sight of how far we still had to go before we met solid ground. The grassy Jenran plains were so far away that they swirled blearily in the distance and my stomach churned. But I forced my mind back onto moving, swallowing my terror with a great effort.

'Dalin?' I eventually heard Noal's thin, wavering voice carry down to me.

'Yes?' I panted back.

'You remember climbing down the Gwynrock wall on that rope?'

'Yes ... I do.'

'Well,' he grunted with the strain. 'This is worse.'

'This isn't so bad,' I lied, flexing my stiff fingers.

'I'm trying not to lose my lunch,' Noal's voice groaned mournfully.

'Keep trying,' I wheezed up testily. 'I'm right below you.'

Everyone froze as we heard a sudden cry from above.

My eyes whipped upward as I registered sickly that the voice had been Tane's.

My dread only eased when I realised the cheerful warrior hadn't yet plunged past me, and at last I heard his voice.

'Thanks Kiana,' he called in a croak. 'I was cramping and lost my balance.'

As we continued grimly on, fearing that every slip of a finger would be the last mistake we ever made, we clung to the comfort of Kiana's invisible touch. Whenever we lost balance, it seemed as if the air was pressing us back towards the wall so that we soon recovered.

'Dalin, your feet are just about to touch down on the first ledge,' I heard Kiana call out at last, just when I was beginning to fear that my arms would rip away from their shoulder sockets.

I let go of the last holds and muttered 'thank the Gods,' as I sank against the wall.

My limbs were shaking erratically and my vision swam as I took deep breaths to steady myself on the sizable platform. We would all fit comfortably on it with no risk of toppling.

I caught Noal as he skidded the last couple of steps, and he slumped joyously down onto his back. Thorin rejoiced loudly when he touched down, lying next to Noal with a million promises to leave tributes to his Gods when he got home.

'My hands are numb. My arms will never function properly again,' Purdor gasped next with wide eyes. 'Must we really do that again?'

Finally we were all laying in moaning heaps on the ledge – Vulcan sprawled face down because Agrudek had passed out and now hung limply against his back.

Kiana only joined us after she had continued downward to make the hand-holds for the next quarter of the descent.

When she landed on the ledge beside me, she had a bottle containing an elixir of her own making. It was an energising draught that she had given Noal and I once while we were being chased by the Evexus, and she passed it around the group until everyone was able to sit up once more. Then she checked everyone's fingers, making us flex them out and shake our hands and wrists before more arm and leg stretches.

'One quarter down,' Kiana said then. She held out one hand to pull me to stand.

'You are ruthless,' I told her ruefully, though I was aware that she looked as strained as the rest of us.

I lowered my protesting body back down to find the first foot hold and began the dreadful process again. And despite having been bolstered by Kiana's drink, the next part of the journey was even less pleasant.

This time Kiana had to steady both Ferron and Phrixus at different points, both of them narrowly missing a fatal fall. Purdor also suffered a finger popping out of its socket under the pressure of his grip, and Kiana had to slip it back into place and bind it.

Ignoring her own fatigue, Kiana's focus seemed total. She was aware of every finger, every slipping foot, every buckling arm, and she was there beside us in a flash with a steadying hand when needed. She was pale and sweating when she sank down beside me at our next stop, collapsing down to rest just as everyone else did.

She only rose to crawl to the edges of the ledge, forcing them to curve upward so that a sort of basin was formed around us. She created a floating ball of heat that hung over our group like a lantern, and we stayed where we had laid from when the sun finished setting, until it rose the next morning.

'We're only halfway through the descent,' Wolf rasped when Kiana smoothed our ledge once more. His legs were quivering despite the night's break.

'Also, I think I can see movement out there,' Phobos tiredly motioned across the valley below, and I blinked as I noticed a band of dust travelling across the plains towards us.

'Are we going to have a welcoming party when we get to the ground?' Thale asked in exhaustion.

'Don't worry too much,' Kiana answered, forcing herself to remain upright. 'They won't shoot at us. Our party is too small to be an attack and too big to not be of interest.'

'A stroke of good fortune,' Vulcan sighed, rubbing the raw marks left across his shoulders and chest from the ropes once again keeping Agrudek on his back. 'So, they didn't fire at you when you came here last?'

Kiana used the wall to support herself. 'They didn't see me. I kept hidden to study them, their ways and their land. They don't get visitors from the outside.' She reached for my hand to pull me up again. 'Time for the next descent.'

And, by the time we lowered ourselves, shaking and gasping, onto the last resting platform, we could make out the approaching Jenran horses and their riders in the distance below.

'We won't start the last part of the descent until we can hold ourselves together and present a show of strength for the Jenrans,' Kiana informed us, and sprawled between Noal and I while we all battled to breathe regularly once more. It was an effort to even raise a finger without it wobbling erratically.

I turned my head and found Kiana's brilliant eyes as she settled at my side. I could see her lethargy as she gazed back and I reached out to take her hand in mine once more.

'Who knew that your hand could warm me just as mine does yours?' she said quietly. Then she smiled her slight smile and closed her eyes.

63

Sixty Three

*D*alin

'This last stage is going to be tricky in a new way,' Kiana told us once we had roused ourselves and struggled to our feet, groaning and pale, but determined nevertheless.

'The rock slopes at such an angle that you won't really be climbing from one handhold to the next so much as sliding,' Kiana continued, wiping a sheen of sweat from her face.

'Won't that be faster?' Ferron sounded slightly relieved. 'It'll take the constant pressure from our hands and arms.'

Kiana cocked her head to the side and sighed. 'It'll be faster to descend from one spot to another, but you'll have to be careful that you don't accidentally slide too far and lose control. You'll also have to be careful not to damage your hands or loose a barrage of stones upon the men below you.'

'At least the wind is weak at this height, so you won't have to save us from getting plucked off the cliff,' Thorin croaked, trying to flex his stiffened claws for hands.

'Yes. It's a good thing,' she answered. 'Because I don't want to hover about too obviously for much longer.' Kiana glanced at the now ever closer Jenran party.

'Soon the Jenrans will be able to see us clearly, and I want to keep my identity a surprise for now.'

Thale snickered hoarsely. 'It'll gain their respect if they think we conquered their mountains without magical help.'

'You basically did. Now, I recommend wrapping your hands with any cloth you can spare,' Kiana suggested. 'Then get started so that we can all reach the ground before the sun sets and with enough time to straighten ourselves out before they reach us.'

She squared her sagging shoulders and her wings flickered back into a whir of action.

'Be careful,' she told us, and then shot upward, away from the ledge. 'I'm going back for our bags.'

We feebly picked the most ragged cloaks between us, shredding them for hand coverings.

'Alright,' I announced at last. 'I'll go first again.'

And with curses, rocks raining down on our heads, and flesh scraping away from our raw, scrabbling fingers, we each slid in skidding bursts down the slope of the cliff, catching ourselves on the outward jutting handholds at each interval.

'Sorry!' Noal called down apologetically when he faltered and a fist sized rock hurtled down to hit my cheek bone. He corrected his course, but a constant stream of loosed pebbles dribbled down the cliff from above and ran past and over me.

At one stage I saw Kiana lowering our packs to the ground far below, holding onto the ropes we had bundled them together with, straining against the weight, and I longed to get down to the ground to join her.

I was beginning to feel that somehow the ground had fallen away and that I would be sliding down endless rock forever, when finally I saw the earth rushing towards my feet.

I quickly propelled to the next handhold, and letting out a whoop of joy I launched myself elatedly downward, ignoring the last hold and almost free falling along the angled cliff for the last league until my boots made contact with solid ground.

My legs gave way with the impact and I let myself flop to the ground, only rolling to get out of the way as Noal did the same thing – laughing all the way down to thud into the grass at the base of the mountain.

Thorin pushed himself away from the rock while he slid so as not to crush Noal, then sank gleefully to the ground.

'Grass!' he sang ecstatically. 'Not blasted rock! It's grass! I thought I'd dreamed that green things ever really grew!'

We all sprang up and moved as Vulcan hurtled into our midst, having slid the entire distance on his front to save Agrudek from being torn to shreds and flattened.

Soon the full band of Krall soldiers were lolling about with exclamations of adoration and declarations of devotion toward whatever blades of grass happened to be sprouting where they'd landed.

A faint smile touched Kiana's lips as she took in the sight of the blubbering pack of flower loving warriors before her, until the fast-approaching group of Jenrans in glittering mail released a mighty blast from a battle horn – and we all froze.

'We have very little time,' Kiana said gruffly then. 'There are at least thirty of them. Try to look tough.'

'We *are* tough,' Tane demurred, daintily picking a buttercup out of his hair as we all dragged ourselves up again.

'Yes. We are already considered worthy of attention,' Kiana murmured triumphantly as the Krall men assembled behind Noal, Kiana and I. 'They have sent their Warlord, Aeron.'

The noise of their approach grew and we made out the solemn, intent expressions of the riders for ourselves before the dust of thundering hooves whirled around our group and the muscular, panting bodies of thirty mountain guard horses surrounded us.

At a fierce cry from their leader, the entire troop reined in and fell silent, ending the confusion of dust and sound.

Encircled, our group stood tall under the scrutiny of every hostile Jenran eye.

Most fierce of all, the unrelenting gaze of the stern soldier who appeared to be the Warlord peered out from under his heavy helm. There were silver streaks in his black beard, and lines furrowed his face so that he seemed particularly foreboding as he studied each of us with intensity.

Kiana boldly stepped forward from her place between Noal and I, but their eyes were all that moved – and they regarded her with interest.

She gave a slight bow before fearlessly addressing the leader, who was towering on his steed above her.

'Larn une Vendara.'

I started at Kiana's words, but a flicker in the proud Warlord's eyes was all that betrayed his own surprise as she spoke what must have been Jenran.

'Ge rev a Awyalkna ra Krall. Ge ush vo presa vo gesh Maelgon,' she finished, and then bowed slightly again.

The Warlord leaned forward, his sharp eyes not leaving her face.

'Gresha,' he said then, his voice deep. 'Gresha os sphita.'

Then he steered his mighty horse around and the other Jenrans stirred into motion.

'I introduced us, asking to see the King, and he answered: 'Come. Come be tested',' Kiana explained in a low voice. 'They are going to escort us to the gates of Jenra. No outsider openly enters Jenra without being tested. And no living Jenran has seen such a test.'

'A test of arms?' Nikon asked, hand on his sabre hilt.

Kiana shook her head. 'We must answer questions correctly. I will speak for us all. But if in the heart of anyone of our group there is the wrong answer, we will face retribution.'

'How can they tell what's in our hearts?' Noal asked.

Kiana frowned. 'I don't know how, but the Jenrans must have some form of magic.'

'Magic?' Wolf was perplexed. 'As long as it is not Sorcery.'

'Try not to worry,' Kiana told us. 'For now, we simply march to create distance from the eyries of the Griffins. To-morrow, when the whole city is awake to witness it, we'll learn what magic they have.'

'Oh lovely,' Cadell muttered. 'Another challenge.'

64

Sixty Four

K^{iana}

In the isolated Jenran basin, the night sky seemed vast and the world felt untouched.

Our escort hadn't lit any fires, for even small campfires, if lit so far from the rest of the civilisation, would serve as beacons to hungry Griffins.

The Jenrans themselves sat alertly in small groups. They were straight backed, dark silhouettes against the starry night, hemming us in even though I was the only one of our group still awake.

Dalin slept beside me, his skin like marble in the moonlight. And despite the rugged roughness about him from the journey, he truly did look princely. Ready to be introduced to Jenra, and to re-enter the world as the Raiden – heir of Awyalkna. Untouchable and surrounded in his true identity.

I turned away with a quick pang of wistfulness and rose to my feet, the wary eyes of the Jenrans following me while I stepped amongst my unstirring soldiers.

'You do not sleep.' A gruff voice spoke quietly from the darkness.

'Nor do you,' I returned in Jenran as I discerned that I'd drawn close to Warlord Aeron.

He inclined his head, the picture of stern grace, and gestured for me to be seated beside him where he had been quietly watching the skies.

I unobtrusively took my place at his side, dwarfed by his height even as he sat.

'You are very young,' he spoke in his quiet voice again.

'In years,' I answered. 'But I have seen and lived through much.'

'You are not afraid,' he asserted, making an evaluation rather than asking a question. 'You are surrounded by foreign warriors,' he said. 'But you are no captive and you have no fear.'

I mirrored his perfect posture. 'I have no need for fear at this time.'

'You are in a fierce land, at our mercy,' he reminded me. 'Perhaps you should be afraid.' His words were not unkind.

'Only those who cannot defend themselves, or who are of dishonest intent should be afraid of you,' I replied. 'I am neither.'

Aeron turned to appraise me more directly. 'Perhaps it is I who should be afraid,' his stern voice was unwavering, but it still pulled a smile from me.

'Definitely. But not of us,' I dispelled any threat.

'I do not feel danger from your group,' he agreed. 'I feel only curiosity.'

'We are a curious group,' I affirmed. 'But for tonight I will answer only questions you have for me personally. All other questions will be answered in your King's test.'

'Of course,' he acquiesced sombrely.

'What would you ask of me?'

He considered for a moment, before he slowly asked: 'what kind of life have you led, to have seen and lived through much already?'

I kept my eyes on him as I answered. 'I am a hunter and a healer. I have both ended and saved lives in my time.'

Even in the dark I could see that the answer surprised him, though I was sure his keen eyes had already picked out my bow and arrows, the dagger hilts protruding from the sheathes in my boots, and my very apparent sword.

'I have experience in such a way of life,' he commented. 'What do you hunt?'

I made an effort to loosen my shoulders as I felt tension seep into my bearing.

'The Sorcerer King of Krall has long sent unnatural beasts to torment not only Awyalknians, but those of Krall, too, and any innocent person who has happened to cross such a beast's path. I made it my focus to end such creatures.'

'Where are your family?' he asked. 'Why hunt?'

'They were ended by the war,' I answered simply, looking out across the plains to where the figures of the Jenran horses grazed.

I felt a moment of yearning for Ila and Amala, but my mind cleared when Aeron held his bunched fist out and then unfurled his fingers gracefully. I nodded my gratitude, recognising a gesture of condolence.

'Where are your family?' I asked him, realising that I had only ever learned of Aeron's professional prowess rather than his personal life when I had secretly visited the city before.

He gestured to the men around us. 'They are my family when I am on hunts of my own.'

I nodded again. 'Will you tell me about your type of hunting?' I asked.

The shadowy face of Aeron looked as if a slight smile was forming beneath his beard, then. 'You must first share with me,' he answered.

I felt my brow rise. 'I am a novice compared to you. I can see that the test starts before I even reach the city.'

Any stories I told would allow him to easily judge the truth in my claims to be a hunter. And beyond that he might evaluate my history, my strengths, my attitudes, possibly my role and my ambitions in his country.

'Let me think of an example.'

I recalled a number of memorable hunts out of the many blurred and savage ones I had experienced and Aeron waited while I gathered my thoughts.

'The villagers I helped in Krall always stand out in my memory,' I began reflectively. 'Their own ruler creates the beasts that threaten them, and they know that no help will ever come from their Sorcerer King or his army.' My mind was stung by images of haggard peasants begging for help.

'I remember finding one obliterated village on the outskirts of Krall,' I went on. 'I came across structural and human remains. Thrown about in the dirt, broken into pieces, gnawed at and played with by what could only have been a massive beast. A beast that would be sure to get hungry and come back. There was only one barn left standing in the whole area, and I found four people still alive and hiding in it.'

'They had stayed in the village?' Aeron asked.

'With no protection for miles, and certainly no welcome from neighbouring villages, they could only wait and hope the danger had gone,' I replied. 'And the family could not have survived fleeing through the border lands – a worn grandmother, a desperate couple and a young man who had been ripped open across his middle.'

I inwardly winced at the memory of the stench coming from their hiding place, and how their desperate, skeletal hands had clutched at my clothes when I'd first walked into the barn.

'Their dirty faces were gaunt and wasted. And they had such hungry eyes as they clung to me for help,' I recounted grimly.

'Yet you would have had little time for comforting or soothing them,' Aeron reflected.

I inclined my head. 'They probably found me to be distant and cruel. But the heat of the afternoon was waning, and with the cool night, the mysterious beast and its appetite would awaken and crawl out of hiding. So, I did my best to futilely bind the wounds of the young man, and ordered the others to make a bonfire outside with the wrecked wood, away from the barn that could be brought down on top of them, or that would be needed by them for shelter if they survived.' I sighed, thinking back over the hollow cries of fear that had escaped the grandmother's lips as I had gestured for the group to huddle near the flames. 'Admittedly, I believed a fire as well as the people around it would attract the beast's attention and draw it out. But I was also sure that the creature wouldn't wish to be too near the flames, and I knew I could keep the beast's focus on myself.'

'So, you preferred to announce your presence and let the animal come to you,' Aeron commented.

'In this instance, yes. Because it seemed this thing was brutish and predictable. I could have tracked it down and tried to surprise it, but I was just as successful waiting for a confrontation in the location of my own choosing.' I shook my head, reliving the amazement I had felt at the sheer size of the thing.

'The thing was not subtle when it arrived,' I went on. 'It seemed that Darziates had warped a bald, mole-like creature into something that was easily the size of two loaded carts. But it snuffled towards us noisily and bumped into the wreckage it had left previously because the three eyes in its pink skinned forehead were so ridiculously small as to be almost useless.'

'That explains the destruction and sloppiness in its previous attacks,' Aeron surmised.

'And faulty eyesight also meant it shied away from the firelight and couldn't stand to even look at the villagers,' I agreed. 'However, I foolishly took for granted that the beast would be quick to slaughter. My arrows did sink into its thick hide, but I could leave no fatal marks and before I knew it the beast had charged me and I was trying to get a grip on its wrinkly skin.' I shivered. 'I was trampled by some very hefty paws and whipped mercilessly by tentacle-like feelers before I realised that no matter how many times I stabbed the beast, I had to find its heart to do true damage. Thankfully, like a boar, I at last discovered that the heart was behind the beast's meaty shoulder.'

'And the villagers?' Aeron asked.

'The young man had passed away while I was engaged, and I left them to their mourning so that I could mend my own injuries without imposing on them. I had to be swift, as I had already heard rumours that a reptile of some kind was feasting on villagers to the south.'

Aeron's broad shoulders rose and fell with a large breath. 'The people of Krall suffer.'

'They have little way of surviving off the land,' I said. 'But they have been exposed to horrors for all of their lives and are more resigned than shocked by it. In contrast, when these beasts started appearing in Awyalkna, the Awyalknians reacted with terror, but also with disbelief and indignation that such a disturbance could happen in Awyalkna at all. Many times, when I saved Awyalknians, they would pile me with a list of complaints instead of thanks.'

Aeron chuckled low beside me.

'What of your own experiences?' I prompted him then.

'Oh, Jenrans do not suffer as those of Krall do,' Aeron answered. 'Yet Jenrans are not dissimilar in their reactions to danger.'

I remembered how, when word was spread of Griffin attacks, the people would shake their heads, but accepted that it was simply an unavoidable factor of their lives.

Aeron's tone was quiet and calm as he spoke. 'The Griffins can be sly,' he continued. 'They sometimes try to take people through windows or balconies. But the guard is always on watch and the Griffins rarely attempt something so risky unless they are starved. It is mostly the valley farmers who face regular abduction.'

'How do you target the Griffins in return?' I asked.

'We exterminate,' Aeron stated fiercely. 'The Griffins are vermin. If we are not careful, and do not cull, they will not only kill us by their violence, but through their germs and diseases. So, we often leave scrap heaps of rotten fish about the mountains, and lure in starving, desperate fiends. We also stalk out the nests of their kings.'

My eyebrows rose at the thought of such an adventure. Breathing would be incredibly hard at such altitudes, and one would have to be nimble and cold resistant to reach the heights of those nests.

'Hazardous,' I commented, approving of the idea of such a venture entirely.

'Only the most hardened squads attempt it. The men must be unnaturally good climbers, and are trained so thoroughly in group tactics that they think as a unit. No one man could take on the king-sized Griffins alone. Especially when faced with the king Griffin's nesting partners as well.' Aeron straightened as he sat, as if remembering an ailment in his back as we talked about such challenges. 'Stealth is key. We must wait for the wind to carry our scent in the opposite direction to our prey, so that we do not become the hunted. And we also use tactics similar to your own in that example.'

'What do you mean?' I questioned.

'Using human bait,' Aeron explained. 'Groups of soldiers put on their brightest uniforms and 'search' the mountains for trouble – parading through the most Griffin infested passes to tempt the enemy to come to us.'

'Are your measures effective?' I asked.

'Each week at least one hundred Griffins are slaughtered. Yet each day a new litter of Griffins is birthed. The cycle will never end. We simply maintain their numbers for them, to make our own lives safer.'

'Are injuries common?'

'The men are trained to handle shields and short swords, but death is not uncommon. The snap of a Griffin beak can easily be the slice of a vital artery or the fatal crack of a bone. Or one misplaced step can mean a nasty tumble out of an eyrie. Though even scratches or gashes have caused many soldiers to sicken and die.'

I winced at the thought, though I was also aware that Jenra was one of the most developed nations of men in the discovery and treatment of different illnesses. They had needed to learn, finding ways to combat the dangers of infections from the Griffins that plagued them.

'Lady Amarantha, Jenra's leading healer, is revered amongst our people for her research and methods of sanitation. She has saved countless lives from infection,' Aeron told me, as if reading my mind. He began to rise as faint touches of light returned to the sky. 'Lady Amarantha is perhaps our greatest warrior against the winged fiends, because of her efforts.'

He towered over me as he stood, and I noticed his soldiers purposely rising too, following his lead.

'It has been pleasant talking,' Aeron concluded our swapping of information, stretching his stiff muscles. 'I thank you.'

'I was glad to have shared the time with you,' I replied, standing as well.

'May I ask,' he started, and then cleared his throat. 'How is it that you know the Jenran language?'

I smiled a slight smile, aware that he wanted to know if I had ventured as far as Jenra before, without their knowledge. Perhaps he thought me to be a skilled spy, for nobody should be able to enter Jenra without having passed the unknown test.

'You are evaluating me again,' I said.

But I would not be elaborating on my lengthy, secretive stay in Jenra, where I had been a hidden presence in their midst, taking note of their healing practices, breathing exercises and even harvesting some of their exotic ingredients for my healer supplies.

'I simply feel it is courteous to know the language of those you wish to speak to.'

'Of course,' Warlord Aeron answered slowly. 'And soon, in the test, you will be heard by our entire nation.'

65

Sixty Five

N*oal*

I woke to Thorin gruffly nudging my shoulder. Every single part of my body ached. I could've sworn that every follicle, every cell, every tendril of hair, was throbbing.

'Agghhhh –'

'We're trying to look formidable, remember?' Thorin whispered, interrupting my moan. 'You need to put your alert face straight back on,' he prodded me in the ribs.

I lifted my head off the ground and saw Thale waking everyone else while our Jenran guards watched on.

'Ugh, Gods,' I gave a muffled whisper back. 'Right. I can do tough.'

I immediately pushed myself up, flexing my arms and stretching, looking for all the world as if I had awoken refreshed and ready to face a whole new nation.

I scooped up my pack and swung it cheerfully across my shoulders, as if it didn't feel like a sack of potatoes.

'Good job,' Thorin commented, resting his hand almost carelessly on the hilt of his curved sabre – back to the image of a warrior.

Kiana and Dalin joined us and our group came together as the Jenrans mounted and the march began again.

Our escorts remained largely silent as we stepped through wide grassy fields sprinkled with yellow, bobbing flowers. We too remained quiet as we drew closer to the Jenran city carved from the mountain and cliff faces.

We only started when our peace was broken by a great boom of noise that suddenly thundered across the countryside. The sound reverberated around the wide landscape, making pebbles on the ground shudder and birds lift off from trees with cries of surprise. Only moments later the boom of noise rumbled around us again, sounding louder than the heartbeat of a God.

'What *is* that?' Nikon asked Kiana disconcertedly, and we all glanced about in search of the source of the sound while still trying to appear undaunted.

'It's fine,' Kiana stated. 'I've read of this. It is the sound of the Jenran drums calling any who would come to witness our testing.'

'I hope that's what it means,' Ferron exclaimed. 'It sounds like we are being led to some kind of sacrificial ritual.'

'That ground shaking racket comes from drums?' Tane asked incredulously.

'Big drums,' Kiana reassured him. 'Very big.'

'And they are being used to summon the Jenrans to watch us?' Thale asked nervously from behind Thorin. 'I'd prefer not to have a nation sized audience.'

'Be flattered,' Kiana told him. 'Those drums are ancient and only used for such occasions as the crowning of new Kings and Queens and the call to war. Or,' she added, 'the testing of strangers.'

'So not very often then,' Purdor winced, not looking flattered or comforted at all.

As we drew closer to the looming gates at the base of the cliff carved entrance, the booming beat of the drums became so powerful that I felt as if my teeth rattled in my head.

'Oh Gods,' I heard Phrixus utter, gazing upward.

Between the many towers and rocky peaks there were countless walkways and halls that had open windows and sweeping balconies. And, filling every spare open space – spilling around every doorway and gap, there were swarms of people. So many thousands in each space that they looked simply like a shifting sea of shapes.

We were close enough now that we could hear the roaring anticipation and cheers of the crowds over the drum beats, the sound forming a roar that was almost as deafening.

Gideon swallowed nervously. 'They are very excited to witness what will happen to us.'

'Because we are the first visitors they have ever seen,' Kiana replied calmly.

My heart raced as Dalin and I at last approached the moment that our original quest had been focused on, and as I saw in the distance that the richly dressed figure of a crowned man, with archers at both of his sides, had stepped up onto the walkway at the gates.

When we reached the foot of the great gates the thunderous drumming stopped and the tumultuous storm of voices ceased, though the atmosphere still seemed to tremble with energy and echoes.

The King atop the gates stepped closer to the edge, and then he spoke in a deep and booming voice that carried down to us with words delivered in the Jenran language.

'You have come to Jenran land, strangers,' Kiana whispered in translation for us. 'But before you may enter into our halls you must first be proven friends. You must pass our test. If you refuse to take the test you will be escorted out of this land. If you fail this test, you will live no longer. If you pass this test, you will be welcomed forth, as dear to us as our own kin.'

The King paused, his gaze boring into us even from the distance. 'Do you agree to take the test?'

Kiana stepped forward, unflinching under the eyes of so many. She raised her hand, held in a fist, to her chest and gracefully bowed before straightening. 'Randaer tren Maelgon. Ge una vo opok gesh sphit ra vo ata lo forvoners,' she called in her clear, carrying voice.

There were muffled exclamations and the crowds shifted. But I couldn't make out if the man above was surprised.

'What did she say?' I asked in an undertone.

To my astonishment the leader of our guards, the Warlord who sat upon his horse beside us spoke in a low voice.

'Your companion has just greeted our King, mighty Durna,' he explained in a thick accent. 'She said: 'Hail great King. We agree to take your test and to accept the consequences.'

I raised my eyebrows.

So, he had known how to speak to us all along.

The King addressed us again, and Aeron translated once more. 'Will you speak for your group?'

'U des.' Kiana affirmed. 'I will.'

The King raised his hands and a servant came forth, opening an ornate box for Durna. Upon a cushion there sat a spiralling, sharp tipped rod of gold, and with reverent hands the King accepted the sceptre-like ornament.

'Beware that no lie is in the hearts of any of your group when you answer. For the golden horn will shine red,' Durna declared, and his voice seemed to project even further, as if the object had increased his personal power.

Kiana was gazing at the 'golden horn' in his hand intently as she answered.

'We will answer with truth and honour.'

I noticed Agrudek clinging nervously to a pendant around his neck, enfolding the flashing red jewel in his hand for comfort.

Then the King asked his first question and I focused back on the Warlord as he translated.

'Do you mean harm to the people of Jenra?' Durna questioned.

'Lin.' No.

I held my breath along with every Krall soldier and every Jenran above as the 'golden horn' judged each of us based on Kiana's unfaltering answer, and was stunned when the horn in the King's hands burst into a blindingly pure, golden light.

I found that I couldn't look away. Awe-struck wonder and joy flooded me as I gazed open-mouthed at it, realising that I could feel the timeless warmth of magic radiating from it even from here.

Only when the wondrous light faded was I able to shake myself out of my stupor, and the entire Jenran population broke into deafening outpours of cheering until King Durna raised the horn again, ready for the next question.

'Are you loyal to Darziates, his Witch, or any other evil?'

I heard the men shifting uneasily behind me and I was aware that Agrudek held his pendent more tightly, but not a shadow of doubt crossed Kiana's face as she answered.

'Lin.' No. Each of the Krall warriors had pledged themselves to the Three, to our quest. I thought I saw a glint of red out of the corner of my eye from Agrudek, but my attention was absorbed again as the horn burst forth with brilliant and enchanting light.

'Who are you?' Durna asked next.

'Representatives of Awyalkna, Krall and the beings of the forest.'

This time there wasn't such rapture and intent focus on the horn as it glowed gold. Instead, there were unrestrained gasps and exclamations that rippled up and down the mountain as word of what she'd said spread.

There were disbelieving calls and the recognisable words of 'Krall?' and 'Sylthanryn!' But the truth of that simple statement had been proven by the horn's glowing light.

Finally, the King asked: 'Why have you come?'

Kiana remained bold and confident. 'We have come to speak with you, King. To ask for the renewal of the ancient alliance between our lands, so that we may triumph over the evil Darziates has brought to this world.'

This time there were so many exclamations and outbursts of chatter that hardly anybody noticed the horn anymore and it took the King a number of moments to achieve silence before he asked his final question.

'I see a troop of Krall men marching with Awyalknians in friendship and co-operation,' the King stated. 'And your group presumes to evoke the alliances of old to bring Jenra into the war,' he said seriously. 'Tell us. Why should we listen to you?'

I held my breath as a hush descended over the scores of people along the mountain Kingdom as they watched Kiana and waited.

She took a step forward and peered up at the crowds keenly.

'The Lady of Sylthanryn foresaw that the world's races would become separate and that a deadly threat would be born at the end of the ninth age. She warned that the world must be united to survive, and that the war is not just between Awyalkna and Krall. Darziates' Sorcery is in fact a threat to all races.

But,' Kiana took a deep breath. 'The Lady has also foretold that there are to be three to lead the world to stand against this threat, and to unite all races against the Sorcerer.'

Total focus bore down on Kiana as the Jenran masses strained to hear her.

'I have travelled with Noal, Prince of Awyalkna, and Dalin, heir to the Awyalknian throne. We have crossed Awyalkna amidst constant threat from Darziates' creatures, and gained the allegiance of his sixteen warriors. We have crossed the largest forest in this world, and met the magical beings dwelling within. We have gained the allegiance of the Elves, the Nymphs and the Lady of Sylthanryn. And we have traversed the Jenran mountains to seek allegiance here, too. For we are the Three. And we mean to unite the mortal and magical races of this world to end the threat of Darziates in another War for the World.'

Kiana paced back to me, putting a hand on my shoulder. 'One to bring the Three and their allies together in their quest,' she called, and a shiver ran down my spine as her words were translated. Then she stood by Dalin. 'One to unite the lands of men, to lead all mortals in this war. The Raiden.'

Then she took her place between us.

'And I,' she called calmly – this time using *Aolen*, 'am the One. The One to summon and lead the magical races to combine with the mortals led by the Raiden.' She stepped forward. 'I am the last of the *Larnaeradee*.'

Aeron's translation stopped and he gaped, appearing as if it was the first time in his life that anything had ever taken him by surprise.

I felt a sudden rushing of air before Kiana's wings had appeared and were lifting her so that she hovered on an equal level with King Durna and his astounded archers on the gate to the city.

Her magic seemed to rain down over us, and it was almost as if I could see it beaming like the rays of the sun upon every person that beheld her.

'We have come to ask if Jenra will rise and unite with us, so that the threat to our world can be ended.'

The whole of Jenra was struck mute as the unmistakably glowing golden horn shone with a light even more brilliant than before. It throbbed and sparkled as if the power in it was somehow rejoicing too.

Then as the light faded, the city erupted with a cacophony of almighty cheers that shook the mountain even more than the drums had. Even if *Aolen* couldn't be spoken widely yet, it was clear that they had understood the message.

Kiana lowered back down to earth, settling between Dalin and I as Durna raised his voice once more.

'Welcome to Jenra!' he called. 'We have much to discuss, but let it be known that the Three and their comrades are as kin to our people and free to roam our halls!'

More cheers punctuated his announcements.

'Enter our city, friends. For we have long awaited you!'

66

Sixty Six

D*alin*

I felt my stomach lurch at the King's words.

'What?' Tane asked in confusion. The King and his archers were quickly disappearing from the top of the gate and there was the groaning sound of its mechanisms while it was pulled open.

'There is another population that has 'long awaited' us?' Noal exclaimed over the thundering crowd. 'I thought only the Lady and the forest dwellers knew about the Three.'

Thorin was frowning up at the city as if the Jenrans were all mad. 'We just delivered as much ghastly news as good news. You'd think mention of war would result in a more subdued response.'

Kiana simply shrugged. 'The King did say that there would be much to discuss. We must wait and learn.' She started toward the gate as the vast city of Jenra opened before us and we followed her while our Jenran guards dismounted and fell in at our sides, guiding us through the gates in a procession.

The gates hulked over us for a moment, before we passed into the incredible mountain kingdom, and were instantly overwhelmed by the sheer size of the endless cavern before us.

The mountain's interior appeared to be made up of a number of expansive, hollowed levels of cool, artfully shaped rock. Light poured in from large balconies and windows in the mountain walls, illuminating the level we were on, which spanned for as far as the eye could see. There were sprawling markets and village areas, dwellings, gardens, stone fountains, stalls, sheds and workplaces all built inside.

And everywhere people were crowded, craning to see us, their voices intensified and echoing excitedly under the high roof. Our Jenran guards parted a clear way for us, and soon the multitudes of voices began to quieten – with people clearing the way and bowing as King Durna approached.

I noted that he was taller than the Jenran officials flanking him, with a frame that suggested he was a man of strength. His dark, short beard was flecked with silver and covered a strong jaw, but despite his steely exterior he greeted us with a wide, welcoming smile and the people he passed watched him with respect as he drew to a stop before us.

Our guards bowed and Noal and I swept ourselves into a similar stance that the warriors of Krall quickly copied. But as we straightened from our bow Kiana was already stepping forward.

'Before we begin, you have heard and understood *Aolen*, but now I will also give you the gift of being able to converse in the language,' she said to the King, her voice carrying across the now hushed crowd. I felt the power laced within her musical words and felt the magic as if it were plucking at my soul, pulling me to step close to her.

'Now you may remember the language of your forefathers and spread this gift to others.'

By pouring power into her words, it seemed that her magic was spreading outwards in an expanding blanket as the people closest to us shifted and murmured in amazement, and the people beyond them slowly began to react too.

I saw a young girl nearby clasping her ears in shock, as if she'd suddenly been granted the gift of hearing.

'I thank you,' the King gasped in halting *Aolen*. 'You can truly perform miracles if you are able to so quickly teach a nation a forgotten tongue. Your presence lightens our hearts. And you are all most honoured guests in Jenra. You will be treated as kin here and will be taken to rooms where you can rest.'

'We thank you for your hospitality,' Kiana answered. 'And will look forward to meeting with you to begin our deliberations before we must cross back through the mountains.'

'After today's undisturbed rest the discussions will begin,' Durna promised. 'Then, perhaps, there will be little rest for any of us.'

Durna gestured to Aeron then, who stepped forward.

I couldn't fail to notice the striking resemblance between the King and his Warlord, and realised that they must be siblings.

'Warlord Aeron will show you to private quarters so that you may have peace for now. I myself will eagerly wait to speak with the Three in council tomorrow morning, and in the night, we will ease our minds from meetings to feast in celebration of your coming.'

I felt the eyes of every member of the public fall upon us once more and there was the deafening sound of everyone within range beginning to speak animatedly at once, testing out the *Aolen* tongue.

We unquestioningly followed the looming Aeron's lead through the thronging, gaping crowds, moving towards a section of the mountain wall that had a lavish stairway.

I noticed that long ladders ran up the wall that we were drawing closer to, and I craned my neck to see that those ladders stretched so high upward that they disappeared through faraway openings in the roof, continuing into the level above us. I realised that there were confident, flitting figures of different Jenrans on those ladders, and they scurried up and down them without fear now that the show was over. Some people had even stopped to have casual conversations with those high up on the ladders neighbouring them.

'I'm glad we're taking the stairs,' I murmured to Thorin, who was cringing as he watched a child sliding down a nearby ladder to the floor. 'I've had enough of heights and scaling.'

'What are those?' Noal asked with wonder, and I diverted my attention toward what could only be described as a series of cages all along the wall. They were being lifted up toward another hole in the roof by a series of incredibly thick, oiled ropes, each carrying heavy cargo inside.

'Elevators,' Kiana answered.

'What are elevators, then?' Noal asked. 'How are they going up and down like that?'

'A pulley system lifts them up and down. They hold things that are too heavy or slow to carry up to the highest levels of the mountain,' Kiana explained as we reached the foot of the smooth stone steps.

It was a short flight of stairs that led to a wide, upward-slanting passage looking out upon the market level on one side, and also overlooking the valleys on the other side. The passage was like one giant balcony winding up the mountain, carved into the inside of the mountain itself.

'Even though it's inside, this city seems far superior to the cramped living in Krall's sectors,' Phrixus commented, wide-eyed as he stared down into the spectacular market.

We reached another spurt of steps and Cadell ran his hand along the cool, neat stone of the balcony ledge. 'Everyone lives together inside one giant mountain palace, and even the lowest ranking people appear to have clean water and paved streets. Did you see those fountains?'

'The King probably lives separately in the highest rooms of the mountain, but he comes down to the lowest levels and walks among his people comfortably,' Tane added with an impressed tone. 'I think he will be a reasonable leader to meet with.'

'It would be nice to have a King like that,' I heard the reserved voice of Lydon from the back. 'I didn't have such a pleasant experience when I was in a crowd where King Darziates happened to appear once.'

'Did you all get blasted out of the way?' Thale asked sympathetically.

'No,' Lydon answered bleakly. 'He didn't need to use magic to clear the way. The automatic surge of people running for cover cleared the market quickly enough, and a few people were crushed in the stampede.'

'Which sector was this in?' Aiolos asked.

'South Krall Domain,' Lydon replied, still looking aggrieved at the memory.

'In North Krall Province, when I was a child,' Aiolos started a memory of his own, 'it was rumoured that Darziates would disguise himself and spy on citizens, listening for betrayal.'

'Who knows if that's true,' Rendor added beside him. 'But unexplained disappearances were common enough that people kept to themselves and kept their mouths closed.'

'There were similar stories in Western Sector,' Wolf grunted.

'And in the Eastern Region,' Roth affirmed, breaking his usual silence.

Purdor spoke up then. 'I never heard of him checking up on the border villages, though. Those people are too exhausted to think up ways to betray the Sorcerer.'

There was a mollified silence for a few moments as we all took in the clean, well-cared for society blossoming on the next level that we passed into.

'That's the kind of life Darziates hopes to impose on every other land as well,' Vulcan commented at last. 'Gods, I hope the Jenrans agree to an alliance.'

'Well,' Kiana sighed, 'absorb all you can about the way this nation functions, anyway. Because you are the only people of Krall to have seen that there are other ways of life. You are the ones who have to carry word back home.'

'I'm no good at explaining systems,' Nikon shook his head.

'We're warriors, not ambassadors,' Phobos agreed. 'And no Sorcerer infected citizen would listen.'

'Nevertheless, Krall will need all of the help it can get,' Kiana answered.

'Relax comrades, old Wilmont ensured that the Raiden and I are well trained for such tasks as setting up a country's ruling system,' Noal announced. 'We'll help.'

'Oh dear Gods, save us,' Tane appealed to the heavens.

Jenrans that we passed as we climbed stared and politely bowed or curtsied as we reached higher levels, but most traffic still seemed to take place on the ladders and at one point a loudly mooing cow swung upward past the balcony in one of the elevator cages.

Each level we wound around was lined with buzzing indoor streets just as busy as the last, though the levels finally began to grow steadily smaller and were filled with grander homes and offices, along with people who were each officially or ornately dressed. And then at last the hallway opened out and stopped at a level that was simply made up of a circular room. There were four stairways leading in different directions.

'No wonder the Jenrans seem so fit,' Noal puffed, holding a stitch in his side. 'With so much climbing.'

'We're not even anywhere near the peak,' Kiana told us with her slight smile. 'Or we would be freezing and struggling to breathe.'

'Your rooms are on the southwest stair, overlooking the valleys,' Warlord Aeron stated, breaking his silence and leading us to that stairway. 'The other stairways lead to the rooms of council members, the King's offices and quarters, and homes of high-ranking soldiers.'

We started up the southwest stairs where there were no longer the sweeping windows, but doors to rooms instead, and we all stopped with relief as Aeron halted at these doors.

'These are the apartments of the princes and princesses from generations past, but King Durna has no children,' Aeron informed us. 'You, as our honoured guests, will have these rooms as your own. Lady,' he said to Kiana, 'I pray you find this chamber comfortable.' He crossed to one door and opened it for her so that I caught a glimpse of a wide balcony and silk decorating the room's roof and walls, shimmering gold and red.

'Thank you, Warlord,' Kiana answered. 'At last – some privacy and a bath.'

For her, his serious face relented, producing a smile.

'This quarter will be for Your Majesties,' he said, turning to Noal and I.

He opened the door to the next room so that I saw another elaborately decorated space.

'And for the Krall guardians of the Three, each of you may choose to share any of these other chambers, with four beds to a room.'

We all thanked the Warlord before he descended the steps, and then at last we were alone again – all twenty of us, and we allowed ourselves to droop our shoulders and sag with the fatigue we felt.

'Rest time,' Kiana stated, before wearily stepping through to her spectacular room and closing the door.

'Agreed,' Thale muttered, trudging towards the closest door and already loosening his roll of armour. A few others followed him and the remaining men began to choose rooms of their own.

Noal and I entered our own chamber, where red silk adorned the golden painted walls and red and gold cushions covered two majestic beds. Wooden doors behind golden, veil like curtains led out onto a glorious balcony, and at the base of one wall there was a small, pristine pool lined with sparkling blue tiles.

However, Noal and I regarded our surroundings with only dull wits, dropping our bags onto a plush, crimson rug before we both sprawled luxuriously on the beds.

67

Sixty Seven

D*alin*

My eyes opened to see the blazing sun setting through the open doors to the balcony.

I blinked as I remembered where we were, and squinted across the room to find that Noal still slept contentedly.

I rose from the bed stiffly, and followed the warm sunshine out to the balcony that continued around to Kiana's chamber.

I found that the doors to her own balcony were open and Kiana was sitting on her bed, combing her freshly washed hair with a golden comb that matched the spectacular dresser against one of the walls.

The red jewel at her throat glittered magnificently in the light as she glanced up with a smile while I leaned in the doorway, watching her movements.

'Did you sleep well?' I asked when she put the comb down.

'Almost as well as I used to in Sylthanryn,' she answered, looking resplendent in the golden light as she rose to lead me out to the balcony ledge. 'There is a different kind of ancient magic here that I can feel running all through this mountain. It makes me feel safe, and as though no malice could live in the city because of it.'

'I wondered if somehow this whole place had been made by pure magic,' I answered, leaning against the balcony beside her. 'The mountain city is huge, and too impossible to be of mortal make.'

She nodded, and I relished the warmth and the slight ticklish tingling of her power dancing from where her arm made contact with mine.

'I am sure the golden horn that tested us is a clue,' she mused, now leaning her head upon my shoulder to gaze at the meadows below in the late afternoon haze.

'You seem to be gaining greater understanding of your own magic,' I commented and felt her nod.

'The effort of channelling the power from the atmosphere and earth became a tiring task as we descended,' she stroked her tourmaline stone. 'But I think as long as I am surrounded by the elements, I will be able to channel their power. The greater the energy around me, the greater I will be able to achieve, and perhaps it will be only the limits of my own mind that gives me any obstacles.'

With that, she reached out her hand, and suddenly an orange ball of wispy fire was flickering upon her palm.

My eyes widened. 'You have only ever made spheres of your own magic with the help of a spark or another flame,' I gasped. 'You are progressing quickly.'

With a flicker of her fingers the flame extinguished. 'The tiniest bit of the heat of the atmosphere and the light of the sun were all I needed. And at night I'm sure the heat of rubbing my hands together or breathing into them would be enough.'

I leaned forward and gingerly put my hand into hers where the flame had been, and her brilliant blue eyes were on mine. But we stirred when there was a drumming knock on the heavy door to Kiana's room.

After a pause Kiana broke away from me and crossed back into the room to find Thale waiting at the door.

'I hope you are well rested,' Thale greeted us rather politely, appearing pensive as Kiana invited him in. At once I joined Kiana in sitting on the silk covered bed, both of us watching Thale questioningly.

He cleared his throat and rubbed at his beard, his deep brows almost meeting.

'The lads and I, we've all agreed, that now that the Three are revealed, and are obviously so revered in Jenra ... Well, we've all decided that we will be your guards. In fact, we are adamant about it. We wish to be aware of everyone around you from now on, because you are too important, we owe you, and we like you too much to let anything happen to any of the Three.' Thale now faced us squarely. 'From now on there will be a guard when you are in your rooms, and when you leave those rooms more of us will accompany you without question. We will take shifts and keep each other updated. I will hear no objections.'

He stopped then and straightened his shoulders with a hardened expression as he awaited our reply.

'It sounds like a good idea,' Kiana answered simply.

'It's an honourable and appreciated idea,' I confirmed. 'There are no others I would trust as highly to guard my back.'

Thale's face broke into a beaming smile. 'We were concerned you would reject us. Of course, none of the Three are inexperienced or helpless, and the Gods chose you for a reason, but we couldn't allow you to face possible danger alone.'

'So, the men all sent you in here to order us to accept your protection,' Kiana smiled her faint smile.

'That is the crux of it,' Thale nodded. 'Except for Agrudek, who has been muttering over his necklace as if he has been driven to the edge of his wits.'

Before I could feel my face darken at the scientist's name, we heard a clatter echo from mine and Noal's room.

I laughed. 'Poor Noal's probably awoken only to fall over with hunger.' I stood to check on him.

'Raiden, this could be my first mission,' Thale suggested. 'I could check on him and you and the One could continue your time together.'

I felt warmth touch my cheeks and was suddenly glad that I remained unshaven, but Kiana's expression simply appeared entertained.

'I'll go settle him back down,' I reassured Thale as if Noal were a fussy baby, quickly leaving for the balcony once more.

'And, I may have to speak to you further about your guard duties,' I heard Kiana begin to deliver a shattering contradiction to Thale's proposal as I left.

'I will be practising the art of flight while I am here,' I heard her say calmly. 'And there is no way I'm going to carry a group of big men along with me. Or at least not just yet.'

'Ahhhhh ...' I could just imagine the defeat on Thale's face. 'But Griffins ...'

I grinned, knowing she would always have some excuse to allow herself independence.

68

Sixty Eight

N^{oal}

I woke suddenly with the feeling of being watched.

I at once tensed for danger, but instead found a pretty blonde woman gazing at me.

She jumped, startled by my quick waking, and slammed a tray of food down on the table in a rush.

I shook myself alert and rushed to sit up, holding my hands out in a placating gesture.

'Sorry!' I told the wide-eyed beauty. 'I didn't mean to frighten you.'

She quickly curtsied and spun on her heel to devote herself to wiping at a spot of ale that had spilled from the two tankards on the tray.

'My apologies, Your Highness,' she said hurriedly in a sweet, nervous voice.

I thanked the Gods for *Aolen* and the fact that I could understand her.

In a flurry of movement, she began to set the table for a meal. 'I shouldn't have woken you. I didn't mean to stare.'

She sounded mortified and I blanched at the formality in her address. I smoothed my hair and noticed that I'd fallen asleep fully clothed, even my sword still belted uncomfortably at my side. But I hardly worried at it.

'What is your name?' I asked her.

Long wisps of blonde hair fell in waves down her back and over her shoulders, and she wore a simple, grey maiden's dress with a white apron.

'My name is Noal,' I prompted.

'... Prince Noal,' she corrected me absently, and then whirled back around with a horrified expression on her love-heart face.

'It loses effect if people have to use my full title all of the time,' I grinned, and saw the wariness fade in her stiffened posture. 'Imagine if even my closest minders had been forced to shout: 'Your Royal Majesty, Prince Noal, put down that frog!'

I mimicked an admonishing carer for her.

A wavering smile broke out across her sunny, cherubic features. 'I hardly think I would need to tell you to leave frogs alone at your age,' she ventured, and my grin widened.

'You have no idea the kinds of things I have to tell him to put down, even at this age,' came a friendly voice at the door, and I looked to find Dalin stepping off the balcony and into the room.

She turned quickly, at once curtsying formally. 'Raiden,' she murmured with reverence, then she scurried to the door and disappeared without having told me her name.

I sighed disconsolately.

'Oops. Sorry to have spoiled your conversation,' Dalin winced as he crossed to me, taken aback. 'I didn't mean to scare her away.'

I nodded. 'You can't help the way people react to you,' I told him glumly.

'She actually looked even more like an angel than you do,' Dalin replied, taking a seat at the small table to begin the dinner she'd laid out for us. 'And obviously she had enough of an effect on what is normally your immediate appetite.'

'She was lovely,' I said honestly, joining him without enthusiasm.

'She will probably be the one to come back for our dishes, and I will likely be gone to visit with Kiana again by then,' Dalin replied tactfully.

And my spirits lifted enough for me to properly enjoy our first quality meal since Sylthanryn as the food disappeared from our plates.

I tried not to rush Dalin out of the room as he took a painstakingly long time to bathe and to scrape away his stubble before it was my turn to bathe, dress and shave.

Then when a faint knock came at the door, I had enough time to swiftly pat my face dry as the maiden slipped back into our room, this time with a flaming torch in her hand. She curtsied shyly, but with a smile.

'You're back,' I grinned, trying not to sound too joyous.

'I pray you enjoyed your meal,' she returned politely, beginning to light the torches in our room.

'Not at all,' I sighed, and lowered myself into a red, cushioned chair.

She paused and frowned with worry. 'You didn't?'

'No,' I shrugged sadly. 'You never told me your name. I was too upset to enjoy the food.'

She laughed a light, clear peal of laughter. 'I could get you something else to see if you enjoy that better,' she tried.

I shook my head. 'It won't do any good. I need just one word and my heart and appetite will be healed,' I informed her.

She crossed to my side of the room to light the last torch. 'I am just a maid; you have no true need for my name.'

'Well,' I reasoned, 'you know mine.'

'Yes. Everyone knows your name,' she rebutted.

'I did also go to some effort for you, so that my appearance might frighten you less than before.' I folded my hands in my lap, reasonable and business-like. 'It's only fair you show me kindness in return.'

'I don't think you could ever look frightening –' she began, but then blushed furiously.

I beamed and she relaxed again. 'What else could I do then, to earn the knowledge of your name?'

She put her free hand on a curvy hip. 'You are a prince. You could order me to tell you.'

I changed to an offended expression this time. 'Abuse my power? When I'm having so much fun charming your name out of you? I don't think so.'

Her features had softened and she became more at ease. 'I can think of nothing else, and I have finished lighting the torches, so I must clear your dishes and leave you.' She set her own torch into a free holder on the wall.

I put a hand to my heart with a pained expression. 'You would leave me in torment?'

'Torment?' she asked. 'You have only just met me and you may not even see me again after this.'

'All the more reason that I should know your name and treasure it.' I paused. 'Will I really not see you again?'

She relented, pleased. 'I have been assigned to your rooms. You will see me.'

I brightened. 'Then wouldn't it be pleasant if I could greet you by your name?'

'If I were doing my job correctly, I would be unobtrusive enough that you would not notice me,' she winced.

'How could I not notice you?' I asked. 'And I don't see that your occupation should be a barrier to me behaving kindly towards you.'

She smiled hesitantly. 'Kindness is always appreciated,' she said. 'I am Maeve.'

'Maeve,' I breathed the name. 'Thank you.'

She swept across the room, took up the tray of our dishes, and returned to the still open door. 'I will see you tomorrow.' She cast deep brown eyes over me with one last smile. 'Goodnight.'

Then she was gone again and I flopped back happily in my chair.

'See you at breakfast,' I announced optimistically to the spot where she'd been standing.

'Oh dear,' Dalin remarked dryly when he returned later and caught a glimpse of my face. 'Does that expression warn me I should make myself scarce after every meal now?'

I nodded. 'You would really only be in the way if you were here,' I told him winsomely.

He dropped down across his bed. 'It is fortunate that I asked Kiana if I could join her for breakfast,' he mused.

'Yes!' I exclaimed eagerly. 'Very fortunate!'

And Dalin was still rumpled from sleep and squinting against the light in only his hurriedly pulled on trousers when I propelled him down to Kiana's room the following morning.

'I feel *unfortunate*,' he grumbled unclearly as I tossed his shirt to Kiana while he groaned and sank down onto her bed. He assumed much the same position he'd been in before I'd rolled him off his own bed.

'You're lively this morning,' Kiana told me as I skipped back onto the balcony.

Then I heard her say to Dalin. 'But you're not.'

I was tactfully leaning on the balcony when I heard the faint knock and Maeve's light footsteps.

'Good morning, Maeve,' I couldn't help beaming when I saw her, and her own smile in return made mine grow wider still.

'Did you sleep well ... Noal?' she asked in her melodious voice as she set down the tray for breakfast.

'Not at all.'

She gave a good-humoured gasp. 'And why ever not?'

'You have told me nothing but your name. I couldn't sleep from wondering about you.'

'Ahh,' she pondered. 'Never fear. You will have a long, tense day today. That will tire your mind for tonight.'

I shook my head. 'What if wondering about you distracts me from my prophesied duties? It could put the world's fate in jeopardy.'

Maeve tapped her rounded cheek with delicate fingers. 'After facing the Sorcerer's creatures and travelling all the way here on your quest, you would let yourself be distracted by a desire to know more about me?'

'It seems a shame,' I nodded, half mesmerised. 'But you must see that it's critical you tell me about yourself when there's so much at stake.'

'It wouldn't be a fair exchange,' she reasoned. 'I – and everybody – already know all about you. An adopted Awyalknian prince, part of the Three.'

I grimaced. 'None of that really describes me. However, it does mean you must provide me with some superficial details about yourself until we're even.'

She grew intrigued. 'I would be interested to learn what more there is to you than all of that.'

I grinned. 'To help balance things out a bit, I need just one fact about yourself for now. It will keep me going through the day so that I can be the prophesied prince you know me to be.'

'One fact?' her petal-like lips quirked up thoughtfully.

I nodded. 'For today.'

She tapped her fingernails on the table she'd set the breakfast out on before her face brightened.

'One fact is that I will be helping the other maids to make the beds of every room on this level when you are out. I have a very different role in life to you.'

I crinkled my nose. 'That's not the kind of fact I meant,' I protested.

'It's a fact all the same,' she told me. 'A fact of life.'

'Is that part of your daily routine then?'

Maeve held up a finger. 'No cheating,' she admonished. 'You said just one for today.'

'Yes, but I'm expanding on that one fact now. That's well within the rules.'

'Is it?' she laughed lightly. 'Well in that case, yes, I do that among other things each day.'

'What other things?' I prompted her audaciously, already making a mental note to ensure everyone in our group got straight onto making their beds nicely.

'Other things ... like picking out what lovely garments you will be wearing to the feast held in your honour tonight,' she said. 'So, if you cheat too much, I may have to pick you something with Griffin feathers.'

'Griffin feathers?' I asked weakly, 'I'd die of the stench.' I felt my shoulders droop slightly as I realised that a feast for dinner meant I probably wouldn't see her again for the rest of the day.

'You must have your breakfast then,' Maeve pulled out the chair I was meant to be sitting in pointedly. 'You'll need your strength.'

Every sense within my body was aware of how close she was as I moved to be seated in the chair she stood behind, and she leaned across quickly to straighten the cutlery.

'Just one more fact?' I pleaded, gazing up at her face.

Maeve slowly picked up her tray again, and I felt sure she wished she could stay with me in that moment, too.

'I love flowers.' She withdrew from the table. 'Despite the risk outside, I travel down the mountain every day when my noon chores are done just to roam the valleys for a short while.'

'And now I will be able to get through today,' I told her confidently.

Maeve smiled warmly before she made her way to the door once more and was gone from the room.

At once the grand bedroom seemed suddenly less brilliant, and I felt an odd tugging in my chest that suggested I was in trouble.

It suggested that perhaps from now on everything would be less brilliant whenever Maeve had to walk away from me.

I forlornly poked a berry with my fork, and when I bit into it, its juices were not as sweet as usual.

69

Sixty Nine

Noal

Thorin and Thale flanked us as we followed Warlord Aeron back down the mountain to a lower-level exit onto the coast side.

A fresh breeze carried the scent of salt and I heard the thunderous crashing of waves and the rushing of the wind even before we had left the tower stairs to stand upon sand.

'Gods,' I uttered under my breath, forgetting the stitch in my side as I stood next to the equally stunned Dalin, Thorin and Thale. We were dumbfounded by the expansive, shifting water before us, and had to stop to at last properly behold the wild, rolling ocean up close. 'It's like a bathing pool for the Gods.'

'Its size seems an impossibility, yet it is part of reality all the same,' Thale shook his head.

'Everything in Jenra exists on unbelievable scales,' Thorin declared, watching while waves lapped against a wide strip of dazzling white sand that sparkled in the early morning sun. 'It is incredible.'

The sand stretched along the bottom of the mountain cliff, but ahead of us the water appeared to reach further than the sky did – the amazing blue-green mass melding with the horizon.

'It's dangerous,' Kiana warned, jutting her chin toward larger, faraway waves crashing and breaking in tumults of white foam. That was a sign that the splashes lapping at the shore were but mere demonstrations of the power of the ocean.

Small fishing boats navigated their way along the coast, but I doubted that the Jenrans had ever developed larger vessels to explore the furious seas, because no stories of mortals finding the lands beyond had ever been told.

We all tore our eyes from the spectacular view only when Aeron cleared his throat. 'It is certainly wondrous and treacherous at the same time,' he stated, and then gestured for us to follow him down a long, pebbled trail at the base of the cliff wall, only stopping us as we approached a large cave opening in the rock face.

'These are the ocean caves of Miridoon,' Aeron went on in his deep voice. 'Only Jenran eyes have seen these caves for generations. They are one of Jenra's greatest secrets, though under these special circumstances our council welcomes you here. Before entering Miridoon, you must pledge to never betray this secret to anyone beyond the rest of your party, who have all passed the test. The power surrounding this place will make your pledge binding, and will also impact on your comrades.' He paused, regarding each of us. 'If you are willing to pledge, you must simply say: 'I shall never divulge the secret of Miridoon', and you will be allowed to pass inside.'

Kiana didn't hesitate to pledge confidently, and each of us repeated the pledge before Aeron nodded, satisfied, and again gestured for us to follow.

I felt bubbles of nervous excitement as we stepped into the cool darkness of the cave, and then a strange tingling crossed my skin. Magic.

We found three archways to different tunnels and followed Aeron to where a flickering golden light glimmered through the entrance to the middle arch. The middle arch opened into another cave-like room carved out of rock and adorned by countless stalactites and stalagmites.

King Durna and eleven of his twelve council members were seated in what appeared to be an ancient ring of rock chairs circling a perfectly rounded and smoothed rock table.

But it was the walls of this cave that caught my attention. Filling every spare space on the rocky surfaces were dazzling images – artworks in such vibrant colours and drawn in such detail that they seemed real, and could not possibly have been drawn by mortal hands.

I shivered as I saw that in many of the images there were three figures.

The three of us.

Aeron took his seat as the twelfth council member and I tried to refocus.

'Welcome,' Durna said with as serious a face, 'to our ocean caves. Where we must hear all facts and must debate before tonight's feasting and before the fate of Jenra will be decided.' He motioned with outstretched arms at the artistry around us. 'As you can see, there are many things to discuss.'

He gestured then to three empty chairs that had been added to the circle and the three of us silently took our places while our Krall guards took posts at the walls behind us.

'All secrets spoken within these caves are kept hidden by the crashing of the waves on the shore,' Durna went on. 'And the artworks of the caves themselves are known only to Jenrans. In daylight we watch so that none come from the sea or air to steal this knowledge, and at night the caves are sealed when the tide comes in.'

I saw that water still dripped from the walls and puddles had been left across the uneven floors as King Durna turned to our real business.

'I must begin by explaining, in a very short time, things that no one outside of Jenra will have heard. I believe once that is done it will be easier for you to share your tale, and then for us to form resolutions together.' The King straightened his shoulders, his eyes keen. 'The Jenrans have known of the prophecies and the forest dwellers perhaps even without the Lady of the forest being aware that it was so. We remained silent lest any messages between the mountains and the forest should fall into the hands of Darziates. The Griffins would not hesitate to advance themselves by intercepting us.' Again, he gestured at the wondrous works of art upon the cave walls. 'The prophecies, and more, have in fact been laid out for us in these images of the past and future, and were given to us by an ancient race that once called this place Karanoyar.'

I heard Kiana's intake of breath, and Durna nodded.

'This was where the original Unicorns first lived. And where the few surviving Unicorns returned as their last hiding place after Darziates' massacre. With them came many of our forefathers, a host of mortals who could not bear to lose the last of the Unicorns. Jenra was but a small Kingdom before they arrived, but in appreciation for the shelter that was offered, those Unicorns used their power to create our city so that we could be safe. Before the remaining Unicorns dwindled further and weakened with age, they used their power to create these images so that we would always remember the Lady's warnings and be ready.'

'The golden horn that tested us?' Kiana asked.

'Was the horn of the last Unicorn to have lived,' Durna supplied. 'She gave it to the line of Jenran Kings as her parting gift so that it might help us. And though we mortals cannot use it for much, finding the truth is but a trifle of what it can do.' King Durna paused. 'For example, the horn can allow us to easily find our way through the mountains. With the horn we have access to the tunnel that runs right through the heart of the mountain you climbed, the very tunnel the Unicorns first used to get into Karanoyar and again to leave it when Treyun met Farne the *Larnaeradee*.'

Awe and relief flooded the features of the three of us as we processed how quickly the brutal mountains could be traversed if there was no need to climb them.

'We kept this secret jealously guarded against Darziates or any strangers, and aside from your party, the tunnel can also never be spoken of to anyone else while the threat to the world remains. Your pledge binds you to silence on the matter,' Durna said, and we all nodded our acceptance. 'Yet, though we do not often leave our home, there are those who are sent outside of the mountains to collect information. We have heard news of happenings in the other mortal lands, and had in fact already held talks over whether the time has come for us to leave our safe mountain home. We feared that Darziates might do to me what he did to Razek, and trap me into an alliance with Krall. Our thoughts have already been heavy with notions of war, alliances and questions about leaving,' Durna explained. 'But now I think the rest of the story is yours to tell.'

Kiana recounted our story in full for them, and I was aware of the eerie fact that as she described each of our pasts and our journey, the eyes of the council members moved from her to cave drawings that depicted the very events she spoke of.

There was an image of Dalin and I in the woods when we met Kiana, an image of Kiana speaking to the willow, of Dalin defending Kiana from sixteen Krall warriors, of the Lady and the forest dwellers. And a particularly spectacular depiction of Kiana with her wings when she first received her earthstone.

'And that is where the tale halts for now,' Kiana said finally. 'We are here at last to seek your help.'

They were all silent for a moment, and Durna sat forward thoughtfully. 'Yes. That is where it halts for now,' he looked to his council. 'We have long debated our reasoning for and against re-joining the world, and now have heard the words of the Three to help guide our decisions further. We cannot ignore that the arrival of the Three is a profound sign. While I suspect that most are ready to vote now, I ask all members of the council to think carefully and to take time to reflect. After our feast tonight we will come together once more tomorrow to decide on Jenra's fate. Much is at stake over our decision, no matter what we decide.'

70

Seventy

K*iana*

I was peaceful as I soaked in the sparkling bathing pool, watching the sun set in a blaze of oranges and pinks through the doors to the balcony.

A fleet of birds dashed across the sun and I considered what it would be like to join them as I let the dripping spout of water trickle droplets down my spine.

The drops shimmered on my nearly transparent wings, clinging like crystals, and I traced a finger over the little blue tiles beneath me, thinking of blue open skies.

At last, I rinsed the perfumed soaps from my body and stood, and I was nearly dry when an almost imperceptible knock came at the door.

'Yes?' I called, drawing a light cotton robe about myself.

The door opened and a pretty face peered cautiously around it. 'My Lady ... One,' the young maid began hesitantly. 'We have come to help you dress, if it pleases you.'

Her rounded face was sweet and honest, and golden hair seemed to float in wisps around it. This must be Maeve, I thought, based on Dalin's descriptions. She had been nervous and quick in visiting my room each time so far.

'You may come in,' I told her warmly. 'But I've been able to clothe myself since early childhood.'

She stepped uncertainly in, carrying an extravagant red gown in her arms, and an equally young and meek second maid followed her inside, closing the door.

They both curtsied daintily, but I shifted uncomfortably under their reverent stares and quickly allowed my wings to disappear so that I might appear more normal.

'Perhaps I will need your aid if I am to dress in something of that scale,' I admitted at the sight of the magnificent gown.

'One,' Maeve shook herself back into action. 'My name is Maeve and this is Kerrin.'

I hid a smirk. I'd heard how Noal had needed to pry a name out of her. This maiden had been teasing him.

'Kerrin picked this dress from the seamstress for you, and is skilled at delicate stitching and refining. She'll make it as if the dress was made exactly for you,' Maeve went on, unaware of how much I already enjoyed her nature. 'I am also very good at arranging hair, if that is acceptable to you?'

I cleared my throat. 'It is nice to meet you properly. Please call me Kiana. I shall follow your lead obediently.'

Maeve set the sweeping red dress down on my bed and then approached to take my cotton robe.

'Every woman in Jenra is going to envy you,' Kerrin said shyly as she came forward with the underclothes.

'In a dress like that,' I shrugged.

'It's not the dress,' Maeve assured me. 'You're quite impressive.'

I was abashed for a moment, unused to such conversation with other females.

'There are too many scars and muscles for this body to be impressive,' I told them then in what was my honest opinion. Though at least Agrona's brand was less grotesque, having turned silver.

There was a tut of disagreement as I let Kerrin guide me into the complex layers of underclothes.

'Scars are the patterns of survival,' Maeve told me. 'Yours are decorations of a life bravely lived. Such marks are quite respected here in Jenra, as most scars of note tell the tale of surviving Griffins or something equally challenging. Unfortunately, most don't get to survive such things to bear the outward signs.'

'Maeve is a volunteer healer,' Kerrin explained her friend's passion, and endeared Maeve to me even more. 'She is especially proud when she can help someone to live with a scar instead of die of an infected wound. Yours are just as much to be proud of.'

I was quietly, surprisingly, relieved and pleased by their words. I wasn't as uncomfortable as I'd feared I would be when they began to work around me.

They became more confident as they focused on their tasks, and I relaxed and let them do as they pleased until, after a session of hair brushing, light powders being puffed across my face, perfume dabbing and lip painting, they stepped back.

'You are flawless,' Maeve told me while I peered into the looking glass to admire how she had swept my hair up.

Kerrin had also stepped back from the now perfectly fitting, striking dress that was closely matched to the colour of my earthstone.

The material of the gown was heavy and flowing. The bodice hugged across my chest down to my navel, where it bunched and wrapped around my hips. From my hips the skirts swept outward and down to the floor, and the whole image I now presented was one of extravagance and elegance. Something that I had never expected to experience, even in my wildest imaginings as a girl dreaming with Joelle.

I thanked the two maidens whole heartedly as they led me from the room, where I was met with an abrupt silence as the banter that had been raging in the corridor cut off.

It appeared that Thorin and the other warriors had been out of their rooms heckling Dalin, Noal, and the selected Krall guards who would be attending the feast with us – needling them mercilessly about their refined appearances.

'Kiana … um … stunning!' Cadell commented hoarsely after a moment.

Suddenly there was a rush of similar comments, but I noted Dalin's speechlessness.

'These two sure look like princelings,' Tane gestured at Dalin and Noal. 'But Kiana, you are a Queen.'

I smiled. 'Maeve and Kerrin were kind to me,' I said, watching Noal's eyes flicker toward the stairway she'd just disappeared down. Both he and Dalin were resplendent in golden brocade vests, shimmering with precious red stones, and tightly fitted maroon trousers. They looked like Jenran lords in the cultural colours.

'Gods, I feel overawed just to stand behind the Three of you,' Phrixus swallowed nervously. 'Does anyone want to swap for my shift tonight?'

'No thanks. The only times I've been in royal halls was when I had armour on and my biggest task was to stare straight ahead and avoid the Sorcerer's notice,' Wolf grimaced.

Purdor and Ferron, also in all their finery, seemed as tense as Phrixus at the idea of their duty at the feast.

'There's no reason to fear,' Dalin reassured them. 'At these kinds of events your greatest challenge will be to maintain a politely interested expression.'

He moved to my side and held out his arm, covering my hand warmly with his own when I allowed him to escort me.

'Well, anyone would be able to maintain an attentive expression with Kiana by their side,' Ferron smoothed his red hair shakily as we moved out to the central stairs, and then upward to join the crowds flooding into the grand hall a few levels above ours. 'But I'm stuck with these dopes.'

Purdor rolled his eyes. 'You clown.'

'Feel free to take my arm,' Noal offered Ferron winsomely, straightening his tunic with a dashing grin. 'I can escort you if you need support.'

However, the three of us were very quickly drawn into conversations with different high-ranking officials and wealthy or important citizens who were curious about such momentous newcomers.

Unlike the boisterous festivals I had grown up with, this function was characterised by polite laughter, tinkling glasses, gently played music and soft candlelight.

My princes were perfectly at ease, formal and gracious as we were swarmed with admiring crowds, while our Krall guards were trying to be alert but obscure in the background, blending in with the other Jenran guards stationed along the walls.

After some speeches of greeting, I watched Dalin and Noal gradually become hemmed in by a swarm of eager listeners. But I withdrew from the crowds – if not from the many intrigued, indiscreet eyes that followed me.

'You must forgive us all for being so obvious in our fascination of the Three,' a deep, musical voice spoke from behind me, and I turned to find a beautifully adorned woman sitting at an impressive table by the wall. 'Not many of us have seen outsiders. Especially outsiders so long awaited.' She held herself gracefully and with dignity, and despite a lock of white amongst her black, pinned back hair, her beauty was profound. She offered me the seat beside her.

'Such fascination is understandable,' I told her, taking the chair she had offered.

The distinguished looking lady nodded. 'And it is good that people wonder about you rather than their fate and the horrors that may await Jenra in war.'

I inclined my head, regarding her respectfully.

I knew from my past travels that she was the nation's formidable leader of healing.

'I am called Amarantha,' she introduced herself, deep brown eyes washing over me. 'And my husband, a council member, spent a great part of this afternoon telling me every detail of your story.'

I felt my eyebrow arch and she gave a quick, melodious laugh.

'It is allowed for a husband or wife of a council member to know their partner's mind and choices. After all, the same details will soon be all over the city, twice as embellished. And no man in his right mind should make any life altering decisions without the adept counsel of his wife in particular.'

She looked over at a group of young men approaching our table bravely.

When caught under her gaze they decided to sidle the other way.

'I simply wish to say,' Amarantha continued. 'That we are grateful you have come and that we believe in what you represent.'

I lowered my eyes, moved. 'Thank you, friend,' I told her.

'One,' a male's voice spoke in greeting, and I glanced up to find a beaming council member standing by Amarantha's chair. 'Please excuse me for taking my lady from your company. But tonight of all nights, above all I wish to dance with my wife.'

I gave him an honest, heartfelt smile. 'Such beauty should not be left to sit at a table in the shadows.'

He nodded happily as Amarantha rose, before he led her through the crowd.

When they were gone one of the young Jenran nobles bolstered his courage once more and advanced to the table again.

'You know, you were right,' he announced, stepping in front of where I was sitting. 'Such beauty should not be left to sit at a table in the shadows. Could I tempt you to dance?'

'I thank you, but I am not tempted. I desire to rest here peacefully for now.'

His smile dimmed slightly. 'Please do not be shy, I will ensure you are swept away into gaiety.'

'Thank you,' I said firmly. 'But if I wanted to be swept away, I could just fly.'

'Ah,' he said, appearing wounded. 'But, perhaps one dance –'

'No.'

When he withdrew, and I sent the next few jaunty young men to try away, I gazed towards where Noal was now surrounded by the wealthy daughters of the high-ranking citizens he'd been conversing with earlier. But as they vied for his attention, the distant expression on his face showed that Maeve had left him unreachable.

Dalin was also nodding graciously at a group of well-bred, high class young ladies, but I found that his gaze sought mine. I watched him courteously conclude his conversations and withdraw, crossing through the crowds to reach me.

As he held his hand out to me, I felt a sudden change of heart about dancing, and allowed myself to be swept away onto the dance floor.

'Remember when we danced together in the mountain pass?' he asked, leaning in closer than the dance required.

'Just the two of us. It was nice,' I smiled a half smile.

'It's just you and I again right now,' he whispered, his green eyes fixed on my face.

'I remember another time of dancing and music, but I did not yet know you,' I told him as he drew us around in an arc. 'You were just the green eyed noble at my stage.'

His brow furrowed and then smoothed. 'You remember me from the festival? It was so long ago.'

'I never forgot.'

'I'm glad I know you and that there's no stage between us now,' he told me, and pulled me in to dance more closely, as if we were hugging instead.

I hardly noticed that time had passed with Dalin, until the musicians had stopped for the night and he was bowing over my hand.

71

Seventy One

Kiana

I dreamed of green eyes and woke to Dalin tapping mournfully at the open doors to my balcony.

'G'morning,' he mumbled as I waved him in. He stumbled past where Maeve and Kerrin had draped my dress after returning to free me from it the night before, and he threw himself onto the bed beside me, embedding his face in the sheets.

'Good morning,' I answered. 'Why so early today?'

'Mmmmmmmmmm,' he moaned and rolled over to face me. 'Maeve must have decided to arrive earlier to give Noal more time to talk before her next duty.' Dalin muffled a yawn. 'He's been a real dictator about everyone making their own beds, so I think she has a few spare moments.'

He closed his green eyes, ready to resume drowsing. 'I had to tactfully make up an excuse to remove myself,' he mumbled.

'That was good of you,' I told him.

He shrugged one shoulder. 'Now you get stuck with me instead.'

'Are you going to fall back to sleep?' I asked him, tickling his arm by tracing down one of the jagged, ferocious scars on his bicep with a fingertip. I remembered what Maeve had said about such marks and how Jenrans prized them.

He shivered and a smile curled drowsily up in one corner of his mouth. I saw goose bumps rise across his chest but he kept his eyes closed.

'We'll have to rise soon,' I reasoned, tracing my finger along the scar that ran over his jaw line this time.

He caught my finger with one hand and cracked an eye open. 'I might smother you in the sheets to keep you from disturbing me.'

I wriggled away as he made as if to roll over to flatten me under his weight.

'You know I can wrestle out of any grip you get on me.'

Dalin laughed, and laid flat on his back. 'You're right of course.'

I lay my head on his chest as he settled an arm around my shoulders, as easily as if this was how we had always behaved.

'You seem to have awoken properly now anyway,' I commented.

'Alas,' he agreed, and I peered up at his face from where I lay.

I could see that with wakefulness had also come worry.

He lifted his head to gaze down at me. 'Kiana, do you think that if the Jenrans vote in our favour, we might truly stand a chance?'

'I think,' I began to reply slowly. 'That if this vote passes and Jenra joins us in war ... then we may at least survive. But if we are able to gain the aid of the rest of the magical races as well, we might even win.'

My head rose and fell with his chest as he let out a big pent-up breath.

'That would mean you leaving us.'

'For a while,' I agreed.

Dalin dutifully rolled over and closed his eyes then so that I could rise and ready myself for the day.

When we had eaten together, I joined him as he returned to his own room, where we found Noal looking stricken to have bidden Maeve goodbye once more.

I patted his golden hair down reassuringly before we headed out to follow Warlord Aeron back down the mountain, back to the glorious coast, and into the dark caves.

Again, Durna and his council were awaiting us and we were seated as Durna distributed a golden stone to each member of the council.

'Today,' Durna began the ceremony, 'I call upon all council members to cast their vote on behalf of Jenra. Your vote must reflect the course of action that you feel best serves our people. There will be no judgement or shame in any choice that you make in serving your country. You must place your stone inside the red or the blue basket upon the table, red being a vote for war and blue being a vote against it, and the majority will decide the vote. The final outcome is to be accepted without question, but if somehow there are six stones for and six stones against war, my thirteenth stone will decide it.'

The King paced to his seat. 'Warlord and council member Aeron, on behalf of the officers and soldiers you represent, I call on you to cast your vote.'

Warlord Aeron came to stand before the table, and lifted his gold stone.

'I vote we join the war,' he stated in his gruff, low voice. 'The army is fit and driven to end any darkness that threatens their land. They know that the Three have been sent to us by the Gods, to lead us in a march to battle. The Unicorns told us of their coming, of their pure cause. The Three's path is Jenra's path.' He leaned over and firmly set his stone in the red basket. With a bow to his King and then to us, he was then seated.

Dalin and Noal sat beside me with straight postures and Thale was tugging at his beard as he nervously watched from the background with Phobos, Vulcan and Thorin.

My heart was throbbing as five more members, each representing different sectors of Jenran society, all set their stones beside Aeron's in the red basket. But inevitably one council member eventually held up a blue stone.

'War is havoc and misery,' the minister for businesses and the economy said, her voice low. 'Apart from depleting resources, straining production and straining the economy, war would mean shattered lives for families left behind and death for those that go. It will take years to replenish what we may lose.'

The next member held up a blue stone as well.

'I also say no to war,' the agricultural council member announced. 'So far Darziates has not turned his eye to us. He has left us alone even after troubling Razek and Glaidin. Perhaps we are removed enough that he will continue to leave us alone, and so we need not risk the survival of Jenra in Awyalkna's war. But, if he doesn't, Jenra is safe in the mountains. We can defend from the upper ground against any siege.'

I kept my face blank as my mind argued that the upper ground would be fine against mortal armies, yet useless against a Sorcerer and a Witch. Especially when they had Dragons.

The following council member for health rose then, showing no expression as to which way he would decide.

'I,' he said slowly. 'Vote for the war.' His gold stone went into the red basket. 'We must do our part in the War for the World, for everyone's survival, including ours. We have an army for this exact purpose. They are fine fighters after a lifetime locked in battle with the Griffins. They are ready, and they understand the risks. We must follow the Three, for they are this world's best chance.'

I remained outwardly calm as I watched the last voters all place their stones in the red basket.

Then Durna stood again. 'It is hardly necessary for me to add my vote. But as it is,' his stone was also housed in the red pile. 'We will aid Glaidin and the world against the threat.

Jenra has never cowered in hopes that danger will pass before. And we will not cower from darkness now. We will follow the Three.'

With that Aeron stood at his brother's side. 'Then I pledge the army to this cause.'

The woman beside him also stood, and pledged for the merchants she represented.

One by one each of them stood and pledged for those they represented. Even those who had voted against joining the war pledged without any hesitation until finally Durna announced: 'and I, as King, pledge the entirety of Jenra as a united whole to this cause.'

'So let it be,' each of them intoned simultaneously, and with their words our original quest was fulfilled.

'Jenra will be going to war,' said Durna, looking neither pleased, nor upset. 'Tomorrow the drums will sound and I will announce the decision. After tomorrow, we prepare.'

72

⬥

Seventy Two

N*oal*

The council disbanded quickly so that each leader could start their preparations before the entire population was informed. The day was still young for us, however, and Aeron left us in the hands of a young peasant man only too glad to stop work for the day to show us around.

Our escort's name was Gern and he thought it would be a good idea to begin on the ground level, back in the bustling village complex, as he wanted to take us through the water feature areas and to homes of the villagers while the market was quiet with many people out in the valley working.

Yet we'd barely greeted the few people milling in the markets, before everyone seemed to have heard of our presence. Soon it felt as if every farmer, blacksmith and washerwoman had stopped work to come and meet us.

Gern was deeply distressed as a horde halted our progress, but Kiana graciously waved at people who were calling out to her and who were craning for her attention while Dalin and I shook hands with the farmers.

After a while the excited crowds stopped pressing in and we were able to be drawn excitedly from one place to the next with a growing mob gathering behind us. Only at one point did a wily elderly woman manage to truly press close to Dalin, past our Krall guards.

He had rolled up his sleeves with the heat of so many people pressing in, and the beginnings of the gashed scars on his arm were visible.

'Well met,' she told Dalin in *Aolen*. Then the woman grasped his scarred bicep and turned to the rest of the yearning crowd, declaring in Jenran: 'Lo Raiden ge e gendaren. Ro des hund ni vo lo fatalem a lo Scaren!'

The crowd cheered rapturously and she bowed respectfully to Dalin before returning back into the swells of people.

Dalin was faintly bewildered, but managed to keep up his smile. 'What did she say?' he asked Kiana out of the corner of his mouth.

Kiana smiled slightly in return. 'The Raiden is a warrior. He will lead us to the downfall of the Sorcerer.'

Many of the people around us already appeared confident with switching in and out of Jenran and *Aolen* after Kiana's gift to Durna had spread. The ability to use the new language seemed to have passed throughout the nation like wildfire, and many voices continued to ring around us until, at last, after being shown a multitude of different homes, shops and features of the market and village area, we began to lose some of our followers as we moved to explore the next level.

'There are so many people!' I exclaimed tiredly as we climbed the sloping walkway. 'It seems as if Jenra has a bigger population than Awyalkna!'

Then we stepped out onto the second floor and realised that the population of this area had heard we were coming, and were now all rushing to meet us.

'No,' Kiana told me as I gaped ahead. 'It's just that Awyalkna is spread out. Here the whole population is condensed into one place, as big as it may be.' Her voice was nearly drowned out by the onrushing masses, all vying for attention.

'Either way, we are at risk of dying under a pile of adoring fans before we ever get to the frontlines,' Phobos asserted laconically.

Gern was obviously frustrated that his tour was being ruined, and as we proceeded onward, we could hardly hear his informative details while he made grand gestures towards buildings or historical monuments. He finally conceded defeat and was placated when a tavern keeper offered us ale and lunch so that we could sit to meet people less formally.

In that way people swelled in and out cheerfully and Gern was pacified with enough ale to get a loud drinking song going so that it started to sound like everyone on the level was making vaguely musical roaring noises.

It was late in the afternoon when we eventually left the crowds behind as they cried out in *Aolen* for us to visit again. We were in good spirits as we ascended to our own rooms for the evening meal. Just in time for Maeve to arrive.

73

Seventy Three

K^{iana}

I rolled over to face the side of the bed where Dalin had lain that morning, and found my thoughts obstinately lingering on him until I at last threw the covers off. I pulled my travel trousers, shirt, tunic and boots out, dressing quickly and sliding my hunting knives into their sheathes.

Then I took a deep breath, and ran at the open doors – leaping over the balcony railing to plunge in a free fall down the mountain.

I was exhilarated by the drop and allowed myself to hurtle for a few moments before I let my wings burst out and catch me. I flipped to face the cliff wall, braced my legs, and kicked away from the mountain so that I tore through the whistling air like an arrow.

I was dashing across the plains so swiftly that the grass rushing by below was nothing but a dark blur, but I pushed my wings to soar through the air even faster so that I could hear them whirring close by my ears, just silvery glints of colour as they flashed with action.

Testing myself, I jerked to a sudden stop and, quicker than the reflex of blinking, my wings had caught me in mid-air.

I launched back into flight, soaring higher and higher while noticing that somehow my eyes weren't streaming with the harsh air and my flesh wasn't stinging with the chill of the wind. My body seemed to have made adjustments to enable flight, and I whirled through the air in delight, calling to a tree full of curious birds as I passed and hearing their returning chirps of joy.

I only sobered when I realised how close I was getting to the watchtowers and, with a swift sweep, I was landing on the ledge of one a moment later.

I crouched in front of the five startled archers on duty so as not to lose my balance with the wind.

'Well met friends,' I said politely.

It took a few moments before one of them was able to bumble a greeting out.

'Is everything alright, One?' the archer asked uncertainly, eyes wide.

'All is well,' I reassured them. 'I have decided to practice the art of flight while the skies are clear and was hoping that you could pass word along so that your archers do not mistake me for a Griffin.'

They all visibly paled at the thought of firing on me.

'Th-Thank you for the warning, One,' a guard stuttered.

'Thank you for ensuring that I won't have to dodge arrows,' I smiled in return. 'Carry on your fine work guarding Jenra while she sleeps.'

Then I plunged off the ledge and let my wings carry me over the glorious landscape until I was close to the beach. Then I simply let myself drift down to where only a thin strip of sparkling sand remained with the high tide.

I sat for a time on the cool, soft sand and watched the waves surging and glimmering in the silvery light, swashing forward and washing back away.

Soon I would need to cross those dark, surging expanses of water, I considered. Soon I would be truly tested.

74

Seventy Four

Noal

I dreamt of a cave where stalagmites and stalactites rose and fell from ceilings and floors like works of art. I dreamt of a picture in that cave where I was not part of the Three's quest, but was living a golden fantasy – settling down in Jenra as a happy farmer, or even as an Awyalknian ambassador. With Maeve.

Startled by some noise that was not part of this dream world, I opened my eyes and stared about the bedroom, which was lightening with the coming of morning.

Dalin was already sitting up in bed, gaping with wonder. For Kiana had opened the doors to our balcony with a soft push of magic, sending her power swirling about our room like an enchanted breeze, and now she swept gracefully down to stand in the open doorway.

The silk drapes stirred against the walls, the light material floating about her as if she was appearing to us out of another dream.

'Kiana,' Dalin gasped, peering at her face. His voice trailed off as we both noticed how changed her features seemed while she gazed back at us.

She looked exotic and wild. Her flashing blue and gold flecked eyes had become somehow sharper and fiercer, like the eyes of a bird of prey. Her wings were translucent silver, yet were longer than I'd ever seen them, ready to slice through the air, and possibly other things too, at great speed. But as we watched, Kiana put a hand to her chest and winced, as if things were changing inside.

Then the pupils of her eyes slowly shrank back to normal, her wings disappeared and she was standing before us like normal. All traces of the wild *Larnaeradee* hiding once more.

'Good morning,' she told us with the glimmer of her smile.

'Were you flying all night?' Dalin asked, still shocked and mussed up in bed. 'You looked ...'

'I was. And the native Jenran rinx birds have already pointed out what illogical physical changes my body undergoes to keep me airborne for longer periods,' she answered. 'My lungs altered so I could breathe the thin air, my eyes sharpened for keener sight and protection against the wind. Even my heart worked harder to keep my blood warm.' Kiana came to sit on the end of Dalin's bed. 'The rinx birds were impressed that magic allowed me to keep my body mass in the air without tiring, when their entire anatomy is developed to help them do as much. But without my earthstone channelling nature's power, it would not be possible.'

'You're a wonder Kiana,' I told her in amazement.

'And you,' she smiled again and stood. 'Are going to run late, so it is fortunate I woke you.'

I tensed. 'What do you mean? Maeve normally wouldn't be here for a long while.'

'Today isn't a normal day,' Kiana reminded us. 'The whole city is already awake and abuzz. Everyone has risen early to hear the announcement. People are already beginning to line the outer walkways on the valley side so that they are able to see King Durna while he speaks. The drums to summon everyone will soon be starting.'

'Oh Gods!' I exclaimed. 'I haven't bathed or shaved!' I hurried out of bed at once.

75

Seventy Five

D^{alin}

The mountain shuddered and reverberated with a colossal beat, and it felt as if my pulse had changed to beat along with the tune of the drums from the sheer force of them.

But as soon as we followed Durna, stepping out onto the walkway of the gates and into the blinding sun, the drums stopped. And over the ringing in my ears, I heard the great uproar of the gathered crowds begin.

I felt miniscule as we squinted up at the entire Jenran population filling every open space throughout the city. We were much closer than when we had been tested, and their waves of sound surged down the mountain to greet the grim-faced King.

After taking the golden horn presented to him once again, Durna turned to speak to his people, and in almost an instant all of Jenra stopped dramatically to listen to his magically amplified voice.

'The Three have come to give us hope and direction against the Sorcerer's threat. But amidst the joy and wonder of this there also exists a great burden. For Jenra has had to decide if she shall join the long awaited Three in their quest against the darkness.'

Even the crowds gathered so high above that I could hardly make out the blurred colours of their clothes were still, though surely his voice only carried up to them as a faint whisper.

'The Three have now spoken with your representatives, and we have considered and voted. So now I stand before you to make known the choice of your council.'

He looked at the thousands before him, all waiting in suspense, and he had the weight of having chosen the fate of his people written upon his brow.

'Jenra is going to war,' King Durna declared loudly. 'We will join in the fight against Darziates to rid this world of the evil he has spread, and the threat he poses to our land.'

There was a barrage of noise with the sudden release of many voices intermingling and lapping over each other, but when Durna gestured for quiet it again came almost instantly.

'Now,' he called, 'is the time for preparation. While we have long bolstered our own city defences in the face of this threat, and have done much to organise ourselves already, we must further prepare for many of us to leave to join

Awyalkna in their march through Krall. And we must do it within fourteen days.'

Now the people's voices rose in earnest, this time a little higher and more urgently.

Two weeks was a very short amount of time to finish readying a whole nation for war, even if it was one that they'd foreseen. It took a few moments longer for the public to quieten before Durna spoke again.

'Our ranks of healers and the army itself are strong and ready. But any citizen who wishes to join their comrades in protecting Jenra must enlist with Warlord Aeron's or Lady Amarantha's assistants. Families to remain behind must ready themselves to farewell their loved ones and make do without their skills. But we all have extra work ahead to ensure our people are armed, stocked and as safe as possible, whether they are staying in the mountains or marching away from them. Much is to be done, and much is to be gained if we prepare properly. Take the time given to you and use it in service of your nation.'

When Durna had finished it took a great deal of time for all of the crowds to slowly dissipate – the reality of the decision setting in.

'Aeron,' Kiana spoke as we followed him from the gate and neared the stairway that led out to the beach. 'There is much for Jenra to do now. Could the three of us use this time wisely, too, and closely inspect the ancient wall pictures in the Miridoon caves?'

He nodded gravely and walked us out to the peaceful strip of sand before returning to his own tasks. And, with only Thorin and Nikon waiting outside for the three of us, we became quiet as we entered the dark caves.

Kiana lit up the middle cave with her luminescent globes of light, letting them bud to life at her fingertips before sending them to different positions around the room, and we each gazed at the scenes that had been depicted about us before we had ever been born.

They filled nearly every spare space on the rocky walls, and were such dazzling artworks that it looked as if each picture was a window looking into the very event taking place.

I stepped over puddles on the floor and shivered at how disturbingly accurate and freakishly lifelike the out of sequence images were, feeling as if stepping too close to them could lead me to fall right through and back to that time.

When I came upon scenes I did not recognise, a scene I was yet to live, my skin would prickle and I could not look too closely for fear of seeing something in my future that would terrify me out of acting when the real moment happened.

Stepping away from one such image about Noal – where he appeared to be surrounded in an odd cloud of red smoke, I crossed to Kiana's side instead and found her studying a picture of what could only be herself locked in a skyward battle with a Griffin.

'Perhaps this is you battling those Griffins in the Pass?' I asked her softly, feeling the need to be quiet in the eerie, echoing cavern.

'No, there's something in that Griffin's talons. I'm fighting for whatever it appears to be holding,' she replied thoughtfully.

'It looks like a bundle of washing,' I frowned. 'But I doubt you would be provoked into mortal combat over some bed sheets.'

She pointed to the next image and I shuddered.

'No one would have understood the outcome of what was going on in this one until they'd lived it or had it explained to them in great detail,' she answered. 'So I won't understand the portrait of the Griffin battle until I've lived it either.'

Noal came over to join Kiana and I in viewing the almost nightmarishly lifelike picture of Agrona attacking us beneath the willow in Bwintam.

Noal cleared his throat. 'There's so much detail in these things, I'm lucky they didn't paint me in a bad moment.'

'Scratching yourself somewhere you shouldn't?' I asked, turning my back on the event.

Kiana moved on to keep gazing at the images while I sat on one of the flat rocks at the foot of a glorious picture. It was of an incredibly huge being touching hands with a tiny, winged, future Kiana while an incredible light surrounded them. Beside that image was a horrific one that portrayed the slitted white eyes of an Evexus peering out of some trees while a raven perched behind it. I gave up mulling over whether that was a past or future image and waited for Kiana to finish.

'You should go,' I told Noal when he sat in a council seat. 'You should spend the afternoon as you want to, in the company you wish to, while you can.'

He regarded me with hesitation. 'Kiana is enthralled here. You'll be amongst these unnerving pictures for a while.'

'I'll be spending my time in the company that I wish to, while I can,' I answered him, and he smiled slowly with understanding and nodded.

'Maeve spends her free time walking through the valley flowers in the afternoons,' he replied, and stood eagerly. 'I'll be with her if you need me.'

When Noal had gone I returned my focus to Kiana.

'Is that him?' Kiana asked in a low voice.

I had been avoiding the dreaded picture she referred to, of the most hated man amongst all races.

Piercing eyes as hard as granite seemed to bare down on us. Those eyes showed the unnaturalness existing within the man.

'Yes,' I told her, coming over and glaring up at the towering, white-blonde, soulless being. 'That is the Sorcerer.'

In the picture a storm so unearthly that the sky flashed red and purple was raging behind Darziates, and in the distant sky – lit up by a fork of lightning, flew the raven that was Agrona.

'Noal and I have seen his likeness drawn on scrolls or described for reports in the palace at home.'

Kiana's face was hard and her body was tense as she frowned up at him, and I reached for her hand.

'Perhaps it is time to look at more lovely pictures, where we can treasure the memories we have made,' I told her, and she allowed me to pull her away towards an image of when she'd descended into Sylthanryn city after she'd first found her wings.

She smiled at me quickly.

'This one is a very lovely memory,' I told her. And I didn't let go of her hand.

76

Seventy Six

N*oal*

Only Nikon's quick reflexes and strong grip catching my shoulder stopped my euphoric exit of the Miridoon caves.

'Bleh!' my excited running turned into a startled grunt as I was caught and jolted back.

'Where do you think you're going?' Nikon drawled, releasing my shoulder.

Thorin straightened from leaning against the rocky cave entrance.

'I'm afraid I'm in a terrible rush and can't chat.' I made to move off again, and this time it was Thorin's quick reflexes that broke my euphoria. His hand shot out and caught my collar, and as easily as if I were a child, he towed me back towards them.

'What's the terrible rush?' he asked.

I sighed. 'Maeve. She goes down into the valleys at this time between her duties every afternoon and today I want to join her.'

Thorin's face softened with a grin.

'Noal,' Nikon growled. 'We are here to guard you. Wait until Kiana and Dalin are ready so that we can accompany you. We must leave soon so that we're not caught by the tide anyway.'

I shook my head. 'I mean no offence, but I don't really desire a bunch of chaperones as well as Kiana and Dalin all trundling along behind Maeve and I.'

Thorin's grin grew wider. 'I'm highly insulted,' he stated, not looking one jot upset. 'I never trundle.' But he let me go and smoothed my collar.

Nikon raised his eyebrows, but followed Thorin's lead.

'Fine. But,' Nikon warned. 'If you get yourself hurt, in any kind of trouble, lost, or are too late in returning to your quarters, we'll tear the mountains apart looking for you, raining destruction upon the Jenrans and likely ruining any alliances.'

'Understood,' I affirmed, straining to go. 'Don't make the soldiers testy. Keep the allies happy.'

'And ...' Thorin added. 'Enjoy yourself.'

'Thanks!' I called over my shoulder as I immediately sped off along the sand.

I moved so quickly through the lower levels that no one had time to notice me, and in barely moments I skidded out into the valleys from the city gates, spotting her floating golden hair glimmering in the sunlight as she followed a trail through the fields.

I didn't pause, but almost soared across the distance between us to close it as fast as I could.

77

Seventy Seven

D^{alin}

I walked Kiana back to her chamber and then followed along as Nikon sauntered back to his room.

We heard roars of laughter and cheers that were coming from further along the corridor, and Nikon paused to listen.

'What's the commotion?' I asked, seeing that Lydon and Roth had their door closed after having spent the night on guard duty. They were probably holding their pillows over their heads, trying to catch up on sleep.

A wide grin spread across Thorin's face. 'Some games are afoot,' he told me, and I realised that it was Wolf and Phrixus that I could hear from their room further down the hall.

They were singing drinking songs and the fact that Aiolos and Gideon's voices could be heard singing along with their roommates as well meant that there must have been quite a quantity of alcohol consumed. The piping music accompanying their sorry excuse for a choir suggested that Rendor, a withdrawn and creative type of man, was also involved.

I followed Thorin and Nikon down to the chaotic room and found Ferron, Purdor, Cadell and Tane lounging in the apartment while Wolf and his musical group performed.

Ignoring the loud songs, Ferron's auburn eyebrows were knitted together in concentration as he tried to work out Tane's next move in a game of runes.

'Come on, take your turn,' Tane was smug as he plotted Ferron's downfall.

He already had a small pile of Ferron's coins gambled away beside him. 'Don't you worry about me, I'm your friend!'

'Of course, don't worry Ferron,' Thorin mocked Tane as we flopped down on the empty beds. 'Tane is too sweet to have sly strategies up his sleeve.'

'Much too sweet.' Ferron glanced darkly at the coins he'd succumbed.

Cadell was polishing his armour on the balcony, and all of the different pieces normally assembled together were spread out in the sun. They gleamed brightly.

'You know, Ferron,' he remarked. 'If in doubt, you could always call for a slip.'

Rendor's piping music cut off on a shrill note and Wolf tripped over Aiolos and into Gideon so that the three of them fell in a heap. Phrixus shrugged and sat himself down too, tired from his out of tune exertions.

'He's going to call for a slip?' Wolf's muffled cry came from under Gideon's armpit.

'Never!' Ferron answered, aghast.

'But it would mean you got half your money back,' Cadell reasoned.

'Come on, I've seen him worse off than this,' Tane laughed as Ferron made his move. Tane flipped his own next rune over and Ferron groaned, giving him another coin and taking a big drink from the deep mug of Jenran ale beside him.

I noticed that there were many empty mugs at his elbow, and only three beside Tane.

'We'll have to send for some more soon,' Tane commented evilly as he noticed that Ferron's mug was emptying again.

'Slow down on the ale and you might win one,' I recommended to Ferron.

His cheeks were becoming as ruddy as his hair.

'I can't, that's the point,' Ferron hiccupped. 'The more you lose, the more you drink.'

'What's this slip thing you can do then?' I asked sympathetically.

'When you call for a slip, you are admitting defeat to both the liquor and the other player's talent,' Cadell informed me. 'The superior player then usually takes pity on their tottering, unskilled opponent, and gives half their winnings back.'

'I guess you could say it's like admitting you made a slip in judgement by playing at all,' Thorin explained with good humour.

Purdor shrugged from where he had been rocking back in a wooden chair at the table, eating fruit from a platter. 'We've all had a slip when playing Tane. Most of us have learned from it.'

'But most of you have not actually verbally requested a slip,' Tane seemed to enjoy reminding them.

'How do you request a slip in any way but verbally?' I asked curiously.

'You pass out,' Thorin laughed.

'I would love to see you beat Kiana,' I commented thoughtfully. 'She would be hard to beat in a thinking game and a drinking game.'

Tane suddenly became very eager. 'I'll have to challenge her to a round!'

'No, that would be unfair, she's probably never played Krall's version of rune gambling,' Purdor said with his mouth full of grapes.

'I bet she knows most gambling games, but if not, I don't think it would matter,' I told them. 'It might actually give Tane more of a chance.'

'Oh, this afternoon could be interesting then,' Tane crowed in delight, right as Noal came trudging miserably into the room.

'How was Maeve?' I asked him cheerfully.

'Beautiful,' he moaned. 'She had to return to work.'

'She's probably got to relieve the other maid,' Cadell stated. 'That one's exhausted from having to fetch Ferron more ale all of the time.'

'Because she was in a rush, she had to use the ladders. I didn't like watching Maeve run up those ladders so quickly, holding her skirts and a basket of flowers,' Noal told us mournfully.

'Don't look up a lady's skirts,' Thorin admonished.

'I miss her already,' Noal sighed, stricken.

'Oh, poor man,' Tane tutted. 'My wife had the same strange power over me when we first met.'

'She still does,' Thorin told him. 'I've never seen a grown man so meek and so adoring. You're like a little lamb for Mil.'

'Just you wait,' Tane warned us all knowingly. 'Women all have these strange powers.'

'Very mystical and frightening,' Purdor agreed.

'Good luck to the Raiden then, seeing as Kiana truly does possess actual powers,' Phrixus commented woozily from the floor beside his sprawled-out comrades.

I rose to put an arm around Noal's glumly drooping shoulders.

'Come on,' I soothed. 'Let's cheer you up.' I steered him towards Tane and Ferron's game and beckoned to the others. 'I'll go get that powerful One now, and we'll see if we can do better against Tane with her playing along.'

Noal acquiesced for a short while, but was gradually cheered more by the idea of saving his coins and withdrawing to encounter Maeve at dinner time once again.

In contrast, those of us who stayed long after the sun had gone down were surrounded by piles upon piles of ale mugs. And most of Tane's money, most of Ferron's money and most of everyone else's money was being counted out by Kiana. She'd been drinking too, but only for the fun of it, or she would have missed out.

Surprisingly, Phobos had been carted back out to his own bed, being the first one of us to 'slip' unintentionally, despite his hulking size.

Aiolos, Gideon and Rendor had admitted defeat early, after already having had a big afternoon of drinking songs. And Agrudek had never surfaced from his rooms while Lydon and Roth had had the sense to stay out of the game altogether.

'I feel as though I have been educated,' Tane stated humbly. from where he was slumped tiredly over the table amongst the messy masses of scattered runes.

His battle with Kiana had been an epic one that had lasted long after everyone else had bowed out.

'A very worthy adversary,' Thale burped into his beard, congratulating Kiana.

'And now we know to avoid *both* Tane and Kiana,' Wolf puffed some smoke out of his pipe from where he lounged against the balcony.

Cadell was only now putting his polished armour away after having been distracted from finishing it all afternoon.

'I feel better that Tane lost my coins again. Even though he didn't lose them back to me,' Ferron chuckled. He was collapsed on his own bed, unable to stand or even sit up straight after having lost so many times and having had to drain so many mugs.

'Poor Tane,' Purdor laughed. 'Even your curls look weary.'

Phrixus leant over from where he was sitting at the table between Kiana and Tane, and pulled one of Tane's locks. Instead of snapping back into a spring like usual, his hair drooped limply.

'Perhaps we should play again?' Thorin asked everyone. 'Kiana might not be able to do it a second time?'

'I definitely could do it a second time,' Kiana replied. 'But you could give it a go.'

'Count me out.' Nikon stretched and made to leave. 'I want to be able to see straight in the morning when we go out to help the Jenran working groups.'

'I agree,' Phrixus yawned. 'Don't want the Jenrans to think we're useless.'

'I'm sure they already know you're useless,' Wolf bantered.

'But what about the rest of us?' Cadell joked, having finally tied his armour into a neat bundle.

'Apart from all that,' Thale said. 'I want to both win the war, and go back to Krall with more than an empty purse to my name.'

'Fine, fine,' Thorin sulked. 'Bunch of cowards.'

78

Seventy Eight

A^{sha}

'AMBUSH!!!!' she roared at the top of her lungs.

The air around the army had suddenly shifted and warped as if it were melting. A violent onrush of tremors shook the earth while it quaked in pain. Four foul blister-like mounds were springing up ahead of the army's front and the mortals lurched and cried out as they lost their balance.

'*What are they?*' Warlord Conall yelled, wheeling his horse around as Asha darted down to him.

Ace had sent five others to follow Glaidin's army – just enough to be helpful, but not enough to appear threatening. Those five whirred to her side now with stricken expressions.

'Rucksha!' Shiva hissed, gnashing his teeth as he blurred to a stop beside Asha.

She heard shouts and cries of alarm from the soldiers at the head of the march as the cracked, quaking dirt ahead of them trembled and surged violently – massive mounds of groaning earth fast rising out of the dust in hardening shapes.

'Bouldermen,' Asha growled, briefing Conall as quickly as she could. 'Ogres in your old stories. They're desert spirits that make themselves bodies out of rock and earth. Darziates has awakened them for the first time since the failing of Deimos.'

Conall paled.

'They're indestructible, but for the failing of the dark magic that roused them from their sleep. When Darziates is ended, they will rest once more. But they can be stopped and sent back temporarily by brute force.'

The Warlord nodded. 'We'll do that, then.'

He accepted her hand as she reached to touch his throat, and the Nymph Catori sent a light show into the air for attention.

'HOLD YOUR POSITIONS!' Conall barked in a magically amplified voice. 'PIKES FORWARD. PROTECT THE FRONTLINE!'

In a flurry of movement, the pikemen at once moved to get through to the front.

'HEAVY CAVALRY, READY!'

The mounds of earth had already swollen into hulking bodies that were quickly casting the army in shadow. Crude facial features were becoming apparent, as if fingers had poked and scraped away some dirt where eyes ought to be.

'Let's burn that leader down,' Asha told Shiva, eyeing the biggest solidifying monster.

'Adahy and I will take the second one,' Catori asserted, and the male beside her nodded.

'Do your best against the third and fourth,' Asha told the males Tate and Dyami.

Without a Giant or a team of Elves handy to smash the Rucksha back to dust, the Nymphs would just have to bombard them with fire and hope the mortals could beat the things down when they were weakened.

Asha and Shiva soared over the frontline, immediately hurling blasts of magic into the face of the tallest, thickest boulderman. The rocky head swivelled and jolted on stone shoulders as it opened a gaping, jagged hole for a mouth; dribbling cascades of dirt and pebbles.

'Go back to sleep!' Shiva yelled, and zoomed in close to send a handful of fire right into the thing's mouth.

It coughed dust and lifted its heavy arms to swat at its tiny assailants – managing to detach its crumbly feet from the dirt at last. It lifted one colossal foot and then stamped it back down with a mighty boom that sent the nearest mortals teetering.

'Heavy cavalry!' Conall's voice roared behind them. 'Charge!'

And the thundering of the horses' hooves rattled the ground almost as much as the Rucksha had.

The lead Rucksha released a shattering bellow, and all of the bouldermen took heavy steps forward now; wading into the charging lances like children splashing into waves on the beach for fun.

Chunks of rock went flying, and cracks and craters were made in boulder bodies. But at least twenty of the lance men were also damaged – unhorsed and hurtling from their saddles.

The Rucksha shook themselves off, ignoring any brittle holes that bled dust from their new bodies. And they stomped and bashed their way into the next obstacle, where they got stuck on a protective border of pikes.

'Swords, maces and axes!' Asha yelled.

Hordes of soldiers scrambled past the pikes to swarm around each of the Rucksha, battering the rocky pillar legs of the bouldermen as best they could.

Huge clumps were chipped out of the bouldermen as swords and axes struck heavy blows, and the Rucksha were slowed enough for the cavalry to regroup and make a new, powerful charge.

'Infantry!' Conall bellowed to the men chipping away at the Rucksha as the cavalry thundered back. 'WITHDRAW!'

Then lances were thrust forward again to poke into the crevices between rocky joints, skewering and levering open key parts of the four beasts, and one of the Rucksha tumbled to the ground – nearly exploding back into a heap of dirt. Another Ruksha's leg broke off and crumbled back into the earth, and immediately the infantry swamped the two fallen bouldermen once more, hacking at them with all of their might.

'We got one!' sounded a chorus of cheers as one boulder-man disintegrated beneath the beatings. Catori and Adahy showered the remains with fire to keep the creature from re-forming.

But the other two Rucksha remained largely intact and angrily ripped pikes and people away to plough on into the ranks at last.

They bashed a savage path through horses and soldiers; Asha and Shiva's huge brute stampeding straight for where another protective pike circle had been formed around the healer and supply carts.

Asha and Shiva redoubled their efforts, throwing continuous explosions into the boulderman while soldiers again sought to hack at the beast's knees.

The Rucksha finally skewered itself again on a dozen pike blades protecting the wagons, and as it tried to push forward the heels of the men holding the pikes dragged backwards in the dirt.

The Rucksha grumbled with a sound like a rockslide, thrusting one pike away, yanking another from its stomach and snapping a third like a twig.

With a snarl, Asha backed up and then hurtled at break-neck speed towards the thing's face, colliding against its rocky cheek with a force that knocked the Rucksha off course. Shiva was quick to throw himself at the boulder-man's other side before it could lash out at Asha, and a gravelly grunt crunched from the thing's gaping mouth hole as it rotated in irritation.

Men dove to avoid getting trampled while Shiva darted at the Rucksha's eyes and Asha pelted a golden globe of light that could normally roast a whole horse into the thing's forehead, leaving a great scorch mark that charred its face.

It roared as tiny pressure cracks formed in its dusty forehead but Shiva was already pelting his own fiery globes into the back of its knee. Asha continued blasting it in the head and back to keep it from getting any good swipes in at Shiva while he aimed to wear away its legs. But it was too strong, and in its fury, it stomped five pikemen into oblivion and pushed over a cart full of healers.

Asha lunged in a state of battle fury that sent the fire spreading from her hands to envelop both of her little arms. She latched onto the stony, oversized fingers reaching for the healers and her fire spread so that the Rucksha bellowed. She scratched and gouged at the dirt making up the rubbly knuckles and they started to weaken and crumble.

For a moment the great brute howled as two of its massive fingers completely broke away into ash and dust. But then the enraged beast struck out at Asha, knocking her from the air with a spatter of blood and cracked bones.

She had no time to recover as the Rucksha lifted its disintegrating leg, ready to squash her.

She heard Shiva roar in rage and Asha reeled with shock as magic suddenly consumed the whole of Shiva's little body, until he was nothing but a wavering torch of aqua light.

When such a burning rage overcame a Nymph, nature's power could no longer be contained within their little body, and then their fire could do near anything. But it was rare, and often extinguished the Nymph's own soul.

'Don't!' she rasped, reaching little broken fingers out to stop Shiva. 'Sati waits!'

But through the billowing dust Asha saw a blinding aqua fire ram into the core of the beast. The boulderman caught Shiva in surprise and agony, doubling over as it was rammed backward to collide heavily with the earth.

The ground cracked and all of the nearest men and horses toppled over.

And the Rucksha was still clutching Shiva while its body caved in and sucked downwards to return to its maker through the earth.

79

Seventy Nine

'The world is biting back,' the Sorcerer's heavy breathing, loyal lapdog – Angra Mainyu glowered at his King. 'That frarshking inventor is only telling half-truths!' he spat so that globules flung from his dirty lips. 'The world is turning on us. Let me tear it all apart. By myself. I'll go.'

Darziates regarded the eager, sweating Warlord with more patience than he offered all other mortals. Mortals were unimportant, momentary parts of the world. They passed through life so quickly, barely leaving an imprint to worry over. Yet Angra Mainyu's particular brand of cruelty left him practically inhuman, and made him very useful. Darziates frequently drew on the state of the Warlord's soul for inspiration. And as a resource.

'I'll hunt down those traitor soldiers and snap their necks,' Angra bunched grimy fists passionately. 'And I'll wipe out them three Awyalknians before they can even become the threat to your cause!'

'Hush.'

Obediently, the hulking, unstable Warlord hunched himself into silence.

The Sorcerer wasn't concerned about any of Agrudek's reports. He was certain that the Krall soldiers he had lost to the threatening 'Three' would easily be swayed when within his reach once more. Just as all of humanity would be swayed when he willed it.

He'd also largely dismissed Agrudek's vague information that a few of the introspective Elves and haphazard, disorganised Nymphs would be lending their support to the Three. Those were dying breeds. He would tip them over to extinction when the Lady finally shrivelled up and died.

Even the fact that Jenra was now prepared to leave its own seclusion to fight against his cause hardly displeased the Sorcerer. If the Jenrans wished to deplete their forces ahead of schedule, the Jenran Kingdom itself would fall under his command just that much faster.

'I want to tear. To rip. To feel the slick of hot blood in my hands,' Angra whined after a moment. 'I could get rid of even just Agrudek if you would only send me there. That twerp's going to snap any day now and spill what he's been up to.'

It had been tricky to correspond with and cover for the scientist lately. When Agrudek had reached out for help in passing a Jenran test against traitors or corruption, Darziates had had to quickly withdraw all of his own influence over Agrudek to leave him with his own good, free nature for a moment. It had probably been the nicest, most confusing moment the man had had in a long while – before Darziates had clamped back down with his own force.

Darziates really only wanted little Agrudek alive now to satisfy his own want for information on the *Larnaeradee*. He was restricted to obtaining just snatches of information so that she did not feel the dark magic and suspect the spy.

But those snatches gave Darziates new purpose. And a slight thawing feeling at the pit of his numb conscience ... similar to times when he had felt traces of human emotion in the beginning.

In an uncharacteristic motion, Darziates touched a hand to a vague ache in his chest at the thought.

'It is worth keeping Agrudek,' the Sorcerer answered firmly.

'Or ... Or I could join the Evexus! I'll go with them when they search for whichever hidey-hole the Jenrans will creep out of!' Angra launched off again excitedly. 'I could go instead of the Witch,' he almost crowed. 'She's hardly fit to serve you. Weak. Failing again and again.'

'Angra,' Darziates uttered softly, and the Warlord stopped ranting once more. 'Have I not already given you much?'

Angra's shoulders slumped. 'Yes,' he growled sulkily. 'You've given me war.' He nodded to himself, an eerie red glint in his eyes. 'I do like that.'

Darziates glanced past his Warlord then, towards the door to the throne room as he felt Agrona's approach.

She cringed at his hardly perceptible glare, feeling the true power behind it as she stepped through the doors.

'Yes?' he saw her shiver at having been addressed.

'My King, the Rucksha have returned,' she told him. 'And they brought someone back with them.'

He'd already felt that and dismissed it unconsciously for himself.

'Their return is as expected,' he answered coldly. 'Your empty-handed return, however, is less desirable.'

'I am nearly rested, and will be back out there soon,' she assured Darziates quickly, hungrily eyeing him. 'I am entirely invested in my search for the *Three*.' Her lip curled for a moment. 'Though I thought you'd like to see what the Rucksha brought home.'

'Well? What is it?' Angra burst out impatiently, throwing a bubble of spittle in her direction.

Her expression became poison as he polluted her moment with the King.

'It's a Nymph,' she informed Darziates.

Darziates reached out with his mind to pin point where the being was.

Agrona was brimming with self-importance. 'It might have information about the Lady's health status,' she told her master coyly.

She flinched for a moment, but Angra roared in jealous anguish as a portal of ice and menace opened and Darziates took a claw-like grip around Agrona's arm. Then the Sorcerer blurred them through the Other Realm to the training grounds, where a small group of curious soldiers crowded around the tiny, prone figure struggling to breathe in the dirt.

'It feels so ... pure ...' one of the men was saying.

But in the instant that the magic of Darziates touched them again, the group of soldiers assumed blank or dark expressions once more, lowering their eyes and stepping out of their King's way to reveal the Nymph.

It was nearly completely crushed by its journey, already practically dead, and it had hardly any recognisable features left.

Agrona gazed up at him expectantly.

'This thing is useless,' the Sorcerer stated. 'It has only moments left, and hardly a flicker of power.'

'No!' Agrona insisted. 'It can be made to please you yet!' Red smoke quickly curled about her fists and, with a blast, she forced her magic into the Nymph to make it wake.

Its body became rigid, and with a great effort the Nymph's eyes opened as wide as narrow slits. The thing's whole dust covered face was blown up disproportionately and cut to ribbons.

At once it let out a rasping moan and only the Witch's magic kept it from going into convulsions of shock and back into unconsciousness.

'You waste my time,' Darziates rebuffed the Witch. But without so much as moving a finger, Darziates swept the Nymph's broken body up into the air so that they all heard its loose bones rattling together.

'Welcome back to the outside world,' he told the tortured Nymph, while Agrona scowled sullenly. 'You should have stayed hidden,' he told it.

With that, the Nymph was dashed back down to the ground again, snapping its neck.

Darziates turned and was instantly back in his throne room as if he'd never left.

He found Angra Mainyu growling and spasmodically ramming his head into a wall – releasing pent up frustration. Losing pieces of his soul was taking its toll.

'I intend to send another Dragon to Awyalkna Palace,' the Sorcerer interrupted his Warlord.

'May I go? Please?' Angra stayed where he was, sagging forward against the stone wall. 'I want to hurt a Queen!' he whined into the cobbles. 'You've sent so many flying lizards and they haven't done any true damage!'

'No. You may not.' The Sorcerer almost showed the flicker of a smile in the very corner of his mouth. 'We want subservience, not complete destruction.'

'Arrhhgg!' Angra clubbed the wall with his forehead again.

80

Eighty

A *glaia*

She had just formally farewelled Dren and his Dragon fighting archers, and she was trying not to wonder how the city would fare without them.

She leaned back into her throne, twisting a golden ivy ring around her finger as she thought.

Before she could catastrophise or reassure herself, a panting sentry was crashing through the doors and running across the hall as if Darziates himself was following.

The sentry came to a skidding halt just before the dais and clutched at a stitch in his side at the same time as hurriedly bowing.

'Majesty ...' he panted laboriously. 'Word from ...' another big breath. 'The Gwynrock Wall ...' and another big breath. 'They said ... there's something ... that wants to see you ... They couldn't stop it.'

'What is this 'it'?' Aglaia questioned in concern. In such strange times 'it' could be anything.

But suddenly there came startled exclamations from the men guarding the hall doors. And then a toddler flew into the hall to answer Aglaia's question.

'*It*,' the flying toddler proclaimed, 'is a Nymph. And,' she continued, '*its* name is Asha.'

'Gods,' Friendly uttered as Aglaia rose.

There was already a babble of voices outside from the many onlookers who must have spotted this creature flying across the city to the palace.

Asha ignored the commotion and came to a hovering stop just above the head of the amazed sentry.

Asha winked as he gaped up comically, and then gave a delicate bow to the Queen.

She was riddled with bruises and her teeth were frighteningly sharp, but the Nymph emanated such an indescribable feeling of goodness that Aglaia didn't even consider questioning if the Nymph might be a creature of Darziates.

'I've been sent by King Glaidin, as I'm much faster than normal messengers,' Asha told Aglaia. 'The King also thought that seeing a Nymph would give your Kingdom further hope.'

Aglaia blinked and removed the stunned expression she could feel covering her face.

'Well met Asha,' Aglaia told the little being. 'You are very welcome here.'

'My thanks,' Asha replied. 'I hope you don't mind if I make myself at home, then. I'm exhausted.'

The Nymph promptly buzzed toward Friendly's chest, and he hurriedly caught her as if she had been thrown at him in a game of catch.

'I just need a brief sleep on the way to your conference room to recharge,' she explained, squishing the muscles of Friendly's arms in a satisfied manner and resting her head so that she looked like a babe in a cradle. 'Might as well nap with something handsome to wake up to.'

'Of ... course,' Aglaia agreed as Friendly gaped at his Queen and then at the cherubic, infantile being.

'You are Queen of a land absolutely brimming with gorgeous men,' Asha informed Aglaia, closing her eyes.

'How good of you to say,' Aglaia managed.

'Wake me when your council are gathered,' the Nymph added, and then abruptly fell into a deep and peaceful sleep.

81

Eighty One

Asha

'You're *that* old?' Asha's man-bed, Friendly, asked in disbelief.

'And there are ... ogres ...attacking our army?' a general rubbed his brow.

Asha's red coloured eyes narrowed and she suddenly shot out of her comfortable, Friendly chest-nest and made everyone around the table flinch.

She cocked her head as if listening to something.

'I hate to tell you,' she scowled. 'But you have your own magical enemy on its way.'

'A Dragon?' Sumantra growled urgently.

Asha nodded. 'You have only moments.'

'Let's move,' Sumantra galvanised the room, and at once there was a flurry of action so that soon the palace guards were sounding their horns and the city was full of people racing through the descending night.

Asha circled above Friendly and the Queen as they rode for the Gwynrock wall. When she caught sight of her fellow air-treader at last, she grimaced.

It was bloated, grey and sick. A mindless beast twisted by Darziates to forget all wisdom, its clan, and its allies.

Still, it was powerful. It released a plume of fire into the Eastern Gate and distant yells came from those who had been thrown by the force.

The corrupted Dragon rampaged onward, yet though the creature could have easily torn the entire city apart, it simply antagonised the people and left a trail of damage.

The Dragon growled as a flaming arrow grazed its wing, and it swerved to avoid the new spikes lining the palace towers. Instead, it thumped its tail into the pavement below and sent a dozen citizens flying through the air.

The Dragon seemed to like that, and swooped low along the pavement, swiping at screaming crowds with its claws.

When a thick, steel woven net was pulled up and stretched between two buildings in front of it, it stupidly ploughed straight into the trap to get entangled.

It snapped its jaws furiously as people rushed forward to swarm it, jabbing with weapons that enraged it further.

Asha winced when an impatient burst of flame obliterated two men and a young woman in a moment, before the Dragon thrashed so violently that the net tore away from where it had been tied.

Some people were crushed under its feet and those not fortunate enough to have let go of the net when it came loose suddenly found themselves being dragged into the air and shaken off at a great height.

Asha spotted a soldier manning an as yet unloaded catapult, and flew in a blur of speed towards him.

'Are you good with this thing?' she asked, her fast arrival surprising him and the men stationed at the catapult more than the presence of the Dragon.

He quickly nodded. 'Aye, but I can't shoot boulders at it until it flies higher and past the walls, or loose rocks will fall into the city.'

'I'm not a boulder,' Asha grinned. 'This catapult could throw me into the Dragon with a greater ferocity than I could achieve by myself.'

The soldier was taken aback. 'You would be killed. I won't throw you.'

She crossed her arms as, in the distance, a giant fireball caused an explosion amongst three houses. Flaming people ran from the area with echoing screams.

'Shouldn't we give anything at all a try?' Asha turned back to him. 'More Awyalknians will be killed if you don't. And besides, I'm stronger than I look.'

The soldier watched in horror as next a horse was ripped from a stable and tossed into the air, before the stallion was caught in savage jaws. As the Dragon chewed, whinnies were replaced by the crackling of bones.

She didn't give the man another moment to think on it. Instead, she flitted to his weapon belt and took the sharp dagger hanging at his hip. With no effort whatsoever her fire exploded to life in her palm and licked along the blade. 'I'm not going to ask again,' she told him.

He nodded and swallowed.

'Aim for its wing the next time it flies by,' she ordered the soldier grimly, settling into place on the massive siege weapon. 'I'll do the rest.'

And it was only moments before the beast began circling back towards them, this time with a man dangling from its teeth by his leg. The man shrieked as he was carried upside down over the city.

'Good fortune!' Asha heard the soldier call mournfully to her, and an instant later the catapult released and she was being flung at top speed towards the oncoming beast.

She forced her body to rocket through the air without spinning, holding her arms and the fiery dagger out so that she was like an arrow when she collided with the leathery underside in the middle of the outstretched wing. The soldier's magic coated blade embedded so deeply that smoke issued from the wound and the Dragon dropped the screaming Awyalknian as it roared in thunderous agony and surprise.

Asha felt her eardrums pop warmly in her head, muting the monstrous noise, and she grimly tugged kicked her feet so that her weight dragged the fiery dagger through the wing's length.

The city spun as the Dragon wheeled around and Asha caught flashing glimpses of starry sky, buildings and then ground while the motion pulled her along until the dagger had burned its way to the tip of the now split wing. Then with one last jerk Asha and the dagger were tugged free, and she was sent spinning away from the Dragon in a ball of her own fire.

She was caught across the chest by a lash of the seething beast's tail as she whirled away, and her fire went out as she smashed into the rock of the Gwynrock Wall – landing conveniently close to where the Queen of Awyalkna and her Friendly soldier watched on in horror.

Aglaia rushed forward, her lips moving, and Asha heard two popping sounds as her ears burst back into action.

Friendly scooped Asha up with an aghast expression, and as he lifted her, she saw the now lopsided Dragon disappearing into the darkness as cheers rose from the city below.

'You are one brave, crazy Nymph!' the burly general called Sumantra cried. 'Listen to them down there!'

Asha gave a smile that showed all of her bloodied, sharp teeth.

'You wait until they see how I can strengthen your traps. Next time the nets won't be pulled free.'

She settled back against Friendly with a wet, but satisfied wheeze.

'Wait until they see me pulling water from deep below the earth to create more natural wells. Then the crops beyond the gates will be safer and homes all over the city will have more water against the fires.'

Aglaia, Friendly and Sumantra gaped at her.

'Just you wait.'

82

Eighty Two

N^{oal}

After days of meetings I had even started dreaming of discussions about carts and weapons, tools and canvas marquees, food rations, armour, healer materials, numbers coming, and numbers staying.

I was glad of the relative break offered as the Three of us were at last free to join the Krall men, who had already been volunteering their physical labour for days.

Kiana had stayed with us all at first, showing herself to be truly content and capable in the valley fields after having been raised in a major harvest village.

However, she had been quickly sought out by the owner of a smithy inside the city, who had heard of her talents in the forge. Her face had lit up and she had immediately disappeared with him without a word – much to Thale's annoyance.

Dalin's motivation for the outdoors had waned a little then, though I had spent the day happily in the fields, helping to load bundles of harvested goods into carts – and watching for the moment that Maeve would appear at the gates.

'I think you've earned your break,' Dalin informed me as he wiped his brow and we both caught sight of Maeve.

'I quite like working in the fields,' I grinned at him, dusting my hands.

'Personally, I'd prefer to find myself work in a smithy tomorrow,' he told me.

'Yes. Fields are rather convenient for me. Not so much for you,' I told him as Maeve approached, and I could make out a coy smile on her delicate lips.

'You and Maeve have been seeing a great deal of each other,' Dalin commented wryly, alluding to how he'd fallen asleep at Kiana's table the night before, waiting for us to finish conversing.

'She's swapped to make our room her final duty, so she can stay a little longer to talk,' I informed him happily. 'We talk about everything now. Last night she talked about the machinations of the Jenran city and how a piping system runs through the entire mountain to carry water to every pool and fountain. Apparently at the top of the main mountain the peak has been flattened into a magical, water holding basin by the Unicorns.'

'I bet you don't really care exactly what she talks to you about,' Dalin laughed, and waved at Maeve as she drew closer before he moved off.

And he was right. She could recite the alphabetic runes to me on repeat if she wished. I kept her talking just to hear her light voice and to keep her with me.

We had both shared much about ourselves that was more intimate than even some of my most open conversations had been with Dalin or Kiana. And as she'd come to know my deepest emotions over my past, Maeve had held my hand and I had for once focused more on the person beside me rather than the memories themselves.

Maeve had also described her own experience of losing her parents to a Griffin attack in the farming fields. Maeve had herself been left on the edge of life after suffering scratches that had nearly become septic.

While she had been recovering, Maeve had befriended the head healer of Jenra, Lady Amarantha, who had already established strong charities and mentoring systems for victims of Griffin attacks. With Lady Amarantha's help, Maeve had been given her safe indoor job and in return she had often volunteered her time to help in Amarantha's wards.

She was so gentle. And so strong.

My heart was swelling almost painfully when she reached me at last, her face like sunshine.

'I did not wish to scare away the Raiden,' Maeve smiled.

I took her basket from her and tucked her hand into the crook of my arm. 'If you hadn't, I would have,' I told her warmly. 'Now if only you could scare our Krall guards away. With such little time, I can't afford to share you.'

We both left unsaid the painful fact that we had only seven more days before I would have to leave for good.

83

Eighty Three

D^{alin}

I watched Kiana send sparks flying into the air as she wielded a mighty hammer with unbelievable strength and precision, somehow creating a delicate curve in the metal, rather than a dent.

'It's definitely not the quality I would usually like, but we don't have time for getting too fancy,' she was saying to a smithy as she set her tools aside and scrutinised the helm she had just finished.

He appeared every bit as impressed as all the other black-smiths she'd worked with after word of her talent had spread.

In contrast, I was leaning my chin on the handle of a scratchy broom after having been relegated to an out of the way corner. I was quite inept as a farmer – only being useful for heavy labour under constant direction. And I was even less useful in a forge.

While Kiana set her tools away, the burly smiths who had worked alongside her for most of the day seemed almost wistful for her to be going. But nobody minded too much when I dusted my hands and leaned my broom in a corner to leave the shop with her.

'I'm tired,' I yawned luxuriously as we moved towards where we had said we would meet Noal, and do a check in with our fast giving up mother hens of Krall.

'Oh dear,' Kiana remarked sympathetically, wiping at the sweat and smudges upon her brow. 'Holding up that broom was a challenge.'

'T'was dreadful,' I agreed.

'Buck up, Noal's on his way,' she commented, her sharp eyes picking him out from the crowd.

'Does he look sorrowful again today?' I asked.

She nodded. 'Poor mite.'

Noal hardly even greeted us as he dolefully clutched a vibrant flower that Maeve had surely picked for him.

'Well ...' I cast around for a distraction. 'Perhaps we should head back up the mountain to wash away the grime of a hard day's work before dinner.'

Kiana raised an eyebrow at my almost grime free appearance.

Noal managed to smile. 'You don't really look like you've had a hard day this time.'

I grinned. 'I think my broom gave me a splinter. Perhaps you should carry me up the mountain in case it's serious.'

Kiana tapped her chin. 'I could always try flying you both up there ...' she offered. 'But I haven't tested how much weight I can really carry yet.'

'You're too kind,' Noal declined politely. 'But I would rather carry a thousand heavy Dalins up twenty mountains than be dropped mid-flight.'

'Heavy?' I asked, wounded.

Noal laughed. 'I meant muscular.'

'Kiana!' we all glanced up to see Thorin fighting through the crowd, his expression betraying true exhaustion after he and some of the others had been recruited to spend the last few days giving Aeron's soldiers insight into Krall's fighting tactics. His hair stuck to his forehead and his shirt clung to his body.

'Kiana,' he panted again when he reached us. 'I'm meant to tell you that Lady Amarantha has some maps for you...' he took a breath. 'She's just finished a healer training session in a courtyard near the market place. I passed her on the way in.'

'My thanks,' Kiana clapped him on his shoulder, and it was my turn to feel a little doleful as she immediately left us to flit her way through the crowds.

'Gods I'm tired,' Thorin grimaced as she left.

'Now *you* actually look like you did a hard day's work,' Noal replied. 'And still you've made the effort to check us Three are still alive.'

'Noal, you may have to carry him up the mountain instead of me,' I commented as Thorin almost sagged on the spot.

'It'll be a heroic effort to carry that big lug,' Noal considered the idea.

Thorin tiredly jerked his head towards one of the ever rising and falling carriages being pulled up and down the walls of the mountain. 'Or we could catch a ride on the cable systems.'

I squinted upwards. 'Those things are for transporting heavy goods like cattle,' I said. 'I am not a cow.'

'Definitely not a cow,' Thorin reassured me. 'But look at the cables running in between those used for raising and lowering big goods,' he persisted, pointing out another set of cables with a smaller carriage attached.

'They're usually used for smaller goods, or by the elderly, the sick, or any injured soldiers. They carry people up to where they need to go so that they don't have to climb,' Thorin continued. 'And the way I see it, it's not so embarrassing if we use those things, seeing as we aren't used to climbing mountains every day.'

Noal and I were quiet for a moment.

'That's not embarrassing at all,' Noal agreed.

'We're very official people,' I agreed further. 'We don't have time to walk for ourselves!'

We were already making our way across to the now overly appealing cable system for the elderly or infirm.

'In fact, I am very upset to only be finding out about this marvel four days before we leave,' Noal complained as the wiry master who manned the elevator waved us in beside a carriage load of bleating sheep.

'Well, this is nice,' Thorin stated smugly.

'Thank the Gods my legs aren't climbing,' I agreed.

'Thank the Gods I found you two alive for the check-in time,' Thorin admitted. 'I don't think I had the energy to rustle up the others and storm the mountain if anything had happened to you.'

'So you're not even pretending to be able to keep track of Kiana now?' Noal snorted as we reached our rooms in a much timelier manner than usual.

'Too hard,' Thorin deadpanned. 'It's just luck if she's spotted half the time.'

He shoved us toward where Purdor now stood guard outside our door.

I felt decidedly unlucky, though, when I left our room for Maeve's evening arrival to find that Kiana still wasn't back.

84

Eighty Four

D*alin*

A strange tingling, ticklish feeling, seemed to be flowing into my fingertips and then into the veins along my arm.

My mind woke to the sensation, but I didn't open my eyes for a moment as I let the simultaneously serene and energising feeling ebb from my shoulder and into my chest.

A fresh breeze brought the scent of flowers and pine with it – such a sweet smell, and I registered that it was close. So I finally turned my head towards it and then opened my eyes.

Kiana, stunning beyond all words, was leaning over me. Her half smile played across her lips and her hand had covered mine, but now she entwined our fingers together so that I felt suddenly very dazed.

Almost breathless.

Starlight filled the room, its silvery beams illuminating her wings and making the blood red stone upon her throat seem dazzling. Her eyes were exotic and wild again.

Kiana squeezed my fingers and the prickling, tingling warmth of her magic danced further across my chest and into my other arm, twirling its way past my elbow.

Kiana straightened, drawing me up to stand beside her before she spoke, and I tried to shake myself out of complete mesmerism.

'I've had an idea,' she said softly, 'that I was hoping you might agree to try.'

Right then I would do anything she ever asked of me.

'I remember what a shock it was for you when my magic touched your vision last time. I swore to get your permission before trying something like this again,' she continued.

'What is it?' I asked huskily. 'Tell me and I'll do it.'

She smiled again as the rest of my body now also seemed to lose touch with mortality.

'I want to see what it would be like to fly with someone else. Properly. Not just carrying them in a short burst.'

I swallowed hard.

'I want to know if your body can adapt and survive just as mine can. If my magic can help you to do that.'

'I am glad to be the one you want to try this with,' I told her, my gaze held firmly transfixed by her wild, bright eyes.

'You're sure?' she almost whispered.

'I trust you,' I answered firmly.

Kiana lifted her free hand to rest it against my chest.

'Then don't fight my magic,' she warned as the wondrous, weightless, bursting feeling erupted into something even greater. It spread rapidly through my core, down my spine and along every nerve ending.

It felt as if the power of the Gods was being poured into my ungainly body until everything about me had been heightened and enhanced.

The stars became brighter. The sound of the breeze in the trees of the valleys far, far below became suddenly clear. The scent of the sea became stronger.

I gasped as I felt the pupils of my eyes readjust themselves to suit a creature of flight, and winced as I felt my lungs change too, but Kiana's steadying hand kept me calm and I peered up to find her smiling widely.

'It worked,' she breathed.

I shook my head dizzily, disappointed. 'I have no wings.'

'But look,' she answered. 'I am your wings.'

I followed Kiana's motion and gasped again as I saw that we had lifted from the floor.

My heart pounded. Elated.

Somehow I felt supported and in control of my weight –holding myself as easily as I always did when on the ground.

I could do this.

With Kiana, I could do the impossible.

I had never felt so free.

'Show me the wonders you have found outside,' I said with longing, and she tightened her hold on my fingers again.

'Don't let go,' she warned, and she guided me across the room – my body somehow floating along beside hers towards the balcony.

I wanted to see the mountains from above. To gaze down on the bobbing yellow flowers of the valleys. To fly above the crashing waves. I wasn't even nervous as we flew together to hover above the railing of the balcony, and peered beyond and below the great mountain. Then with a gentle push, we were floating slowly away from the security of the stone walls, gracefully treading the air as if it were water.

The cool wind didn't sear my face or lash at my eyes. I felt no paralysing fear. Spiralling upwards and twirling around each other like shooting stars, we were synchronised as we dipped and soared and somersaulted – our bodies entwining over the monstrous height as if we had been doing it for all of our lives.

'Is this how you felt when you first got your earthstone?' I asked Kiana with a thick voice.

'This is how I feel every time I use my magic to fly. It is as if I am made whole,' she replied. 'It's good to have someone to understand that with me.'

I listened but couldn't understand when a cloud of birds swirled about Kiana, chattering so that she laughed.

'They're picking out what they seem to think are your faults,' she told me.

'And what are my faults?' I asked archly.

'No feathers,' she said with amusement. 'A flat mouth. You wouldn't be able to provide me with the grubs or worms that they could.'

'I see,' I replied. 'Tell them that they aren't the ones you're holding hands with.'

'They have no hands,' she pointed out with mirth, and I smirked.

'Exactly.'

Then the night was ours alone, and Jenra was our glorious stage to soar over as dancers would.

When we started drifting easily back toward the mountain, I still hardly felt ready to let her go.

85

Eighty Five

Kiana

The sharp cry of my hammer beat out the tune played in every smithy. The taut feeling of the muscles burning between my shoulder blades, along my neck and through my triceps, was a nostalgic familiarity.

My cheeks radiated with the warmth of the fires and the metals heating. I made another strike against the sword on the anvil, sending sparks dancing, and all around me there was the song of the smithy's' hammers and the hissing of glowing blades as they were plunged into water.

Steam rose from our bodies as well as our creations while we followed the rhythmical routine of our toil, and I felt incredible peace in the mindlessness and precision.

Until I saw Dalin daydreaming out of the corner of my eye.

He had once again come to find me after having spent his time training with the Krall and Jenran soldiers. His narrow chin rested on top of his hands as he leaned over an unused work bench and gazed at the flurry of action about the shop. His green eyes seemed to flash as the fires flared. He was watching the dance of the blacksmiths as they instinctively wove and dipped around each other, stepping to the song of many ringing tools.

I would miss those green eyes.

I would miss Dalin.

When I finished at the smithy Dalin was still waiting, and we walked together quietly for some time, in no rush to return to our rooms.

'What do you want most in the world, right now, apart from our quest to be successful?' I asked him after a while.

I waited while he was thoughtfully silent, before he reached for my hand.

'To have you all to myself,' he answered in a candid tone. 'Like last night.'

I regarded him for a moment before I pulled him to a stop beside a wide window in the walkway that overlooked the valley. Nobody was about as the sun began to set and people returned home.

'Very well,' I said. 'Then that is what you shall have.'

His eyes widened and a smile played about the edges of his lips as I let the magic that swirled within me now spread outward to flow through him.

It wasn't uncomfortable. Not like I was losing or completely giving myself over, but simply like expanding my living being and awareness. As if I was pouring a second self, my shadow, into another so that I could share for a time.

The green pupils in his eyes sharpened and we both stepped up onto the wide sill together as my wings flickered into sight at my back.

'What would you have wanted?' Dalin asked as we gazed down from the great height and felt the wind plucking at our clothes.

'Oh ...' I smiled. 'It was definitely you.'

I leant forward to draw a lingering kiss from him that made the magic dance more furiously between us.

Then I launched us from the window's edge, and we soared upward, spiralling around the watch towers and racing along the rocky walls.

I slowed our progress for just a moment when our eyes, sharpened by the magic, found Noal and Maeve at their balcony in the distance.

I could see their features changing with disbelief as we drew close.

'Dalin ...' Noal coughed in shock. 'You didn't tell me you could fly.'

Dalin shrugged. 'I only just learned.'

'You can learn too if you like,' I offered.

Both Noal and Maeve eyed our dangling feet as we hung suspended above the mortifying drop and shook their heads.

'Thank you, but perhaps another night ...' Maeve managed politely.

I laughed gaily and allowed the wind to sweep Dalin and I away once more, pulling us upward and then gusting us in the direction of the ocean.

We clung together and spun through the air with abandon until, in exhaustion, we stopped to watch the night deepen from the beach.

The salty breeze played through our hair and the cool waves swirled and tickled about our ankles, refreshing us right down to the soul. The sand shifted beneath our feet, ever changing, and the stars glittered their reflections upon the surface of the sea – billions of lights floating on the waves.

'Thank you,' Dalin murmured as he looked out at it all. 'This was exactly what I wanted.'

I placed my hand on his scar lined jaw and turned his face to me. I let my lips gently caress his again, our kiss slow as he moved to hold me closer.

And it was my heart, this time, which took flight with a magical leap for him.

86

Eighty Six

N*oal*

Kiana had tired of pouring over ancient maps for the day. The maps simply guessed at where the lands of the magical races might be, and offered no way of navigating the sea with any certainty, so Kiana had left them upstairs and rounded up the Krall soldiers so that we could all spend our second last afternoon together properly.

Now the tavern she'd chosen on the lowest level of the Jenran mountain was bursting with raucous gaiety.

'I can't believe you convinced my mistress to excuse me for tonight,' Maeve whispered into my ear.

'And tomorrow,' I reminded her. 'Though for a moment I thought nothing would sway that hard faced woman to agree.'

'How could she not obey the request of one the Three? And the Raiden personally visiting her was an impressive touch, too,' Maeve added. 'You went above and beyond to secure me a break.'

'I guess Dalin *can* be impressive when he stops slouching and puffs himself up,' I grinned, peering over at where he was sprawled out on a large armchair, roaring with mirth at Tane and Thorin's ale racing antics.

I felt Maeve's small hand slip into mine under the bench. 'I am glad to spend time with you.'

'Gods know it is all I've craved,' I assured her, and she rested her head on my shoulder to watch Ferron and Phrixus arm wrestling over a mead barrel nearby.

When we all at last bundled back into the room I shared with Dalin, continuing the merrymaking from the tavern in there, I felt incredibly natural as I sat with my arm around Maeve. We sat together on my bed, our backs against rich red cushions, the men perching anywhere they could. Anyone who didn't fit inside the room spilled out comfortably into the hall, revelling just as easily from their seat on the floor.

It was only when Kiana had retired for the night, and we heard her voice carrying from where she sang in her room, that the men began to quiet down.

She sang the 'Isilia Isiltha' – a song about great journeys and courage, and Tane sighed, shaking his curl covered head when she got to the part about sad partings.

Wolf groaned from where he was dangling on the edge of a sofa that was already being accosted by Thale and Vulcan's weight.

'I am going to miss her,' he said ruefully.

'We pledged to follow the Three,' Purdor agreed in exasperation. 'It doesn't bode well to see one of the Three journeying far from our aid.'

'No fear,' Dalin told the subdued soldiers solemnly. 'Noal and I are actually the hopeless ones out of our group. We need your aid more than Kiana does.'

'We know,' Thale reassured him, rising to move to his room. 'We'll have a great task ahead of us.'

The room began to empty out as Gideon and Lydon stood too, and others began to gradually wander off to find their own beds after that.

'But, I'm not tired enough to sleep yet,' Thorin complained as he watched them go. He turned to Dalin. 'How about a friendly round of runes?'

Dalin sat up from where he had stretched out on a rug and shrugged a shoulder. 'Friendly, you say?'

'We're up for that!' Ferron cried, dragging a merrily humming Phrixus up with him and gesturing to Phobos so that, in a matter of moments, the eager hubbub of men exiting our room had finished, and Maeve and I found ourselves in peace.

She gazed up at me with a smile at their energy, and, emboldened, I cupped my hand under her chin and gently brought her face up to mine.

I stole a kiss.

And after a moment of hesitation, she kissed me back.

Slowly we pulled away from each other, but her face stayed close to mine and I could see a tiny furrow in her brow.

'What's wrong?' I whispered, tracing her lips with my fingertip.

'We ... can't be together,' she said. 'Even if you stayed here as an ambassador and took me for a bride, people would be disappointed that a more advantageous pairing had not been made. We are not an acceptable match.'

I grinned. 'You're right.' I stroked her hair. 'You are much too good for me.'

I hugged her close, and after a faltering moment, this time she took my face into her hands, kissing me harder, as if we could keep ourselves from being dragged apart by the war.

My heart was racing and I was sure hers was too as our embraces became more fervent. More desperate. More intimate.

We found ourselves kneeling up together on the bed, holding each other tight, our lips dancing together. I felt her hand on my chest and my own hands stroked her neck and back, then bunched her golden hair.

My lips began to move down her throat and she held me close, her hands warm and tight around my arms.

Then I felt her fingers pulling the tie of the front of my shirt loose just as my own were fumbling at her blouse.

I was hot and cold all over and her lips fluttered over my chest and back to my mouth.

I pulled her closer to me. Hugging her. Wrapping her in an embrace I never wanted to let go of while I ached at the knowledge that I would have to.

I had never wanted to tell a lady that I loved her. Until that very moment when I knew I meant it. That I was in love with Maeve. And I kissed her even harder, her body pressing against mine.

My heart was speeding up, and this time I definitely felt hers pounding just as hard because our chests were pressed together.

I leaned forward, pushing her backward, holding her suspended underneath me with one arm while pressing my lips to hers. I was about to lower her down to lay on the bed when Dalin and Thorin waltzed back in to find us.

Maeve's lips sprang away from mine and our heads whirled to stare at them, both of us caught with sudden awareness of the gravity of what we had been doing.

Dalin quickly apologised and dragged Thorin out by his collar, shutting the door.

And Maeve muffled a cry – pressing her face into my chest for a moment before she wriggled free and our bodies parted.

Maeve was off the bed in an instant, quickly readjusting her dress and tidying her hair, her face pale. I stayed frozen in shock.

'We've only known each other for a short time …' she was saying faintly as she bustled about and wrung her hands. 'I have to do something …' she turned to me abruptly. 'I have to go.'

She was gone before I could apologise for my foolishness. And before I could admit my true feelings for her.

87

Eighty Seven

N^{oal}

The maid Kerrin delivered the morning meal.

I cringed to think of what I had nearly done to the girl I loved, and while Dalin mentioned nothing of it, my misery over Maeve and what was ahead for the Three surrounded us as we spent our last day with Kiana.

We were mostly quiet, wandering along the beach at the bottom of the cliffs and dawdling in the valleys. The guilt and disappointment bubbled in my stomach as the usual time of our walk passed without a single glimpse of Maeve.

I was feeling so wretched that I parted with Kiana and Dalin to return to our rooms, and I was staring glumly at my feet as I reached the door and didn't see the Jenran in my way, bumping into the maiden.

'My apologies, miss,' I mumbled dejectedly as I passed.

There was a soft, familiar laugh. 'I forgive you.'

I spun around in my open doorway.

'Maeve!' I breathed in disbelief, standing stock still.

'Yes.' With a smile she rushed towards me, flinging her arms around my neck, and propelling us into the room.

'I'm so sorry!' I gushed at her, holding her tightly. 'I should not have let that happen, it was not the time, we may never meet again,' I gulped. 'I could have ruined you,' I groaned remorsefully. 'I don't want that life for you. You deserve someone that can take care of you, not soil your reputation. Gods, I feared I wouldn't get to say goodbye!'

Maeve peered up and put a hand over my lips to shush me. 'Last night,' she began meaningfully. 'I wasn't upset about that, not really.'

The air rushed out of me. 'Then, why didn't I see you today?' I asked in confusion.

She pulled me gently to sit on my bed beside her. 'I was upset that I would be losing you. It was obvious you feel as seriously for me as I do for you. I would do anything not to lose you,' she smiled. 'And you didn't see me today because I had some very important tasks to do.'

The swirling mass of nerves began to dissipate from my stomach. 'What did you have to do?' I was ecstatic as I stroked her golden hair, drinking her in.

'I had to speak to my mentor, Lady Amarantha, before she is to leave,' Maeve told me. 'But it is nothing for you to worry about.'

'Gods, I am just so relieved to see you,' I groaned, pulling her into my arms.

We sank down to lie on the bed, glad to simply be together, refusing to let go of each other even when night began to set in.

88

Eighty Eight

D*alin*

The dawn had not yet come and a chill hung in the air from the night.

A white cloud of mist erupted from my cold lips, with each breath becoming vapour in the dark.

Though the Jenrans were massed at the base of the mountains the many voices around us were muted as sorrowful partings were made and brave faces were assumed. Subdued soldiers pulled carts into place and joined their assigned ranks with resolutely, ready to leave their homeland – possibly forever.

I waited near where the hidden mountain tunnel was supposed to appear, standing out of the way atop a jutting rock while the crowds gathered quietly to farewell us all on our quest.

Our starting signal was to be the breaking of dawn, and I could see Noal, quiet and grimly focused, standing in wait with Thorin and Thale a small distance away.

I could also see Kiana conversing quietly with Durna and Aeron. She was sombre and dressed for travel.

I sighed, with more white mist erupting from my lips into the dark. But I held up the brave face of the Raiden.

I scanned the Krall men, who were forming their ranks directly behind Aeron's elite team in places of great honour. They were hulking and intimidating again, carrying their spiked armour, and only Tane's face still managed to show cheer.

He seemed to be telling Phobos to put his helmet on so that less moon would be reflected from his head for Griffins to target.

The little skulking figure of Agrudek was hovering by itself on the edge of the crowd, nervously clutching his little ball pendant. I ignored his piteous form, and instead looked to the slowly lightening sky.

I found no comfort there either as I saw that, at the peaks of the mountain we gathered below, there appeared to be countless watching shadows.

'There are hundreds of Griffins up there,' Kiana's voice affirmed for me. 'Just observing and waiting.' She launched herself up lithely to stand beside me on the rock.

'Why?' I breathed in dismay.

'They are going to see how good the defences we left are. If they find a weak spot, they will aim to make the entire city their dinner.' She glared upward. 'But Aeron, Durna and the council have prepared well. The moment one Griffin leaves its perch on those mountain peaks to swoop above the valleys, a hailstorm of expertly launched arrows will fell as many of them as is possible.'

'They're not witless,' I croaked. 'Why would they even try when they must realise the consequences that await their attack?'

'Because even if they aren't daft, they are hungry and greedy. It is within their nature to send their smallest and weakest to at least test the remaining defenders before they rule out the possibility of a Jenran meal. Such a meal would almost make leaving for Krall's battlements pointless.'

'Sacrifice their most useless brothers to test us out,' I shook my head in disgust.

'Aeron seems to think the Unicorn horn will addle their memories and motivation,' Kiana mentioned with interest. 'So, they won't remember the opening of the tunnel and pass the information on.'

I moved my eyes from their foreboding shadows to gaze at Kiana. She carried only a very light pack and her daggers and sword. She had left her healer bag and her Unicorn figurine in my care while her bow and quiver remained back in her Jenran chamber.

A sudden wistful desire to kiss her just once more burned through me, and her sharp blue eyes flashed to my face, feeling my scrutiny.

She raised one perfect eyebrow and then smiled faintly, as if she had understood my thoughts.

Kiana wrapped her arm lightly around my waist and I rested mine about her shoulders, and with the rest of Jenra we watched the first rays of the golden sun lightening the sky.

89

Eighty Nine

The Witch

Darziates' magic curled around her limbs and dragged her out of existence. Agrona rolled through time and space, buffeted by the evil of the Other Realm.

It burned and stung, and she would have been reduced to ashes without his guidance, but if he was pulling her to him, then surely the Sorcerer had missed his Queen of Darkness!

Agrona began to blur into existence again, re-materialising triumphantly – only to find herself summoned into the planning room, where her Sorcerer was in conversation with Angra Mainyu.

Agrona had hoped for their reunion to be more intimate. Or that her master would at least glance up from his discussion with the inferior, crazed mortal. But instead, it was Angra Mainyu who stared up from their battle plans to rake her body with his red tinged eyes. Then even he turned back to the plans and she was left neglected, waiting for them to finish.

The Witch inwardly glowered until Angra had been dismissed, and she waited hungrily for Darziates to acknowledge her.

For an agonising amount of time the Sorcerer remained outwardly passive. He simply continued to observe his parchments, leaving her to hover near him like a starved child staring at a banquet.

When he at last rose and turned, she waited expectantly for his greeting.

'Agrona.'

That deep, velvety voice! Her breath abated.

'You have work to do.'

She stepped closer and was bold enough to take his hand, grovelling over it, and he did not draw it away. 'My Dread Lord, I shall serve you in any way you wish.'

He had no idea how far she was willing to go.

'Agrudek has spoken to me. The Three will soon be out in the world again, beyond the mountains.'

'Of course, master,' she crooned. 'I know. I must make sure that the Three are brought to you.'

'Her.' His granite gaze was overwhelming. 'Bring *her* to me. Alive.'

Agrona felt as if a sharp hook had just been tugged through her insides.

Beware, her visions had told her.

Forces beyond the physical planes – Gods or demons – had chosen to warn her. Had chosen to reveal that the wretched *Larnaeradee* would ensnare the Sorcerer.

Why?

Simply to torment the Witch? To tell her to give up on her Darziates? Or ... to tell her to rise up as her own kind of force to be reckoned with?

Agrona felt herself harden inside. She drew a cloak of red magic about her feelings and her mind. And for the first time since she had met him as a child, Agrona was able to shield every single thought from the Sorcerer.

He didn't even notice.

His mind had been corrupted by pure magic. He needed her help to ensure he was able to complete his quest before the tenth age.

The Three had to die. Kiana had to die. And the magical races of the world had to be completely destroyed. Only then could life begin anew – rising from the ashes with a new world belonging truly to Agrona and her King.

It was up to her to help him to preserve his ideals, when his own mind had become clouded.

'I will serve you to my very best, and to my very last breath,' Agrona replied.

'As I expect,' the Sorcerer told her, before pushing her back through the icy flares of the Other Realm, and thrusting her out into the wastelands where the Evexus waited.

After so long in ill favour and isolation, Agrona at last flew proud in the sky once more while the magnificent

Evexus ran below her – their design now perfected and powerful Other Realm spirits seething beneath their skins.

They spoke intelligently together in their forbidden, foul language, now clever as well as cruel.

They would not fail. And she would not fail against that savage little *Larnaeradee* this time, so that her King would have no one to love but her, for saving his great quest.

A viciously exultant screech rent itself from her beak, to be echoed back up from the Evexus listening below.

The Three did not stand a chance.

The Evexus were coming.

Agrona was coming.

Other Books By Shelley Cass

The Raze Warfare Series

'A Fairy's Tale' Epic Fantasy Series:
Book One – 'Huntress'
Book Two – 'Raiden'
Book Three – 'Krall'

Dystopian Future:
'Awaken Dreamer'

Contemporary/Action/Fantasy/Erotica:
'Darkling'

The Sleep Sweet Series for children:
Book One – 'Little Pixie's Christmas'
Book Two – 'The case of the bored baby Ace'
Book Three – 'Mum and Me'
Book Four – 'The Cloud and the Flower'
Book Five – 'Hush'

Reader Gift

Access bonus Raze Warfare stories at shelleycass.com as a thank you for being one of my appreciated readers.

About the Author

I was an awkward, reserved year 8 student – totally in love with the escape and comfort offered by novels I read. I could hear the voices of the authors' characters, I could tune out my stresses and uncertainties as I journeyed with each protagonist through their own troubles. And then one day I could hear the voices of characters who hadn't been written yet, in places that hadn't been created, and I decided to write my own world.

It took a quest of over fifteen years to get that world perfected in three novels – because of course the real world kept getting in the way.

In the real world I became a high school teacher, and faced the epic battle of staying afloat in all the papers that must always be assessed. And in the real world the magic was also sometimes hard to find. Stress and disunity surface like cancer – making the nightly news too hard to watch on most days.

But in the real world there was also inspiration – incredible students, loved ones, golden memories, growing up, warm hugs, big laughs and good people.

So I wrote of the things that threaten the world, and of the things that save it.

I wish for a real world where the air is clean, the trees can grow without concrete borders, the darkness can be cured with the switch of a light, and the people can all have long days and happy lives.

Acknowledgments

Thank you so much to the friends who have encouraged me with my writing of this series, a process that has taken over fifteen years.

Thank you to those who put such time into helping me, by reading this novel and offering advice, even when the manuscript was triple the length it is now. Wendy Glover (the most helpful neighbour to have ever lived), June Laurie (the first author I ever befriended, and creator of the 'Blake Collider' series), my uncle, Lee, and my mum, Linda.

Thank you so much mum, dad (Robert), Melissa, Andrew and Leigh, for being the warmth in my world.

Thank you Jack, Elyssia and Sophie, for making the future world worthwhile.

Thank you to my extended family, for being everything I needed.

Thank you to Jarryd and baby Myla, for being the magic and loves of my life.

And thank you to the hesitant little Junior High School version of myself, for picking up that pen to write.